Trust

Trust

HERNAN
DIAZ

Riverhead Books ✦ *New York* ✦ *2022*

RIVERHEAD BOOKS
An imprint of Penguin Random House LLC
penguinrandomhouse.com

Copyright © 2022 by Hernan Diaz

Library of Congress Cataloging-in-Publication Data

Names: Díaz, Hernán, author.
Title: Trust / Hernan Diaz.
Description: New York : Riverhead Books, 2022.
Identifiers: LCCN 2021018182 (print) | LCCN 2021018183 (ebook) |
ISBN 9780593420317 (hardcover) | ISBN 9780593420331 (ebook)
Classification: LCC PS3604.I17 T78 2022 (print) | LCC PS3604.I17 (ebook) |
DDC 813/.6—dc23
LC record available at https://lccn.loc.gov/2021018182
LC ebook record available at https://lccn.loc.gov/2021018183

International edition ISBN: 9780593541548

Printed in the United States of America
1st Printing

BOOK DESIGN BY LUCIA BERNARD

Hernan Diaz is available for select speaking engagements. To inquire about
a possible appearance, please contact Penguin Random House Speakers Bureau
at speakers@penguinrandomhouse.com or visit prhspeakers.com.

To Anne, Elsa, Marina, and Ana

Trust

Contents

Bonds

A Novel

by

HAROLD VANNER

ONE

B
ecause he had enjoyed almost every advantage since birth, one of the few privileges denied to Benjamin Rask was that of a heroic rise: his was not a story of resilience and perseverance or the tale of an unbreakable will forging a golden destiny for itself out of little more than dross. According to the back of the Rask family Bible, in 1662 his father's ancestors had migrated from Copenhagen to Glasgow, where they started trading in tobacco from the Colonies. Over the next century, their business prospered and expanded to the extent that part of the family moved to America so they could better oversee their suppliers and control every aspect of production. Three generations later, Benjamin's father, Solomon, bought out all his relatives and outside investors. Under his sole direction, the company kept flourishing, and it did not take him long to become one of the most prominent tobacco traders on the Eastern Seaboard. It may have

been true that his inventory was sourced from the finest providers on the continent, but more than in the quality of his merchandise, the key to Solomon's success lay in his ability to exploit an obvious fact: there was, of course, an epicurean side to tobacco, but most men smoked so that they could talk to other men. Solomon Rask was, therefore, a purveyor not only of the finest cigars, cigarillos, and pipe blends but also (and mostly) of excellent conversation and political connections. He rose to the pinnacle of his business and secured his place there thanks to his gregariousness and the friendships culti-vated in the smoking room, where he was often seen sharing one of his figurados with some of his most distinguished customers, among whom he counted Grover Cleveland, William Zachary Irving, and John Pierpont Morgan.

At the height of his success, Solomon had a townhouse built on West 17th Street, which was finished just in time for Benjamin's birth. Yet Solomon was seldom to be seen at the New York family residence. His work took him from one plantation to another, and he was always supervising rolling rooms or visiting business associates in Virginia, North Carolina, and the Caribbean. He even owned a small hacienda in Cuba, where he passed the greater part of each winter. Rumors con-cerning his life on the island established his reputation as an adventurer with a taste for the exotic, which was an asset in his line of business.

Mrs. Wilhelmina Rask never set foot on her husband's Cuban es-tate. She, too, was absent from New York for long stretches, leaving as soon as Solomon returned and staying at her friends' summerhouses on the east bank of the Hudson or their cottages in Newport for entire seasons. The only visible thing she shared with Solomon was a passion for cigars, which she smoked compulsively. This being a very uncom-mon source of pleasure for a lady, she would only indulge in private, in the company of her girl-friends. But this was no impediment, since she was surrounded by them at all times. Willie, as those in her set called her, was part of a tightly knit group of women who seemed to constitute a sort of nomadic tribe. They were not only from New York but also from Washington, Philadelphia, Providence, Boston, and even as far as Chicago. They moved as a pack, visiting one another's houses and vacation homes according to the seasons—West 17th Street became the coterie's abode for a few months, starting in late September, when Solomon left for his hacienda. Still, no matter in what part of the country the ladies happened to dwell, the clique invariably kept to itself in an impenetrable circle.

Limited, for the most part, to his and his nursemaids' rooms, Benjamin had only a vague notion of the rest of the brownstone where he grew up. When his mother and her friends were there, he was kept away from the rooms where they smoked, played cards, and drank Sauternes well into the night; when they were gone, the main floors became a dim succession of shuttered windows, covered furniture, and chandeliers in ballooning shrouds. All of his nurses and governesses said he was a model child, and all of his tutors confirmed it. Manners, intelligence, and obedience had never been combined as harmoniously as in this sweet-tempered child. The only fault some of his early mentors could find after much searching was Benjamin's reluctance to associate with other children. When one of his tutors attributed his student's friendlessness to fear, Solomon waved his concerns away, saying the boy was just becoming a man of his own.

His lonely upbringing did not prepare him for boarding school. During the first term, he became the object of daily indignities and small cruelties. In time, however, his classmates discovered that his impassiveness made him a dissatisfying victim and left him alone. He kept to himself and excelled, dispassionately, in every subject. At the end of each year, after bestowing on him all available honors and distinctions, his teachers, without fail, would remind him that he was meant to bring much glory to the Academy.

During his senior year, his father died of heart failure. At the service, back in New York, relatives and acquaintances alike were impressed by Benjamin's composure, but the truth was that mourning simply had given the natural dispositions of his character a socially recognizable form. In a display of great precocity that baffled his father's attorneys and bankers, the boy requested to examine the will and all the financial statements related to it. Mr. Rask was a conscientious, tidy man, and his son found no fault with the documents. Having concluded this business and knowing what to expect once he came of age and into possession of his inheritance, he returned to New Hampshire to finish school.

His mother spent her brief widowhood with her friends in Rhode Island. She went in May, shortly before Benjamin's graduation, and by the end of the summer had died from emphysema. The family and friends who attended this second, much more subdued memorial barely knew how to speak to the young man orphaned in the course of a mere few months. Fortunately, there were many practical issues to discuss— trusts, executors, and the legal challenges in settling the estate.

Benjamin's experience as a college student was an amplified echo of his years as a schoolboy. All the same inadequacies and talents were there, but now he seemed to have acquired a cold sort of fondness for the former and a muted disdain for the latter. Some of the more salient traits of his lineage appeared to have come to an end with him. He could not have been more different from his father, who had owned every room he had walked into and made everyone in it gravitate around him, and he had nothing in common with his mother, who had probably never spent a day of her life alone. These discrepancies with his parents became even more accentuated after his graduation. He moved back from New England to the city and failed where most of his acquaintances thrived—he was an inept athlete, an apathetic club-man, an unenthusiastic drinker, an indifferent gambler, a lukewarm lover. He, who owed his fortune to tobacco, did not even smoke. Those who accused him of being excessively frugal failed to understand that, in truth, he had no appetites to repress.

THE TOBACCO BUSINESS could not have interested Benjamin less. He disliked both the product—the primitive sucking and puffing, the savage fascination with smoke, the bittersweet stench of rotten leaves—and the congeniality around it, which his father had enjoyed so much and exploited so well. Nothing disgusted him more than the misty complicities of the smoking room. Despite his most honest efforts, he could not argue, with any semblance of passion, for the virtue of a lonsdale over a diadema, and he was unable to sing, with the vigor that only firsthand knowledge can impart, the praise of the robustos from his Vuelta Abajo estate. Plantations, curing barns, and cigar factories belonged to a remote world he had no interest in getting to know. He would have been the first to admit he was an appalling ambassador for the company and therefore delegated daily operations to the manager who had served under his father for two faithful decades. It was against the advice of this manager that Benjamin, through agents he never met in person, undersold his father's Cuban hacienda and everything in it, without even taking an inventory. His banker invested the money in the stock market, together with the rest of his savings.

A few stagnant years went by, during which he made halfhearted attempts at starting different collections (coins, china, friends), dabbled in hypochondria, tried to develop an enthusiasm for horses, and failed to become a dandy.

Time became a constant itch.

Against his true inclinations, he started planning a trip to Europe. All that interested him about the Old Continent he had already learned through books; experiencing those things and places was of no importance to him. And he did not look forward to being confined on a ship with strangers for days on end. Still, he told himself that if he ever would leave, this would be the proper moment: the general atmosphere in New York City was rather glum as the result of a series of financial crises and the ensuing economic recession that had engulfed the country for the last two years. Because the downturn did not affect him directly, Benjamin was only vaguely aware of its causes—it had all started, he believed, with the burst of the railroad bubble, somehow linked to a subsequent silver crash, leading, in turn, to a run on gold, which, in the end, resulted in numerous bank failures in what came to be known as the Panic of 1893. Whatever the actual chain of events might have been, he was not worried. He had a general notion that markets swung back and forth and was confident that today's losses would be tomorrow's gains. Rather than discouraging his European excursion, the financial crisis—the worst since the Long Depression, two decades earlier—was among the strongest encouragements he found to leave.

As Benjamin was about to set a date for his journey, his banker informed him that, through some "connections," he had been able to subscribe to bonds issued to restore the nation's gold reserves, whose depletion had driven so many banks to insolvency. The entire issue had sold out in a mere half hour, and Rask had turned a handsome profit within the week. Thus, unsolicited luck, in the form of favorable political shifts and market fluctuations, led to the sudden and seemingly spontaneous growth of Benjamin's respectable inheritance, which he had never cared to enlarge. But once chance had done it for him, he discovered a hunger at his core he did not know existed until it was given a bait big enough to stir it to life. Europe would have to wait.

Rask's assets were in the conservative care of J. S. Winslow & Co., the house that had always managed the family's business. The firm, founded by one of his father's friends, was now in the hands of John S. Winslow Jr., who had tried and failed to befriend Benjamin.

As a result of this, the relationship between the two young men was somewhat uneasy. Still, they worked together closely—even if it was through messengers or over the telephone, either of which Benjamin preferred to redundant and laboriously genial face-to-face meetings.

Soon, Benjamin became adept at reading the ticker tape, finding patterns, intersecting them, and discovering hidden causal links between apparently disconnected tendencies. Winslow, realizing his client was a gifted learner, made things look more arcane than they truly were and dismissed his predictions. Even so, Rask started making his own decisions, usually against the firm's counsel. He was drawn to short-term investments and instructed Winslow to make high-risk trades in options, futures, and other speculative instruments. Winslow would always urge caution and protest against these reckless schemes: he refused to put Benjamin in a position to lose his capital in hazardous ventures. But more than worried about his client's assets, Winslow seemed to be concerned about appearances and eager to display a certain financial decorum—after all, as he once said, laughing shallowly at his own wit, he was, if anything, a bookkeeper, not a bookmaker, in charge of a finance house, not a gambling house. From his father, he had inherited a reputation for pursuing sound investments, and he intended to honor this legacy. Still, in the end, he always followed Rask's directives and kept his commissions.

Within a year, tired of his advisor's priggishness and ponderous pace, Rask decided to start trading on his own account and dismissed Winslow. Severing all ties with the family that had been so close to his for two generations was an added satisfaction to the feeling of true achievement Rask experienced, for the first time in his life, when he took the reins of his affairs.

THE TWO LOWER FLOORS of his brownstone became a makeshift office. This transformation was not the result of a plan but, rather, the effect of meeting unforeseen needs one by one, as they came, until, unexpectedly, there was something like a workspace filled with employees. It started with a messenger, whom Benjamin had running all over town with stock certificates, bonds, and other documents. A few days later, the boy let him know he had to have help. Together with an additional messenger, Benjamin got a telephone girl and a clerk, who soon informed him he was unable to cope on his own. Managing his people was taking vital time away from Benjamin's business, so he hired an assistant. And keeping books simply became too time-consuming, so he engaged an accountant. By the time his assistant got an assistant, Rask lost track of the new hires and no longer bothered to remember anyone's face or name.

The furniture that had remained untouched and under covers for years was now handled irreverently by secretaries and errand boys. A stock ticker had been installed on the walnut serving table; quote boards covered most of the gilt-embossed foliage wallpaper; piles of newspapers had stained the straw-yellow velvet of a settee; a typewriter had dented a satinwood bureau; black and red ink blotched the needlework upholstery of divans and sofas; cigarettes had burned the serpentine edges of a mahogany desk; hurried shoes had scuffed oak claw feet and soiled, forever, Persian runners. His parents' rooms were left intact. He slept on the top floor, which he had never even visited as a child.

It was not hard to find a buyer for his father's business. Benjamin encouraged a manufacturer from Virginia and a trading company from the United Kingdom to outbid each other. Wishing to distance himself from that part of his past, he was pleased to see the British prevail, thus sending the tobacco company whence it had come. But what truly gratified him was that with the profits from this sale he was able to work on a higher plane, manage a new level of risk, and finance long-term transactions he had been unable to consider in the past. Those around him were confused to see his possessions decrease in direct proportion to his wealth. He sold all remaining family properties, including the brownstone on West 17th Street, and everything in them. His clothes and papers fit into two trunks, which were sent to the Wagstaff Hotel, where he took a suite of rooms.

He became fascinated by the contortions of money—how it could be made to bend back upon itself to be force-fed its own body. The isolated, self-sufficient nature of speculation spoke to his character and was a source of wonder and an end in itself, regardless of what his earnings represented or afforded him. Luxury was a vulgar burden. The access to new experiences was not something his sequestered spirit craved. Politics and the pursuit of power played no part in his unsocial mind. Games of strategy, like chess or bridge, had never interested him. If asked, Benjamin would probably have found it hard to explain what drew him to the world of finance. It was the complexity of it, yes, but also the fact that he viewed capital as an antiseptically living thing. It moves, eats, grows, breeds, falls ill, and may die. But it is clean. This became clearer to him in time. The larger the operation, the further removed he was from its concrete details. There was no need for him to touch a single banknote or engage with the things and people his transaction affected. All he had to do was think, speak, and, perhaps, write. And the living creature would be set in motion, drawing beautiful patterns on its way into realms of increasing abstraction, sometimes following appetites of its own that Benjamin never could have anticipated—and this gave him some additional pleasure, the creature trying to exercise its free will. He admired and understood it, even when it disappointed him.

Benjamin barely knew downtown Manhattan—just enough to dislike its canyons of office buildings and its filthy narrow streets filled with prancing businessmen, busy displaying how busy they were. Still, understanding the convenience of being in the Financial District, he moved his offices to Broad Street. Shortly thereafter, as his interests expanded, he got a seat on the New York Stock Exchange. His employees were quick to realize that he was as averse to dramatics as he was to outbursts of joy. Conversations, stripped down to the essentials, were conducted in whispers. If there was a lull in the typing, the creaking of a leather chair or the rustle of a silk sleeve on paper could be heard from the opposite end of the room. Yet soundless ripples disturbed the air at all times. It was clear to everyone there that they were extensions of Rask's will and that it was their duty to satisfy and even anticipate his needs but never approach him with theirs. Unless they had vital information to impart to him, they waited to be spoken to. Working for Rask became the ambition of many young traders, but once they parted with him, believing they had absorbed everything that could be learned, none of them could quite replicate their former employer's success.

Much despite himself, his name started being uttered with reverent wonder in financial circles. Some of his father's old friends approached him with business propositions he sometimes accepted and with tips and suggestions he always ignored. He traded in gold and guano, in currencies and cotton, in bonds and beef. His interests were no longer confined to the United States. England, Europe, South America, and Asia became a unified territory to him. He surveyed the world from his office, in search of venturesome high-interest loans and negotiated government securities from a number of nations whose destinies became inextricably entwined because of his dealings. Sometimes he managed to take entire bond issuances to himself. His few defeats were followed by great triumphs. Everyone this side of his transactions prospered.

In what was becoming, increasingly and against his will, Benjamin's "world," there was nothing more conspicuous than anonymity. Even if gossip never reached him, Rask—with his fastidiously unremarkable appearance, his abstemious habits, and his monastic hotel life—knew he must be regarded as somewhat of a "character." Mortified at the mere thought of being considered an eccentric, he decided to conform to the expectations of a man of his position. He built a limestone *beaux arts* mansion on Fifth Avenue at 62nd Street and hired Ogden Codman to decorate it, certain that his ornamental achievements would be touted in all the social pages. After the house was completed, he tried but ultimately was unable to host a ball—he gave up once he understood, working on the guest list with a secretary, that social commitments multiply exponentially. He joined several clubs, boards, charities, and associations at which he was seldom seen. All this he did with displeasure. But it would have displeased him even more to be thought of as an "original." In the end, he became a wealthy man playing the part of a wealthy man. That his circumstances coincided with his costume did not make him feel any better.

New York swelled with the loud optimism of those who believe they have outpaced the future. Rask, of course, benefited from this breakneck growth, but to him, it was strictly a numerical event. He did not feel compelled to ride on the recently inaugurated subway lines. On a few occasions, he had visited some of the many skyscrapers being erected all over town, but it never occurred to him to move his offices to one of them. He viewed automobiles as a nuisance, both on the streets and in conversation. (Cars had become a pervasive and, to his mind, endlessly tedious topic among employees and associates.) Whenever possible, he avoided crossing the new bridges that tied the city together, and he had nothing to do with the multitudes of immigrants who landed every day on Ellis Island. He experienced most of what happened in New York through the newspapers—and, above all, through the ciphers on the ticker tape. And still, despite his particular (some would have said narrow) view of the city, even he could see that although mergers and consolidations had resulted in the concentration of the wealth in a handful of corporations of unprecedented size, there was, ironically, a collective feeling of success. The sheer magnitude of these new monopolistic companies, a few of them worth more than the entire government budget, was proof of how unequally the bounty was distributed. Yet most people, no matter their circumstances, were certain they were part of the soaring economy—or would be, soon enough.

Then, in 1907, Charles Barney, president of the Knickerbocker Trust Co., became involved in a scheme to corner the copper market. The attempt failed, wrecking a mine, two brokerage houses, and a bank in its wake. Soon thereafter, it was announced that checks from the Knickerbocker would no longer be accepted. The National Bank of Commerce met the requests of the depositors for the next few days, until Barney saw no choice but to shut his doors and, about a month later, shoot himself in the chest. The failing of the Knickerbocker sent waves of panic through the markets. A widespread run caused general insolvency, the Stock Exchange plunged, loans were called in, brokerage houses filed for bankruptcy, trust companies defaulted, commercial banks failed. All sales stopped. People trooped down Wall Street, demanding to withdraw their deposits. Squadrons of mounted police officers rode back and forth trying to preserve public order. In the absence of cash on hand, the call-money rate skyrocketed to over 150 percent in a matter of days. Vast amounts of bullion were ferried over from Europe, yet the millions flowing across the Atlantic failed to assuage the crisis. As the very foundations of credit were crumbling, Rask, who had robust cash reserves, took advantage of the liquidity crisis. He knew which companies hit by the panic were resilient enough to survive it, and he picked up assets at preposterously undervalued prices. His assessments in many cases were one step ahead of those of J. P. Morgan's men, who often swooped in right after Rask, driving the stock up. In fact, in the midst of the storm, he received a note from Morgan, mentioning his father ("Solomon's were the finest maduros I ever had the pleasure to smoke") and inviting him to confer with some of his most trusted people at his library, "to help safeguard our nation's interests." Rask declined without providing an excuse.

It took Rask some time to find his bearings in the new heights to which he ascended after the crisis. A humming halo surrounded him wherever he went. He felt it between him and the world at all times. And he could tell others felt it, too. His visible routine remained the same—he kept to his mostly deserted home on Fifth Avenue and, from there, maintained the outward illusion that he led an intense social life, which, in reality, was limited to a few appearances at functions where he thought his ghostly appearance would have the greatest impact. Still, his coup during the panic had turned him into a different person. What was truly surprising, even to himself, was that he had started to look for signs of acknowledgment in everyone he met. He was hungry to confirm that people noticed the hum enveloping him, the quiver, the very thing that estranged him from them. However paradoxical, this desire to confirm the distance separating him from others was a form of communion with them. And he was new to this feeling.

Because it had now become impossible for him to make every decision regarding his business, Rask was forced to develop a close relationship with a young man at his office. Sheldon Lloyd, who rose through the ranks to become his most trusted assistant, sifted through the daily matters that demanded Rask's attention, letting only the truly important issues ever reach his desk. He also took several of the daily meetings—his employer joined him only when a show of force was necessary. In more than one way, Sheldon Lloyd embodied most of the aspects of the financial world that Benjamin abhorred. For Sheldon, as for most people, money was a means to an end. He spent it. Bought things. Houses, vehicles, animals, paintings. Talked loudly about them. Traveled and threw parties. Wore his wealth on his body—his skin smelled different every day; his shirts were not pressed but new; his coats shone almost as much as his hair. He brimmed with that most conventional and embarrassing of qualities—"taste." Rask would look at him, thinking only an employee would spend the money someone else gave to him in such a fashion: looking for relief and freedom.

It was precisely because of Sheldon Lloyd's frivolity that Benjamin found him useful. His assistant was a shrewd trader, yes, but Rask also understood that he personified the stereotype of what many of his clients and fleeting associates considered to be "a success." Sheldon Lloyd was the perfect mouthpiece for his business—a much more effective presence, in many contexts, than his employer. Because Sheldon so faithfully complied with all the expectations of what a financier should look like, Benjamin started to rely on him for matters beyond his official duties. He asked him to organize dinners and parties, and Sheldon was delighted to oblige, crowding Rask's home with his friends and eagerly entertaining board members and investors. The true host invariably slipped away early, but the fiction that he led a somewhat active social life was strengthened.

In 1914, Sheldon Lloyd was shipped to Europe to finalize a deal with Deutsche Bank and a German pharmaceutical company and to conduct some business in Switzerland as his employer's agent. The Great War caught Sheldon in Zürich, where Rask had sent him to acquire interests in some of the thriving new local banks.

Back home, Benjamin directed his attention to the tangible foundations of his wealth—things and people, which the conflict had merged into one single machine. He invested in sectors related to the war, from mining and steelmaking to munitions manufacturing and shipbuilding. He became interested in aviation, seeing the commercial potential airplanes would have in times of peace. Fascinated by the technological advancements that defined those years, he funded chemical companies and financed engineering ventures, patenting many of the invisible parts and fluids in the new engines driving the world's industry. And, through his proxies in Europe, he negotiated bonds issued from every nation involved in the war. Yet, despite how formidable his wealth had become, this was only the starting point of his true ascent.

His reticence increased with his reach. The further and deeper his investments extended into society, the more he withdrew into himself. It seemed that the virtually endless mediations that constitute a fortune—equities and bonds tied to corporations tied to land and equipment and laboring multitudes, housed, fed, and clothed through the labor of yet other multitudes around the world, paid in different currencies with a value, also the object of trade and speculation, tied to the fate of different national economies tied, ultimately, to corporations tied to equities and bonds—had rendered immediate relationships irrelevant to him. Still, as he reached and passed what he thought was the midpoint of his life, a dim sense of genealogical responsibility, together with an even vaguer notion of propriety, made him consider marriage.

TWO

The Brevoorts were an old Albany family whose fortune had not kept up with their name. It had taken three generations of failed politicians and novelists to reduce them to a state of dignified precariousness. Their house on Pearl Street, one of the first built in the city, was the very embodiment of that dignity, and Leopold and Catherine Brevoort's existence revolved, to a large extent, around its upkeep. By the time Helen was born, they had closed down the upper floors to make sure they could give the lower ones, where they entertained, their full attention. Their parlor was one of the centers of Albany's social life, and the Brevoorts' dwindling means did not prevent them from receiving Schermerhorns, Livingstons, and Van Rensselaers. If their gatherings were so successful, it was because they achieved a rare balance between lightness (Catherine had a knack for making others feel like gifted conversationalists) and gravitas

(Leopold was widely acknowledged as one of the local intellectual and moral authorities).

In their set, meddling with politics was seen as something rather ignoble, and literature smacked of bohemianism. Mr. Brevoort, however, combined his ancestors' ungentlemanly love of public service and the written word by penning two volumes on political philosophy. Embittered by the perfect silence that met his work, he turned to his young daughter and took her schooling in his hands. Since Helen's birth, Mr. Brevoort had been too preoccupied with his failing affairs to pay any serious attention to her, but now that he had decided to take charge of her education, he delighted in every facet of her personality. At age five, she was already an avid reader, and her father was surprised to find in her a precocious interlocutor. They went for long walks along the Hudson, sometimes well into the night, discussing the natural phenomena around them—tadpoles and constellations, falling leaves and the winds carrying them, the moon's halo and the stag's antlers. Leopold had never experienced this sort of joy.

He found all the available schoolbooks insufficient, questioning both their content and pedagogical approach. Therefore, when he was not teaching or tending to the social obligations his wife always seemed to create for him, Mr. Brevoort was busy writing manuals and composing workbooks for his daughter. They contained instructive games, riddles, and puzzles that Helen enjoyed and almost invariably solved. Along with science, literature was featured prominently in their educational program. They read American transcendentalists, French moralists, Irish satirists, and German aphorists. With the aid of obsolete dictionaries, they attempted the translation of tales and fables from Scandinavia, ancient Rome, and Greece. Encouraged by the utterly absurd result of their efforts (Mrs. Brevoort often had to break into their little study to ask them to stop laughing "like horses" when she was entertaining), they started a collection of fabricated, outrageous myths. The first two or three years of Helen's studies under her father's tutelage would remain the happiest in her life, and even if, in time, the details and contours of these memories faded, the general feeling of excitement and plenitude remained as bright and vivid as ever in her mind.

In his effort to widen his syllabus, Mr. Brevoort's capricious research methods led him to defunct scientific theories, derelict philosophical edifices, deranged psychological doctrines, and impious theological dogmas. Trying to marry religion and science, he became absorbed in the teachings of Emanuel Swedenborg. This was a turning point in his life—and his relationship with his daughter. Guided by Swedenborg's teachings, he believed reason, rather than penance and fear, was the road to virtue and perhaps even to the divine. Mathematical treatises became second only to Scripture, and Mr. Brevoort was delighted at the elegant ease with which Helen, at age seven or eight, solved recondite algebraic problems and could give detailed exegeses of a number of biblical passages. She was also asked to keep meticulous dream journals, which they parsed with numerological fervor, looking for ciphered missives from the angels.

Some of Mr. Brevoort's former joy had wilted in the shadow of his newfound passion for theology. Still, for as long as she could, Helen carried on with the good-humored spirit of their previous years. To lighten the thickening tedium of her daily lessons, Helen learned how to toy with her increasingly distant father. True, there were many aspects of the largely improvised curriculum that she enjoyed and applied herself to—arithmetic, optics, trigonometry, chemistry, astronomy—but she found the more mystical parts of Mr. Brevoort's syllabus dull, until she discovered how to twist and bend them for her amusement. She created anagrams with biblical prophecies to foretell their family's future; she designed her own cabalistic interpretations of Old Testament texts, backed by esoteric mathematical arguments her father always found impressive, whether he understood them or not; she filled the pages of her dream journal with shocking entries, many of them verging on the indecent. Leopold had demanded that the accounts of her dreams be uncompromisingly honest, and Helen enjoyed watching his chin quiver with ill-concealed horror as he read her faintly filthy fabrications.

If making up her dreams had begun as a prank, eventually it became a necessity. Around the time she turned nine, insomnia started lengthening her nights, depriving her not just of dreams but of peace. Icy spores of anxiety colonized her mind and reduced it to a wasteland of fear. Her blood, thinned, seemed to course too fast through her veins. Sometimes she thought she could feel her heart gasping. These terror-filled vigils became more and more frequent, and the days that followed them were a haze. She found it almost impossible to do her part in upholding reality. And yet it was this dampened version of herself that her parents preferred—her father followed her uninspired work with great pleasure; her mother found her more approachable.

Helen soon came to realize that in addition to being her father's pupil she had become his object of study. He seemed interested in the concrete results of his teachings and tracked how they shaped his daughter's mind and morals. When he examined her, Helen often thought someone else was peering out from behind his eyes. It was only in hindsight that she saw that all this prying had driven her to create a quiet, unassuming character, a role she performed with flawless consistency around her parents and their friends—inconspicuously polite, never speaking if it could be helped, responding with nods and monosyllables whenever possible, always looking away from people's eyes, avoiding the company of adults at all costs. That she never shed this persona made her wonder, later in life, if that was not who she had truly been all along or if, rather, over the years, her spirit had shaped itself after the mask.

The gatherings at Pearl Street remained well populated despite the family's reduced means, a testimony to Mrs. Brevoort's charm and dexterity. Neither the declining quality of her tea nor the multiple desertions among her help had deterred her visitors from calling. Not even her husband, whose behavior had become as erratic as his words had become cryptic, had been able to turn her guests away. By the sheer force of her charm—and some deft political maneuvers—she made sure her parlor remained at the heart of Albany's social and intellectual life. But the point came where they had to reopen the upper floors, furnish them as best they could, and take in lodgers. Mrs. Brevoort would have been able to circumvent the shame of having government employees clumping up and down her stairs, but her habitués thought it more tactful, for her sake, to move their gatherings elsewhere. It was around this time that the Brevoorts decided Albany had become too provincial for them.

They spent a month in New York City before embarking for Europe, staying at the house of one of Mrs. Brevoort's friends on East 84th Street at Madison Avenue, a mere few blocks away from the mansion nobody suspected would become Helen's future home. In fact, years later, she would often look back at that time in New York and wonder if her eleven-year-old self might have spotted, during one of her walks with her mother, the already successful businessman who would become her husband. Had the girl and the man ever seen each other? It is certain, in any case, that, as a child, she spent several dull hours in the company of many of the people who would compete for her attention and friendship as a married woman. Her mother brought her to every daytime engagement she was able to attend in the course of that month—lunches, lectures, teas, recitals. What she could learn at these events was more essential to her education, Mrs. Brevoort often said, than the botany lessons or the Greek she received from her father. As was her custom, Helen remained quiet during these gatherings— watching and listening, without guessing that about a decade later she would recognize many of those faces and voices, without imagining how well it would serve her adult incarnation to know who pretended to remember or forget her.

THEIR LIFE IN EUROPE would have been impossible without Mrs. Brevoort. Upon first arriving in France, they took modest rooms in Saint-Cloud, but Catherine soon discovered it was simply too removed from the center of Paris. Since she had many errands to run, she went to visit the Lowells on Île Saint-Louis for a few days, on her own. From there, she called on the people she knew or had been asked to see, bringing news, letters, and sensitive messages from New York. Before the end of their first week, they had been invited to stay at Margaret Pullman's house on Place des Vosges. This situation repeated itself almost everywhere: the Brevoorts would arrive in Biarritz, in Montreux, in Rome and take reasonable lodgings at a *pension* or an *albergo* in a somewhat lesser yet respectable section of town. Mrs. Brevoort would then spend about a week visiting her friends, delivering messages, and making new acquaintances among American expatriates, after which she and her family were invited to become the guests of one of them. In time, however, the roles were inverted: if at first it had been Mrs. Brevoort who had relied on the kindness of her more prosperous compatriots, after a year or so, the demand for her company was so high she had to start declining invitations, which only made her more desirable. Wherever her family went, she became the node that connected all wandering Americans worth knowing.

It was not uncommon for Americans abroad to avoid one another. Not only because, according to an unspoken protocol, it was the tactful thing to do, but also because no one wanted to be perceived as friendless in Europe and provincially dependent on acquaintances from back home. Well aware of this code, Mrs. Brevoort made use of it and became a courier of sorts among the self-isolated foreigners who heartily welcomed her services, which allowed them to sustain their pretense of aloof autonomy. She was the person to turn to for a much-desired introduction that, in other hands, would have been an awkward affair; she mended broken bonds and created new ones; she managed to include people in select circles while, crucially, preserving the sense that these circles were closed; she was, everyone agreed, a peerless anecdotalist and a consummate matchmaker.

Traveling alongside mountains, by the sea, or through cities (following the seasons), and staying, lingering, or making haste (following convenience), the Brevoorts drew the map of their own peculiar Grand Tour. Mr. Brevoort devoted most of this time to tutoring his daughter and seeking out different mystical circles—spiritism, alchemy, mesmerism, necromancy, and other forms of occultism had become his all-absorbing concerns. Helen was already heavyhearted to have lost a friend and her only European companion in her father, but it was around this time that her spirits sank to new depths: she was older, well-read, and educated enough to realize that Leopold was becoming a hoarder of nonsense. She was being displaced by dogmas and creeds that a few years before would have been the object of their shared ridicule and served as inspiration for their absurd tales. It was sad enough to see her father drift away, but it was crushing to find her respect for his intellectual worth vanish with him.

Still, Mr. Brevoort was not altogether oblivious of his daughter's talents. A few years into their travels, he had to admit that her aptitude for languages, numbers, biblical hermeneutics, and what he called her mystical intuitions had developed beyond his abilities, and he started planning part of the family's itinerary around various scholars who could further her education. This brought them to humble boardinghouses in small country villages or hostels in the suburbs of university towns where mother, father, and daughter were forced to spend time with only one another for company. Isolated and out of their element,

Mr. and Mrs. Brevoort became quarrelsome and mean. Helen retreated further into herself, and her silence opened up a battleground for her parents' increasingly acrid arguments. Still, when the time finally came for the interview with an illustrious professor or an authority on the occult, a transformation always took place in Helen. She was suddenly crystalline with confidence—something about her hardened, shone, and sharpened.

Whether in the center of Jena, the fringes of Toulouse, or the suburbs of Bologna, the routine remained, for the most part, the same. They hired rooms at an inn, where Mrs. Brevoort claimed some sort of indisposition that demanded bed rest, while Mr. Brevoort took his daughter to see the great man who had brought them there. Leopold Brevoort's lengthy and for the most part unintelligible introductions always made their host look at him and his daughter with apprehension and regret. Not only had his doctrines become quite arcane, but they were delivered in a hodgepodge of mostly fictional French, German, and Italian. Some of these academics and mystics were impressed by Helen's intimate knowledge of Scripture, her scholarly attainments, and her fluency in different esoteric dogmas. Sensing their interest, Mr. Brevoort would try to say something, but he was stopped by a raised palm and ignored for the rest of the interview. A few of these tutors asked him to leave the room. And some, with pedagogical warmth, grabbed Helen's leg but soon withdrew their hands, frightened by her lethal impassiveness and unyielding glare.

◆

HELEN HAD LEFT HER CHILDHOOD in Albany. Being constantly on the move, she met few girls her age, and those casual encounters never had a chance to blossom into full friendships. To pass the time, she taught herself languages with books she shifted between different homes and hotels—she would take a copy of *La Princesse de Clèves* from a bookcase in Nice and then reshelve it in a library in Siena after removing from it *I viaggi di Gulliver*, with which she filled the gap created by borrowing *Rot und Schwarz* in Munich. Sleeplessness kept claiming her nights, and she used books as shields against the onslaught of her abstract terrors. When books proved insufficient, she turned to her diary. The dream journals her father had made her keep for a few years had instilled in her the daily habit of recording her thoughts. Over time, as he stopped reading her entries, her writing turned away from her dreams and toward her musings on books, her impressions of the cities they visited, and, during her white nights, her innermost fears and yearnings.

Early in her youth, a quiet but decisive event took place. She and her parents were staying at Mrs. Osgood's villa in Lucca. Helen had been walking through the grounds and then, stunned by the heat, around the empty house. They were the only guests. The servants scurried away at the sound of her steps. A dog, splayed out on the cool terra-cotta floor, its half-open eyes staring into its cranium, was having convulsive dreams. She looked into the drawing room: her father and Mr. Osgood had fallen asleep in their armchairs. Helen felt softly vicious, possessed by a vague desire to do harm. She realized she was peering through the bottom of boredom. There was violence on the other side. She turned on her heels and went back out into the garden. As she reached the shady spot where her mother and her host were having lemonade, she simply announced that she was going for a stroll in town. Perhaps because her tone was so peremptory, perhaps because her mother was in the middle of an emphatically whispered conversation with Mrs. Osgood, or perhaps because hazel-and-copper Lucca glowed with benevolence that afternoon, there was no objection—just a quick side glance from Mrs. Brevoort, who told her daughter to enjoy her *passeggiata* but not to go too far. And so, unnoticed by everyone other than herself, a new chapter began for Helen. For the first time in her life, she was out in the world on her own.

She barely paid attention to the country road and its surroundings, lost in her fulfilled dream of independence, but she was woken up by the stuccoed silence that first met her in town. The dry echo of her shoes on the cobblestones was all she could hear in the empty streets. Every few steps, she gently dragged a foot, just to feel the skin on her neck tingle with delight at the murmur of leather on stone. With each block, the small city became livelier. Trying to prolong the sense of elation she had found in the initial stillness, she walked on, with buoyant aplomb, away from the voices crashing at distant intersections, away from the mercantile clatter coming from the square, away from the liquid hoofbeats clip-clopping around the corner, away from the women yelling from window to window as they unpinned their laundry, and into alleyways with houses shuttered against the heat, where she could hear, again, her solitary steps. She knew, then, that this solemn form of joy, so pure because it had no content, so reliable because it relied on nobody else, was the state for which she would henceforth strive.

Trying to avoid the hubbub of the square, where some sort of jubilee or religious *festa* was now taking place, Helen found herself on a street with a few shops. One of them was a double anachronism. A photographic studio could only be an incongruity in that small city, with its Etruscan past that made medieval churches feel new. But on closer inspection, this dissonant apparition from the future revealed itself to be, in fact, old. The portraits in the window, the cameras on display, the services offered—all remitted to the early days of photography. And somehow, Helen experienced those thirty or fifty years by which the shop was outdated more acutely than the twenty centuries elapsed since the city's foundation. She went in.

The shop, chalky with the light streaming through the delicately unclean windows, revealed a strange sort of indecision. At first, Helen thought the beakers, pipettes, and oddly shaped glassware, along with labeled flasks, bottles, and jars, were part of the great assortment of props that cluttered the room—bicycles and Roman helmets, parasols and stuffed animals, dolls and nautical accoutrements. But gradually she understood the place was stuck somewhere between the realms of science and art. Was this a chemist's laboratory or painter's studio? It seemed as if both sides had given up a good while ago, leaving the dispute unresolved.

A small man with kind or exhausted features came out from behind a curtain in the back. He was delighted to find that this foreign young lady spoke Italian so well. After a short conversation, he produced an album with cabinet cards, the old-fashioned kind Helen's mother used to collect as a child. She recognized many of the objects the legionaries, hunters, and sailors held in the photographs. The man said she should make an imposing Minerva. He unrolled a backdrop of the Parthenon, placed Helen in front of it, and rummaged through the props for a helmet, a spear, and a stuffed owl. Helen declined. But before disappointment set in on the photographer's face, she said she would very much like to have her picture taken. No costume, though. No backdrop. Just her, standing there, in the shop. The photographer, pleased and confused in equal measure, proceeded to record the first day of Helen's new life.

HAVING REACHED THEIR FOURTH YEAR on the Continent, the Brevoorts had been to all the capitals and vacation sites frequented by American expatriates, while also tracing what, on the map, looked like a demented trail in their attempt to further Helen's education. Because they had traveled so widely and for so long, following both their social and academic pursuits, Helen—very much despite her reserved disposition and mostly because of her mother's indefatigable efforts to promote her family's triumphs—had turned into a bit of a sensation. Whenever Leopold was away on one of his short trips to visit a salon of particular interest, attend a séance, join a meeting of the Theosophical Society, or see one of the people he called his colleagues, Mrs. Brevoort would bring her daughter to some of her engagements, claiming she was now old enough to start learning how the world truly worked. But according to form, Helen was, of course, too young to be out in society. Mrs. Brevoort, then, brought her along not as another guest but as entertainment.

Prompted by Mrs. Brevoort, men skeptically swirling snifters of brandy and ladies sipping thimblefuls of sherry with bemusement had Helen read passages from two random books, sometimes in different languages, which she would quickly memorize and then repeat verbatim as an after-dinner diversion. The distracted guests found this somewhat charming. But when Mrs. Brevoort, after that initial demonstration, asked her daughter to alternate sentences from each one of them, and then do the same thing starting at the end, smug smiles invariably slackened into gaping awe. This was only the first feat in her routine, which included a variety of mental stunts and always ended in a murmured ovation. Soon, her presence started to be requested. She became somewhat of a "thing." There was no need for

Mrs. Brevoort to tell her daughter to keep these performances, which were doing so much for the family's renown, a secret from her father.

But there is no such thing as confidential publicity, and in the end, while the family was visiting with the Edgecombs in Paris, Mr. Brevoort was furious to learn that his wife had been using his daughter's talents as a parlor trick. Over the previous year or two, as their inclinations diverged and their marriage deteriorated in proportion, Catherine and Leopold Brevoort had tried, for the most part, to stay out of each other's way, hoping to avoid the bickering in which most of their exchanges ended. When the truth about Helen's performances came to light, however, the anger that had hardened and sedimented in heavy layers of resentment came crashing down in a landslide. Mrs. Brevoort was sick and tired of her husband's self-absorbed gibberish, his dubious science, and all the celestial nonsense that kept him from addressing his family's very terrestrial needs. If things had reached the point where they depended on the kindness of increasingly distant friends, whose hospitality they enjoyed thanks to her resourcefulness and her hard work (and Mrs. Brevoort gave this last word its full weight by pointing at her own chest), and if she needed to enlist Helen's talents to maintain and expand those friendships, it was only because he could not be relied upon to ensure the well-being of his family. Mrs. Brevoort had spoken in a venomous hiss, knowing better than to engage in a shouting match while staying in the Edgecombs' guest room. But Mr. Brevoort had no such qualms. The gift that God had given his daughter to converse with Him, he screamed, was not to become a sacrilegious circus act. His daughter would not be dragged into the frivolous mud in which his wife so much enjoyed to plod. His daughter would not be subjected to this intellectual harlotry.

Helen looked at her shoes throughout the entire fight. She could not face her father; she did not want to see his mouth forming those senseless words. It would be a confirmation that someone else was now speaking through him. This way, it was just a ranting voice—a disembodied scream, unrelated to her father. More than the threatening tone, what she found terrifying was the incoherence of his tirade, because she thought there was no greater violence than the one done to meaning.

After this row (it would take Mrs. Brevoort an embarrassed conversation with Mrs. Edgecomb the next morning, followed by several weeks devoted to a tactful counter-gossip campaign around Paris, to partially undo that evening's damage), Helen's talents continued to flourish, against all odds, under the most rigid surveillance. Although she disliked being subjected to her father's rigorous and rambling tutelage, she did not find his strictures more oppressive than her mother's gregariousness.

ONE OF THE FEW TRAITS the Brevoorts had in common, even if for entirely different reasons, was their disdainful lack of curiosity regarding current events. Mrs. Brevoort viewed the irruption of public affairs into her private life as a personal affront. She cared about the administrative, financial, and diplomatic intricacies that kept society going as much as she was concerned about the engine under the hood of a motorcar or the fire room below a steamer's deck. "Things" should simply "work." She had no interest in a mechanic explaining to her what the problem was with some greasy piston valve. As for Mr. Brevoort, what could the daily news possibly mean to someone occupied with eternity? Since they both lived on the outskirts of political reality, they did not immediately understand the grave implications of Archduke Franz Ferdinand's assassination.

Everyone told them they were lucky to find themselves in Switzerland and advised them not to leave the country until the situation became clearer. As they made their way to Zürich—where they had planned, months earlier, to meet some friends and then go on a summer excursion—they saw the Swiss army being mobilized and heard the borders were being militarized. It was the very height of the season, and there were thousands of Americans scattered around mountain, valley, and lakeside spas—from convalescents spending their savings at hostelries by municipal baths to New York grandees taking the cure at stately hotels. Orme Wilson, for example, found himself in Bern, Chauncey Thorowgood in Geneva, Cardinal Farley in Brunnen, and Cornelius Vanderbilt in St. Moritz. Regardless of rank, however, all the Americans the Brevoorts met along the way were in a state of frenzy. There was talk of war. Total war.

When they first arrived in Zürich, the Brevoorts stayed with the

Betterleys, who had just spoken with Mr. Pleasant Stovall, United States Minister to Switzerland. Should they go on with their vacation or go home? Mr. Stovall said that concerns over war were not uncommon in Europe. But every seasoned diplomat was well aware of the disastrous consequences of an open conflagration, and he therefore hoped reason and friendly interventions would manage to avert this major disaster. Within a few weeks, Austria, Serbia, Germany, Russia, and Great Britain had issued formal declarations of war. Soon, the conflict engulfed most of Europe.

During the strange months that followed, the improvised American community in Switzerland was dragged, as a whole, into something that resembled what had been the Brevoorts' everyday reality for years. There was neither cash nor gold at hand; checks, even those issued by sound American banking houses, were repudiated; letters of credit were refused. Millionaires depended on the goodwill of hoteliers and had to borrow pocket money from them. People brought their own sugar to tea. Everyone received rationing cards, and at dinner parties, the guests, in gowns and white ties, would give theirs to the hosts providing the meal. There was a widespread state of indigent precariousness. And Mrs. Brevoort had never felt so relieved and relaxed in her whole life.

Still, there was the reality of the war encroaching on them—a reality of which the belligerent airplanes grazing the Alps on their way toward the front were a constant reminder. Most shipping lines had had their vessels interned or their sailings canceled. Obtaining a ticket on a small, crowded boat was a luxury that required connections of the highest order. While Mrs. Brevoort was doing all she could to secure safe passage out of Europe for her family, Mr. Brevoort seemed to have taken permanent residence in a remote land ruled by occult conspiracies, mystic hierarchies, and labyrinthine laws. Everyday tasks became unmanageable, and each morning found him more and more disoriented. He spoke, day and night, in a mélange of increasingly imaginary tongues, struggling to understand the rules he had created for himself and getting lost in the antinomies and paradoxes that beset his mind. He became irascible.

Helen tried to meet her father in the trackless territories of his delirium. She sat with him and listened as he talked without interruption. Sometimes she asked a question, more as proof that she was paying attention than to get a proper answer. Her efforts to understand him were sincere and based on the hope that if she could find any shred of sense, any thread, she would be able to hold on to it and lead her father out of his maze. Yet her attempts always met the same end: Leopold's thoughts curved and curled on themselves, forming a circle that Helen could not enter and he was unable to leave. As if to prove the possibility of physical movement, she was compelled to go on long walks after experiencing this mental claustrophobia.

Mr. Brevoort's condition made it untenable for the family to remain the Betterleys' houseguests, and they had to move to a nearby inn. He covered one notebook after the other with alchemic formulas and calculations in digits and symbols of his invention. His face was besmirched with ink at all times; his monologue, which his obedient hand seemed to be forever transcribing, was never to be interrupted. It became clear to Mrs. Brevoort that it would be impossible to traverse the war-ridden continent and then the Atlantic Ocean with her husband in that condition. Thanks to Mr. and Mrs. Betterley, who pleaded on her behalf to Ambassador Stovall, she was able to secure a spot for Mr. Brevoort at Dr. Bally's Medico-Mechanic Institute at Bad Pfäfers, whose waters, rich in carbonate of lime and magnesia, in conjunction with massage and physical activities at high altitude, were known to be beneficial to patients with nervous ailments.

Mrs. Betterley was glad to look after Helen while Mrs. Brevoort took her husband to the sanatorium. Helen bid her father farewell at the inn. He never looked up from the notebook on which he was taking dictation from himself. It was the last time Helen would ever see him.

Helen's parentless days in Zürich confirmed the intuition she had first had during her walk in Tuscany—that she somehow felt elevated by solitude. She strolled, euphoric and serene, along the promenades skirting the lake; she took random tramways to the end of the line and ambled back; she went to the old town and visited museums and picture galleries. And she always found herself returning to the botanical garden, where she liked to sit with a book in the shadow of the arboretum. It was there where, one afternoon, a foppish American, encouraged by the volume in English she was reading, approached her with some vague horticultural excuse. They introduced themselves, and there was a flash of interest in his eyes when she uttered her last name—a half-concealed spark of recognition many Americans often showed, as if to discreetly let on that they knew of the Brevoort pedigree. He struck up a conversation, emboldened by the fortuity of having found another New Yorker in such a peculiar place. Helen, calmly annoyed at the intrusion, responded with monosyllables to his pleasantries. During a lull, he plucked a flower for his lapel and then one for Helen. She looked at it but did not take it. Repressing a flash of irritated confusion, the man used the flower to point to different parts of the city while expounding on the different historical aspects of each vista. It did not seem to bother him that Helen paid little attention and even looked away from the sights he spoke about. He simply enjoyed explaining things, and under this pretext, he managed to learn where Helen lived and invite himself to walk her back so he could show her some of the city's hidden treasures along the way. When they finally arrived, Sheldon Lloyd introduced himself to Miss Brevoort's hosts.

Mr. Betterley exchanged a meaningful look with his wife, asked Sheldon to supper the following evening, and then escorted him to the door, where the two men lingered for a hushed chat.

Mr. Lloyd did come to supper the following evening, followed by a porter from his hotel carrying two baskets full of provisions, and called again at lunch, dinner, or teatime during the next five or six days. The Betterleys were more than welcoming and made sure to give their guest an hour of laxly supervised time with Helen after each meal. He devoted most of those moments to talk about his achievements and the life they afforded him, describing each single detail concerning his clever dealings, started right before the war on behalf of his firm, with Deutsche Bank; all the paintings by European masters hanging in his apartment or on loan to the Metropolitan Museum; every facet of the investments he had been asked to pursue with Krupp; his house in Rhinebeck, partially built and then torn down and rebuilt following unanticipated needs; how he had outsmarted his employer, who thought he had outsmarted the board of directors at Haber Pharmaceuticals; the string of horses in his stable and his glass-roofed riding ring; the bureaucratic convolutions inherent in setting up the bank his employer was opening in Zürich, encouraged by the city's blossoming financial industry; his motor yacht, which he sailed down the Hudson for his summer commutes to Wall Street. Sheldon, it seemed, had taken Helen's distracted silence for speechless awe.

After almost two weeks, Mrs. Brevoort returned from the sanatorium. Mrs. Betterley gave her a few moments to display her grief about her husband's condition and bemoan her uncertain future before telling her about Helen's new acquaintance. Mrs. Brevoort took a moment, as if riffling through her brain in search of just who this Sheldon Lloyd might be, before asking, with studied hesitation, if that young man was not by any chance Mr. Rask's right hand. In an unusual defeat for Mrs. Brevoort, Mrs. Betterley did not dignify this poor performance with a response.

When Mrs. Brevoort and Sheldon met, she was quick to understand that he was very much impressed with Helen's lineage and that he hoped to attach an old name to his new money. And if Sheldon had felt flattered by Helen's silence, he was delighted to find in Mrs. Brevoort an unequivocally vocal admirer who uttered all the expected exclamations of amazement and gasped at every right moment. During their daily banquets, she made sure not only that he felt even more important than he thought he was, but also that he felt in charge—above all, by giving him the chance to gallantly rescue them from the fearsome grip of war. Little by little, through small trivial anecdotes, Mrs. Brevoort told Sheldon about her husband's disorder and her daughter's precarious circumstances. But she waited until his departure was a mere few days away to share with him, in its full lachrymose extent, the family's distressful situation. Sheldon, incapable of suspecting that his chivalrous spontaneity had been carefully induced, offered to drive mother and daughter to Genoa and invited them to join him on the *Violeta*, a Portuguese ship that would take them to New York.

THE ALBANY HOUSE was still rented out, and there was no point, really, either in subjecting Helen to such a provincial atmosphere after their time in Europe or in stressing Mr. Brevoort's absence by being around his relatives. Mrs. Brevoort was therefore glad to welcome Sheldon, yet again, as their savior and accept his generous offer to let them stay at a deceased aunt's apartment on Park Avenue he had neglected to sell.

The friendships forged on the Continent served Mrs. Brevoort well. Not satisfied with having most doors in the city open to her, she also wanted to open her doors to the city. The soirées at her new apartment soon became a fixture. Without making any kind of fuss about it, she started to have Helen out at these functions. Those who were unaware of her talents wondered how someone as charming and outgoing as Mrs. Brevoort could have such a reserved and even pensive daughter—a rumor the hostess was well aware of and manipulated to deepen the impression of Helen's intelligence and complexity of character.

Sheldon Lloyd never attended these occasions. The fact that Catherine and Helen were staying at a family home, added to the stories about the close relationship he had developed with mother and daughter in Europe and during their subsequent crossing of the Atlantic, made him—guided, in part, by Mrs. Brevoort's counsel—careful to ensure that people saw his aid had been disinterested. Still, during Sheldon and Helen's heavily chaperoned walks around the park, Mrs. Brevoort always made sure to bring up his virtuous magnanimity and remind him how absolutely indebted they were to him for the heroic deeds that, in the strictest sense, had saved their lives. On these strolls, Mrs. Brevoort circled back, over and again, in a manner so casual it made her persistence quite undetectable, to Mr. Lloyd's elusive and mythical employer. Was it true that Mr. Rask was omnipotently rich? Was he really still a bachelor? Why on earth? Did he ever go out? What were the tastes and pleasures of such a unique man? Sheldon was delighted to answer all these questions at length, understanding that his own stature grew with the financier's outsized, eccentric legend. It was, in fact, his vanity that made him reveal that Mr. Rask was too misanthropic (or lost in his work, he corrected himself) to have people over at his house and that it fell on him, Sheldon, to organize the lavish parties from which the host was mostly absent. And it was his arrogance that prompted him to invite mother and daughter to the gala for the Red Cross to be held at Mr. Rask's home. Sheldon wanted Helen to see for herself how magnificent his arrangements for the party would be.

Helen understood her mother's schemes all too well and realized that once the ideal suitor had been found, she would have to accept him. Having no marital or material ambitions of her own, Helen nevertheless believed she owed her mother a good marriage—it was their only chance to stop living at the expense of others and, finally, settle down. However, though she did not oppose Mrs. Brevoort's matchmaking maneuvers, her limp assent made it clear she refused to play an active part. Her unapproachable silence, which some thought a display of petulance, and her perennial abstraction, which many mistook for sadness, were not passive forms of disobedience but manifestations of ennui. She simply could not engage with the pleasantries and platitudes that moved her mother's matrimonial campaign forward. This very inability led her to realize that braggarts like Sheldon Lloyd, consumed as they were in self-contemplation, could, paradoxically, afford her some degree of autonomy. But instead of giving the obviously eager Mr. Lloyd the final push toward proposing, Mrs. Brevoort had kept him at a prudent distance, while still encouraging him in many subtle ways. Helen hoped her mother's ploys would go on long enough for them to backfire by the time she had become too old to marry.

The temples dedicated to wealth—with their liturgies, fetishes, and vestments—had never managed to transport Helen to a higher realm. She failed to be raptured. Nothing, as she first arrived at Mr. Rask's fastuous home, made her tingle with desire or even feel the momentary and vicarious thrill of a life unfettered from every material constraint. Sheldon was waiting for her and her mother next to the footman at the edge of the red carpet that cascaded down the steps and flowed across the sidewalk. Emboldened by his role as the surrogate host of one of the most splendid functions of the season, he walked Helen in by the arm, with Mrs. Brevoort in tow, annoyed at having been left behind unescorted—although her irritation soon dissipated in the glow of the surroundings. After they had handed their cloaks to a servant at the door, a butler announced their arrival in a soft yet projecting voice to a slender man standing on the shore of invisibility. Mrs. Brevoort managed to convey a curtsey through an almost imperceptible nod. Benjamin Rask might have nodded back or simply looked down. While she arranged her daughter's hair in the ladies' reception room, Mrs. Brevoort told her Mr. Rask looked much younger than she had expected. And was it not queer how uneasy he seemed to be in his own home? She supposed it was natural, after all—it would take an enormous personality to fill such an enormous place. Her monologue was interrupted by the arrival of other guests. Mother and daughter left for the drawing room, where Mrs. Brevoort could well have passed for the hostess. Sheldon was whispering a story to a group of men and making them roar with laughter. Helen retreated to the shadowy fringes of the room and stayed there until the butler told Sheldon dinner was served.

Helen and Catherine were placed at the opposite ends of the table, next to Mr. Lloyd and Mr. Rask, respectively. As they sat, Sheldon told Helen that, knowing how keen Mrs. Brevoort was to meet their host, he was certain she would appreciate this rare opportunity to talk to him (and enjoy being envied for her coveted spot at Mr. Rask's right side). All the way up to the fish course, Sheldon graciously made the conversation revolve around Helen and told their dining neighbors all about her travels, her talent for languages, and her bravery in the face of the perils of war, which she must have inherited from her illustrious revolutionary ancestors. But by the time the roast arrived, he had turned to his friends and colleagues, eager to make them laugh again, leaving Helen free to dismiss, with short answers, the questions the well-intentioned women around her asked. At the other end of the long table, her mother monopolized Mr. Rask's attention. Helen recognized all too well his absent nods and was therefore surprised when, during dessert, she could detect traces of genuine interest in Mr. Rask's face, as her mother, who now seemed to have lowered her voice, talked on. The time finally came for the gentlemen to smoke their cigars while the ladies gathered in the drawing room. Helen took this opportunity to slip away and wander through the house on her own.

The farther she got from the din of the party and the garishness of Sheldon's arrangements, the more the house changed. She entered an orderly, discreet world. There was a calm confidence to the silence, as if it knew it would always prevail with little effort. The faint coolness in the air was also a scent. It was not the conspicuous tokens of affluence that impressed her—the obvious Dutch oil paintings, the constellations of French chandeliers, the Chinese vases mushrooming in every corner. She was touched by smaller things. A doorknob. An unassuming chair in a dusky recess. A sofa and the void around it. They all reached out to her with their heightened presence. These were all common-enough objects, but they were the real things, the originals after which the flawed copies that littered the world had been made.

A shadow hesitated, right next to hers, on the threshold leading to a sitting room. Helen noticed that her own black shape on the floor expressed the same vacillation—the regret of having been seen, the lack of courage to leave, the unwillingness to come forth. The faceless silhouettes seemed to look at each other, as if wishing they could resolve the situation between themselves, without having to trouble their owners. Helen was not surprised when Benjamin Rask emerged from the sitting room.

Stiffly, they exchanged a few pleasantries. In the ensuing silence, they shifted from one foot to the other at the same time. Benjamin apologized and gestured to a sofa facing a window. They sat and looked more uncomfortable than when they were standing. Their reflections, half sunken in the dark pool of the window across the room, peered back at them. Benjamin told Helen he had heard, from Mrs. Brevoort, about her travels. Slowly, Helen drew the tip of her shoe against the grain of the silk carpet, leaving a small wake. Benjamin seemed to understand she would not respond unless it was necessary. After a pause, he started telling her how he had never really traveled or even left the East Coast but, feeling he was being unclear, kept interrupting himself, and finally fell silent, as if realizing that Helen, whose gaze examined the room in segments, was not listening to his muddled explanation.

Helen erased the wake she had left on the carpet by drawing her shoe in the opposite direction. Benjamin looked at her and then away, into the window.

"I."

When his pause became long enough to be final, she turned to him, curious about the rest of his sentence. His inability to finish it had hardened his features.

Sitting in the twilight of that hushed room, Helen understood at once that her mother had triumphed. She knew, with total certainty, that Benjamin Rask would take her as his wife, if she let him. And she decided right then that she would. Because she saw that he was, in essence, alone. In his vast solitude she would find hers—and with it, the freedom her overbearing parents had always denied her. Depending on whether his loneliness was voluntary, he would either ignore her or be grateful for the good companion she would try to become. One way or the other, she had no doubt she would succeed in influencing her husband and obtaining the independence she so longed for.

THREE

I ntimacy can be an unbearable burden for those who, first experiencing it after a lifetime of proud self-sufficiency, suddenly realize it makes their world complete. Finding bliss becomes one with the fear of losing it. They doubt their right to hold someone else accountable for their happiness; they worry that their loved one may find their reverence tedious; they fear their yearning may have distorted their features in ways they cannot see. Thus, as the weight of all these questions and concerns bends them inward, their newfound joy in companionship turns into a deeper expression of the solitude they thought they had left behind.

This was the sort of dread Helen sensed in her husband shortly after their wedding. Knowing that powerlessness has a way of turning into rancor—just as someone who undervalues himself eventually will blame others for his depreciation—she did her best to dissipate Benjamin's anxieties. Even if securing his peace ultimately meant safeguarding her own, Helen's motivations were not entirely selfish. She had been quick to develop a genuine fondness for Benjamin and his quiet habits. But being of a quiet nature herself, it was hard to find the right vocabulary, the proper gestures, or even the adequate venues to express her kind feelings, which (and she knew this was the main obstacle) by no measure matched his timid ardor.

A brief engagement had been followed by a rather unconventional winter wedding. There was nothing Mrs. Brevoort could do to put the whole affair off until at least early spring. And her indignant cries were also disregarded when it came to the ceremony and the celebration. Benjamin and Helen got married in the sitting room where they had first talked to each other, joined only by Catherine Brevoort and Sheldon Lloyd, who seemed eager to dispel any rumors about his previous informal courtship of the bride. The few guests invited to the luncheon following the ceremony were either Catherine's or Sheldon's friends. Ever since her engagement had been announced, Helen had perceived a general change of attitude in all of them. Those who, in the past, had bothered to try to bridge the distance she had always imposed between herself and the world had done so unceremoniously. Now that same distance had become a literal symbol of her new station. People tiptoed across the gap, trying to confirm with every hesitant step that they were indeed allowed to approach her. Often confused with shyness or arrogance, her silence was now, she could tell, taken to be the becoming attitude for someone of her standing, and her ill-concealed ennui was all of a sudden welcomed as sophisticated detachment—it would have been vulgar for someone like her to show an interest in anything. Everyone expected and even wanted her to be intimidating. But she had not felt the full extent of the prudish obsequiousness that would encircle her for the rest of her life until the wedding lunch, where she made her first appearance as Mrs. Rask.

The following morning, the newlyweds met for an almost wordless breakfast. Helen glanced at her husband across the table, relieved to have learned that she would be able to endure nights like the previous one without physical or moral pain. Benjamin, sensing he was being watched, put additional care in the cracking of his egg, trying to conceal that he was as disoriented and abashed as when he had left his wife's bedroom.

They had no desire to travel, but Benjamin still had taken two weeks off work for a brief honeymoon at their home, which was sufficiently alien to both of them to make it a bit of a holiday. Newspapermen loitered outside at all times, and some of them had mounted their cameras on tripods across the street, in case the couple ever looked out a window. Helen and Benjamin strolled around the rooms, making vague, halfhearted plans for their use. This took them to the third floor. After examining a parlor, a study, and a few bedrooms, they paused halfway down a corridor—a tunnel of wood and damask that amplified every small sound but dulled their voices. Trying to lead Helen away from the door at the end of the hallway, Benjamin said that was the one room they should not enter. Helen asked why by narrowing her eyes and cocking her head. It was a side door to his office, he said and paused. She did not repress a slightly impatient sigh. Turning away from the door, he told her he found it hard to leave once he went in. Helen, however, walked around him and opened it to reveal one of the largest spaces in the house, designed to impress and overwhelm but failing to do so because everything in it looked inert and unused. It was a big room, yes, but there were no papers, files, typewriters, or any other sign of real work. And it was not just that the place happened to be tidy, because on closer inspection it became clear that there was nothing there to be tidied up. Helen could not understand how this could be the office Benjamin claimed to be unable to leave until, in an unassuming nook next to a fireplace the size of a small room, she spotted a table on which, by a telephone, stood a glass dome with a device that she initially mistook for a clock or a barometer but was, she soon realized, a stock ticker. The patch of carpet in front of it was threadbare.

Once again, he tried to walk away from the office, claiming there was nothing to see; once again, Helen remained in her place. Benjamin, always looking away from his wife, allowed himself to ask her if she would not find her new home and circumstances oppressive. Perhaps if she made a few changes to the house to make it her own, she would ease into her new life? Yes, they probably should make some adjustments, he confirmed when she remained silent. Renovate. She touched his shoulder, smiled, and told him, with serene warmth, that neither of them really cared about such things. He did not know how to receive the unexpected gift of her affection. She nodded toward the ticker and, before leaving him in the room, said she would see him for dinner.

◆

During the war, Helen had been unable to reach her father at Dr. Bally's clinic in Switzerland. Once regular communications were restored, not too long after her wedding, she was stunned to learn, from a brief letter in German responding to her latest request for information, that Mr. Brevoort had left the facilities shortly after having been checked in. He had given no notice but simply vanished in the middle of the day, during garden activities. The staff had conducted an extensive search of the surroundings but had failed to find him. The doctor signing the letter regretted the delay in imparting this sad news and explained that even if the postal service had not been disrupted by the war, they had no address of a next of kin to write to until they received Mrs. Rask's letter.

Helen could not remember when she had last cried, and now she wept for reasons she initially failed to understand. The portion of her unaffected by grief could see that it would be natural to mourn the loss of a parent and almost thought her tears were the result of an innate reflex that did not, in actual fact, involve her emotions. This same part of her also experienced a clear sense of relief from knowing that her father, with his unbending dogmas and his burdensome madness, was gone. But gone where? And with this question, sorrow engulfed her completely. He could have been killed by shellfire or a stray bullet; he could have died of cold; he could have starved to death. But he could also be alive, a mumbling idiot roaming the countryside or begging his way through cities whose languages he did not speak. Or he could have recovered somehow and started a new family, dismissing the confused memory of his daughter as one of the hallucinations that had haunted him during his illness. In the most absolute sense, she had lost her father.

The moment Benjamin learned that Mr. Brevoort had vanished, he contacted his associates in Europe and instructed them to hire investigators to comb the entire continent. Helen knew it was all in vain but let him proceed and feel as if he were helping. As she thanked him, she also asked him to keep the news of her father from her mother, who was finally happy and safe after so many years of uncertainty. Helen's hidden intention, however, was to see whether Mrs. Brevoort would ever bring up her husband again. She did not.

Catherine Brevoort had taken permanent residence in the Park Avenue apartment, which Benjamin had bought for her from Sheldon Lloyd. Her social horizons had expanded considerably after Helen's wedding, and her gatherings had never been more successful. It was plain that most of the newcomers to her soirées attended in the hopes of meeting Mrs. Brevoort's elusive son-in-law. To Catherine's credit, these guests kept frequenting her salon even after it had become clear they would never get to see Mr. and Mrs. Rask there. Helen had stopped going to her mother's get-togethers as soon as she moved in with Benjamin, not only because she had always disliked social occasions, but also because she had found her mother increasingly difficult since the engagement. She knew that Mrs. Brevoort's newly acquired eccentricities, her heightened frivolity, her calculated impertinence, and her gratuitously flamboyant behavior were not simply manifestations of unbridled joy but acts of a festive sort of aggression directed straight at Helen both as a dare and as a lesson—"*This* is the life you should be living." The most eloquent declarations in her mother's unspoken monologue came in the form of bills and receipts. Mrs. Brevoort's parties (and her wardrobe and her furniture and her floral arrangements and her hired cars) had become rather extravagant affairs, and all bills were sent to Benjamin's office. They were never refused or even questioned, but Helen always had them forwarded to her once they had been paid, and she kept them as if they were a collection of one-sided letters from her mother.

During the first few years after the wedding, Rask's fortune experienced unusual growth. He and his men started conducting a rather shocking volume of trades in the widest imaginable array of instruments with a precision many of his colleagues found uncanny. These transactions were not necessarily spectacular coups, but put together, their often slim profit margins added up to formidable numbers. Wall Street was perplexed by Rask's accuracy and his systematic approach, which not only led to consistent earnings but also was an example of the most rigorous mathematical elegance—of an impersonal form of beauty. His colleagues thought him prescient, a sage with supernatural talents who simply could not lose.

It was in this period that Helen came to understand what Benjamin had realized a long time ago—that privacy requires a public façade. Since having some semblance of a social life seemed unavoidable, she decided to put hers to good use. Instead of following in her mother's footsteps, which were very much in keeping with the merry spirit of the times, she became involved in numerous philanthropic endeavors. Over the next several years, hospitals, concert halls, libraries, museums, shelters, and university wings appeared all over the country bearing plaques with the name of Rask on them.

At first, philanthropy had only been a part of Helen's social front. In time, however, she developed a genuine interest in cultural patronage. Since her marriage, she had been left free to pursue her love of literature, inherited from her father and then cultivated during her European travels. She was particularly interested in living authors, although she initially refused to meet them, knowing the distance between the work and the person could be covered only by disappointment. But in return for her support, many of these writers began to offer their advice and suggest causes worthy of her generosity. It seemed unreasonable not to pay heed to their counsel. With their help, she made the most of her philanthropic efforts, and in the process her sphere of action expanded. She was introduced to the foremost artists, musicians, novelists, and poets of the day. And much to her surprise, she started looking forward to meeting with these new acquaintances. Conversation had never been one of Helen's pleasures. Yet now, in the presence of the right interlocutors, she relished the verbal dexterity, quick erudition, and improvisational talent on display in their exchanges—although she preferred listening to joining in the discussion (to later record the liveliest, most thought-provoking moments in her journal, which by then comprised several thick volumes). It was not lost on her that by uniting her passion for the arts with her charitable endeavors she was reconciling her father's intellectual fervor with her mother's social skills.

Much as she enjoyed her work with artists, the cause closest to her heart was the research and treatment of psychiatric illnesses. She found it baffling and inexcusable that the medical sciences, which had made so much progress in every field, should lag in such a neglectful way when it came to mental disorders. In this regard, she worked closely with her husband, who had always manifested a keen interest in the chemical and pharmaceutical sectors and had invested heavily in them during the war. He was the majority shareholder in two American drug manufacturing companies and owned a large stake in Haber Pharmaceuticals in Germany, which Sheldon Lloyd had helped him obtain shortly before meeting Helen in Zürich. It became a priority for these companies to develop effective medications for the wide spectrum of psychiatric conditions so far treated with little more than morphine, chloral hydrate, potassium bromide, and barbital. The multitude of soldiers who had returned from the front with deep psychological scars and clear signs of mental trauma—and no adequate therapies to address their symptoms—made this research particularly urgent.

Helen and Benjamin invested considerable time poring over reports from their companies and meeting with scientists. Both of them having predatory minds (supple, swift, voracious), they learned fast. Soon, they were able to read fairly abstruse papers and academic treatises and talk about them with fluency. Their desire to learn about the latest developments in the field of chemistry was sincere, but it is also true they both held on to this pursuit because in pharmacology they had finally found a shared interest, a topic they could discuss passionately, while also marveling at each other's intellectual prowess.

Since the early days of their courtship, they had admired each other's intelligence and, above that, their mutual ability to understand the silences and empty spaces on which both of them thrived. While Benjamin folded back into his work, Helen was left free to widen the horizons of her literary world. She received crates and boxes full of books every week, for which she had to make some accommodations. One of the only two alterations she made to their home started by doing away with the decorative morocco-bound books in the library, whose gilded spines had never been cracked. Helen filled the shelves with her own volumes and created a real reading room. When she ran out of space, she tore two walls down; when her collection became unmanageable, she hired a librarian. In this enlarged library, she hosted readings, lectures, and informal gatherings.

The other change to the house consisted in converting one of their drawing rooms into a small concert hall. Almost by chance, Helen and Benjamin had discovered that they rather enjoyed concerts. What had started as a compromise—music performances, they learned, were the perfect way for them to be seen "out" without having to engage in inane conversations to fill uncomfortable gaps—grew into a passion. As both developed a taste for chamber music, they translated this principle to their own relationship. They organized private recitals at their home, and on these occasions, they could be together, in silence, sharing emotions for which they were not responsible and which did not refer directly to the two of them. Precisely because they were so controlled and mediated, these were Benjamin and Helen's most intimate moments.

Their evening concerts became somewhat of a legend in the musical community and beyond, both for the caliber of the performers they attracted and for how limited and select the audience was. No more than two dozen people were ever invited to the monthly recitals, and yet a large portion of New York society claimed to attend them regularly. Some of the guests were businessmen who had to suffer through Brahms so that their host did not have to suffer through chitchat. But most of the audience was made up of Helen's new acquaintances—other musicians and writers. During the first few seasons, socializing after the performances was unambiguously discouraged. After the applause died off, Helen would thank performers and guests, following which she and her husband would be the first to leave. Yet as Helen's philanthropic work expanded, it could only intersect with her concert series. At the end of a *Lieder* recital, a writer in the audience would come up to Helen to finish a discussion about a library program; after a cycle of cello sonatas, one of the players would approach her during intermission to let her know about an orchestra in need of funding; following a clarinet quintet, a young composer, knowing he would probably never set foot in her house again, would muster the courage to ask for her patronage. Over time, these conversations grew longer until they became part of the program. Helen started serving fruit juices after each performance—Prohibition had no influence on the household's innately temperate habits—and people lingered until midnight. Benjamin never stayed for these abstemious cocktail parties, which came to be almost as mythical as the concerts themselves, always being the first to bid everyone goodnight.

DISCIPLINE, CREATIVITY, and a machine-like consistency were essential factors in Rask's new level of success—but not the only factors. His prosperity matched the roaring optimism of the times. The world had never experienced anything like the growth of the American economy in the 1920s. Manufacturing was at an all-time high, and so were profits. Employment, already burgeoning, was on the rise. The automobile industry could barely keep up with the insatiable demand for speed that had taken hold of the entire nation. The industrial wonders of the age were advertised from coast to coast on radios everyone wanted to own. Beginning in 1922, the valuations of securities seemed to ascend vertically. If before 1928 few thought it possible that five million shares would ever be traded on the New York Stock Exchange in a day, after the second half of that year this ceiling almost became the floor. In September 1929, the Dow closed at its highest point in history. Around those days, Yale professor Irving Fisher, the nation's leading authority on economics, declared stock prices had "reached what looks like a permanently high plateau."

Thanks to the government's lenient oversight and its reluctance to disturb this wonderful collective dream, opportunities were there for anyone who saw and took them. Through his banks, for example, Rask borrowed cash from the New York Federal Reserve at five percent, only to then lend it in the call market for at least ten and even up to twenty percent. It just so happened that, at the time, trading on margin—purchasing stock with money borrowed from brokerage firms by using those same securities as a collateral—soared from about one to seven billion dollars, an obvious sign of the fact the public had flocked in and people, most of them thoroughly unfamiliar with stocks, were speculating with money they did not have. And yet Rask somehow seemed to be a step ahead at every turn. His first investment trust predated the proliferation of similar institutions in the late twenties by at least half a decade. As a premium for his fame as a financial genius, Rask valued his portfolio well above the market price of the stocks it contained. Not only that, but in his double capacity as investment banker and sponsor of several trusts, he was able to produce some of the very securities he sold—and he repeatedly issued common stock that he would buy in its entirety (or distribute among favored investors) and then trade to the public for up to eighty percent above his original purchase price. Whenever he wanted to avoid the scrutiny of the New York Stock Exchange, he traded in San Francisco, Buffalo, or Boston.

Every man and woman felt entitled to partake in the prosperity that reigned during the ten years after the war and enjoy the technological marvels that came with it. And Rask helped to fuel this sense of limitless possibilities by creating new lending institutions and banks that provided cash under tempting terms. These banks (between which the occasional fictitious rivalry was fostered to attract clients) were nothing like the august marbled institutions with starched clerks that had intimidated customers for generations. On the contrary, they were friendly spaces with welcoming tellers—and there was always a way to get that loan for an automobile, a refrigerator, or a radio. Rask also experimented with financing credit lines and installment plans with stores and manufacturers so that they could offer these payment options directly to their customers. All of these countless and sometimes trifling debts (from his lending services, smaller banks, and different credit ventures) were bundled together and traded in bulk as securities. He saw, in short, that the relationship with the consumer did not end with the purchase of a good; there was more profit to be extracted from that exchange.

He also created a trust meant exclusively for the working man. A small amount, the few hundred dollars in a modest savings account, was enough to get started. The trust would match this sum (and sometimes double or even treble it) to then invest it in its portfolio and use that stock as security. A schoolteacher or farmer could then settle her or his debt in comfortable monthly payments. If everyone had the right to become wealthy, it was Rask who would fulfill that right.

At the peaks and lows of this boom, during trading frenzies fueled by either optimism or panic, it was not uncommon for the ticker to fall behind the market. If the volume of trades was large enough, the lag could be of over two hours, rendering the tape obsolete by the time it came out of the machine. But it was in these moments of utmost darkness that Rask truly soared, as if he could reach the greatest heights only by flying blind. This was not a small contribution to his legendary status.

The speed at which Benjamin enlarged his fortune and the wisdom with which Helen distributed it were perceived as the public manifestation of the close bond between them. This, together with their elusiveness, turned them into mythical creatures in the New York society they so utterly disregarded, and their fabulous stature only increased with their indifference. Their family life, however, did not fully conform to the fable of a harmonious couple. Benjamin's admiration for Helen bordered on awe. Finding her unfathomable and intimidating, he desired her with a form of mystical, mostly chaste lust. Doubt, a feeling that had never visited him before his wedding, increased year after year. If at work he was always self-assured and resolute, at home he became indecisive and timid. He wove intricate conjectures around her, threaded with contrived causal links that quickly expanded into vast nets of suppositions, which he would unspin and weave again in different patterns. Helen sensed his hesitation and tried to appease him.

But much as she tried (and she did try), she was unable to fully recipro-
cate Benjamin's feelings. While she was impressed by his achievements
and touched by his devotion, and although she was always kind, atten-
tive, and even tender to him, there was a small but ineluctable force,
much like the repulsion between two magnets, that made her recoil in
proportion to his closeness. She was never cruel or dismissive toward
him—quite the contrary, she was a considerate and even affectionate
companion. Still, from the very beginning, he knew something was
missing. And knowing that he knew, she tried to make up for this in
many thoughtful yet insufficient ways. Benjamin always experienced
an incomplete thrill on these occasions.

Around this core of quiet discomfort, they managed to build a
strong marriage. Perhaps part of that strength came precisely from the
dissonant void and their willingness to make up for it. But it is also
true that there existed a connection between them. They both knew
that, despite their differences, they were uniquely well suited for each
other. Until meeting, neither of them had ever known anyone who
would accept their idiosyncrasies without questions. Every interaction
out in the world had always implied some form of compromise. Now,
for the first time, they experienced the relief of not having to adapt
to the demands and protocols inherent to most exchanges—or devote
part of their attention to the awkwardness that prevailed whenever
they refused to follow those conventions. Even more importantly, in
their relationship they discovered the joy of mutual appreciation.

If the Rasks never ceased to be a captivating enigma in the circle
immediately surrounding them, public attention dwindled at a rate
proportional to its distance from the center. The purely fictional accounts of the couple's life in society pages and tabloids became shorter,
sporadic, and finally extinct; the swarm of photographers lurking
around the family home dispersed; the scant and exceedingly grainy

footage of the newlyweds, used over and over again in fanciful reports, disappeared from the newsreels. Because of his ever-expanding business interests, Benjamin appeared regularly in the press, but within a year, there was no mention of Mrs. Rask in the newspapers, except in connection with her charitable work. Alone in the house (Benjamin's hours at the office only grew longer), mostly unnoticed out in the streets, and having found, for the first time, a group of like-minded people with whom friendship seemed possible, Helen was finally living the sort of life that had always seemed unattainable to her.

Despite Benjamin's initial desire for a successor, they found no need to either question or discuss the causes of their childlessness.

◆

MOST OF US PREFER to believe we are the active subjects of our victories but only the passive objects of our defeats. We triumph, but it is not really we who fail—we are ruined by forces beyond our control.

During the last week of October 1929, it took most speculators—from the high-powered financier in downtown Manhattan to the amateur housewife trading at the San Francisco Stock Exchange—a matter of days to shift from the agents of their success, with nothing to thank but their own acumen and relentless will, to the victims of a profoundly flawed and maybe even corrupt system, which was the sole responsible for their demise. A dip in the indexes, an epidemic of fear, a selling frenzy driven by pessimism, a widespread inability to respond to margin calls . . . Whatever caused the slump that, in turn, became a panic, one thing was clear—none of those who had helped to inflate the bubble felt responsible for its bursting. They were the blameless casualties of a disaster of almost natural proportions.

Very much as in the Panic of 1907, all through the week of the 1929 crash, the chairmen of the biggest banks in the country, together with the head of the New York Federal Reserve and the presidents and senior partners of the main trust companies and brokerage agencies, held secretive meetings to try to find the best strategy to shore up the market. Once again, as in 1907, the night-long talks took place in Morgan's library, this time presided over by Pierpont's son, Jack. Once again, Rask was summoned to lend his advice and material help. And once again, Rask declined.

Despite the organized support of bankers, the intervention of industrialists, and the assurances of politicians and academics who claimed, time and again, that the conditions of the market were "fundamentally sound," stocks kept plummeting. On Monday, October 21, about six million shares were sold, an absolute record that set all the stock tick-ers in the country back two hours. This historical volume was dwarfed by the trading hysteria of the following days. On Thursday 24, almost thirteen million shares were traded; on Tuesday 29, over sixteen mil-lion. The ticker lagged for nearly three hours. Crowds thronged Wall Street and gathered at the doors of banks and brokering houses around the country. As investment trusts shipwrecked and self-cannibalized, there was a tidal wave of sell orders but no buyers. Inevitably, that wave broke, leaving behind a stagnant ocean of unsalable stocks and a ravaged market.

Only one man seemed to have been immune to the catastrophe. It took Rask's bewildered colleagues a few days to realize the full scope of his situation. The press soon followed suit. Rask had not just sailed through the storm unscathed; he had, in fact, profited colossally from it. Discreetly and through his subsidiaries, during the summer months leading up to the crash, he had started liquidating his positions and buying gold, as this asset, attracted and devoured by speculation, grew scarce both in Wall Street and London. What drew even more scrutiny was the precision with which he had been short-selling vast amounts of shares from the very companies that later were particularly damaged and even destroyed by the crisis. He had negotiated piecemeal loans of shares from a myriad of brokers when they were at their peak and immediately sold them, while they were still at the cusp. As if he had known the market would take a plunge, he simply waited until these same stocks hit rock bottom, bought them back for nothing, and re-turned the now worthless shares to the brokers, making a gargantuan profit in the process. There was something chilling in the systematic rigor with which he had proceeded, from the targeting of the compa-nies to the timing and stealth of his trades. Meanwhile, as this opera-tion was under way, he had severed every remaining tie to those debts that he had packaged and sold as securities—all of which defaulted shortly after. He had even divested from all his trusts, including the one he had designed for the working man. On Wednesday, October 23, an epic flood of unexpected sell orders inundated the trading floor. Nobody knew the source of this rush, but when Wall Street closed, only two hours later, the market was down by more than twenty points. The following day would be remembered as Black Thursday. Five days later, on Black Tuesday, the Dow fell eighty points, and by that time stocks had depreciated by the equivalent of half the total national product.

In the general desolation, amidst the rubble, Rask was the only man standing. And he stood taller than ever, since most of the other speculators' losses had been his gain. He had always benefited from chaos and turmoil, as his masterful operations during the ticker delays repeatedly had proven, but what happened over the last months of 1929 had no precedent.

Once this picture became clear enough, the public was quick to react. It had been Rask who engineered the whole crash to begin with, people said. Slyly, he had whetted a reckless appetite for debts he knew all along could never be honored. Subtly, he had been dumping his stocks and driving the market down. Artfully, he had leaked rumors and stoked paranoia. Mercilessly, he had overthrown Wall Street and kept it under his thumb with his selling spree the day right before Black Thursday. Everything—the breaks in the market, the uncertainty, the bearishness leading to panic selling, and eventually the crash that would ruin multitudes—had been orchestrated by Rask. His was the hand behind the invisible hand.

Despite the inflamed speeches, the caricatures in magazines and newspapers (where Rask was depicted, mostly, as a vampire, a vulture, or a pig), and the proliferation of fuzzy or downright fabricated exposés about his career, nobody in his right mind believed that one single man could bring down the entire economy of a nation—and, with it, that of most of the world. Yet almost everyone found it convenient to have a scapegoat, and the eccentric semi-recluse fit the bill perfectly. Still, even if he had not designed the crisis, it was beyond doubt that Benjamin Rask had turned an incalculable profit from it. In financial circles all over the globe, even among the legions of enemies he had made, this lifted him to divine heights.

Dear Helen,

You know how consumed I've been with work—lectures, reviews, articles, et tedious caetera. Everything seems to conspire against my writing. And I do need to finish this manuscript. I am ever so sorry, but I will have to politely bow out of the reading program at your lovely library for the remainder of the season. Please do wish me good luck with this wretched novel of mine!

All best wishes,
  Winnie

Dear Mrs. Rask,

I trust these brief lines will find you in good health. For about three years I have been organising a concert series for the working people of Catalonia that brings the world's best soloists and conductors to laborers, farmers and students. I fund the Workers' Concerts Association by giving private recitals, much like the one I was to offer next week at your home. Having recently learned in greater detail about the terrible crisis that has shaken your country for the last few months, I find that silence may be more pertinent than music. Through this silence, I hope to honour the plight of the American brothers and sisters of the Catalonian workers for

*whom next week's recital ultimately was intended. I hope you
and your guests will forgive this last-minute cancellation.*

Yours sincerely,
   P. Casals

———

Dear Mrs. Rask,

*Thanks so much for yours. I wish I could repay you for your
support over this last year or two. But as you know my
publisher has gone under and business in general is lousy.
Come to think of it, perhaps I HAVE repaid you after all.*
   *Becoming a farmer and growing my own food doesn't
seem like such a bad idea. Failing that, bricklayer. Failing
that, Hollywood and write for the pictures. But perhaps the
revolution will come first.*

My best to you and your husband,
   Pep

———

Mrs. Rask,

*Perhaps you will be so kind as to help me settle an argument
I had with some fellow poets the other day. Where do you
think Dante would have lodged the savants of Wall Street?*

In the fourth or the eighth circle of Hell? Greed or Fraud? In fact, this could be a stimulating topic for one of your upcoming salons. Please share your thoughts, if you ever can spare a minute. And if you can't spare a minute, I'll take a dime.

Yours in so many ways,
  Shelby Wallace

———

H Dear,

Sorry to cancel on such short notice. Frightful cold. Hope reading tomorrow goes well.

As ever,
  Maude

DURING THE MONTHS following the crash, the air had been suctioned out of the house, leaving only a tight, high-pitched void behind. It was as if reality itself, independently of anyone's perception, had become light-headed. People around Helen simply vanished. Not everyone. Those who had always tried to approach her only to be closer to Benjamin saw an opportunity in the public outrage and presented themselves as staunch supporters, brave and faithful enough to weather the storm by their maligned friends' side. Helen cared as little for this obsequious set as she always had. It was her new acquaintances who had left en masse. Without the writers and musicians who had enlarged her world over the past few years, she found herself back in the quiet inner hideaway that had sheltered her in her childhood and early youth, and drew comfort from her old solitary habits, her books, her journal, her walks. In the past, she had thought this space within herself to be as vast and serenely inexplicable as a cosmos. Now she deemed it narrow and flat. None of the people who gave and attended her readings and concerts had become, in a true sense, a friend, but together, all of them, as a group, had come to be a necessary presence in her life. She had lost her taste for loneliness.

As the city sank into the depression that followed the crash, Helen found it harder to leave the house. She knew that looking away from the destitute families, the breadlines, the shuttered stores, and the despair in every thinning face was a gross form of self-indulgence, but she also understood that the anguish she felt when confronted by this bleak reality was yet another of her luxuries. Helen had to acknowledge this paradox each time she went for a walk—until what would become her last excursion south of the park. She experienced something different that afternoon. It started with a concave oppression in her chest. A disturbance in the air. She was unable to understand what brought about that dread until she realized she felt watched. Stares. Scowls. Whispers. Everywhere. Smirks. Slurs. Hisses. Everywhere. It was plausible, even expected, that some people would recognize and despise her. But everyone? Hate rang in every sound—every horn, every whistle, every scream was a curse. Hate streamed from every window—she felt narrowing eyes training on her from behind every curtain and every pane of glass quicksilvered by the sun. Hate was twisted into every grimace and every hand gesture—every passerby a merciless, obscene judge. Did the woman with the cardboard suit-cases spit at her feet as she crossed the street? Did that newsboy mut-ter those brutal words between an extra and a headline? Were those men signaling each other to follow her? For the first time, in broad daylight, she was possessed by the same kind of terror that had so often filled her nights since her childhood. She knew that part of the hostility she sensed walking down Lexington Avenue must be—as it was during her sleepless nights—only in her mind. But much of it was, beyond doubt, real. Her inability to distinguish between the two was her greatest source of panic. The world became granular; all sounds echoes; her blood too thin; the air too thick. It—everything—tingled.

She would later have a faint recollection of rushing back home, her skirt and shoes restricting her to an inefficient trot over puddles. Laughs.

Helen was ready to accept and, also, to atone for the real causes of the rush of panic that had nearly pulverized her that afternoon. She would pay for the suffering that had helped make her husband rich beyond measure. Her confinement to her home was part of the punishment—although she could see that this seclusion was, to a great extent, motivated by fear and shame and, therefore, self-serving. Still, even if she seldom left the house, she toiled without pause and gave herself completely to her philanthropic work. She created countless jobs by building new residences all over the country (which she then practically gave away to homeless families), reopened factories and workshops whose entire production she sometimes bought (and distributed for free), gave credit at no interest to businesses that promised to keep their doors open (never enforcing collection). All this, she did as anonymously as possible.

Benjamin's wealth was such that he could fund his wife's altruistic enterprises without much thought. Thoroughly unmoved by the reality around him, he felt no need or moral obligation to assist anyone. His life, always limited to his office and his home, remained unaltered. The recession was, to him, nothing but a healthy bout of fever, after which the economy would rebound, stronger than ever. The crash, he believed, had been a lancet applied to an abscess. A good bleeding was necessary to do away with the swelling so that the market could find its true bottom and rebuild on solid foundations. He was even quoted as having said that because there had not been one single bank failure as a result of the crisis, it had merely been part of a healthy purge.

If he helped Helen with her endeavors, it was only out of concern for her well-being. She had changed, even deteriorated, quite visibly over the previous few months. Helen assured him that her work was her only solace, and he, not without reluctance, kept financing her undertakings, while attributing her decline to lack of sleep and rest. He was partially right. It was true that Helen barely slept, but not because she was absorbed by her charities. Work, rather, was a welcome distraction from the true causes of her insomnia. The fears clawing at her mind in the dark were no longer abstract and incoherent. And they were not erased by sunlight. Not even her tireless humanitarian duties, which addressed the more concrete sources of her anxiety, gave her comfort.

Because what she dreaded now, ever since that walk down Lexington Avenue, was that the illness that had possessed, transformed, and consumed her father might also be at work in her brain. She could feel herself think differently and knew that, in the end, it did not matter whether this feeling was based on reality or fantasies. What mattered was that she was unable to stop thinking about her thoughts. Her speculations reflected one another, like parallel mirrors—and, endlessly, each image inside the vertiginous tunnel looked at the next wondering whether it was the original or a reproduction. This, she told herself, was the beginning of madness. The mind becoming the flesh for its own teeth.

Because she felt increasingly lost in the new tyrannical architecture of her brain, and because she no longer trusted her thoughts or her memory, she started relying on her journals, which she kept with daily rigor. She hoped her future self, the one reading her diaries, would be able to use those writings as a measure of how far into her delirium she had gone. Would she see herself on the page? She addressed herself constantly in her entries, asking herself to believe that it was, in fact, she who had written those words in the past—even if her future self refused to believe it; even if, as she read, she were unable to recognize her own handwriting.

Helen had never shared her innermost worries with Benjamin, and she was certainly not about to start now. Given the depth of her anxiety, she was relieved that he happened to be so utterly consumed by his own concerns. Following the crash, the Senate held hearings before the Committee on Banking and Currency "to thoroughly investigate practices of stock exchanges with respect to the buying and selling and the borrowing and lending of listed securities, the values of such securities and the effects of such practices." Benjamin Rask's appearance before members of the Seventy-Second Congress is a matter of public record, and the printed version of his statement, included in a 418-page-long tome, is readily available to anyone who cares to examine it. The hearings served the ceremonial function of presenting the indignant citizen with a few obvious fiends so that he could shake his head at their picture on the front page of his newspaper, mutter a few curses, and then forget all about them. Nobody was expected to actually read the transcripts. The few who did, however, found that many of the assumptions regarding Rask's dealings were not far from the truth. His answers to the senators' accusatorial, convoluted questions were reduced, for the most part, to "yes, sir" and "no, sir," but they confirmed that he had indeed divested from his most volatile vehicles in the months preceding the collapse, that he had flooded the market with sell orders the day before Black Thursday, and that he had shorted, quite spectacularly, the ensuing crash. Despite his interrogators' inflamed rhetoric, it was apparent that none of his actions had been illegal.

◆

WITH PERVERSE SYMMETRY, as Benjamin rose to new heights, Helen's condition declined. Unable to sleep, she spent her nights wandering around the house. Benjamin tried to keep her company during these walks, but she refused him; he fully staffed the house for the night, but she dismissed all the servants; he got her crates of books from Europe, but she left the pages uncut. Her instructions pertaining to her charitable work became erratic and contradictory. Only one pattern seemed to be consistent: all her impatient exchanges with her aides ended with the conclusion that they were simply not doing enough. She started writing checks for extravagant figures and authorizing expenses that were unmoored from reality. Benjamin intercepted all these transactions and let Helen keep imparting inconsequential orders to her assistants. In the end, however, she seemed overwhelmed. Almost crushed by the vast numbers and the complex operations she had invented for herself, she withdrew from her imaginary work. An excited sort of exhaustion paralyzed her, and she started taking her meals in her room. Every time, however, the service trolleys were picked up with their plates still domed. She only drank the fruit juices that had been the signature of her cocktail parties.

Benjamin and Helen had been working for a long time with physicians and pharmaceutical chemists to find better treatments for psychiatric disorders. He now understood that his wife might not have been moved solely by altruism or the memory of her father. Still, he was loath to involve anyone outside the family, especially since Helen's quiet form of mania did not conform to any of the symptoms he had read about in the past. Sometimes he listened at her door. The active silence within was terrifying. It was interrupted only by the sporadic rustle of papers, which confirmed that Helen was not asleep but writing in her journal, filling page after page in one thick notebook after the other. Benjamin respected her privacy too much to pry, but on one occasion, when he knew she was at the other end of the house, he inspected her diaries. German, French, Italian, and, perhaps, other languages (he wondered if they were, indeed, proper languages) were intertwined in each sentence, forming braids that Benjamin, confined to English, could not untangle. In one of her notebooks, he found a photograph of young Helen he had never seen before. She was standing amidst a jumble of disparate props and stuffed animals, looking straight into the camera, her eyes stirring with defiance. For a curiously long time, Benjamin stared at the photo. He had never looked into his wife's eyes for that long. She had never looked into his eyes for that long. He came out of his trance, pocketed the picture, made sure all the papers were as he had found them, and left the room. But as he was closing the door behind him, he paused, reopened it, and went back to the desk. He returned the photo to the journal where he had found it and then, at last, walked out with brisk, quiet steps.

It was around this time—and Benjamin could not help but think that it was because she had sensed that he had gone through her papers—that Helen hid all her journals and started writing as she walked. Sometimes she seemed to mumble, as if taking dictation from herself. Her ramblings around the house were reduced to narrowing perimeters, until they were limited to just her bedroom floor. One morning, Benjamin saw her looking up the flight of stairs. She seemed to be staring through the ceiling and into the sky. Cautiously, she touched the first step and withdrew her foot immediately, as if she had dipped her toes into frigid or scalding water. She paused and did it again. Paused and did it again. Then she tried the staircase leading down to the dining room. Her gaze was lost in depths beyond the downstairs landing. Much as she tried, the tip of her slipper could not make it beyond the edge of the first step.

If Benjamin had found it difficult to approach her during their happier years, now he was completely at a loss. The more he tried, stutteringly, to connect with her, the further she withdrew. And if he insisted too much or showed any sign of concern, she would retreat to her rooms and could only be coaxed out by being left completely alone for days. After one such attempt—he had come with some new books he offered to read to her—Helen shut herself in for a particularly long time. The juice remained untouched out by her door. She would not respond to her maids' pleas. Footsteps and the rustle of paper could be heard within.

Helen had gone two full days without sustenance when Benjamin decided to take action. He told her, through the closed door, that he would force the lock unless she opened right away. After some audible signs of hesitation, she did. Benjamin took a step back, stunned first by the smell and then by the sight before him. Worse than the stench of decay was the sweet, flowery reek of the many perfumes sprayed in the attempt to conceal it. He tried to blink the smell away and then, as his eyes adjusted to the twilight within, saw the blood on Helen's arms and chest. There was no question as to the origin of the wounds. She never stopped scratching the oozing blisters as she stood there, gaunt and abstracted. The scales and vesicles of her eczema were making their way up her neck, and the red lichen had already colonized her jaw.

This broke Benjamin's spirit. Only now, by seeing the violence on the surface, did he understand the turmoil within. He cried, alone, in his office.

The best course of action, he decided, would be to speak with Mrs. Brevoort, who would be in a unique position to compare her daughter's condition with that of her husband and thus determine whether Helen's illness was of a hereditary nature.

Mother and daughter had drifted apart over the years. After learning about her father's disappearance, Helen stopped making an effort to put up with Mrs. Brevoort's loud way of life. She barely went to her mother's apartment and never had her over at the house. Instead, Helen would telephone once a week or so, and Mrs. Brevoort would always be cheerful, lighthearted, and fizzing with anecdotes. But she would never call back, so Helen, as an experiment, stopped ringing. Almost a year had passed since they had last spoken. On that occasion, Mrs. Brevoort had described, in great detail, interrupted by her own giggle fits, some prank she and her friends had played on a milliner. This time, however, when Benjamin called to tell her about the situation at the house, she adopted a tragic tone, decided she had to see her daughter at once, and would not be convinced that her presence might upset Helen more. Mrs. Brevoort hung up on a beseeching Benjamin and a few minutes later was at his door, giddy with the drama of it all and visibly pleased to be agitated and slightly out of breath.

Once more, Benjamin questioned the wisdom of confronting Helen—all he wanted was to describe the symptoms to her mother and confirm whether they reminded her of her husband's condition. Mrs. Brevoort would have none of it. Without taking off her coat and hat, she rushed, with determined distress, up the stairs that led to her daughter's rooms. Benjamin trailed behind. Mrs. Brevoort did not even pause at the door; she opened it without knocking, in one abrupt swing. Mrs. Brevoort and Benjamin froze, shocked by the figure in front of them.

Helen was standing in the middle of the room, facing the door. There was something regal in the Grecian simplicity of her nightgown, something martial in her tousled hair and scars, something angelic in her victorious stillness.

After a moment, she took a step forward, looked for her reflection in her mother's eyes, and proffered her a sheet of paper. Mrs. Brevoort first focused on the stains the fresh ink had left on her kid gloves and then read the hasty lines on the page.

I smelled your scent.
I heard your strut.

Medico–Mechanic Institute.
You shall deposit me in Switzerland.

FOUR

Helen was indeed admitted at the Medico-Mechanic Institute, but her mother had nothing to do with the arrangements or the transport to Switzerland. In fact, she rushed out of the house after seeing her daughter in such a diminished condition and was unable to visit her again—it was simply too painful, she said, without wiping off her tears, and she was simply too heartbroken.

It was Benjamin who took care, in person, of the preparations. At first, he thought Helen's request to be taken to Bad Pfäfers was a response to her mother's sudden appearance, which must have sharpened the pain of having lost her father to the disease that was now claiming her. He also suspected the demand had been made only as an attack on Mrs. Brevoort, and a very successful one at that. But through the ensuing weeks, Helen remained adamant in her request. It was in Bad Pfäfers where she would find peace and, she knew, be cured.

Benjamin had his associates at Haber Pharmaceuticals, in Berlin, look into every aspect of the Institute—from its financial statements and its infrastructure to the records of every staff member and the profiles of its patients. If at first he thought he might take Helen there for a short spell to satisfy her whim (although he nursed the secret, groundless hope of seeing her miraculously cured by the shock of visiting this traumatic site), after getting the report from Haber he believed that Bad Pfäfers might, in fact, be just the right place for his wife.

Dr. Bally, the director who had admitted Helen's father, had died some five years after the war, and it was now Dr. Helmut Frahm who was in charge of the establishment. According to Benjamin's men, under Dr. Frahm's direction, the Institute had earned an excellent reputation in the treatment of mental illness, especially emotional disorders—different forms of neuroses, phobias, acute varieties of melancholia, and so forth. Before the war, the clinic had been more of a spa, with a blanketed, rather vague approach to nervous ailments that relied on rest cures and hydropathy. Now, however, it offered more focused clinical treatments, and it was pioneering a study into the psychiatric applications of lithium salts, which Haber Pharmaceuticals was following with great interest. Dr. Frahm's credentials, in sum, were impeccable, and descriptions of his modern methods and his line of pharmacological research could be found in the many papers the doctor had published, in German, in a number of peer-reviewed medical journals, copies of which were included in the report. In short, Benjamin's informants concluded that the Medico-Mechanic Institute was a reputable establishment. They did, however, object to Dr. Frahm's slight psychoanalytic slant and took the liberty to recommend, instead, Dr. Ladislas Aftus, in Berlin, whose work they knew firsthand. Dr. Aftus was developing a promising new drug for Haber Pharmaceuticals, and Mrs. Rask seemed to be exactly the kind of patient who would benefit from his innovative treatment.

Benjamin found the report on Frahm and the Institute encouraging. For a moment, he considered Dr. Aftus and his new drug—it would have been convenient to keep Helen's condition within the domain of Haber Pharmaceuticals, an environment he controlled. But he was reluctant to bring such a delicate family situation into contact with his business. And Helen was so emphatic about Bad Pfäfers and the Institute. Perhaps there would be a therapeutic value to the location itself, which appealed to Benjamin for reasons of his own. Bad Pfäfers was far from any major city, inconvenient enough for well-meaning acquaintances who might consider a visit while summering in the region, and decidedly out of the way for the press.

Always through his German intermediaries, Benjamin requested an entire wing at the Medico-Mechanic Institute. After studying the sanatorium's blueprints, he concluded that the northern section of the compound, away from the chapel and the baths, would afford the most privacy. Benjamin's representatives drew up a proposal for the Institute outlining his requests. Mr. Rask wanted the pavilion vacated of patients at once—and promised to pay for the equivalent of room, board, and full course of treatment for all the empty rooms for as long as necessary. The building, however, should remain fully staffed, and Mr. Rask reserved for himself the right to bring in outside physicians at any time to consult on his wife's condition. A few minor renovations would have to be promptly undertaken to make the wing fully autonomous from the rest of the Institute and ensure Mrs. Rask's comfort. All modifications, which Mr. Rask would (it went without saying) fund, had been marked up and described on the blueprints. The document concluded by offering the director a substantial sum in compensation for any disruptions these arrangements might cause.

Dr. Frahm, in a few dryly polite sentences to Benjamin's agents, declined the offer. The institute did not require renovations, was not looking for the endorsement of outside physicians, and, fortunately, was not in need of financial assistance. Benjamin, in turn, replied with a personal letter, where he tried to impress on Dr. Frahm the urgency of the case and the personal connotations Bad Pfäfers had for his wife. In closing, he pledged a generous unrestricted endowment—and the funding of an entire new building for any branch of research the director saw fit. Dr. Frahm did not respond. Two weeks after the arrival of Benjamin's letter, there was a brief article in *Deutsche Medizinische Wochenschrift* raising doubts about Dr. Frahm's research protocol concerning clinical applications of lithium salts and other new substances on which the scientific community had scant and inconclusive information. The journal stated that an inquiry into Dr. Frahm's methods was ongoing and promised to follow up as further reports became available. Shortly after the publication of this article, the Institute experienced a shortage of many drugs critical to the treatments it provided. All these drugs were patented by Haber Pharmaceuticals.

Before the end of that month, the northern wing had been cleared of patients and renovations were under way.

Just as his wife had tried to distract herself from her initial symptoms by working incessantly on her charities, Benjamin fled from his grief by fixating on every detail related to the Institute. Refurbishing the pavilion, securing the best staff available, and readying Helen for the trip became his only concerns. For the first time in his life, business was an afterthought, a chore—he had delegated daily operations to Sheldon Lloyd and became irritable when approached with work-related questions. It was only in his active dealings with his wife's illness that he found some solace. He had always feared he would lose Helen—lose her interest, lose her to someone else. And now it had happened. She was gone, having abandoned him for something that called to her with irresistible vehemence. He discovered that he was jealous of the illness, which demanded and got all her attention and energy—and he was ashamed to admit that he was angry at Helen for doing everything her dark master commanded.

Benjamin tried not to indulge in this irrational and rather shapeless resentment, suppressing it as soon as it emerged and never letting it affect his relationship with Helen. He was a tender nurse who understood that his love was best manifested by its inhibition—he was present but unnoticed, solicitous but removed. Weakened by her long fast and her relentless mania, Helen was for the most part confined to her bed. The merciless red flat monster gnawing on her skin brought her to tears at all times. Doctors and nurses were now involved in her care, mainly to address her malnourishment, dress her eczema with compresses, and administer the morphine that afforded her some calm. She was in a haze, always falling asleep or just waking up, yet too excited and talkative to get any real rest. On the few occasions Helen requested or acknowledged his presence, Benjamin proved to have a talent for following her incoherent monologue, smiling at the right places, showing sympathetic indignation whenever pertinent, and responding to her questions without a hint of condescension. He always held her hand when they talked. Sometimes Helen, even if her gaze was fixed on distant visions, would stroke his thumb with hers.

MORNING BROUGHT OUT a deeper sort of white from the changeless snows capping the peaks on either side of the valley, which, later, in the midday sun, would become blinding splinters. A pastoral bell echoed across the sky, dappled with flocks of small solid clouds, while unseen birds found themselves, yet again, unable to break their bondage to their two or four notes. The air was laced with the scent of water, stone, and the long-dead things that, darkly, were finding their way back to life deep under the dew-soaked dirt. During that unpopulated hour, the buildings ceased to be objects of artifice and industry to reveal the nature fossilized in them and come forth in their mineral presence. The breeze dissolved in stiller air; the treetops, so green they were black against the blue, stopped swaying. And for a moment, there was no struggle and all was at rest, because time seemed to have arrived at its destination.

Then a nurse with a compress, an orderly with a rake, a doctor with a clipboard, a server with an infusion would set it all in motion again. The itching, the exhaustion, the words, the thoughts behind them, and the noise of her being, so much louder than the world.

Upon her admittance at the Medico-Mechanic Institute, she visited her father's room. All the patients staying at the more modest eastern wing, mossy and damp in the perennial shadow of two sharp cliffs, were taken out to the garden while Helen toured the facilities together with her husband and Dr. Frahm. She seemed distracted in her father's narrow quarters. Her eyes focused a bit beyond each object. It was her fingers that engaged with the space, gently gliding over every surface or tentatively touching a basin or the back of a chair, as if unsure of their consistency and temperature.

Dr. Frahm signaled Benjamin to leave the room. Indignation rippled across Rask's face, and he turned his back to the doctor, feigning to have missed his gesture. But he could not ignore Frahm's hand on his shoulder and his heavily accented request to give them a moment. Benjamin looked at the soft hand on his shoulder; Dr. Frahm lifted it to show him the door; Benjamin lowered his outraged eyes and announced he would wait outside.

Once they were alone, Frahm invited Helen to lie down on the bed, placed a chair behind the iron headboard, sat down, and asked, in German, what image of her father was conjured up in that room. Was it the man presiding over her childhood or the invalid of her adolescence?

Helen seemed calmer in German. Although she spoke it with remarkable ease, she also had vast lacunae, as is usually the case with those who have somewhat haphazardly taught themselves a language. Because she often had to pause and find circumlocutions to bypass grammatical voids and lexical gaps, she gave the impression of having slowed down, of having mastered, in some measure, her anxiety. But her German, like all her foreign languages, had come from unusual sources, detached from everyday speech—outmoded books and the affected chatter of dispossessed aristocrats and drawing room diplomats. This gave her words a baroque, theatrical quality that, to some extent, undid the illusion of sanity created by her slower pace, because, despite her innate elegance, she could sound like a bad actress in too much makeup.

She laughed quietly at the doctor's question. Only a fool would distinguish past from present in such a way. The future irrupts at all times, wanting to actualize itself in every decision we make; it tries, as hard as it can, to become the past. This is what distinguishes the future from mere fancy. The future happens. The Lord casts no one into hell; the spirits cast themselves down, according to Swedenborg. The spirits cast themselves into hell by their own free choice. And what is choice but a branch of the future grafting itself onto the stem of the present? Past father? Future father? Helen laughed again and moved on to consider the subject of gardening in relation to alchemy. Dr. Frahm, however, knew that Swedenborg had played an important part in her upbringing and gently insisted on this point of access into her childhood—while pursuing Helen's implication that her father had chosen hell for himself. She talked on, her eyes fixed on a mold stain on the ceiling that resembled a black peony.

Dr. Frahm started to wean his patient off her medication shortly after her arrival at the Institute. He wanted to observe her symptoms in their purest form, without any interference, he said, and then try the smallest dose of lithium salts. After a gradual withdrawal, when she was about to be completely taken off her sedatives, her mania reached its highest point. Benjamin demanded that his wife be put back on her drugs. The psychiatrist, unmoved by his threatening tone, said he needed a few days more. About a week later, disproving Benjamin's worst fears, there were signs of mild improvement. Helen was still incoherent and verbose, yes, but failing, time and again, to find a way out of her verbal mazes had made her exhausted, which, in turn, had made her somewhat calmer. Dr. Frahm explained that he was turning her manic condition against itself: her insomnia and frenzied mental activity, together with the natural depletion of certain hormones and her physical regime, would end up having a narcotic effect. She needed to be drained of energy; she needed exercise; she needed air.

And so it was that Helen, after each sleepless night spent talking to silent snooded nurses, was taken out into the garden with the first light and left alone on a chaise facing the mountains. She continued with her soliloquy while freeing herself from under the tightly tucked blankets. As the sun rose, however, her monologue declined into sporadic mutterings, which, in turn, melted into silence. For an hour or so, she would enjoy the bliss of impersonality—of becoming pure perception, of existing only as that which saw the mountaintop, heard the bell, smelled the air.

BENJAMIN WAS OUT OF PLACE, removed from his element by several layers of estrangement. He had never been a foreigner before, and although he had reproduced his American life almost flawlessly by taking with him his closest servants (and his chef and his furniture and most of the accessories that surrounded him in New York), he was irritated and even offended by every "European" peculiarity that managed to filter through to him. The German language, with its indecipherable serrated sounds, was part of a widespread conspiracy against him. The uninhabited hills, the vertical horizon of the Alps, the barely tamed nature encircling the Institute made him feel like a castaway. And although his wife was still his topmost concern, being away from his business had started to take a physical toll on him—a blend of light-headedness and mild suffocation. Telephone lines had yet to reach the Institute, radio signals were too weak in that deep valley surrounded by tall mountains, and the relay system he had designed to transmit information from New York and London to Bad Pfäfers was much too slow. The developments of the market reached him only as "news," which is how the press refers to decisions made by other people in the recent past.

Reduced to an idle spectator in the realm of business, Rask turned his full attention to his wife's treatment. Since the opening negotiations, when Benjamin was trying to secure a whole wing of the Institute, the director had made it clear that he was not intimidated by the financier's wealth. At the time, Rask, fed up with the sycophantic acquiescence of lackeys and yes-men, had found this response refreshing and even encouraging. He respected Dr. Frahm's passion for his art, his refusal to submit to external demands, and his indifference to the vulgar enticements of money. All this made him believe that

Helen was in good hands. But now, when the day-to-day evolution of the treatment was all he could concentrate on, the firmness and moral rectitude he had previously admired in the doctor had become a source of constant frustration and resentment. Frahm avoided him and only provided brief, elusive reports during their meetings, which invariably were cut short by a nurse or a colleague demanding *Herr Direktor*'s attention—a pathetic ruse every secretary in New York had been taught to perform. Benjamin's suggestions, referrals, and connections in the pharmaceutical world were declined with, he was quite sure, some disdain. Contact with his wife had been reduced to a minimum so that she could get enough "air." What were this doctor's methods after all? No drugs? What were those salts? And all those conversations. What were they about?

Nothing in Dr. Frahm's approach seemed regular or predictable. He either met with Helen many times in one single afternoon or suspended their sessions for several days for no apparent reason. Consultations could take place anywhere—her room, the grounds, his office, the gymnasium—and could end, suddenly, after only a few minutes. All these anomalies baffled Benjamin, who ascribed them to unprofessional whims and a general lack of method. Frustrated, he confronted Dr. Frahm and demanded an explanation.

Dr. Frahm's English was academic, imperfect, and brusque. Rather than containing Mrs. Rask's free-flowing rants and redirecting them into the realm of normalcy (or gagging her with sedatives), he said, he wished to encourage her monologues. She could not stop talking because she could not stop trying to explain her illness—and her desire to understand her illness *was*, to a large extent, the illness itself. If he listened and taught her to listen, they would find that her never-ending rant was full of ciphered instructions. Symptom, disease, and cure were three in one. Each time he came across one of those revealing moments in Mrs. Rask's speech, where her illness threw light on itself, an abrupt interruption underscored the epiphany and forced her to listen to herself. This is why so many sessions were so short. And they took place anywhere (at any time) to impress the idea on the patient that her self-examination was not restricted to an office but a continuous process. With these "raid" sessions, he wanted to teach her to ambush herself.

Rask accused the doctor of Freudianism and said he would not have his wife exposed to any such nonsense. Frahm laughed and dismissed the charges with a wave of his hand. He had met Professor Freud, yes, and learned a thing or two from his approach to talk therapy. But what Mr. Rask was ignoring, the director explained as he was called away by a nurse, was the emphasis the Institute put on the body. Thermal baths, calisthenics, induced repose, hiking, treatments with galvanic and faradic currents, *Luftliegekur,* a strict vegetarian diet, Contrology, homeopathy, and, above all, the salts. As Herr Rask surely could see, they did not reduce the body to a metaphor at the Medico-Mechanic Institute. Bad Pfäfers was not Vienna.

Aside from her habit of taking long walks, Helen had never engaged in any kind of regular physical exercise. Once she was off all tranquilizers, however, her daily routine started to revolve around the activities Frahm had listed to her husband, and she engaged in them wholeheartedly. The more she exerted her body, the quieter her mind became. She particularly enjoyed the boxing lessons that followed her calisthenics. Sparring, she felt flashes of her old self in the confused darkness within. Every afternoon, before supper, she would take the waters and doze off as her warm muscles melted into the warm healing spring. Little by little, her body was teaching her how to be quiet again. Sometimes, after a good day, there was only a panting silence. Even her skin had quieted down. Perhaps as a result of the waters, her eczema, which had turned each one of the pores on her skin into a small screaming mouth, had subsided. She no longer needed to be gauzed and poulticed at all times and was even able to apply her camphor and calendula ointment on her own.

Helen's busy schedule allowed for two visiting hours, one after breakfast and another during tea, both of which she spent with her husband. At first, Benjamin's presence did not seem to affect her in any way. She barely acknowledged him and kept talking to herself, usually while writing—Dr. Frahm had learned about her diaries and had encouraged her to start keeping them again. As time went by and her mind seemed to settle down, Helen started to feel safe without having to surround herself with a moat of words. Her sentences still had a tendency to become torrents of wild associations, but they sprang from reasonable sources and often came to some sort of conclusion, sometimes even followed by a pause. It became possible to have a semblance of a conversation with her. And with this improvement, the distance that had always separated Helen from Benjamin was reinstated and, perhaps, increased. She recognized him, yes, and was even polite to him, but in a way he found chilling. Her former efforts at trying to close the space between them had now ceased. Those affectionate attempts had been at the foundation of their marriage, and Benjamin had been touched by her exertions over the years, finding them of even more value than spontaneous love (which, he believed, was not a matter of choice or the result of labor, but merely some sort of fatal hex that reduced its victim to a passive trance). But now all he saw in his wife's most lucid moments was good manners and courteous consideration. Perhaps he was asking too much of her precarious convalescence, but the undertow of her illness seemed to have pulled her far away, and she had emerged on some new, remote shore from which he was visible only as an outline.

Benjamin would have accepted Helen's detachment as part of her healing process or even as the permanent terms under which she had recovered her sanity, had her apathy been universal. But as she improved, her coldness appeared to be reserved only for him. Lately, he had seen her smiling during her exchanges, in German, with the nurses. Her tone with them, despite the harshness of the language, was softer. She looked them in the eye. Gestures enlivened her words. Once, returning from a short stroll, he spotted her sitting on the grass with Dr. Frahm. She was giggling.

QUIETLY, Rask's American servants started packing the trunks and crates they had brought across the Atlantic. Benjamin decided that he had honored his wife's request by spending almost two months in Bad Pfäfers, but now it was time for him to be back in command and determine the direction of her treatment. Sensing that Helen would oppose their departure (and knowing Dr. Frahm would advise against it), he continued with his arrangements in secret. Only the day before their trip would he share his decision with everyone. He had already contacted his associates at Haber Pharmaceuticals with the notion of taking Helen to Germany to have her examined and diagnosed by doctors recommended by them. Everything was almost ready—a furnished house in Berlin, the few things they would take with them, the arrangement to have the bulk of their belongings shipped back home to New York. They were a mere few days away from leaving when he was told that Helen was gone.

During the half hour between her first bath and breakfast, there had been some miscommunication between the nurse on duty, who did not speak English, and the handmaid, who did not speak German. Each of them believed Helen to be in the care of the other. It soon became apparent that Mrs. Rask had created this confusion deliberately so that she could slip away. As soon as Dr. Frahm was notified, he sent out squadrons of nurses, orderlies, and waiters to go through the northern wing. He then expanded the search to the remaining buildings and grounds. Once he was sure she had left the compound, he called for Mr. Rask.

Benjamin knew better than to lose his composure when he needed it the most. In the subdued voice that so many in New York's business circles had failed to imitate, he dispatched his cars to the villages north and south of the Institute with orders (and cash) to enlist their inhabitants in the search. Helen could not have climbed the abrupt mountains to the east and west; she must have followed one of the roads to then roam the gentler hills around them. The villagers, combing the surroundings of the two roads leading to the Institute, would find her. A few hours later, plowmen, dairymaids, and herders had fanned out over slopes, forests, and glens.

While waiting for news, Benjamin summoned Dr. Frahm to his rooms to let him know they were leaving. The director walked in, looked around at the pieces of luggage, and said he was sad to hear the rumors of their departure were true. Benjamin was indignant to learn they had been spied upon and gossiped about. The rumors must have reached his wife, prompting her to flee. Benjamin blamed her disappearance on the staff's indiscretion and the director's negligence.

Dr. Frahm ignored these charges and in a few impassioned yet cool sentences tried to explain how much progress Helen had made, how responsive she had been to the salts, and how much better she now understood her illness thanks to her sessions with him. It was imperative, he said, that Helen stayed and finished her treatment. The fact that she was reenacting her father's escape had to be taken, odd as this might seem, as a sign of improvement.

Benjamin called Dr. Frahm a fabulist and a quack. Just as the director was saying that the dislike he and Benjamin felt for each other should not get in the way of Mrs. Rask's well-being, there was a knock on the door. One of the drivers walked into the room. Mrs. Rask had been found. A farmhand had spotted her drinking from a brook. As Benjamin rushed out, the chauffeur told him he should know the blisters on her face were bad, very bad indeed.

THE NORTHERN WING severed its ties to the Institute. The gates leading to the rest of the compound were locked; all the local nurses and supporting personnel, from cooks to janitors, had been dismissed. Benjamin had consolidated his American staff in a few rooms at the far end of the building. He resumed his place at Helen's bedside, assisting the nurses and maids he had brought from New York. But there was little to do because Helen was now under heavy sedation. Benjamin had decided on a dose he believed, based on his previous experience, to be the strongest one within the realm of safety. It had been impossible to calm her down when they brought her back. In her loud jumble of German and English, the only clear thing was that her words were unable to keep up with her thoughts. She would not allow anyone to touch her and was, for the first time during her illness, aggressive. Her face was bleeding from her compulsive scratching, and she refused to have her wounds dressed. She had to be pinned down to be sedated.

Dr. Frahm had not been allowed to see Helen or even set foot in the northern pavilion since she had been brought back. If Benjamin had started to take control of the situation by packing up and arranging the trip to Germany, the last series of incidents had fully restored him to his adamant self. There would be no further treatments based on superstitions and unquantifiable guesswork; there would be no private "sessions"; there would be no spying, no gossiping; there would be nothing that did not make sense to him, nothing that eluded his authority. Now, being in command again, he looked back on the past few weeks, when he had sheepishly accepted his ailing wife's decisions and submitted to Frahm's charlatanry, as if they had been part of some disorganized dream. He would have left Switzerland at once, but Helen was in no condition to travel. He therefore dispatched a courier to

Berlin with instructions for his associates at Haber Pharmaceuticals. They were to spare no expense or effort in finding the best specialists and to send them over—with equipment and supplies—to Bad Pfäfers at once.

For most of the day, Helen seemed to be floating on her back, half submerged in unconsciousness, mumbling to herself. Her eyes appeared to have been left open by accident. Eventually, her eyelids would droop, slowly, as she drifted away, still murmuring, until falling asleep for a short moment. She always awoke with a gasp, as if she had run out of air down in her inner darkness and had kicked herself back up to the surface and out into the world again. Rather than finding rest in her narcotic torpor, it only seemed to deepen her exhaustion. Her face was barely visible under the bloated mask of the drugs, studded with the blisters and scales of her eczema. The compresses only brought temporary relief. Benjamin understood that all this—her confusion, her physical deterioration—would be rectified once help from Berlin arrived. What distressed him and, he knew, would always haunt him was Helen's wrists. She would take the compresses off her face and scratch her scabs open with great violence, as if digging into herself. The nurses put gloves on her hands and tried to restrain her with snug sheets and tight swaddles, all to no avail. In the end, Benjamin ripped one of Helen's robes and, swallowing his tears, tied her wrists to the bed railings with the silken shreds. Every time she woke up and saw her bonds, Helen was surprised, then angry, then inconsolable. Once she managed to calm down, she started mumbling until she drifted away, and the cycle started again.

Time was a smudge in this restless monotony. The only traces left by the passing days were the accumulating signs of neglect, resulting from Benjamin's lockdown. To make the most of their limited resources, the American maids wheeled Helen into a new room every day, leaving behind dirty sheets, bandages, and basins. The drivers made daily runs to the neighboring villages for produce, dairy, and other essentials. But Benjamin barely ate. For the first time in his life, he grew a beard. He hated it but somehow thought it had to be there. A calendar of sorts. He would shave it when the Germans came.

And the Germans did come. Benjamin went out to meet the small convoy—two slate-gray trucks and a black sedan. The trucks contained supplies, medical equipment, and six nurses; the sedan produced Dr. Aftus. As the nurses unloaded the boxes and crates and moved them into the building, Benjamin led the doctor to his room. After a few pleasantries, Dr. Aftus handed Benjamin a letter signed by the board members of Haber Pharmaceuticals.

Esteemed Mr. Rask,

We trust the following will find you in good health.
We are pleased to introduce Dr. Ladislas Aftus to you through this letter. As you can see from his curriculum vitae (enclosed), he comes with the highest academic credentials.
Dr. Aftus's current line of research is centered on the use of pentylenetetrazol in the treatment of schizophrenia. This drug is known for its benefits as a stimulant that addresses certain respiratory and circulatory maladies. But Dr. Aftus has discovered new applications for it. After careful statistical research, Dr. Aftus found that epilepsy is antagonistic to and virtually incompatible with schizophrenia. He concluded that the high concentration of glial cells in epileptic brains had to be the cause of the low incidence of schizophrenia. He further concluded that artificially inducing epileptic seizures would augment the presence of glia in a schizophrenic brain, thus curing it. And he realized that he was able to induce these convulsions with a special compound based on

pentylenetetrazol, which, used in high dosages, produces convulsions not unlike grand mal seizures. Our clinical trials, conducted recently at a psychiatric clinic in Budapest, have shown a great rate of success.

Convulsive Therapy, which Haber Pharmaceuticals is in the process of patenting, is the future of psychiatry. And we believe Mrs. Rask to be an ideal candidate for it. Dr. Aftus, naturally, will be able to supply all the details better than we ever could and address any concerns you may have.

Our thoughts remain with you and your wife during these trying times.

Yours truly,
  Lorenz Rantzau
  Wilhelm von Bültzingslöwen
  Dieter Elz
  Julius Birk
  Reinhardt Liebezeit

THERE WAS A WAITING PERIOD while Helen, once again, was weaned off her sedatives so that Dr. Aftus could see her symptoms "in full bloom." During this time, Aftus and Rask got to know each other. Perhaps because he had been instructed by Haber Pharmaceuticals' board of directors to take special good care of their main investor, Dr. Aftus was available at all times to answer questions and discuss every aspect of the treatment in the utmost detail. Benjamin was delighted at the contrast with the elusive Dr. Frahm and his cryptic mumbo jumbo. He took every meal with Aftus and was educated on the chemical composition of the drug and its metabolism. In his fluent yet laborious, fictitiously patrician English, Dr. Aftus told Benjamin about his first experiments with camphor and how he had discarded this convulsant for its slow action, which patients and physicians alike found terrifying. His new compound was swift and therefore humane, a central aspect of this procedure in particular and his medical philosophy in general. Benjamin was quite touched by this emphasis on compassion and kindness, since it reminded him of the principled ardor with which Helen had once devoted herself to the development of new psychiatric therapies. Dr. Aftus also provided him with exhaustive statistics from his clinical trials and furnished him with charts, graphs, and diagrams. These calculations, derived from empirical facts—these numbers—gave Benjamin a sense of security: here was a treatment based on observation, experimentation, and the uncompromising laws of nature; here was scientific work that could be measured by objective standards.

The day to administer the first injection came. Benjamin was taken aback when he was denied access to Helen's room. He asked one of the nurses to fetch Dr. Aftus. A few minutes later, they were having a hushed conversation in one of the vacant neighboring rooms. Before Benjamin could speak, Aftus pleaded with him by raising his hands and closing his eyes. He had been reluctant to discuss this with Mr. Rask earlier, but the convulsions were not an easy thing to witness— especially for a layman. It would be deplorable if watching the most unpleasant part of the treatment made him doubt its enormous benefits. And above all, would it not be reasonable to spare Mrs. Rask her husband's anxiety and concern? The procedure would be short, and Mr. Rask could come visit as soon as it was over and his wife had rested.

Benjamin spent the morning overseeing the details concerning the trip back to the United States. Dr. Aftus had assured him they would be able to leave soon, possibly within the next ten days. The effect of his convulsive therapy was almost instantaneous. Mrs. Rask would be weak, yes, but Dr. Aftus had volunteered to come along and look after her during the journey across the Atlantic and to continue the treatment in New York, in the comfort of her home. Nothing could have pleased Benjamin more. He was eager to return to his office and be in charge, once again, of his business. Chief among his many projects was a complete takeover of Haber Pharmaceuticals, which, given Dr. Aftus's revolutionary findings, seemed a most promising investment.

A nurse knocked on the door, announced Mrs. Rask was ready for him, and left. As Benjamin was adjusting his tie, he realized he still had a full beard. He took off his shirt and hastily shaved for his wife.

Dr. Aftus met him halfway down the corridor and gave him a brief report as they walked to Helen's room. She had responded more than favorably to the treatment. He had started with a low dose to measure her tolerance. It had been such a success that he was considering increasing the dosage to make the most of each session and shorten the process. When they reached the room, Aftus paused before turning the doorknob. Mr. Rask should keep in mind that his wife would be under the effects of phenobarbital, used to control the seizures, and thus somewhat befuddled. Perhaps even speechless. And above all, he ought to remember what he had been told numerous times—that convulsive therapy was based on shock and that Mrs. Rask would, therefore, be, well, yes, shocked.

Benjamin approached the bed with reverent caution. Helen's face was turned to the wall. Her chest rose and sank shallowly and a little too fast. Intentionally, Benjamin made some noise with his shoes on the tiles, trying to announce himself. Helen turned to him. Her face was a desolate ruin. A thing broken and abandoned, exhausted of being. Her eyes did not look at Benjamin but seemed to be there only so that he could peer into the rubble within. He leaned over, kissed her scorched forehead, and told her she had been so brave and done so well. He hoped he was smiling.

A SOUNDLESS VACUUM. No one, in the airtight hush, dared disturb Helen's prostrate silence. Because she did not speak, everyone was quiet; because she did not move, everyone was still. Nurses and maids became white shadows. Benjamin took his modest meals alone in his room, where he spent all his time. There was an underwater quality to the sounds that came wafting from the other parts of the Institute—patients joking in different languages as they made their way to the thermal baths, the rumble and thumping of coordinated feet following a calisthenics instructor, occasional music, janitorial clatter. The dissonant concert of life seemed to be performed as a provocation to the sequestered inhabitants of the northern pavilion and their vows of silence.

Dr. Aftus had described to Benjamin, in great detail (but never before the information was strictly necessary), the aftereffects of the first injection of pentylenetetrazol. The account had been unambiguous, even brutal. He had also mentioned the deplorable fact that some in the medical community mistook his treatment for a punitive act of violence against the insane—such was the intensity of the convulsions that, regrettably, were essential to his therapy. Still, nothing Benjamin had been told could have prepared him for the state of catatonic trance in which he found Helen after her first session. He had never refused to confront any of his wife's facets, however hurtful or confusing he found them. He had looked squarely at the tender lovelessness she had shown for him during all of their marriage; he had watched as she turned away from him for her writers and musicians; he had faced, unblinkingly, her new self, possessed and disfigured by disease. But the breathing carcass he had seen after the treatment was more than he could take. That vacancy—while she was still, physically, there—was the most sinister and literal embodiment of his fear of Helen leaving him. He found little relief in the fact that Dr. Aftus had anticipated her current state and assured him that this was the expected, standard reaction to convulsive therapy, a reaction that, in the future, would be considered "textbook." It usually took three injections to see clear results, which, he guaranteed again, were just short of miraculous. It would be, he used to say, as if Helen suddenly woke up from a long dream. Sometimes, a mild improvement could even be perceived with the second shot. Heartbroken but with his faith in Aftus intact, Benjamin authorized the next session.

Benjamin waited on a bench by the main entrance to the building. A faint half-moon notched the daytime sky; the Alpine walls felt taller; the thin, electric air made him light-headed. Aside from his school years, he had never been away from New York City this long. He was tired of feeling foreign—tired of nature, of Switzerland, of idleness, of doctors, of receiving explanations, of subjecting to those explanations while refusing them. Knowing he would be on his way home in about a week made him even more intolerant of his surroundings. He looked back up, offended, at the misplaced moon.

The door swung open, and one of the American nurses stumbled out, sobbing. She came to an abrupt halt and bent over, resting her palms on her knees, crying and catching her breath. As she shook her head, saying no to the ground, she caught sight of Benjamin. He could have sworn that, the instant she overcame her surprise and embarrassment, hatred flashed in her eyes. But it had all been too fast. Almost immediately, she turned her back on him and ran away to the nurse's living quarters. Shortly thereafter, he was summoned to Helen's room.

Two days had passed since he had last seen her. He paused at the door, wondering if he should wait for the next shot and the visible improvement that was supposed to come with it. Finally, he went in. This time, Helen was propped up with pillows and facing him as he opened the door. Was there a faint hue of triumph in her exhausted features? Involuntarily, he thought this had to be the expression on women's faces after giving birth. Did he also see the hint of a sad smile? He took a few steps forward and then, beyond doubt, saw his wife mouth his name. Kneeling by the bed, he held her (collarbone, shoulder blade, spine) and wept, believing, for the first time since the illness had claimed her, that she would be cured.

For the next three days, Helen remained motionless and quiet. There was something unquestionable about her silence, much like an animal's wordlessness. Still, to Benjamin, her improvement was beyond doubt. Even in her hazy exhaustion, she was more present, and, if not fully engaged with her surroundings, at least tenuously aware of them. During her brief visiting hours—Dr. Aftus was adamant about rest—she looked at Benjamin, seemed to recognize him, and even appeared to convey soft signs of affection through her gaze. When she closed her eyes to rest, she would give his hand a gentle squeeze, as if saying goodbye for a little while.

Most of their belongings had been packed up and sent away in hired trucks while their home in New York was being readied for Helen along Dr. Aftus's guidelines. They were set to leave three days after the next injection. Now that his faith in Helen's recovery was fully restored, Benjamin's attention shifted back to his work. Although he did not have information from direct sources (he still suffered the ignominy of having to read newspapers), he sensed there were many opportunities in the reshaping of financial practices taking place in the United States. It was the perfect time to insert himself in the new order that was rising after the crash. And, of course, he was moving ahead with the acquisition of Haber Pharmaceuticals. He had already dispatched an envoy to Berlin with a letter stating his intentions.

Benjamin was not a superstitious man, but on the afternoon of Helen's third and last injection before their departure, he resumed his place on the bench by the entrance. He was pleased to experience, after so many weeks of inactivity, the contraction of time that took place when he lost himself in work. If asked, he would have been unable to say exactly what his thoughts were during that hour, and yet there was an untranslatable clarity to his mental process. During this focused vagueness that preceded all his great business ideas, the world somehow vanished from his senses. Even his self dissolved into the stream of impersonal thoughts. This is why he did not immediately accept Dr. Aftus's presence, although his eyes had seen him approach with slow steps. It was only when he sat down next to Benjamin that Aftus acquired the solidity of the real.

Dr. Aftus put his palms together, making sure each finger exactly mirrored the other, then separated his hands, took a deep breath, and said that in some occasions numbers and statistics have no meaning: each loss is absolute and can never be mitigated by past or future triumphs.

Benjamin blinked at the doctor's words.

After another sigh, Dr. Aftus went on to say that Mrs. Rask's heart, which had previously responded so well, had given in. He knew his condolences would always be insufficient and was, of course, at Mr. Rask's disposal, should he decide to conduct an inquest.

The mountains, the ground, Benjamin's body were drained of substance and weight. All was hollow.

He didn't get up; the planet sank.

Benjamin walked into the building and down the hall to Helen's room, surprised to see his feet move and his hand turn the doorknob.

The nurses froze. He approached the bed. They stepped away.

As if it were the skin of a delicate fruit, he lifted the sheet. There was nothing restful about Helen's face. All the pain had remained sealed within. Her body was somehow distorted. Benjamin took a step back, trying to rearrange it in his mind.

Someone mentioned her clavicle. He turned around. It was the American nurse who had rushed out of the building in tears a few days before. She said Mrs. Rask's convulsions had been so violent she had broken her collarbone.

◆

BY THE TIME BENJAMIN RETURNED to New York, it was too late for
condolences, cards, and memorial services. Few people dared to speak
to him; fewer had the nerve to impart advice. Those who did always
told him he should sell the house—it was too crowded with memories, and no one could live in such a haunted place, no matter how
friendly or loving the ghosts might be. He never bothered to respond.
All rooms were left untouched. Not as in a museum. Not as if he were
waiting, unhinged by pain, for something miraculous to happen in
them. In fact, he seldom ventured beyond his quarters and his office.
They were preserved simply because without them, the universe would
be a poorer place. As it was, it contained Helen's rooms.

The house, however, was not among Benjamin's most prominent
thoughts. If anything reflected his grief, it was the redoubled zeal with
which he returned to his work. He tried to make one of his discreet yet
decisive interventions in the market and focused primarily on currency
manipulation. Following the Emergency Banking Act, the Federal
Reserve had printed money in a large volume to meet every possible
call after the 1933 bank run. Almost simultaneously, the government
had suspended the gold standard, letting the dollar float on foreign
markets. Making use of his vast gold reserves around the world (and
foreseeing executive orders regulating its trade), Rask made a strong
bet against the dollar, assuming that, as a result of the vast amounts of
currency the government was emitting, its value would be depreciated.
He invested heavily in the pound sterling, the Reichsmark, and beyond, all the way to the yen. The markets, for a moment, responded
to his influence. But in time the economy reacted favorably to the set
of government policies, and Benjamin's profit was only marginal. He
also decided that the New Deal was doomed to fail and that Wall

Street would suffer from the series of regulations introduced by the Securities Act. Based on these intuitions, he decided to replicate his 1929 play and orchestrate short positions on a massive scale. Halfway into his maneuvers, he had to recognize he was wrong. The market was responding well to the government's actions, and Benjamin had to backtrack. His monetary loss was not as large as the damage done to his reputation. People on the Street said his currency speculation had been wrongfooted from the beginning and that his failed stock market coup, mimicking his old success, showed that he had only one tattered card up his sleeve. The public at large—or at least the average reader of the financial pages in the paper—was indignant to see Mr. Rask gambling against the nation's recovery.

During this time, Mrs. Brevoort was exuberant in her grief, exploring all the social possibilities of mourning. She found unsuspected radiance in the deepest shades of black and made sure to surround herself with particularly plaintive and misty-eyed friends so that she could highlight her arrogant form of sorrow, which she called "dignified." It is not unlikely that she felt genuine pain under the somewhat farcical spectacle of bereavement she put up for her circle. Some people, under certain circumstances, hide their true emotions under exaggeration and hyperbole, not realizing their amplified caricature reveals the exact measure of the feelings it was meant to conceal.

Immediately after Benjamin's return, she visited every day, whether he was in or not. She organized things around the house, tyrannized the staff, and made a show of being in charge. He, however, was submerged in work, oblivious of Mrs. Brevoort's displays and seldom available to her. Over the course of the few conversations they had during that period, Mrs. Brevoort hinted, more than once, at the possibility of moving into the house—Benjamin could use the comfort and the company only someone close to Helen could provide, someone who knew her and understood him. These insinuations were never acknowledged. It did not take long for Mrs. Brevoort and Benjamin to drift apart, until their only connection was the bills she kept sending to his office.

As time went by, Benjamin had to own up to a frightful fact: Helen's death had not altered his life. Nothing, in substance, had changed—there was only a difference in degree. His mourning was simply a more radical expression of his marriage: both were the result of a perverse combination of love and distance. In Helen's life, he had been unable to bridge the abyss that separated her from him. His failure had never turned into resentment or stopped him from looking for new crossings. But now, even if his love remained unchanged, that distance had become absolute.

He kept funding Helen's charities and made recurrent donations to orchestras, libraries, and organizations for the arts. Attached to endowments and fellowships, her first name became synonymous with excellence—"a Helen" was one of the most prestigious honors a composer or a writer could aspire to, and this pleased Benjamin to no end. Her charitable work related to research into new psychiatric methods, however, was discontinued. This was a world he did not wish to revisit. Although in the end he did not buy out Haber Pharmaceuticals, he retained his shares in the company—his emotions had never beclouded his business decisions, and this was no exception. Despite Dr. Aftus's failure, Benjamin still believed Haber to be profitable, and it did indeed generate steady and impressive returns. Convulsive therapy laid the ground for what, a few years later, would become electroshock therapy. But by that time, Benjamin had steered Haber away from pharmaceutics altogether (and dropped the second part of its brand name) to focus on industrial chemistry and the pursuit of government contracts in different nations.

Had Benjamin been content with conservatively managing his assets, his fortune still would have been comparable to the economy of a small nation. But in the years following Helen's death, his fascination with the incestuous genealogies of money—capital begetting capital begetting capital—remained intact. He was still an effective investor, and he was still, now and then, capable of some creative flair. Yet despite the continued growth of his portfolio, there was a widespread perception that he was in frank decline, that there was something stale about his approach. Nothing came close to the margins of his golden days. After all, everyone concurred, it did not take extraordinary talent to make money from so much money. Some believed he was out of step with the new political reality. Others thought he never recovered from losing his wife. Many simply said he was old. But most agreed: He had lost his touch. His mystical aura had faded. Gone was the genius who had found profit where everyone else found their ruin. Benjamin Rask's time, it was generally held, was over.

Still, he remained as committed as ever to his business. And his later years were not unlike his early days, when he was first operating out of his parents' house on West 17th Street. All he did was work and sleep, often in the same place. Cared not for entertainment. Spoke only when necessary. No friends. No distractions. Aside from a slower body and some minor ailments, there might have been just one substantial difference between his former self and who he had become: while that young person had believed he would renounce everything in favor of his calling, this aging man was sure he had given life a fair try.

My Life

ANDREW BEVEL

CONTENTS

Preface

My name is known to many, my deeds to some, my life to few. This has never concerned me much. What matters is the tally of our accomplishments, not the tales about us. Still, because my past has so often overlapped with that of our nation, lately I have come to believe that I owe it to the public to share some of the decisive moments of my story.

I cannot say, in all honesty, that I am writing these pages in order to indulge the desire, so frequent in men my age, to talk about myself. Over the years I have been loath to make statements of any kind. This ought to be proof enough that I have never been inclined to discuss my doings out in the open. Rumors have surrounded me most of my life. I have grown accustomed to them and take care never to deny gossip and tales. Denial is always a form of confirmation. Yet I confess that the urge to address and refute some of these fictions has become pressing, especially since the passing of my beloved wife, Mildred.

Mildred was the quiet, steady presence in my life that made so many of my achievements possible. I take it to be my duty to ensure that her memory does not fade and that her placid moral example endures through time. I offer here my wife's loving portrait, resigned to knowing it shall fail to fully honor her dignity, candor and grace.

One further reason has moved me to gather my thoughts and recollections into this book. For about a decade now I have witnessed a woeful decline not only in the business of our country but also in the spirit of its people. Where perseverance and ingenuity once dwelled, apathy and despair now loiter. Where self-reliance reigned, beggarly submission now squats. The working man is reduced to a panhandler. A vicious circle has taken hold of our able-bodied men: they increasingly rely on the government to alleviate the misery created by that same government, not realizing that this dependency only perpetuates their sorry state of affairs.

My hope is that these pages will serve as a reminder of the unflagging boldness that has hitherto defined our people. I also hope my words will steel the reader not only against the regrettable conditions of our time but also against any form of coddling. Perhaps this book will help my fellow countrymen remember that it is through the sum of daring individual actions that this nation has risen above all others and that our greatness comes only from the free interplay of singular wills. It is in this spirit that I offer the narrative of my life to the public.

I know the days ahead of me are fewer than those I have left behind. There is no escaping this most basic fact of accounting. A certain amount of time is allotted to each of us. How much, only God knows. We cannot invest it. We cannot hope for a return of any kind. All we can do is spend it, second by second, decade by decade, until it runs out. Still, even if our days on this Earth are limited, we can always, through toil and industry, hope to extend our influence into the future. And so it is that, having lived my life with an eye set on posterity in the hopes of improving the lives of later generations, I enter these remaining years of mine not with nostalgia for all that is gone but with a sense of excitement for what is yet to come.

New York, July of 1938

I

Ancestry

I am a financier in a city ruled by financiers. My father was a financier in a city ruled by industrialists. His father was a financier in a city ruled by merchants. His father was a financier in a city ruled by a tight-knit society, indolent and priggish, like most provincial aristocracies. These four cities are one and the same, New York.

Although this is the capital of the future, its inhabitants are nostalgic by nature. Every generation has its own notion of "old New York" and claims to be its rightful heir. The result is, of course, a perpetual reinvention of the past. And this, in consequence, means there are always new old New Yorkers.

The early descendants of the Dutch and British settlers who passed for our local nobility wanted nothing with the German immigrant who became a trapper, then a fur trader and finally a real estate tycoon. And they had only contempt for the Staten Island ferryman who turned into a shipping and railroad magnate. Yet once these traders and builders joined the upper echelons of society, it was only to look down on the newcomers from Pittsburgh and Cleveland with their sooty, oily fortunes. Because their wealth was vaster than anything hitherto imagined, they were scorned and even called robbers. Still, after taking over the city, these industrialists, in turn, spurned the bankers who were reshaping America's financial landscape and ushering in a new era of prosperity, pegging them as speculators and gamblers.

Today's gentleman is yesterday's upstart. But behind these shifting characters there is a constant presence: the financier. Investing, lending, borrowing and, more widely, the efficient administration of capital is what sustained the city at each of those periods, regardless of what was being produced and sold. Nonetheless, just as this town has changed from one generation to the next, so has the meaning of the word "financier."

I am not a historian and do not intend to offer a scholarly account of the evolution of American finance. Neither am I a genealogist, bent on exhuming every detail of my family's past. These pages, rather, will be limited to the events and characters found in the intersection of these two circles.

WILLIAM

My forefathers were, in many ways, one-man banks before banking had truly been established throughout our country. This lineage of businessmen within my family began not too long after the Declaration of Independence, at a time when, aside from the First Bank of the United States, chartered in 1791, there were only four private financial institutions. I am honored to walk in my ancestors' footsteps and humbly carry on the duty of upholding their name.

My great-grandfather William Trevor Bevel left his native Virginia for New York with the intention of expanding the family business. His father grew tobacco on a modest scale. They made a handsome living, but William saw more potential in the operation. Why should he limit himself to only exporting goods produced in America? Why not also supply the growing demand prosperous local landowners showed for imported European goods?

William's designs were momentarily upset by Thomas Jefferson's embargo of 1807, which brought our economy, rather than the British against which it was aimed, to its knees. In the midst of its war with France, England resorted to seizing American merchant ships, confiscating their cargo and forcing their crew into the service of the British Navy. In response Jefferson decided to wage a commercial war. No English goods were to be imported into America. And, more significantly, no American wares were allowed to leave our shores for theirs. The hope was to cripple British industry, so dependent on our raw materials. Instead it was our nation that suffered the most. Entire harvests went to waste. Planters were forced to let the fruit of their labor gather dust in storehouses.

The unpopularity of this gross form of government intervention was patent. Its effects were discussed on every street and felt in every home. William understood it was an untenable situation. And he knew the embargo would have to be lifted in time for the 1808 presidential election. This, however, was a year away. He therefore devised a plan.

William acquired a sizable loan against his father's property and then borrowed more upon that sum. He went deep into debt with the intention of buying from those who, like his parents, were unable to sell their goods. But rather than tobacco, which he would have been unable to store properly, he purchased non-perishable goods, especially cotton from farther south and sugar from the newly acquired Louisiana. This venture was based on the assumption that he would be able to sell the merchandise in Europe once the embargo was lifted and clear his debt while making a profit.

Producers everywhere were struggling just to keep their estates in the family. William, a mere twenty-six-year-old, was welcomed as a savior. Prices dropped sharply as plantation owners fought one another to secure a deal with him. And for as long as possible he did his best to assist as many of them as he could, bringing much-needed relief to countless families.

This all happened quickly and ceased to be good business in a matter of months. Other buyers followed his lead, and soon there were no more bargains to be had. But by then William was in possession of an impressive stockpile. Shortly after, the embargo ended. By the time he had sold all his inventory in Europe he had amassed a substantial capital.

Almost overnight my great-grandfather became a financial authority. People came to him for both counsel and loans. His rates were always much lower than those of the few banks in existence. And as these loans multiplied it occurred to him that he could start trading them, thus creating, almost singlehandedly, a thriving secondary market. From this, new profitable associations and investing opportunities arose.

He was an innovator and a visionary. His experiments with currencies for his European transactions, for example, were ahead of his time. He led the way with futures contracts (by which buyer and seller fix a price, immune from market fluctuations, for commodities that do not even exist at the time, such as crops yet to be sown) when these were exotic financial instruments few had hitherto tried. He bolstered, both to his and the country's great benefit, the treasury notes issued to fund the War of 1812, which led to our nation's first paper money, circulated in 1815.

More examples of his business acumen.

Show his pioneering spirit.

Even if at the time there was an established mercantile class in New York and the city revolved to a large extent around business, it was also understood that it was in poor taste to talk about money. Furthermore, involvement in any form of industry was frowned upon. A true gentleman was supposed to be a man of leisure. But the financial enterprises that made such leisure possible were not to be discussed in society. This put my great-grandfather in an awkward place. While his services were greatly appreciated he was also shunned by those who benefited from them. It would take three generations to begin to correct this hypocritical tendency, not yet fully overcome.

Through all his endeavors William always took care to remember his beginnings during Jefferson's embargo. This experience taught him two lessons he took to heart. The first one was that the ideal conditions for business were never given. One had to create them. If the embargo had initially shattered his dreams, he found a way to turn the situation to his favor. And his second and main discovery was that self-interest, if properly directed, need not be divorced from the common good, as all the transactions he conducted throughout his life eloquently show. These two principles (we make our own weather; personal gain ought to be a public asset) I have always striven to follow.

This is not the only resemblance between my ancestor and me. It just so happens that my great-grandfather was artistically inclined. He was, in fact, the only one in the family who ever displayed any such dispositions, aside from me. Without ever receiving a formal education in the fine arts he was a consummate draftsman. Although I have no skill with either charcoal or ink, I like to believe I have inherited his eye. And I hope my art collection, of which I shall speak later, is a testimony to this. But there is a further and more literal resemblance between us. Among William's many sketches there are several self-portraits. I have one of them before me right now. Looking at it is like looking in a mirror.

CLARENCE

Despite his success, or perhaps because of it, New York never quite opened up to William. He therefore married a relation of one of his associates in Philadelphia. Louisa Foster was a loving companion to him. She was also a practical woman of great taste who oversaw every detail of the house they built on West 23rd Street. They lost their first two children within months to a rare respiratory condition. This is why their third, Clarence, born in 1816, led a rather secluded life. During his early years he barely left the house, where he was kept away from sudden gusts of wind, pollen, dust and every other conceivable threat to his lungs.

Clarence had a great mathematical mind. His passion for numbers thrived during his isolated upbringing. But solitude and studiousness turned him into a bit of a hermit. Although I have no memories of my grandfather, I know he had a severe stutter, which, of course, made social interaction even harder for him. He possessed all the qualities commonly attached to men of intellectual genius. He was absent-minded, withdrawn and focused on his work to the detriment of the most basic everyday tasks, at which he was charmingly inept.

Much against his wife's wishes, William sent his son to Yale College. The sheltered world of academia suited Clarence, who for the first time was among his intellectual peers. He excelled at geometry, algebra and fluxions. Shy and for the most part friendless, he still managed to attract the faculty's attention and become something of a scholarly legend.

His math treatise. Title. Summarize.

Close to graduation he was urged to stay on and further his studies so he could become a professor in mathematics, a title just added to the Yale catalog. He almost did. But trouble was brewing back home, in New York.

The price of cotton had plunged while that of wheat, which sustained the labor force, had risen as a consequence of poor crops. Because cotton was used as collateral security for most loans there was a groundswell of defaults. This, together with a climb in interest rates, led to the Panic of 1837. It required great strength and cunning of William to reallocate his investments. Only through his immense dexterity was he able to shield his legacy and hand it down, almost intact, to Clarence. But I fear this came at a cost. It is not unlikely that this crisis played some part in the heart attack that took William toward the end of the following year.

The recession that followed the panic left no time for mourning. Clarence had an uncanny ability with numbers. He had his father's connections. He had a reputable name. He had capital. There was, however, one thing he lacked: social deftness. No enterprise can fully succeed without a true understanding of human behavior. Yet to Clarence finance was a pure mathematical abstraction. This is why, under his guidance, the family entered a period that favored stability over expansion.

His unique, discreetly creative approach. Free Banking Era. Opportunities in currency fluctuation, etc. 2–3 examples.

Despite his reserved personality, Clarence married young. This might have been the most fortunate event of his life. Thomasina Holbrook, my grandmother, loved him precisely for all those qualities that kept him apart from the rest of the world. Tommy, as she was known to those close to her, always took good care of him and tenderly laughed away his eccentricities, which she found endearing.

More Tommy.

EDWARD

After the Civil War the family business faced the most challenging time in its history. Clarence saw the need for a drastic turn. He divested from the family's cotton, tobacco and sugar concerns, not because prices had dropped or because plantations had been ravaged by the war or confiscated by the federal government, but because it was the right thing to do. In this, he followed his father's teachings, according to which personal gain ought to be one with the good of the country. Then he stepped down and passed the torch on to his son, my father.

Edward was the reverse image of his father in almost every way. Where Clarence was withdrawn, Edward was expansive. If one moved only after thorough calculations, the other acted on impulse and had an infallible intuition. The older man was short and his soft features seemed to reflect his gentle soul, whereas the younger one had a towering, muscular build that spoke of his strong character.

Neither nurses nor tutors could restrain Edward, and almost everyone claimed he was a rebellious child. He ran up and down the stairs of the house on West 23rd Street, took over every room with his games, painted outlandish scenes on the walls, dismantled the furniture to build forts. A born leader, he enlisted other children and even adults to do his bidding. What all this shows is that from the tenderest age he had the ability to shape the world to his will.

Tommy, always intuitive, understood the issue was not her son's behavior. It was just that his surroundings were too narrow for him.

She therefore had a summer house built in Dutchess County. In La Fiesolana, a magnificent Florentine villa right on the Hudson River, Edward was in his element. There he was allowed to be wild and was given free rein to exhaust his energy. He picked up every imaginable sport, excelling at all of them. As he grew up he turned out to be a natural horseman, and in his early youth he discovered hunting, which ultimately became his main passion. His trophies from all over the country are still with me. Soon La Fiesolana became more than a mere summer house. It was, to the end, my father's true home.

Clarence sent his reluctant son to Yale. Athletic, imposing and rustically charming, my father soon became the center of attention at every game and gathering. He was one of those rare men who, without meaning to do so, upsets every rule of propriety and etiquette while somehow making everyone more comfortable for it. But although he did well enough at his studies with minimal effort, he was impatient to get out into the real world and leave his mark. And truth be told, my father had no need for a formal education. His talents were fully formed at birth.

Clarence was disappointed but not surprised when his son announced he would not leave La Fiesolana for New Haven at the end of the summer to begin his junior year. A compromise was reached. My grandfather demanded that Edward come with him into the office every day. He complied begrudgingly but soon got into the spirit of things.

The competitive nature of the work and his immediate success at it satisfied the sportsman in Edward. He proved to be a natural businessman, as my pages dedicated to his life and legacy will prove. It did not take long for him to become the public face of the business and steer it into an even more successful pathway. Details.

At one of the many functions he now had to attend he was introduced to Grace Cox. Many believed her to be the biggest "catch" of her day. Some thought the same of Edward. No one was surprised, then, to see their first encounter develop into courtship. Their courtship quickly led to their engagement and then to their wedding.

More about mother.

Grace made Edward's new life complete. The couple was at the center of New York's society for several seasons. And in the summertime they brought New York with them to La Fiesolana. If that stretch on the Hudson has flourished to become what it is today, it is partly because friends and associates built their houses in the neighboring plots just to be close to my parents.

More about mother's wonderful qualities in next chapter. Suffice it to say for now that Grace did honor to her name. Her beauty, elegance and sense of ease gave her an air of gentle authority. Universally admired. And in moments of darkness she was the beacon people turned to for a reminder of their best qualities and noblest aspirations.

One such moment came in 1873, four years after my parents' wedding. That spring, markets all over Europe collapsed. Shortly after, Jay Cooke & Company, America's premier investment firm at the time, failed. A bank run ensued. Meanwhile a shortage in the currency supply, combined with the overabundance of goods created by the manufacturing boom after the Civil War, led to unprecedented levels of deflation. The following years, until the end of the decade, were known as the Great Depression. Uninventive newspapermen have recently hijacked this name to describe our latest recession, an ordeal that seems almost benign when compared with the 1873 original.

It was during these trying times that Grace became the beating heart not only of my parents' circle of friends but also of several of the charitable associations that sprang up to mitigate the blow of the crisis. Self-possessed and soberly cheerful, she soothed and brightened up even the most anxious of those around her. A few little stories.

Meanwhile Edward, with his unerring intuition, had called in his loans before the panic and had successfully negotiated bonds of the New York Central Railroad. This, together with other daring yet shrewd decisions I shall later describe, left my father with readily available cash at a time when money was scarce. He was now in a unique position to help ease the contraction of the economy. And once again he proved, just as his ancestors had, that personal profit and the common good were not at odds with each other but could become, in capable hands, two sides of the same coin.

I was born in 1876, a few years after these events. This was, by all accounts, the beginning of my parents' happiest period. They discovered the joys of domesticity and withdrew into family life. After a few months we moved to La Fiesolana together with my grandparents Clarence and Tommy. My father would come up from work on the weekends and leave, forlorn, every Monday, making up for his absence by going on shopping sprees in the city so he could return with gifts for me and my mother. It saddens me to be unable to remember those days, but I find solace in knowing my father's last years were also his most blissful ones.

The affliction that ended his life had been developing, unnoticed, for quite some time. A ruptured aneurysm took him one afternoon as he was getting ready to leave his office. How this could have happened to such a paragon of health is a question that haunts me to this day. In just an instant my family was robbed of the happiness so recently acquired. I was four years old.

It did not take long for tragedy to strike again. Clarence, my grandfather, was overcome with grief at the sudden death of his son. Always withdrawn, now he refused every interaction. He spent his days under an old oak tree, staring at the river. It was there where his broken heart stopped.

By degrees my mother overcame her sorrow enough to run the house and become the loving presence that shaped my existence. She took an active part in my early education, supervising my governesses and tutors and closely following their programs of study. It was during this time that I started to show an unusual aptitude for mathematics.

My mother found the best possible instructors to foster those talents and engaged teachers with the highest credentials in the city. Her belief in my gifts, no doubt magnified by motherly love, was such that she even brought a young scholar down from Cambridge to lecture me. Yet this too she found insufficient, and shortly after my eighth birthday she sent me off to school in New Hampshire.

In most regards it was the right decision, since I owe my seemingly spontaneous accuracy and ease with numbers to the rigorous training I received throughout my early years. There is only one reason why I wish I had never gone away. Halfway into my third year at school my mother became severely ill. I was unable to make it back home in time to say our last farewells. This is one of the greatest pains of my life. Stalwart as ever, Tommy remained lovingly at my side until I started college. I believe that once she saw I was on the right track in life she allowed herself to finally rest.

II

Education

My school and college years revealed an interesting genealogical amalgamation: in me, my father's temperament was alloyed with my grandfather's spirit. Without being quite the man-about-campus I still led
an active social life. And without being a reclusive scholar I managed
to excel academically, especially in the field of mathematics. I have my
mother to thank for this. She was the first to see, early on, my innate
aptitude for numbers and nurtured my inherited talent for algebra,
calculus and statistics.

Every financier ought to be a polymath, because finance is the
thread that runs through every aspect of life. It is indeed the knot
where all the disparate strands of human existence come together.
Business is the common denominator of all activities and enterprises.
This, in turn, means there is no affair that does not pertain to the
businessman. To him everything is relevant. He is the true Renais-

sance man. And this is why I gave myself to the pursuit of knowledge in every conceivable realm, from history and geography to chemistry and meteorology.

I have a scientific approach to business. Every investment requires profound knowledge of a myriad of specific details. For a venture to succeed one needs to become a specialist, sometimes overnight, in all of its aspects. I have always said that my real work begins after the closing bell, when I pore over binder upon binder of industrial records, detailed summaries of world affairs and reports on the latest technological developments. My years as a student gave me a solid foundation for this sort of disciplined curiosity.

This chapter will show that no investment pays higher dividends than education. I still live by this creed and consider myself to be a perennial student. And over the years Mildred and I have worked tirelessly to ensure that others receive the opportunities I had.

Father. Describe early memories of him. He became a child once again building forts, playing in the woods, making up adventures. The incident on the riverbank.

Edward was truly Tommy's son. Brilliant strategist. His coalition during Panic of '73. Brings back family business. NYCRR bonds whole issue: trophy.

Mother

MATH in great detail. Precocious talent. Anecdotes.

COLLEGE

Coming to own true self.

Making lasting friends and testing character. As essential in business as having a good grasp of numbers.

The boys. Colorful anecdotes. Archie, Cager, Dick, Fred, Pepper, etc. Hint at Society. Overall lightness. Humorous?

Riding accident. Bedridden. Finding perspective and focus. End of juvenile distractions.

Eyes open to art.

Prof. Keene first true math mentor. He saw talent and potential. Eulogy.

Alumni, library, etc.

APPRENTICESHIP

III

In Business

Exactly one century separates my great-grandfather's breakthrough in business from mine. William found his opportunity during the Embargo of 1807. I seized my chance during the Panic of 1907. Both of us saw the need of rising to the occasion in these times of crisis. Back then William did not hesitate to mortgage the family estate several times over and invest it all in his venture. And just like him, I had no qualms about using the capital he had acquired and my ancestors had expanded over decades.

Panic as opportunity for forging new relationships. (Following Edward's example in 1873.)

WHOLE SECTION: "A Rational Approach to Business"?
Expanding some mathematical models developed under Prof. Keene.
Adapting formulas for business. Make accessible for average reader.
"New Ventures" section?
Consolidation.

End of laissez faire, beginning of government regulation: antitrust
suits, currency policy, central banking, National Monetary Commis-
sion.

First run-in with the press. Public opinion. The value of silence.

Bevel Investments portfolio. Limited the amount of stock available
and protected shareholder value.

Safeguarding nation's future. Preemptive measures.

WHOLE SECTION: "Clouds Thicken"?

Jekyll Island. Walked out over disagreement regarding national reserve
bank.

Fed. Was first to see it, acted in consequence.

Art. Collecting, etc.

Recession of 1920–21. Fed.

IV

Mildred

It has now been almost two decades since Mildred first entered my life and changed it forever. In her I found not only comfort and support but also inspiration. I am not given to flights of lyricism, yet I cannot help but say that Mildred was my muse. Because of her, an already successful career soared to new heights. It is not by mere coincidence that my most prosperous years were also my happiest ones.

Some people are exceptionally clear-eyed. To them, nothing is ever too complex or mysterious. Answers invisible to most are in plain sight to these enlightened few. Their approach to the world is elementary and, without fail, right. They see through false complications and find the simple truths of life. Mildred was blessed with this lucidity. Additionally the trials of her tender years and her always delicate health had given her the innocent yet profound wisdom of those who, like young children or the elderly, are close to the edges of existence.

She was too fragile, too good for this world and slipped away from it much too soon. Words are not enough to say how dearly I miss her. The greatest gift I have ever received was my time by her side. She saved me. There is no other way to put it. She saved me with her humanity and her warmth. Saved me with her love of beauty and her kindness. Saved me by making a home for me.

A NEW LIFE

In the fall of 1919 the wife of a business associate gave a dinner to introduce Mrs. Adelaide Howland and her daughter, recently back from a long stay in Europe. They barely knew anyone in New York, and the evening in their honor was meant to enlarge their social circle.

The circumstances of their journey were rather peculiar. What had begun as a pleasant tour to further the child's education ended in a protracted, almost permanent stay abroad. First Mr. Howland's drawn-out, sadly fatal lung condition and then the outbreak of the Great War kept them in the Old Continent for years.

Originally from Albany, mother and daughter decided to remain in New York, where they disembarked in the spring of 1919. They had only a few friends here, but Mrs. Howland wanted a fresh start for her daughter and thought New York would be more welcoming to a foreigner. Because that is what the child had almost become after spending her formative years overseas. She even had a delightfully slight accent that was impossible to place. Although it faded over time, fortunately she never quite lost it.

It is far beyond my verbal abilities to describe Mildred's features. I could never do justice to her delicate elegance. But I can say that it struck me as soon as we were introduced. This first impression never waned. On the contrary. The better I got to know her, the more her beauty deepened, because her charm and poise were the outward manifestations of her spirit. Picture 1,000 words: reproduce here Birley's portrait of Mildred hanging in Fiesolana.

Her mother allowed her to walk with me in Central Park. I cannot say that we got better acquainted during these strolls, because it felt as if we had always known each other. Still, all through that spring we shared details of our past and hopes for our future. But never like two people introducing themselves. It was rather as if two old friends were reuniting after a long time apart. The feeling of closeness was immediate, as was my certainty that I had finally found my tender helpmate.

Because her parents had been consumed with the hardships of illness and war, Mildred had been, for the most part, in charge of her own education. She was drawn to the arts, and her natural good taste proved to be her best mentor and teacher. The inherited status of a piece meant nothing to her. She ignored the opinions of critics and found academic dogmas worthless.

Above painting she loved literature. She was a tireless reader who followed her inclinations rather than the rules dictated by the guardians of taste, thus making her own path. More.

Of all the arts, however, music was uppermost in her heart. Her biggest regret in life was that she had never really learned to play the piano or the violin. Moving from place to place during her childhood she was unable to take regular lessons and rarely found herself in settings conducive to practicing an instrument. It might have been possible to overcome these obstacles, but her parents were reluctant to encourage her artistic tendencies.

It was through music that Mildred's loving presence made itself felt in our house. Without her beautiful recordings playing on the phonograph at all times, without the little recitals we now and then hosted for a few friends, our home would have been as cold as a museum. The warmth she radiated was her most wonderful quality and the single greatest contribution she made to my life. She saw the beauty in the world, and for as long as she found strength in her delicate body, her mission was to allow for others to see it too.

Mildred's all-too-brief stay among us left indelible traces. She touched everyone with her kindness and generosity. Examples. And I know her kind hand will still be reaching out to generations to come, long after I am gone.

HOME

Years before our wedding I had acquired a townhouse on East 87th Street, near Fifth Avenue. Although it always remained vacant, I had plans for it from the very start. Over time I purchased a string of adjacent properties. My intention was to own the remaining westward portion of my block and also the equivalent northward stretch around the corner, on Fifth Avenue. This would allow me to build a house facing Central Park.

It just so happened that shortly after our wedding I found myself in possession of the final piece of this jigsaw puzzle. At long last our lot was consolidated. Anyone who knows anything about New York real estate will understand that realizing this comparatively modest aspiration was one of the greatest triumphs of my career!

George Calvert Leighton and his firm drew up architectural plans, the row of houses was swiftly demolished, and we broke ground at once. During this part of the project Mildred and I moved up to La Fiesolana. She was delighted. Having spent so much time in Tuscany, she truly appreciated how perfectly Tommy, my grandmother, had replicated the best of Italy up in Dutchess County.

Once Mildred settled in, infusing life and warmth into every room with her little touches, I resumed work in Manhattan. Those were busy days, as I was helping to steer the economy out of the recession that choked the nation after the Great War, which I have described in chapter III. From Monday through Friday, after work, I would go by the construction site. And each weekend I found myself making the trip up to La Fiesolana with a carload of gifts to compensate for my absence. Just like my father.

Two years later the house was completed. Mildred's joy after moving in was, in turn, the most overwhelming joy I have ever experienced. She relished in the smallest tasks and found the highest satisfaction in the simplest pleasures of life. That her greatest luxury was a cup of hot cocoa at the end of the day should speak eloquently to her modest, unassuming nature.

Small everyday stories.

Cruel fate would have it that Mildred's illness should strike shortly after she made herself at home in our new residence. An incessant fatigue was the first symptom of what became a long agony. Doctors prescribed bed rest and a fortified diet, but no amount of repose or food was ever enough to restore her. At first she was unable to muster enough strength to keep up with our social engagements. Nevertheless, although weak, she was still up and about the house. Before too long, however, she found herself unable to attend the music performances so dear to her heart.

Since she could not go to concert halls, she brought music home by organizing small recitals in our library. These were unpretentious, informal gatherings. A soloist or a chamber ensemble would play in the second-floor parlor, which has excellent acoustics. A few friends often joined us for these after-dinner programs. I can still see Mildred's wistful smile, her enraptured gaze and her hands gently hovering over her lap, as if she were conducting.

Soon after we started hosting our little performances she was forced to give up her beloved strolls around the park. But this did not discourage her love of nature. She spent the cool hours of the morning in our greenhouse and developed a keen interest in flowers. Throughout the year she received exotic specimens from different parts of the world. Her painterly eye found endless delight in arranging bouquets of all sizes and shapes, many of them inspired by the art on our walls.

A particularly charming hobby of hers consisted in reproducing the floral arrangements in some of our paintings to the very last detail. A vase in the background of an Ingres, Fragonard's gardens and all his nosegays and corsages, van Thielen's vivid garlands and bouquets, Boucher's cascading blossoms . . . All these Mildred quite literally brought to life. Her passion was such that I even purchased some paintings by de Heem, Ruysch, van Aelst and other Dutch artists who specialized in flowers just to indulge Mildred's enchanting pastime.

More home scenes. Her little touches. Anecdotes.

Because of her waning strength she found herself confined to either her rooms or a comfortable chair in the central gallery, where she enjoyed spending most afternoons and evenings. There she would sit with a book and a cup of hot cocoa, surrounded by music, art and flowers. She was an avid reader, attracted to every genre, from Italian poetry to the great French classics, both of which she read in the original. But as her health deteriorated, she developed a taste for mystery novels. Even though Mildred always showed an utter disregard for the established prestige of a work, at first, like a sweetly mischievous child, she kept her newfound passion a secret from me. Then she dismissed it as a mere distraction or as a bit of slightly embarrassing entertainment. Those books were not real literature, she said. Perhaps she was right. But truth be told, as she got frailer we both found something to enjoy in them.

Among my fondest memories of those years are our suppers together where she would tell me about the books she had read. I cannot quite remember how it first happened, but gradually we fell into somewhat of a ritual. After finishing a novel she had liked she would retell it to me over dinner. Her memory was prodigious, and she had the sagacity of Miss Marple. No detail was small enough to escape her attention. The way she parsed every scrap of information would have put the most meticulous detective imaginable to shame. From the first course to the dessert she would narrate a whole book back to me, footnoted with conjectures and predictions. I must say I learned to enjoy those little mysteries. But only in her passionate rendition. It was so lovely to look at her, lit up, lost in her storytelling. She was so captivated by the plot and I was so captivated by her that the food on our plates would grow cold. How we would laugh when we noticed! She always asked me to guess who the killer was, but I had been too distracted looking at her, and it was never the butler or the secretary I offered up as prime suspects. This made us laugh even harder, while I pretended to reprimand her for having made our food cold.

She remained uncomplaining and gay even through her hardest times. And she never stopped taking care of all sorts of invisible yet wonderful details around me. All these little niceties made my life better, without my fully realizing it. Although I loved and appreciated her from the moment we met, only once she had left it did I notice how far-reaching and pervasive her influence was in my everyday world . . .

BENEFACTRESS

It is no accident that the beginning of Mildred's philanthropic work should coincide with the decline of her health. In her intuitive wisdom she understood that every moment mattered. If she was unable to get better, she would make the world better.

Mildred's active support of the arts in general and music in particular began at the moment when she found herself unable to attend concerts anymore. I have always found this extremely touching. And it is an incontestable proof of Mildred's self-abnegation that she should become such a tireless benefactress exactly at the time when she found herself unable to enjoy the fruits of her generosity.

More on Mildred's spirit.

In 1921 she became a patron of the Metropolitan Opera with a sizable gift. As an expression of gratitude, Mr. Gatti-Casazza, the general manager, sent the choir to sing Christmas carols under our window. I shall never forget Mildred's tears, a mixture of thankfulness and utter disbelief, as she looked down at the singers in full costume for the exquisite Nativity pageant they had set up just for her. This was only the first of such gestures from a variety of artistic institutions and individuals. Knowing that Mildred was too weak to attend public performances, some of the musicians came to pay their respects in person. These calls usually took place at teatime, when I was away at work. This was most likely for the best, as my absence helped Mildred overcome her shyness and cultivate the artistic friendships that would become so important in her life.

During those years she also became a continuing supporter of both the Symphony Orchestra and the Philharmonic Society of New York, endowing each of their concertmaster's chairs. She also did much for the Philharmonic's Young People's Concerts, a series of matinées for the whole family she helped establish in 1924. It was of paramount importance for Mildred to make sure young people got the musical education she never received. This is why I stepped in when she decided to help the Institute of Musical Art acquire the Vanderbilt family guesthouse on East 52nd Street to create the Juilliard Graduate School that same year. More details on transaction and personal meaning of taking over Vanderbilt house.

Mildred's love of music did not mean she neglected her passion for books. She became an ardent champion of public libraries. Not just in city. Also in manufacturing towns around native Albany, where culture had not followed industry. And all over country. Ritual of asking a child to cut ribbon in her stead. Refused to use family name for buildings or display her generosity publicly.

It is hard work to give money away. It requires a great deal of planning and strategizing. If not managed properly, philanthropy can both harm the giver and spoil the receiver. Expand. Generosity is the mother of ingratitude.

As Mildred's charitable endeavors grew I saw the need to organize them after a rational fashion. This is why in 1926 I created the Mildred Bevel Charitable Fund. Not only did I endow it amply, but I also managed the funds so that the giving followed a systematic approach and did not deplete the capital. General financial architecture of MBCF. Why it was so innovative. Milestones.

At regular morning meetings in the greenhouse, before I left for work, Mildred and I discussed how to allocate the funds. Oh, her excitement! The thrill so many women seek in extravagant shopping sprees she found, redoubled, in giving. She picked causes and chose institutions with irrepressible enthusiasm, but she also heeded my calls to reason and followed my guidance whenever her choices were financially unsound. My methodical approach reined in her understandable passion. I ensured her noble efforts had the widest reach and greatest impact possible. List some beneficiaries and causes.

Proof of the Mildred Bevel Charitable Fund's success is that it thrives to this day, improving lives of both budding and established artists all over the country. And I

FAREWELL

Managing Mildred's illness was perhaps the greatest challenge of my life. As her condition declined I brought in the foremost physicians in the country. I conferred with them in private after each new examination, only to have the findings of the previous one confirmed. Unanimously, the doctors said they were surprised at how relatively strong she seemed, considering the advanced state of her malignancy. We all attributed this to her positive spirit and optimistic outlook on life.

This is why I kept the prognosis away from her for as long as I could, while always displaying a cheerful attitude and making sure all the little rituals and pleasures that made up her life remained intact. I simply feared she would not have the strength to bear the truth. The hard facts would destroy the joyful disposition that had sustained her so far. It pains me to say I was not mistaken. When I finally told her what the diagnosis was, the very word filled her with dread, which in turn accelerated her decline.

Short, dignified account of Mildred's rapid deterioration.

After extensive consultations with doctors, both in New York and in Europe, I found a sanatorium in Switzerland where some patients with supposedly incurable diseases had made near-miraculous recoveries. The place, a secluded resort somewhere between Zurich and St. Moritz, piqued my interest. But just as I was loath to share unnecessary bad news with Mildred, I was also disinclined to give her false hope. Nothing more harmful to the sick than disappointments.

Soon trip would become too much for Mildred.

Her apprehensions. Race against time.

Settling Mildred's affairs in New York. Making sure New York office kept running while away.

Well wishes from friends. Taking ship. Quick account of trip.

The health resort was in a well-sheltered situation, finely set in richly wooded environs. In a valley halfway up the slope of a mountain, it commanded charming views of the pastures below. Strong and bracing air acted as a tonic, and from the very first I could see its invigorating effect on Mildred. Her face recovered its color, her step regained its spring.

European countryside reminded Mildred of her girlhood. Something brief about her time in Europe with her parents.

She settled in at once. Doctors and nurses alike were smitten with her, etc.

Tests. Daily routine. Taking the waters. Diet, exercise, modest walks, etc. Pain.

Not too long after our arrival, once the doctors had conducted all their tests, the director of the establishment asked to see me. There was no need for him to speak. I know all too well what a man with bad news looks like. After the usual delays and grave preambles he did me the courtesy of being blunt. A cure was beyond the reach of science. I wish I could say I was shocked. The director assured me, however, that I had made the right decision in putting Mildred under his care. The sanatorium and its setting would provide the best possible conditions during this difficult period. This turned out to be true.

Mildred must have sensed or guessed her condition was incurable. She was as sweet as ever, but her joviality and gaiety had given way to a newfound serenity and aplomb. Part of her had already ascended to a higher realm.

Examples of Mildred's innocent wisdom during this period. Her thoughts on nature and God. Our last walk in the woods. Sweet incident with an animal.

Only once dared I interrupt her quiet routine, when I managed to bring the string quartet from the Grand Hotel St. Moritz to the health resort for a private concert. The director and some of the doctors joined us for this unforgettable evening. I had asked the quartet to play some of Mildred's favorite pieces. Name a few. It would not be excessive to say she was transported. At the end of the recital she looked so full of life and vigor, almost as if she had been magically cured. Such was the power music had over her.

This slight improvement encouraged me to leave, reluctantly, on a daytrip to take care of a critical situation that had just presented itself. Zurich, a mere sixty miles away from the resort, is the seat of the Swiss stock exchange and, needless to say, one of the banking capitals of the world. Pressing business demanded my presence there. It was the only time I left her side, and I wish I had never heeded this summons.

I shall always remember how she rested the back of her hand on my forehead before I left. And I shall never forgive myself for not realizing that this unusual gesture was her farewell. When I returned from the city she was no longer with us.

V

Prosperity and Its Enemies

Every life is organized around a small number of events that either propel us or bring us to a grinding halt. We spend the years between these episodes benefiting or suffering from their consequences until the arrival of the next forceful moment. A man's worth is established by the number of these defining circumstances he is able to create for himself. He need not always be successful, for there can be great honor in defeat. But he ought to be the main actor in the decisive scenes in his existence, whether they be epic or tragic.

Whatever the past may have handed on to us, it is up to each one of us to chisel our present out of the shapeless block of the future. My ancestors offer abundant proof of this. We Bevels have lived through numerous crises, panics and recessions: 1807, 1837, 1873, 1884, 1893, 1907, 1920, 1929. Not only have we survived them, but we have emerged stronger, always keeping our nation's best interest at heart. If neither my ancestors nor I had understood that a healthy economy, prosperous for all, had to be safeguarded, our careers would have been very brief indeed. A selfish hand has a short reach.

This is why I find the baseless, libelous accusations directed at my business practice incensing. Should not our very success be convincing enough evidence of everything we have done for this country? Our prosperity is proof of our good deeds.

As I shall lay out here in irrefutable detail, my actions during the 1920s contributed not only to create but also to prolong the growth we experienced throughout that decade. And they helped to safeguard the health of our nation's economy. Newspapermen and overeager historians refer to those years as a "bubble." By using this word they are implying that this period of abundance was a precarious fantasy doomed to burst. The fact, however, is that the time of prosperity we enjoyed before 1929 was the result of carefully designed economic policies, with which a succession of felicitous administrations had the good sense of not interfering. This was no passing "boom" predestined to "crash." This was America's destiny fulfilled.

A DESTINY REALIZED

After the Old World had driven itself to the brink of destruction it became clear that the future belonged to America. While Europe was debt-ridden and torn by nationalistic animosities that the Great War had only deepened, the United States entered a decade of great prosperity.

It was an age brimming with inventions, a new Renaissance. At the end of the war electricity powered only a quarter of American manufacturing. Ten years later steam engines had all but vanished, and our production was almost completely electric. Incandescent lights became ubiquitous. Washing machines, vacuum cleaners and other appliances came to the aid of three quarters of American housewives. Motion pictures and the wireless brought new enjoyment to millions during their hours of leisure.

The mass production of the automobile created a phenomenal circle of prosperity, in which consumption and employment fueled each other. A number of adjacent industries, from oil refineries to rubber factories, flourished around the motor car. Millions of miles of roads were paved. Fleets of trucks expedited commerce. At the beginning of the century there were some 8,000 cars registered in the United States. By 1929 that figure had risen to almost 30,000,000.

But the greatest American industry of that time was finance. After the deflation of 1920, explained in chapter III, a period of unprecedented economic growth began. With general inflation at zero, interest rates were kept down. Stock prices were low and the returns good. Never in our history had such a large portion of the national income been invested as in this period. Profits during the first half of the decade went up 75 per cent, and most of this surplus flowed into the stock market, enormously increasing the value of securities. To provide some perspective, in 1921, right after the recession, the Dow reached its lowest point of 67. In 1927 it broke 200 for the first time. This was the force powering America's manufacturing. This is what financed all those dizzying technological innovations and their consumption. President Coolidge could not have said it better: "The business of America is business."

How did this era of abundance begin? After the recession of 1921, as a way to support the prosperity plan, I felt the duty to do what I could to bolster the market and restore the confidence the recession had erased. In late March of 1922 I took on a string of motor, railroad, rubber and steel stocks. Over the course of the next few days I drove United Steel common up to a record of 97 5/8. Shares of the independent steel companies rose in sympathy, as did Baldwin Locomotive, International Nickel, Studebaker and others.

The breadth of the market on April 3, 1922, was "rivaled only once before in the history of the Exchange," as even *The New York Times* would concede the following day. Unwilling as always to give me any credit, the *Times* called the force rallying the market a "mystery movement."

I am citing these particular transactions from early 1922 only because they are a historical milestone. That day in April inaugurated a period that had nothing to do with a "bubble" but established the foundations for a future of great plenty. Over the following years I conducted many operations of this kind that allowed a multitude of American businesses, manufacturers and corporations to increase their stock issues and capitalize themselves. This is my record. And this is the background against which the reader needs to look at 1929.

Financial robustness: more hard facts and figures. Make accessible for average reader.

I have always shunned politics and declined all the positions offered to me. But I am proud to say that during this time I helped to steer the official monetary and trade policies in the right direction by providing informal advice whenever requested. This amicable relationship with the government started in 1922, when President Warren G. Harding summoned me and other businessmen to the White House to help him fulfill his campaign promise to bring prosperity to our people by putting "America First."

Thanks to the implementation of the tax cuts and protective tariffs for which we had advocated for so long, production was at an all-time high and employment rose steadily throughout the country. In 1921 the top marginal tax rate was 77 per cent. By 1929 we had managed to bring it down to 22 per cent. Rather than filling Washington's coffers this money went back to businesses, generating new jobs for hard-working Americans. I am glad to have been able to lend a hand in shaping these monetary and fiscal policies, and to have helped lead the market down the right path.

Fabulous success of 1926. Unparalleled triumphs. Historical.

During this time I saw not only the destiny of our great nation fulfilled but also my own. Mildred and I had moved into our new home on East 87th Street just a few years earlier. For a brief time, before she was stricken by the fatigue that would become the first symptom of her illness, life was

Brief paragraph Mildred, domestic delights. Home a solace during these happily frantic times.

METHOD

Much fiction has been written about my role in the market. And for too long the public has discussed my "prescience" regarding stock fluctuations, especially during my historical achievements of 1926 and the events that unfolded three years later. I may, then, be pardoned for briefly pausing here to state the facts.

They say the education of a child begins several generations before it is born. I believe this to be true, and my financial education started more than a century ago, with my great-grandfather William, from whom I inherited a sense of entrepreneurial audacity. This instruction continued with my grandfather, who bequeathed me a mathematical mind. It concluded with my father, who passed along part of his unerring intuition. Toward 1922 I organized this rich intellectual inheritance around a method of my own devising.

My real work starts after the closing bell, when I conduct my research and analysis. For years I have been keeping thorough records and charts on financial and industrial movements from all over the world. As I wrote in chapter II, a true businessman is also a polymath. But the breadth of my interests is such that I would never be able to manage the wealth of information collected. I therefore recruited statisticians and mathematicians to form a veritable brain pool. Under my direct supervision these researchers study stock records, evaluate industrial statements, predict future trends from past tendencies and detect patterns in mob psychology.

I then subject all these facts to a rigorous mathematical analysis and contrast them against statistical and probabilistic patterns I have developed over the years. My point of departure for this system was my early work under Professor Keene's tutelage at Yale, described in a previous chapter. Throughout the course of my career I expanded and adjusted those discoveries to the specific demands of finance. The result was a radically new web of calculations and algorithms, adaptable to a wide variety of business contingencies.

The reader will understand the need for discretion and forgive me for not going into further details regarding this particular point. Suffice it to say that the conclusions reached at the end of this process inform my trading, daily operations and long-term plans. The rest, what happens on the floor, is the mere execution of those decisions.

Quite a bit has been made of my ability to "fly blind" during the times when the tape was unable to keep up with the trading volume. Intuition has served me well throughout my career, and I owe a great part of my reputation to it. But to be consistently successful an investor must follow rules. Adding science and the objective interpretation of great volumes of data to my intuition is the source of my advantage. The result is what has so often been taken for "divination." It is this unique combination of instinct and method that has always allowed me to stay ahead of the ticker tape. Even in these calmer times, hampered by suffocating regulation, I am still able to prosper thanks to this formula of mine. But I shall talk about my current achievements in the final chapter of this book.

A DESTINY BETRAYED

The market is always right. Those who try to control it never are. Yet during the second half of the 1920s, at the height of America's hard-earned and legitimate success, two misguided forces burst onto the scene with the intention of doing just that. On the one hand, in-and-out speculators and buccaneers looking to make a quick dollar by recklessly inflating prices on borrowed money. On the other, the blundering machine of the Federal Reserve, inefficiently trying to curb those gamblers through artificial, ill-conceived and poorly timed actions that only managed to hurt legitimate investors. Together, these greedy amateurs and bungling bureaucrats eventually would manage to wreck the prosperity market.

The events that led to the 1929 debacle were nothing but the perversion of everything that was great about the preceding years. Flexible credit, high employment and an ample supply of novel goods were inextricably tied to one another. Encouraged by their steady paychecks and the abundance of the first half of the decade, people became unafraid of debt and started buying motor cars and appliances on installment. The resulting overexpansion of credit stopped no one.

Workers became consumers. And in short order consumers became "investors." Because debt no longer carried the stigma it used to, the masses did not hesitate to gamble with money that was not truly theirs. These new operators did not own the securities on which they were betting. The bulk of their trading was done on margin, through call loans. With rediscount rates low, unscrupulous lenders lured the general populace in with their cheap money. People who had never even seen a ticker before 1924 became financial experts overnight. It never seemed so easy to "get rich." No one was concerned that this reckless gambling undermined the foundations of our hard-earned prosperity.

Trading became America's favorite indoor sport. The debauchery of leveraged speculation attracted endless small fry with big dreams, always the most irresponsible actors in the market. Minor millionaires fooled themselves into believing they had "made it big" and could multiply their loot indefinitely. Gangs of undisciplined parvenus, speculative tourists and riffraff encouraged by unscrupulous croupiers rode on the coattails of the success of hardworking businessmen.

Everyone was playing finance with toy money. Even women got in on the market! The tabloids gave investing "hints" and "tips" mixed in with sewing patterns, recipes and gossip about Hollywood's latest heartthrobs. The *Ladies' Home Journal* ran editorials penned by financiers. Widows and scrubwomen, flappers and mothers alike "played the stocks." Although most reputable brokerage houses adhered to a strict policy banning lady customers, trading rooms for females sprang up all over New York, and in smaller towns housewives with a "hunch" neglected their domestic duties to follow the market at the local wire house and phone in their transactions at the end of the day. Women represented only 1.5 per cent of the dilettantish speculators at the beginning of the decade. At the end they neared 40 per cent. Could there have been a clearer indicator of the disaster to come? The descent from collective illusion to hysteria was only a matter of time. I knew it was my duty to do what I could to rectify this situation.

But as I have indicated above, there was a second force at play during these years: the Federal Reserve. I have made it abundantly clear in chapter III that I always opposed the creation of this regulatory body, but since we are burdened with it, one would have expected it to at least curb the orgy of speculation. Yet the Federal Reserve Board was too hesitant to pull the reins and then, in a desperate attempt at correcting its previous mistakes, pulled much too hard. Between January and July of 1928 the Board raised the rediscount rate from 3.5 per cent to 5 per cent. These actions were too weak to curtail the use of credit in securities distribution but too suffocating for the economic health of the country. It was a classic example of the state's attempting to correct artificially a situation the market would have rectified naturally, if only left to operate freely.

The signs of a slowdown and eventual collapse were there for everyone to see. For quite a while there had been evidence of business recession, such as heaviness in the motor industry and the overproduction of other durable goods. Whoever could afford an automobile, a refrigerator and a radio had already bought them. Commodity prices sliding. Furthermore, the high rates the Board had instituted by that time could only unsettle monetary conditions in Europe and hurt American trade. A correction of the value of securities was inevitable.

Yet in 1929 the speculative saturnalia reached unprecedented levels. That summer the Dow almost doubled, going from 200 to a record high of 381.17. This was not growth. It was insanity. On September 3, 1929, Wall Street recorded its peak of brokerage loans. Just around then, in a flailing attempt at exerting more pressure, the Board raised the interest rate by a whole additional point, all the way up to 6 per cent.

Also: Fed ordered banks to stop providing money for call loans, snuffing out demand for securities. Did Fed honestly believe the massive volume of newly issued stock would be bought in cash?

Understanding these conditions, on September 5 I started clearing my decks. The *Times* reported that "out of a clear sky, a storm of selling broke on Wall Street," resulting in "one of the most hectic hours in the history of the Exchange." In a bitter irony harking back to 1922, I began with Steel common, which dragged down General Motors and General Electric, and then Radio, Westinghouse and American Telephone. The sharp break soon went beyond the blue chips. The ticker kept going till five in the afternoon to catch up with the 2,500,000 shares liquidated that day.

I regret to say that my actions failed to sober up the market. More drastic measures were required. I have always been a guardian of public interest, even when it may seem that my actions go against the public interest. My record of long investments in enterprises that led to America's growth speaks for itself. In 1929, however, disgusted by the depraved greed disrupting the affairs of the Exchange on the one hand and disturbed by the unchecked interventionism of the Federal Reserve on the other, I felt obliged to take a short position. This was not only because it was the reasonable thing to do as a businessman. It was also my attempt, as a concerned citizen, at correcting and purging the market. And just like my forefathers I proved that profit, when responsibly made, is one with the common good.

As I had foreseen, the Federal Reserve's interventions finally managed to send banks and lenders into a panic. Brokerage loans were called in. Bulls became bears overnight. Soon the securities that served as collateral for the call loans would not be worth the paper they were printed on.

The bottom fell out on October 23. During the last two hours before the closing bell the Dow lost almost 7 per cent of its previous day's value. A staggering number of margin calls went out. The following morning *The New York Times* stated that the sudden wave of liquidation had been caused by "the necessity for the readjustment of price levels, the result of over-enthusiastic public buying." So far so good. But then the article slides into falsehoods and conspiracies. Not content with singling out the real cause of the debacle, it also has to add a touch of intrigue. In order to appease the "over-enthusiastic public" it has just denounced, the *Times* goes on to mention a supposed "pool manipulation" and cloak-and-dagger operations involving "strategic selling for the decline by many powerful bears, who picked vulnerable spots for heavy selling."

It does not take a Sherlock Holmes to deduce that these lines are directed at me. But as any true professional will confirm, it is impossible for one single person or group to control the market. The picture of a cigar-smoking cabal pulling the strings of Wall Street from a drawing room is ludicrous. On October 24, known as Black Thursday, an astounding 12,894,650 shares were sold off at the New York Stock Exchange. On Monday 28, prices kept plunging. The Dow experienced its most drastic fall in history, sinking 13 per cent or 38.33 points in one trading session. The following day, Black Tuesday, all records were shattered when 16,410,030 shares were dumped on the floor. The tape was delayed two and a half hours at the close. These vast numbers indeed confirm that the market was facing forces larger than one man, pool or consortium.

At the end of it all, the Dow had dropped 180 points, almost exactly what it had gained over the deranged summer months. Over half of the brokerage loans had been pulled. In this avalanche of liquidation there were no takers, regardless of price. By then I had closed all my positions, and it gives me a certain satisfaction to say that by covering my shorts I was able to step in and provide at least some relief to a multitude of sellers in dire need of a buyer.

My actions safeguarded American industry and business. I protected our economy from unethical operators and destroyers of confidence. I also shielded free enterprise from the dictatorial presence of the Federal Government. Did I turn a profit from these actions? No doubt. But so will, in the long run, our nation, freed from both market piracy and state intervention.

VI

Restoring Our Values

July 8, 1932, Dow hits low of 41.

Since the Panic of 1907, when even the most prominent of my colleagues supported the creation of the Federal Reserve, I have been against this institution. Where they saw a preemptive mechanism I saw the forge from which the shackles of regulation would come. Now, 30 years later, in this age of unlimited government intervention, history has proven me right.

A slew of poor decisions that blighted

Banking Acts of 1933–35. Disturbing factor antagonizing business community. Enemy of American idealism. Usurpation of power. Machiavellian deception of the public. Reckless assault on financial

"Federal Open Market Committee." Joke! We either have an "Open Market" or we have a "Federal Committee." But we cannot have the former fenced in by the latter!

Recent achievements, since Mildred's passing. Prospering despite grief and hostile political conditions. List.

VII

Legacy

Every single one of our acts is ruled by the laws of economy. When we first wake up in the morning we trade rest for profit. When we go to bed at night we give up potentially profitable hours to renew our strength. And throughout our day we engage in countless transactions. Each time we find a way to minimize our effort and increase our gain we are making a business deal, even if it is with ourselves. These negotiations are so ingrained in our routine that they are barely noticeable. But the truth is our existence revolves around profit.

All of us aspire to greater wealth. The reason for this is simple and can be found in science. Because nothing in nature is stable, one cannot merely keep what one has. Just like all other living creatures, we either thrive or fade. This is the fundamental law governing the entire realm of life. And it is out of an instinct of survival that all men desire

Smith, Spencer, etc.

Gospel of Wealth, American Individualism, The Way to Wealth, The Individual and His Will, etc.

Philosophical Testament.

Etc.

A Memoir,
Remembered

———◆———

by

IDA PARTENZA

I

The paneled doors, shut to most of the world for decades, are now open to the public Tuesday through Sunday from 10 a.m. to 6 p.m.

For years I avoided the main entrance to Bevel House on 87th Street between Madison and Fifth Avenue. Now and then, walking through the park, I would catch a glimpse of the building's top floor through the foliage. The limestone darkening with the seasons; the blinds closed regardless of them.

About six years ago, however, I found the shuttered windows open. A piece in the Times appeared a few weeks later, saying that after a protracted litigation over the estate, work would finally start to turn the house into the museum it had been intended to become following Andrew Bevel's death. Shortly after, the mansion was scaffolded and wrapped up in mesh. Renovations began. Some two years later, in the spring of 1981, every publication in New York featured articles on Bevel House, the city's latest "gem," a historical *"treasure," a cultural "jewel."* The New Yorker *asked me to write something on the reopening of the house, without knowing I was once connected to it. I declined.*

Four years went by. The flurry of attention around Bevel House died down, and the building became one more dutiful stop on Museum Mile. I, too, forgot about Bevel House. Living downtown, I found it easy enough to avoid the building and even exile its image from my mind. Sometimes a random chain of associations would take my thoughts back to the house and reawaken my curiosity. Whenever I was visiting a friend or running an errand on the Upper East Side and chance took me to that stretch of Fifth Avenue, I would pause by the elaborate fence that separates the set-back garden from the sidewalk and look up at the windows. Those preposterous new paisley drapes. Still, moved by a wordless superstition, I always kept away from the entrance on East 87th Street.

But then, a few months ago, around the time of my seventieth birthday, I happened to read in Smithsonian Magazine *that the Bevel Foundation had recently placed the personal papers of Andrew and Mildred Bevel at the collection. "The archives include correspondence, engagement calendars, scrapbooks, inventories, and notebooks, documenting the lives of Mr. and Mrs. Bevel," states the brief article. "These materials provide a unique insight into the history of a couple whose philanthropic legacy continues to shape America's public and cultural life to this day."*

Perhaps because I had just turned seventy, this news—learning those documents were available—had a profound effect on me. I have never cared much for anniversaries or decimal fetishes of any kind. Still, I could not stop thinking about the events that have shaped my writing life throughout almost five decades. And the Bevel papers are at the beginning of it all.

The same force that had kept me away from Bevel House for so long now pulled me toward it. In a reverse echo, questions that had faded out of my mind returned, obstinately, from out of the silence, growing louder with each

196

repetition. Events, scenes and people I had forgotten came back with a vivid-
ness that challenged the physical reality around me. And perhaps because they
came from so far back at such great speed, these questions and memories im-
pacted and sometimes even pierced through the very image of myself that had
solidified over the years.

In more than one way I owe the fact that I am a writer to the Bevels, even
if Mildred had been dead for several years when I first met Andrew. But I
have never allowed myself to tell the story that links me to them. Possibly
because I was still afraid of Andrew's retaliation, even beyond the grave.
But more likely because I have always felt, in an inarticulate way, that my
relationship with Mr. and Mrs. Bevel is one of the two or three sources from
which all my writing springs—another of those sources is, more predictably,
my father. So much of what I have written over the past decades is a ci-
phered version of the story of that relationship. Sometimes, in the middle of
a project—a novel about a street photographer, an article on astronomical
observatories, an essay on Marguerite Duras—I realize it is about the Bevels
again. No one besides me would ever notice this connection, of course. Still,
these encrypted and often involuntary allusions have fueled my work from the
very start. So again, in an imprecise way, I believed for all these years that if
I tapped into that spring directly it would be contaminated or even dry out.
But now, at seventy, it is different. Now I feel strong enough.

And this is why I find myself facing these implausibly open doors on this
fall morning. To revisit the place where I became a writer. To look for the
answers to the enigmas I thought had to be left unresolved so they could feed
my work. And to finally meet, even if it is only through her papers, Mildred
Bevel.

It is dusky inside. Two women hesitate on the edge of darkness, pore over
a map and finally vanish.

After staring at the façade for a while, I realize it is not the building I am
looking at but my memories that, like tracing paper, cover it.

I once worked in this house. But I never used the main door. I was always admitted through the service entrance.

That was almost half a century ago.

All I see beyond the paneled doors is shadows.

I walk in.

2

There was no need to confirm the exact address on the newspaper ad. Although I was almost an hour early, when I reached Exchange Place the line of young women outside the building had already bent around the corner of Broad and almost reached Wall Street. Several men walking by slowed down to inspect the girls and, without ever coming to a full stop, make a joke or a comment. Almost all of them adjusted their ties or straightened their jackets, ensuring they looked neat and proper before making their lewd remarks.

The ashen skyscraper took up most of the block. Because I had only seen its pyramidal crown from the Brooklyn waterfront, I could not help but pause and look up. Stern, clean lines coursed up the limestone panels only to be interrupted by copper cornices with overly ornate tracery, gothic arches and busts of futuristic-looking gladiators.

Greedily, comically, the building claimed all of history for itself—not just the past but also the world to come.

Around the corner, a new high-rise was being erected. The angular skeleton seemed ready to pounce on all neighboring buildings. Somehow, the hollowness of the structure made it grander. Like impossible canoes, steel beams hanging from unseen wires cruised through the sky. Below, their magnified shadows drifted down the streets, making a few confused passersby look up at the brief eclipse. I had a sudden dizzy spell when I noticed that one of the beams floating up above was dotted with men.

I felt something in my neck and turned around to realize the women waiting along the wall were looking at me, probably thinking I was an awestruck out-of-towner.

I took my place at the end of the line, recognizing a few faces from other similar lines. And just as on those other occasions, we were all wearing our best clothes. For some this meant a herringbone tweed suit, for others an evening dress, even if it was a summer morning. My skirt was a bit too tight. It didn't show, but it was uncomfortable. My jacket had to remain unbuttoned. Both these pieces, so plain they were impervious to changing trends, had belonged to my mother.

Except for small clusters of friends chatting animatedly, most of us kept to ourselves. I took out my pocket mirror and fixed my lipstick. In the glass I saw the woman behind me do the same. By the time I had put my things back in my purse, at least five more women had joined the line. I went through the newspaper with the ad. There was a review of Graham Greene's *Brighton Rock*, a book I had never heard of—and still have not read. I remember this only because, according to the review, the hero's name was Ida. I thought this was a good omen.

This detail made it easier, decades later, when I was browsing through reels of microfilms of *The New York Times*, to establish that morning's date. June 26, 1938.

I was twenty-three and living with my father in a railroad apartment in Carroll Gardens. We were dangerously behind with rent and in debt with everyone we knew. Although there was a strong sense of solidarity among the neighbors of the small Italian enclave by the river between Congress and Carroll Street (a mere eight blocks by three), many of our friends and acquaintances were as hard-pressed as we were, and our credit around the neighborhood was almost exhausted. Realizing at an early age that what my father made as a printer would never be enough to cover our basic expenses, I found employment at nearby stores—cleaning, organizing the stock, running errands and, when I was older, working behind the counter. But these were all temporary jobs, and my pay seldom made up for my father's meager income as a typesetter.

Like many young women back then, I thought becoming a secretary would allow me to "tap . . . tap . . . my way into economic independence," as a popular advertisement for Remington from that time put it. With the help of some library books and a borrowed typewriter I learned the basics of bookkeeping, stenography and typing while applying for positions all over town. In the beginning I never made it past the first round of tests. But each one of those failed interviews was a priceless lesson, and as time went by, I got closer and closer to being hired. For about a year I worked for a temp agency, and it was at the end of this period that I found myself waiting in the unmoving line that led to the skyscraper on Exchange Place.

3

My first book, a collection of short stories, was published when I was nine years old. One of the stories was about a conspiracy of fish and their failed plans to depose humanity and take over dry land. The unhappy hero of another tale was a girl who died in parts, limb by limb, until she was reduced to an eye. There was also a story of a nine-year-old who lived at the top of a mountain alone with her father, a jewel thief whom the girl broke out of jail again and again.

I have the only existing copy of this book here, before me. It is a tight little volume in octavo. More of a chapbook, really. The blue of the cover has paled over the years, making the words in black stand out more than the original design had intended. I think the font may be some variation of Bodoni. The words are placed far away from one another on that small, faded skyscape:

Seven Stories

IDA PARTENZA

My father printed and bound it. A run of one.

He would also letterpress congratulatory posters, often decorated with rudimentary woodcut illustrations, for my birthdays or at the end of the school year. Sometimes, for no reason, he made me business cards with outlandish titles: "Ida Partenza, Mezzosoprano"; "Ida Partenza, Meteorologist"; "Ida Partenza, Postmaster General." Around that time some of the reports I wrote for school were surreptitiously collected and put together in a volume titled *Essays*.

For a while, during this same period, my father and I edited and printed a newspaper together, *The Carroll Gardens Weekly*, a folded sheet that was far from weekly. I interviewed shopkeepers, policemen and neighbors in search of stories—usually involving births, lost pets, people moving into or out of the surrounding buildings and so on. The paper also included highlights from the news (between issues I collected clippings in a scrapbook), a serialized novel (which I wrote under the pen name of Caroline Kincaid), a horoscope (entirely made up) and other miscellaneous, inconsistent sections. No copies of this short-lived paper have survived.

Flipping through the pages of *Seven Stories*, the same question always comes up. Did my father preserve my numerous spelling errors out of respect for my writing or because they were invisible to him? Suspecting the latter, I never dared to ask him. Ever since his death I have inexplicably felt that those misspellings bring us closer to each other. That we meet in them.

Around 1966, several years after my father's death, I wrote an essay about him that was collected in my fourth book, *Arrow in the Gale*, a title I borrowed (and slightly adapted) from a collection of poems by Arturo Giovannitti. As I recount in that piece, this poet helped my father and me bond. When I was ten or twelve years old, we went through a phase during which we used to read his work, usually after dinner, and laugh together until we wept. He intensely disliked Giovannitti, despite the poet's good heart and even better intentions. Because the worst literature, my father would say, is always written with the best intentions. And so I was taught to dislike those poems, too.

The last stanza of "Utopia," addressed to a "Master," will give a good idea of Giovannitti's style:

> A day shall come when gold shall not enthrall thee,
>> When theft and murder cease to be thy rule;
> So I, who call thee now a friend, shall call thee,
>> Forsooth, a true and upright man, "Thou fool!"

At my father's request I would recite verses like these in an inflamed declamatory style, with histrionic emphasis, making sure to highlight all the archaic words and dubious rhymes with a buffoonish Italian accent and vivid gestures. And we would choke with laughter.

Now, years after the publication of that essay about my father, I find myself reviewing my life with him once again. And once more, our readings of Giovannitti's poems come to mind. Something has changed, though. Our kitchen table parodies appear in another light. There is a different resonance to my frenzied and almost violent laughter. I realize now it was not the poet whom I was laughing at.

Giovannitti was born in the region of Molise (right next to my father's Campania) in 1884 (just five years before my father) and left

Italy in 1900 (not too long before my father), first for Canada, where he worked, briefly, in a coal mine (my father had a stint at a marble quarry in northern Italy), and then for the United States, where he immediately started collaborating with a political newspaper for immigrants, which, in short time, he went on to edit (my father set type for one such paper). He became an activist who quickly rose to national prominence after being unjustly incarcerated in Massachusetts for helping organize the 1912 Lawrence textile strike in response to the brutal conditions to which the mill workers, most of them Italians, were subjected by the American Woolen Company—at the Lawrence mills thirteen-hour-long shifts often led to severed fingers and limbs; child labor was a common practice; women were consistently abused by their managers and, when pregnant, sometimes worked right up to the moment they gave birth, in some cases between the looms; life expectancy was twenty-five years. During this prolonged strike Giovannitti gave passionate speeches and recited his poetry to the workers. Some of these poems took the form of religious addresses—the best known of which, "The Sermon on the Common," was later included in the book my father and I used to mock.

Almost a month into the strike Anna LoPizzo, a mill worker, was slain by a police officer. Giovannitti was charged for having incited a strike that had led to bloodshed, even though he was miles away from the scene where LoPizzo was shot. A two-month trial ensued, during which he was displayed, with two of his comrades, in a cage. He wrote a lengthy prose poem, "The Cage," about this experience. "Like crippled eagles fallen were the three men in the cage. . . . No more would they rise to their lofty eyries. . . . Strange it seemed to them that they should be there because of what dead men had written in old books." After workers around America created a fund for his legal defense and picked up his cause as a banner for labor rights and freedom of speech, he was acquitted. A year or so later he published *Arrows in the Gale*, with a stirring introduction by Helen Keller.

I admitted in my book that, as an adult, I found my father to be right: the poems are, for the most part, as horrible as they are well intentioned. And I still stand by that judgment. But now, several years later, I have made a discovery. Looking back, I cringe at the recollection of my childhood performances in the family kitchen. Because I can see now that the truth is my father was jealous. He never cared for poetry and had no standards or frame of reference to judge lyrical works of any kind. Why fixate on this one book with such zeal? It was not for literary reasons or even because Giovannitti was "a mere socialist." He simply could not stand that Giovannitti, who was almost his same age and had led a life so similar to his, had achieved such prominence.

They were almost doppelgängers, but where one thrived and shone, the other labored in obscurity. Giovannitti was a public figure, an effective fighter who organized strikes, spoke eloquently from jail, gave public addresses and wrote books. He had a voice. And this is what my father wanted me to mock. He was the director of this vaudeville act, and I the performer—a living caricature of Giovannitti, represented as a grotesquely pretentious Italian who overcompensated for his foreignness and heavy accent by flaunting archaic, pompous English words. The voice we created for the poet came with flamboyant hand gestures and all sorts of mannerisms, and it was so cartoonish it made Chico Marx's persona or Paul Muni's rendition of Tony Camonte in *Scarface* seem like nuanced portrayals of Italian Americans. But I have come to see that, through this caricature, my father—with his unattainable ambitions, lofty proclamations and indelible accent—was asking me to mock *him*. It was himself he was laughing at. And now, so long after his death, this makes him dear to me in ways he would have found detestable.

Nothing in my father invited pity. Even his face was hard in a way that, as a child, I thought of as Roman in the imperial sense: his nose a bony triangle, his lips a hard line, his brow often knotted with determination. There was something soldierly about his lean body.

If he never admitted to any weakness, how could he solicit compassion? Even his failures were evidence of his heroic spirit. They proved that the world had wronged him—and his mere presence was a testimony to his resilience. This is why his rigid and often misinformed opinions became irrefutable dogmas, especially when reason and common sense, in unison, contested them.

As I have written in *Arrow in the Gale*, my father's account of the years leading up to his trip to America is inconsistent at best. The more or less undisputed facts are few. He was born in the small town of Oliveto Citra, in Campania, not too far away from Santa Maria Capua Vetere, the birthplace of Errico Malatesta, one of the founding fathers of anarchism. Had it not been for a young priest who took him under his wing, he would probably have been illiterate like his parents and most of his friends (until his final days he hid his hesitant spelling and unsure hand behind a theatrically brisk penmanship). He turned away from the church and to politics in his early adolescence, when he and his father went to work for a season at a marble quarry in Carrara. It was an entirely different young man who returned down south—estranged from his father, his faith and his country. He had a newly acquired, deep-seated hatred for the Italian state brought about by the Risorgimento. The word itself, "Italy," he would often say with disdain, referred only to a centralized bourgeois power. After visiting neighboring towns and villages, he became acquainted with several anarchist groups around Oliveto Citra. Politics took up his life. He claimed to have spent entire nights immersed in books and whole days walking the fields, talking to peasants and laborers about land and freedom. During the production of propaganda materials it became clear that he was a natural typesetter.

It did not take long before the pressure around his group started tightening. Several of his comrades were imprisoned, and it seemed that with each raid the authorities were getting closer to my father. He had also been blacklisted and found it impossible to get work. This is why, in the end, he decided to leave for America together with one of his closest friends from the anarchist circle.

To this day the extent and depth of my father's political involvement remain a mystery to me. Because his comrades are dead and the documentation is scant, his narratives are often my only source, but he was a spirited storyteller who seldom hesitated to sacrifice truth for effect. There could even be several versions of each of his stories, which he tailored to his audience. In some of his accounts his participation was limited to his work with the press and to help distribute the clandestine papers and pamphlets he printed. In other versions he claimed to have been involved, always in unclear ways, in "actions" against "bourgeois institutions." Sometimes he was a nobody, a mere tool for the cause like his letterpress; other times he seemed to have been a rather prominent figure, both back in Italy and here, in New York, where he claimed to have been close to Carlo Tresca and to have given speeches to standing ovations at Circolo Volontà up on Troutman Street or at the famous picnics down in Ulmer Park. Some whispered accounts involved, vaguely, violence.

He never quite ventured beyond the shores of the insular life he built for himself in Brooklyn. Racism and discrimination against Italians, who were so often perceived as dark outlaws, were very real and went beyond stereotyping and mockery. The flow of immigrants from Italy to the United States at the turn of the century constituted, at the time, the greatest exodus on the planet. And the reactions against it could be equally outsized. The lynching of eleven Italian Americans in New Orleans in 1891; the Palmer Raids of 1919 targeting left-wing activists, with a special zeal for Italians; the Emergency Quota Act, signed into law by President Harding in 1921, effectively limiting the influx of Italian immigrants while still welcoming people from northern Europe, followed by the even more stringent Immigration Act of 1924, signed by Coolidge; the judicial murder of Nicola Sacco and Bartolomeo Vanzetti in 1927—these were some of the events that shaped, in part, the lives of Italian Americans at the time. He never confessed this to me, but I know the slurs he so often had to endure (sometimes in front of me) made him withdraw further into the little Italian section of Carroll Gardens and deeper into his anarchist group. Except for his customers, his exchanges with people outside his immediate community were limited. He was marooned on his dim, rancorous islet, caught between the country he had left and resented and the land that had taken him in without fully accepting him.

It is beyond doubt that this insular position was also the result of my father's stubbornness. He had created a marginal, displaced situation for himself in several orders of life. His work embodied this very clearly. My father took pride in his craft's obsolescence. He was a hand typesetter who found the new automated systems offensive. The human touch, he said, was lost. The linotype and all the other machines had cast the soul out of the page. Each line used to be *composed*, he always said, waving his hands like a conductor. They were *melodic* lines, he added without fail, in case the parallel with music had been lost on his listener. No talent was needed now, though. Just mindlessly punching letters and words into a keyboard. He was young enough when this new technology was introduced and could easily have mastered it. But he had refused. Man had become the machine's machine. He would fight back.

The little money he made came from printing elaborate invitations on heavy paper stock for weddings, christenings, graduations, memorials and other occasions. Yet he resented this kind of work. Frivolous bourgeois trash. And his dislike went beyond those who hired him. It extended to the institutions that were behind those ceremonies and celebrations. Church. Family. State.

Still, despite his rants, he always got lost in his work and was delighted when a card or an envelope he had printed looked particularly handsome. His uncompromising perfectionism earned him a solid reputation all over New York City and beyond. But business was slow. Few people had the means and the disposition to throw parties in the thirties.

Between jobs he printed flyers and leaflets for his anarchist group. Over time the pamphlets became far more frequent than his elegant invitations in *intaglio rilevato*. So, while working part-time at a bakery on Court Street doing some bookkeeping and at the register during the weekends, I learned stenography from a manual and taught myself how to type on a Smith Corona with a missing "M" that I borrowed from the bakery, hoping to find a better-paying position.

My father disapproved. Secretary was a demeaning occupation, he said. It promised independence but was another knot in the millenary subjection of women to the rule of men.

4

The line started moving. Because we were admitted in groups, rather than slowly shuffling forward, we took several steps every five or ten minutes. There was something exaggeratedly liberating in these short walks. As we reached the entrance, I saw applicants going into the building but never coming out of it. I assumed (and later confirmed) they were dismissed through a back door, probably to prevent us from learning anything from those who were done.

If we had, for the most part, remained quiet during our wait, the closer we got to the door, the more the silence tightened. We were on our own. And, although there was no sense of hostility in the air, against one another.

The doorman, wearing a brass emblem of Bevel Investments as if it were a medal, counted to twelve by pointing at our heads with his index finger as we were let into the reception. We were told to wait by a desk. The walls of green marble vanished toward a remote ceiling. What was not made of stone was made of bronze. Nothing shone but everything emitted a pale glow. Sounds had a tactile quality, and we all did our best not to litter the space with any audible objects of our own. A man appeared behind the desk and, like the doorman, pointed at us, one by one, with his pen. We understood he wanted our names. "Ida Prentice," I said, feeling the blood throbbing in my cheeks as it always did whenever I used this fake name.

The two eldest women in our group, together with a young thickset girl, were shown to a side door; the rest of us were led to an elevator.

We were let off on the fifteenth or seventeenth floor. Looking out at the gridded pattern of streets full of silent little cars, the river with its tugboats and, beyond it, the docks and Brooklyn's modest skyline, I realized I had never been so high up. The city seemed so tidy and hushed from above. Later I would learn the building was seventy-one stories tall.

A set of double doors at the end of the reception hall opened to reveal a large space saturated with the angry, precise clatter of hammers and the dark, oily smell of ink. All the employees were women. Although I had worked in some typing pools, none of them came close to this in size. It is hard to recall the exact figures, but there must have been at least six rows of about eight desks each. And at each desk, a girl roughly my age, her head slightly cocked to better see the page she was copying. In fact the whole trunk was shifted to the right, dissociated from the hands, which remained centered. The center was the typewriter.

I had never seen so many women working under one roof.

We were led down the aisle between two rows of desks and turned the corner to find, again, six rows of eight desks each. At each desk, again, a secretary absorbed in her work. However, they were not at typewriters but at counting machines. My heart sank. I had only seen these machines in books and magazine ads and had no idea how to operate one. The women here seemed slower than the typists. They punched in each number with great deliberation and then pulled the crank to add the figure to the running total. Because there were always several cranks being pulled, the effect was that of a constant mechanical roar. Once more we were led down one of the aisles. I was relieved when we got to the end without stopping.

We turned the corner to find, for the third time, the same rows of desks. Fortunately, this was another typing room, but it was empty. Each of us was assigned a typewriter. Next to it was a page facing down. We would be told when to turn the page and start typing.

The test began and ended in a minute. I knew it was one minute because I had tested myself over and over again until that segment of time had become internalized. I also knew I had typed around 120 words and made a few minor mistakes.

After this we were given pen and paper and asked to get ready for a dictation test. We were told this was one of the most important aspects of the position, and whoever would move forward to the next stage had to be an impeccable stenographer. A woman read a purposefully labyrinthine text, designed to trip us up. I forget what it said, but it was, in essence, gibberish like this: "The contractual obligations entered into by the contracting parties stipulate, within the limitations and stipulations stated in the aforementioned clause, that, according to the best of their knowledge, the abovementioned parties shall proceed according to their previously prescribed duties." It was read fast.

As soon as she started, the girl next to me made a mistake, ripped out her sheet and began afresh on a new one. She was asked to leave on the spot.

The test continued for a few more minutes. Once done, we handed over our pages and were escorted back to the reception hall and instructed to wait while our transcripts were being marked.

5

My father never called himself an immigrant. He was an *exile*. This was an all-important distinction for him. He had not chosen to leave; he had been chased out. He had not come to the United States to prosper; revolting against the very idea of prosperity had been what had pushed him to America in the first place. Visions of gold-paved streets never lit up his dreams, and he was deaf to the gospel of thrift and industry; he preached, rather, that all property is theft. There was nothing in common between him and his more mercantile-minded compatriots, and he made sure to stress this at all times.

As a self-described exile, his views on both his homeland and his adoptive country were often contradictory—an amalgamation of resentment and longing, of gratitude and antipathy. He claimed to detest the nation that had killed and persecuted his comrades and cast him out. Yet the United States could offer nothing that came even close to the songs, dishes and traditions from Campania—and they were all part of our daily life through his humming, his cooking and his stories. He declared his disdain for the imbecilic people who had surrendered to Mussolini and his black-shirted thugs. Yet he treated Americans with the paternalist condescension often dispensed to slow learners and obedient pets. He resented his parents for not sticking with the vernacular of his ancestors and having submitted, voluntarily, to the "Tuscan babble" that represented the oppression of the central state. Yet even if in protest against "Italian" he had, not without difficulty, embraced English, he still found it an expressively deficient language, limited in its vocabulary and rustic in its constructions, never conceiving that these shortcomings were, in fact, his own. Invariably these personal contradictions were resolved with sweeping universal statements: "I have no country. I don't want one. The root of all evil, the cause of every war—god and country."

While grateful for it, he was suspicious of the American notion of freedom, which he viewed as a strict synonym of conformism or, even worse, the mere possibility of choosing between different versions of the same product. Needless to say, he objected to consumerism and the alienation fueling it—in a perverse circle, workers kept dehumanizing jobs in order to both produce superfluous goods and purchase them. It was for this reason that he welcomed the Great Depression, believing that, thanks to it, the exploited masses would finally wake up to their true historical circumstances and material conditions, thus precipitating a revolution.

Above all, he detested finance capital, which he viewed as the source of every social injustice. Whenever we found ourselves walking along the waterfront, he would point at lower Manhattan, tracing the skyline with his finger while explaining that none of it really existed. "A mirage," he called it. Despite all those tall buildings—despite all that steel and concrete—Wall Street was, he said, a fiction. I heard this speech many times and knew all the main phrases, motifs, crescendos, cadenzas and the grand finale by heart.

"Money. What is money? Commodities in a purely fantastic form." A grave nod, a suddenly furrowed brow, a sigh. "I don't like Marxists, you know that. Their state and their dictatorship. The way they talk, with those bricks of meaning, reducing the world to one single explanation. Like religion. No, I don't like Marxists. But Marx . . ." Again he made that face, as if he were tortured by an excessively beautiful sight. "He was right about this. Money is a fantastic commodity. You can't eat or wear money, but it represents all the food and clothes in the world. This is why it's a fiction. And this is what turns it into the measure with which we value all other commodities. What does this mean? It means that money becomes the universal commodity. But remember: money is a fiction; commodities in a purely fantastic form, yes? And this is doubly true for finance capital. Stocks, shares, bonds. Do you think any of these things those bandits across the river buy and sell represent any real, concrete value? No. No, they don't. Stocks, shares and all that garbage are just claims to future value. So if money is fiction, finance capital is the fiction of a fiction. That's what all those criminals trade in: fictions."

In my teens a strange sort of impulse took hold of me and refused to ever really let go until well into my adult life—the compulsion of eliciting from my father the same reactions that had frightened me as a child. Once he went on one of his tirades, he could never be contradicted. He was untroubled by the possibility of error; he never considered different perspectives; he seldom thought there could be another side to any issue. The normal disagreements and differences that make up any lively exchange of ideas were, to him, personal affronts. His were not arguments up for debate; they were facts. Although he claimed to be an anarchist, he was an authoritarian in this regard: there was no room for dissent when it came to his beliefs, which were presented as mathematical laws. To question any of these principles resulted in disproportionate anger. Pushing back after that prompted a stubborn silence, his final and irrefutable argument. Partly because, over time, his reaction had gotten to be more exhausting than threatening, partly because it was an easy and entertaining form of rebellion, provoking him became my main sport for a while. It was not always intentional (I often found myself in the middle of a fight not knowing how it had started), and it could get nasty, but sometimes I just could not help it. I had to talk back, even at the cost of having to endure his cold hostility for days.

"But if they trade in fictions, how can they be criminals? Fictions are supposed to be harmless, aren't they?" This was the typical kind of objection I would present just to make him angry. I might have capped it with an additional condescending rhetorical question. "You see the contradiction, right?"

"Fiction harmless? Look at religion. Fiction harmless? Look at the oppressed masses content with their lot because they have embraced the lies imposed on them. History itself is just a fiction—a fiction with an army. And reality? Reality is a fiction with an unlimited budget. That's what it is. And how is reality funded? With yet another fiction: money. Money is at the core of it all. An illusion we've all agreed to support. Unanimously. We can differ on other matters, like creed or political affiliations, but we all agree on the fiction of money and that this abstraction represents concrete goods. *Any* goods. Look it up. It's all in Marx. Money, he says, is not one thing. It is, potentially, *all* things. And for this reason it is unrelated to all things."

"Wait. Which one is it? Is money all things or none? Because if . . ."

"This," he would half scream over me, "is why money doesn't say anything about the people who have it. Nothing. Money says nothing about its owner. As opposed to having, I don't know, talent, which defines a person. Money's relationship to the individual is completely accidental."

"What possession or what individual quality would *not* be accidental to you? Where would you (or Marx) draw the line? Let's say I have some particular talent. Let's say I'm a gifted violinist. You could say my musical talent defines me because I have it from birth. But isn't my birth the purely accidental effect of you and mom meeting? What's essential about that?"

Mentioning my mother (and the claim that their relationship, far from being a predestined event, had been a mere accident) was always a calculated attack, and my father's ensuing silence would prove it had been effective.

Silence.

More silence.

"Are you done?" he would ask after an uncomfortable while. "Can I finish now? Or do you want to add something? I can wait."

"Dad, this is not how conversations work. When people have a conversation . . ."

"Right. Just let me know when you're done. I'm listening. Go ahead."

"I'm done."

Nothing.

"Please go on, Dad."

"Because money is all things (or can be all things), something strange happens to the person who has it. As Marx says, it's like someone finding, by pure chance, the philosopher's stone. You know the philosopher's stone?"

"Yes, I know what the philosopher's stone is."

"The philosopher's stone gives you all the knowledge. All of it. All the knowledge of all the sciences. Imagine that someone just finds this stone. By luck. Suddenly he would have all this knowledge, regardless of his individuality. Even if he's a perfect idiot. All of it. All the knowledge."

"Yes, yes. I understand."

"Having money puts you in the same place regarding social wealth as the stone puts that man regarding knowledge. You know why?"

"Isn't this a bit of a stretch? I mean, if . . ."

"I'll tell you why. And I'm quoting Marx here. Because money represents the divine existence of commodities. Real, concrete commodities (these shoes, this loaf of bread) are simply the terrestrial manifestation of this divine idea (all possible shoes, the bread that hasn't even been baked yet). Money is, as Marx said, the god among commodities. And that," his upturned palm drew an arc encompassing downtown Manhattan, "is its holy city."

Having had this exchange with my father countless times, I decided to be blunt when I told him about the interview for the position at Bevel Investments. Yes, we were behind with rent and were in debt with most of the shops in the neighborhood, but I admit to deriving some satisfaction from the idea of working at a financial firm. I enjoyed the provocation. And because we needed the money, I thought my father would just have to swallow his principles.

I was wearing my mother's clothes the morning of my first interview. This always made us both feel visibly strange, so I was not surprised when his eyes turned back to his press as soon as he saw me walk in. I had saved my announcement for the last possible moment, right before I left the house. It was to be direct and concise.

"I'm applying for a job in Wall Street," I told him.

My intention had been to leave it at that. Let the force of this brief sentence stun him. Perhaps even wake him up to the fact that we desperately needed the money. But I was unable to follow my plan. He just kept loading his composing stick.

"The salary is really good, if I get it," I remember adding, immediately realizing that by justifying myself before he had even responded, I had lost.

He must have realized this, too, and that is probably why he never replied or looked up from his type case.

And he did not respond a few hours later, when I returned and told him that I had been the only one of my cohort of twelve who had made it to the following round, a personal interview.

I went to the kitchen and washed the dishes that had been sitting in the sink all morning.

6

Two days later I was back at Exchange Place. There was no line this time. I simply went through the door, walked up to the green marble desk, announced myself and was given a slip of paper, which I was then asked to hand to the elevator boy. He must have taken several applicants to that floor, because instead of unfolding the paper, he just looked at my clothes and punched a button.

I was let out on a low floor that looked like an archive or records office. The walls were lined with boxes and binders all the way up to the ceiling. There was a studious atmosphere. Eventually a woman looked up from her ledger and walked over to greet me while whispering an apology. As she approached, smiling, I realized she was the oldest woman I had seen in the building. She must have been in her mid-forties. After confirming I was there for the position, she took me to a desk in the back, asking little trivial questions to make me feel more at ease. The typewriter was ready with a sheet of cream-colored paper with Bevel Investments' letterhead in hunter green. It was obviously expensive stock, heavy, watermarked and with a beautiful grain. Next to me there was another applicant typing on the same kind of paper. The friendly woman explained that I was to write a brief autobiography. A self-portrait, she called it. Just a quick page. Half an hour. She wished me good luck and returned to her desk.

I had taken countless secretarial tests. All of them included transcribing or taking dictation. But not once had I been asked to write something original, much less about myself. My surprise, however, did not last long. Wonder quickly gave way to terror—an effervescent dryness that still fizzes over me in situations of danger. The self-taught daughter of an Italian anarchist would never stand a chance at Bevel Investments.

Almost without thinking, I started typing with unexplainable assurance. I lived in Turtle Bay, a neighborhood I had never been to, but whose name I had always liked—and it was not Brooklyn. My father, Mr. Prentice, was a sales clerk at a haberdashery. In a few melodramatic yet dignified strokes I narrated the death of my mother. I found solace in church work (I managed to mention I was of sturdy Episcopal stock) and literature. After these brief sentences, knowing all the other girls would write a linear account of their lives, I decided to take a bold approach. I said that since most of my life lay in the future, I felt compelled to write a prospective autobiography. The rest of the text was a combination of my sincere desires (traveling and writing) and what I thought was expected of a woman's ambitions (wife and mother). The style was florid enough to make it stand out while still showing restraint. I closed with a reflection on time and how it was up to each one of us to carve our present out of the shapeless block of the future—or something to that effect.

Once I was done, the room became quiet. None of the archivists used a typewriter. And the applicant next to me, I realized only then, had already left. The nice lady noticed the silence and came over to me. She held my shoulder and, again, asked me comforting questions as she led me back to the elevator. As we waited, she asked to see my text. I read along with her, hardly believing what I had written. Her nods while she went through it lifted my spirit. She handed me back the page with words of approval. The elevator came, and she told the operator to take me to a floor halfway up the building. Before the doors closed, she waved with her fingers crossed.

When the elevator doors reopened, it was to reveal a fictional living room, much more comfortable than any of the real ones I had ever visited. There were four or five other applicants with their cream-colored page, most of whom greeted me with a nod and a half smile (one of them was the girl who had been typing next to me). I can still recall what I felt as I sat down on the edge of the velvet chair, looking around at the sober décor, feeling the delicately chilled air on my calves and listening to the short-lived sounds in the room before they were sponged up by the thick carpet and the plush upholstery—I felt I did not know my city.

All of us, while we avoided looking at one another and corrected hopeless or invisible imperfections in our clothes, felt something similar, I think. All except for one. She was the only one wearing an appropriate outfit, not only seasonally adequate and color-coordinated but also impeccably tailored. Her face failed to be completely disdainful. After a while I realized it was because she barely had any eyebrows. She got up and moved around the room several times, seemingly for the sole purpose of proving that she could get up and move around the room—that she was not intimidated by it, that she belonged in it. One of these little parades led her to the secretary's desk. She whispered a few words to her, curving her lips up into something that was not a smile. They giggled under their breath.

Outside the window two swinging cranes seemed to be about to crash against each other—a trick of perspective. A jackhammer started up, and then another. Screeching circular saws. The rumble of bulldozed debris. All this noise reached the waiting room as little more than a hum—as if the construction site were a playground, and all the tools and trucks toys.

The door opened. An applicant in a brown suit was let out. Although she was empty-handed, her posture was that of someone clutching something very precious to her chest. She seemed pained. With downcast eyes she walked to the elevator; with downcast eyes she stood waiting for it. The secretary told the well-dressed woman she could step into the office. Rummaging through her purse, the woman pretended not to have heard her. The secretary said, again, she was expected inside. This time the woman gave the secretary an irritated look. She closed her purse and walked into the office. The elevator finally came, and the girl in the brown suit rushed in, pressing herself against a sidewall, where she became invisible.

Unlike the girl who had been interviewed before her, the well-dressed woman could be heard from where we were, even if discrete words were indiscernible. She talked fast and with animation, interrupting herself, now and again, with bursts of laughter. There were only a few brief pauses during which, presumably, the other person spoke. The secretary started folding papers and stuffing them into envelopes. The rest of us pretended not to notice anything, fully committed to our awkwardness.

All of a sudden the woman's gabble stopped. A pause. She spoke again but seemed to be interrupted. A pause. Now she spoke in a lower voice, in both volume and register. A final pause, and the door opened so abruptly that the air upset the pile of envelopes on the secretary's desk. The woman walked out.

"Well, I hope you find one of *these* more suitable," she said, pointing at us with a disdainful chin. "My uncle will just love to hear about this."

She called the elevator, and now it was her time to stand there, waiting, indignant and wounded. It arrived a good while after the next applicant had been called in.

About half an hour later my turn came.

I had only seen such grand and austere examples of art deco in films—the stereotypical offices of captains of industry, financiers and magnates of the press, all of whom were usually depicted as heartless despots. Parallel lines chased one another in angular trajectories from the chromed furniture down onto the patterned stone floor, up the wood-paneled walls, onto the window frames and out into the city, continuing on the façades of the surrounding buildings and beyond, following the streets crisscrossing all the way into the horizon.

A fastidious, bespectacled balding man who looked like a witch—thin-faced, yellow-eyed, a mole on his upcurved chin—pointed to a chair as he sat down on his side of the desk. Next to a massive brass lighter there was a sign with his name. Shakespear. "No final *e*," as I would later hear him repeat day after day. Only now did I notice the strong smell of cigarettes and mint in the refrigerated air.

"Please have a seat, miss . . ." He flipped through his papers, made a checkmark and wrote a few words. "Prentice. Your typing test was impressive."

"Thank you."

The jackhammers started again.

"And your steno . . . Yes, impressive."

"Thank you."

"May I?" He pointed to my typed "autobiography," which I handed over to him.

It took him an inordinately long time to read it. Once done, he filed it together with my other tests, jotted down some notes in a book open on his desk and looked at me.

"While we understand that these are pretty trying times and most of you girls are applying for pretty much every available job, we also want to make sure that we hire someone who doesn't just *need* this job but also *wants* it. Do you *want* it?"

"I do."

"Why?"

I never expected to answer the way I did. It was not part of a plan. It was nothing I had prepared. The words simply came out.

"Why work at a place that makes one thing when I could work at a company that makes all things? Because that's what money is: *all* things. Or at least it can become all things. It's the universal commodity by which we measure all other commodities. And if money is the god among commodities, this," with my upturned palm I drew an arc that encompassed the office and suggested the building beyond it, "is its high temple."

A long pause.

"I would like you to come back Monday afternoon for a final interview. Announce yourself downstairs at five o'clock sharp. They'll tell you where to go."

7

This is the only picture of my mother, taken before she got married. She must be around the same age I was during my interviews for Bevel Investments. A little younger, perhaps. She is wearing a high-collared dress with a row of small buttons down the middle, confident in its plainness, navy blue in my imagination. Her hair is gathered loosely at the top. A bold softness defines her face. This resolute kindness is also in her gray eyes. I have always been sorry that her face has not lived on in mine.

This single photo has colonized the few memories I have of her. Over time I realized that in almost all the scenes I was able to recall, she appeared in the same dress and with the same hair. It was impossible to stop this simplification of my mother's image, which now has become pretty much all I have. Strolling through Carroll Park, giving me a bath, walking down Sackett Street, putting me to bed, she is always in the hypothetically navy-blue button-up dress and with gathered hair. I find it devastatingly sad that a woman could disappear to this extent, leaving no trace other than a daughter who barely remembers her.

For years, between books, I worked on a novel about her. It remains both unfinished and the greatest mistake of my writing life. Because I labored unsuccessfully on that book for so long, my mother acquired, forever, the texture and weight of a half-formed character in my mind. I have even come to distrust my love for her.

The facts are few. She was born in a small village in Umbria and came to America with her older brother and her cousin. My father said she had a gift for languages and learned English quickly and spoke it with great elegance. She was a consummate seamstress and had many clients in the neighborhood, where she was universally liked.

She started seeing a young man, Mattia. Her brother and cousin disapproved—Mattia was an anarchist, and the last thing they needed in America was trouble. I am not sure how it happened (I learned about this almost by accident and pieced the story together over the years), but it did not take long for my mother to fall for Mattia's best friend, the comrade with whom he had sailed across the Atlantic and faced the first hardships in New York.

Soon she was pregnant with me and living with my father. Mattia somehow vanished; my uncle and his cousin left for some Midwestern town. It is unlikely that she or her relatives were pleased with my father's refusal to submit to the bourgeois institution of marriage. Still, I think my parents had a good life together. My father always claimed there was no happier couple. This may be true. Most of my memories, real or fictional, are of a cheery family. When I was alone with her, she would speak to me in Italian. I have forgotten most of the words and, with them, the sound of her voice.

She died like so many women throughout history have died—giving birth. The baby, a boy, was stillborn.

I was seven years old, disoriented in my sadness. For months on end I experienced, relentlessly, that crushing, desolate form of homesickness known only to children.

It would be hard for me to say what I did during that time. For a year I simply stopped going to school. I spent days loitering and walking around the neighborhood. Played checkers with my father. Helped him at the press. In time I discovered the Clinton Street branch of the Brooklyn Public Library. It is impossible to pinpoint the moment when I became a regular patron, but I must have been around nine or ten when I started spending my afternoons in the reading room and checking out books. Detective fiction became an obsession. First it was Conan Doyle, S. S. Van Dine and Agatha Christie. These books (and a friendly librarian) led to others. Dorothy Sayers, Carolyn Wells, Mary Rinehart, Margery Allingham. Well into my adolescence these were the women who took care of me in the absence of my mother.

I was comforted by the idea of order in their novels. It all started with crime and chaos. Even sense and meaning themselves were challenged—the characters, their actions and their motives seemed incomprehensible. But after a brief reign of lawlessness and confusion, order and harmony were always restored. Everything became clear, everything was explained and everything was well with the world. This gave me enormous peace. And, perhaps more importantly, these women showed me I did not have to conform to the stereotypical notions of the feminine world. Their stories were not just about romance and domestic bliss. There was violence in their books—a violence *they* controlled. These writers showed me, through their example, that I could write something dangerous. They showed me that there was no reward in being reliable or obedient: the reader's expectations and demands were there to be intentionally confounded and subverted. They were the writers who first made me want to become a writer.

In fact retelling these books was an essential part of my literary education. Over dinner I would narrate entire novels to my father, footnoted with conjectures and predictions. Spellbound, he followed every little detail of the plot, and I learned how to lead him down false trails and make him chase red herrings to heighten his surprise at the final revelation. He would be so captivated that he forgot to eat. "Look! My food! Cold again! All your fault," he often said at the end, mock-scolding me as we laughed.

Eventually, just like in the detective novels I read at the library, a new order of sorts arose from the devastation following my mother's death, one with its own logic and rituals. This new regime, for lack of a better word, was the result of need.

My father had never done any household chores, except for cooking his "special dishes," which created an extraordinary amount of work for everyone around him. His press was in the middle room of our railroad apartment, and soon the boundaries between his work and our family life, between bathroom and kitchen, between food and garbage, between clean and dirty, faded and disappeared. It fell on me to keep things going. Eight years old and fully in charge of the house. If I did not do the washing, there were no fresh linens; if I neglected to sweep, our footprints became visible in the dust; if I left the dishes in the sink, they remained in the sink; if I went without putting my father's tools and supplies away, gunky dots of contagious ink multiplied all over the walls, beds and clothes.

After my mother's death I found this new role, which I performed inexpertly and in an improvised fashion, natural. I had become the woman in the house. My father, the anarchist, found the fact that child labor was required to keep the gender status quo intact equally natural.

Aside from this photograph not much was left from my mother. I remember her few possessions in her drawer—a pewter hairbrush, a manicure kit, a few medals of saints hidden behind her underwear, a broken watch with a mother-of-pearl dial, the gold-plated ring with a watery-blue stone she never dared to wear (and I never take off) and some clothes. I have no doubt my father, who never lived with another woman after my mother, loved her very much. But it was not out of love or because of his inability to "let go" that he had left the things in her drawer untouched. It just never occurred to him to clean them out.

8

During my tests and interviews at Bevel Investments I first learned something I had the chance to corroborate many times throughout my life: the closer one is to a source of power, the quieter it gets. Authority and money surround themselves with silence, and one can measure the reach of someone's influence by the thickness of the hush enveloping them.

In the reception area on the top floor there were four secretaries, two of whom were uninterruptedly on the phone. People went in and out two side doors, occasionally stopping for brief, whispered conversations. Clerks picked up and delivered documents. Yet nothing above isolated murmurs could be heard. It was as if, together with the intimidating furniture, the carpets one avoided treading on and the oppressively ornate wood panels, the room had been provided with a soft pedal.

I was glad to see that the painfully shy girl in the brown suit from the last round of interviews had made it to this stage as well. We smiled at each other as I sat across from her and a young woman in a lavender dress, clearly also an applicant. My gaze wandered from one to the other. They looked remarkably alike. Identical straight black hair, same dark brown eyes, comparable height, similar build. Their faces were slight variations on the same idea of a face. My face. Because by looking at them, I realized that I, too, was a variation on that idea. The three of us were different embodiments of the same type.

The shy girl was told she was expected in the office. As she left, I caught the applicant in the lavender dress staring at me, and from her intense expression, fusing disbelief with outrage, and the vehemence with which she looked away after we paused on each other's eyes, I could tell that she also had noticed the disturbing likeness between us. But this uncomfortable moment was fleeting. Almost as soon as she had entered the room, the shy girl came out, once again with her downturned, mortified gaze. I was called in next.

At the other end of a colorless office that made me think of a swimming pool (and stepping into it felt like immersing myself into a different element), behind a desk, with the back of his swivel chair turned to me, sat a man looking out the window, while out there, looking back at him, was a welder sitting on a beam that seemed to be floating in the sky. A cold wave of vertigo washed over me, and I froze by the door. Each man appeared to be hypnotized by the other. But when the welder adjusted his cap and his coat, always staring at the man in the chair, I realized that, to him, the window was an impenetrable mirror.

The welder's audacity and his unknowing irreverence (oblivious of the abyss, he kept fixing his attire while staring, without realizing it, at the powerful man in the swivel chair) might have inspired me to proceed as I did. Whoever was sitting in that chair surely was tired of his subordinates' stuttering genuflections. I decided he would welcome a bold approach—someone taking the reins of the conversation.

"Soon you won't have much of a view," I said.

"I expect to be unable to see the river by the end of the month."

"And it looks as if that building will be taller than this."

"It will be," he said as he swiveled around to look at me.

There was no meaning in Andrew Bevel's face. Just like in the pictures I had seen so many times in the paper, it was a face that had given up on expression. Mimicking his impassiveness, I pretended to be unaffected by his presence.

"Sorry to hear that." I was surprised to discover that my voice did not tremble.

"Don't be. I own both of them and will be moving to the new one as soon as it's done. Please." He gestured to the chair across his desk.

It was a long walk.

"You're not Ida Prentice," he said as I sat down.

I felt myself blush and could see I would soon lose the ground gained with my initial show of confidence.

"Somehow I thought I wouldn't have gotten here as Ida Partenza."

"Somehow I think you're right. But I'm certainly glad you did get here."

"Thank you."

Up close I discovered that Bevel's face was almost two faces: the surprising boyishness of the upper half, with its very blue eyes and almost imperceptible freckles, was rebuked by his thin lips and exacting chin.

"Your father is a printer. You live with him roughly over there." He pointed across the river, in the general direction of Red Hook. "I'm so sorry about your mother. I, too, lost my parents, both of them, at an early age."

I hoped my face did not show that he had managed to intimidate me.

"The story you made up for yourself in your little essay was very convincing, though." He held up the cream-colored sheet that had been lying on his desk.

"It seems my life is almost as public as yours."

He laughed, motionlessly, through his nostrils.

"Oddly, you've managed to get straight to the point. This is, indeed, all about my public life. Having one is an unwelcome offshoot of my work. I've tried to nip it, stamp it out. It grows back. Always. With renewed strength. So I've decided to take control over it. If I'm to have a public life, I'd rather have my version of it out there."

The beam with the welder on it moved behind him. Noticing my eyes shift and focus beyond him, Bevel turned around.

"I was wondering why that was taking so long." He turned back to me. "Anyway. This is not about me, actually. It's about my wife."

"I am so sorry for your loss."

"Thank you. The fixation of the public on my life is one thing. But when this obsession touches and sullies my wife, that's a whole different business. She—her image, her memory—won't be desecrated." He pursed his lips as if to make sure his indignation remained sealed within him and then took a book out from a drawer and placed it on his desk. "Have you read this?"

He slid the book over the desk. I picked it up. The dust jacket was sage green and the font was black and gray—a palette reminiscent of a dollar bill. There were no illustrations or adornments of any kind. It simply read:

Bonds

A Novel

HAROLD VANNER

As I type these words, I am looking at that very book that Andrew Bevel gave me that day. The dust jacket is now brittle with age, its flaps holding on by a thread to the sun-bleached spine. But underneath these tatters the cover retains the colors that have faded from the jacket. Some of the bound sections are slightly separated from the rest, like little booklets. I find this fragility becomes the book.

"No," I answered, leafing through the pages.

"Well, you are one of the lucky few, then. It came out about a year ago. This scribbler, Mr. Harold Vanner, had almost been forgotten. Not that I would know. But they tell me he had a bad run. After a few moderately successful novels about ten years ago he fell into disfavor. His books didn't sell. Drink. Dipsomania, it seems. The regular squalid story. And then, shortly after my wife's death, he started writing this thing. He met her, Mildred, a few times. Socially. Superficially. Like so many other people. I think he may even have met me on one of those occasions."

He turned around to take a quick look at the beam's progress. It was out of sight, but uncannily, given the height, voices could be heard out the window.

"At all events, he wrote the book. It came out to favorable reviews. Everyone I know seems to have read it; everyone is still talking about it. I'm not a critic. I'm not interested in literature. I haven't even read the reviews. But I can tell you why this book is a sensation: because it's patently about my wife and me. And because it makes us look bad."

He looked at me, perhaps expecting a reaction. I thought my silence would be better than any questions or remarks.

"Friends and acquaintances tell me how sorry they are about the book. Do you understand how irritating that is? Because through their show of sympathy they're letting me know they've read this garbage.

Everyone seems to have read this garbage. And everyone can tell it's about us. You'll see for yourself. It couldn't be anyone else. Maybe because there are a few vaguely correct details in there, people think this is a creditable source. There even are reporters following leads and clues in the book, trying to corroborate certain scenes and passages. Can you believe it? The imaginary events in that piece of fiction now have a stronger presence in the real world than the actual facts of my life."

Something like anger started to gather behind his face. He took a deep breath.

"Let me be plain. This is nothing but libelous trash. Opportunistic defamation. My business practices are grossly misrepresented. I come off as a gambler. As a con man. And he claims that I'm done. That I'm old and my time is over. That I've lost my touch and am in frank decline. Look out the window. Does that new building speak of defeat?" He made a somber pause. "Anyway, this is all irrelevant. I'm used to being smeared. But Mildred . . . What this scoundrel has done to Mildred . . . The gentlest of women portrayed as a raving . . ." He shook his head. "I won't allow for this opprobrious fabrication to become the story of my life, for this vile fantasy to soil the memory of my wife."

I put the book back on the desk, not wanting to be associated with it by proximity.

"My attorneys are already taking care of Mr. Vanner. But I fear the time has come for me to speak up. Rumors of all sorts have surrounded me all my life. I've grown accustomed to them and take care never to deny gossip and tales. Denial is always a form of confirmation. I'm loath to make public statements of any kind, but this fiction demands to be countered with facts. And facts I shall provide. I would like you, Miss Partenza, to help me write my autobiography."

We looked at each other for a moment.

"But, sir, I'm not a writer."

"Goodness knows the last thing I want is a writer. Damn them all. A secretary is what I need. I know you are an extraordinary stenographer and typist. I shall speak; you will take dictation. And from your essay here I can see you have a way with words." He looked at the page again. "'Carve our present out of the shapeless block of the future.' You also have a penchant for storytelling that may come in handy."

He looked at his watch.

"Let's start next week. At my house. In the meantime I must demand your discretion. Not a word of this to anyone."

"Of course."

"Talk to the girls outside. They'll give you all the details. Thank you." He attempted a smile. "And take the book."

As I was walking back to the door, I heard Bevel pick up a receiver.

"Let the other girl go."

9

Jack was having beer and sandwiches with my father when I got home. I just could not get used to his moustache. It looked fake, as if it had been pasted onto the face that otherwise had remained unchanged since our childhood.

I had known Jack since the time he was Giacomo. His family moved to the neighborhood shortly after my mother died. Back then, in my grief, I was beyond reach and uninterested in making new friends, but some years later, in our early teens, we dated for a short while. At the time, this meant going for long weekend walks along deserted streets by the river, during which he silently calculated what the best spot for the next kiss would be while I tried to figure out whether I wanted to be kissed again or not. This lasted for a few weeks, and then we grew apart and mostly avoided each other around the neighborhood. Eventually he left for college in Chicago, which I found impressive.

He returned two years later, a different person. Like in a dream, it was him but not him. He had acquired a new wardrobe, a larger vocabulary and that moustache. A whole new persona for a whole new Jack: he was a journalist now. College had become a waste of time, he said. The truth was out there, in the streets. He was impatient to get out into the real world and leave his mark. We started seeing each other in a loose, unclear way. I think my desire for being smitten was stronger than my desire for him.

My father's brow clouded for a moment when he saw me in my mother's clothes again, but he immediately raised his glass and asked me to join them. Jack gave me part of his sandwich.

"Anyway. I'll finish the story quickly," my father said. "They've captured Paolo, so I can't go back, and right ahead of me is this group of people by the road. One of them is a carabiniere. I can see him. But he hasn't seen me."

Jack listened with an enraptured half smile.

"What can I do?" My father shrugged.

"Yes, what did you do?"

"I move forward, hoping for the best. I need a story for the carabiniere. Maybe that I left my bag at the market for a moment and someone just planted those pamphlets in it. But remember I also had the gun. Maybe I could explain one of those things. But both? No."

"But the carabiniere hadn't seen you. Couldn't you just ditch the bag and the gun and pick them up later?"

Jack did not notice the flash of irritation in my father's eyes.

"No," my father said quickly, cleared his throat and resumed his story with his previous enthusiasm. "So I walk on, holding the gun open over my arm like this." He hung a kitchen towel over his forearm. "Like I'd seen hunters do. 'I'll walk by the carabiniere,' I think, 'and wave like I'm a hunter on a stroll,' you know?"

"Nice."

I asked Jack to pass the salt, and he handed it to me.

"Ah! No, no, no, no!" my father yelled at Jack. "Put it down, put it down, put it down! What kind of Italian are you? Never pass salt from hand to hand. Terrible luck! And you spilled some, too!" He tossed a pinch of salt over his left shoulder. "There. That should do it."

He collected himself.

"So I'm getting closer. They notice me. I'm sweating. The carabiniere now looks straight at me. I'm smiling and sweating. The carabiniere starts walking toward me. And it's not just those pamphlets in my bag. It's also all this information about my group. So I'm sweating. I can see now the carabiniere has his gun in his hand."

"No!"

"We keep walking toward each other. He waves at me. The people by the side of the road move. I see now they're standing around a big black bulk on the ground. 'Is that gun loaded?' the carabiniere asks. He's agitated. 'No, sir,' I say. 'Do you have bullets?' he asks. I decide to stick with the hunter story. 'Of course,' I say. 'I'm hunting.' 'Good,' the carabiniere says. 'Come with me.' And as we approach the people by the road, I can see they're standing by a horse. A fallen horse. Wounded."

"What?"

"Yes. It's hurt. You can tell it's in pain. 'My gun is jammed,' says the carabiniere. But from his look, I know. I can tell. His gun is not jammed. You're telling me that his horse broke a leg *and* that his gun is jammed? His gun is not jammed. He loves his horse, and he can't shoot it. I can tell."

My father paused to make sure Jack was properly enthralled.

"Now. The bullets are in my bag. I put it down. Open it. Reach for the bullets, which are under the bundle of pamphlets and documents, close the bag and load the gun. My hands are shaking a bit. When I'm done, I hand over the gun to the carabiniere."

"Unbelievable."

"Wait. The carabiniere doesn't take the gun." Pause. "He says to me, 'You do it.'"

"What? He tells you to do it?"

"Yes. He's bullying me into doing it. Because he loves his horse. I can tell. So he can't do it. But I can't do it either." My father laughed. "I can't kill a horse! It's looking up with its big black eyes, breathing, asking for mercy. I can't kill that horse!"

"So what happened?"

"I say to the carabiniere, pointing at the horse, 'Sir, your good friend needs you.' And then I look at the people standing around us. 'Right?' I ask them. Some of them nod. 'You can't fail your good friend now,' I tell him. So there's nothing he can do. You know. People talk. A carabiniere who couldn't shoot a horse? Imagine! So he takes the gun. His hands are trembling more than mine. He aims, still trembling. And then, after a long pause, shoots the horse in the head."

Dramatic pause.

"And then he gives me back my gun, thanks me, and I walk away."

"Incredible. Just incredible," Jack says, shaking his head. "Ida, did you know this story?"

"Yes."

"Incredible." And then he looked back at my father. "You should write these stories down, you know?"

"Bah."

"No, these are important stories. Maybe I could help you? We could write them together. Get them published."

"Bah . . . We'll see." My father got up and brushed off the crumbs on his chest, letting them fall all over the kitchen floor. "But the story is not over! The struggle continues! In fact I should head out to this assembly."

"Wait," I said. "Before you leave, I have some news. I just got a job."

"Just now?" Jack asked. "So that's why you look so pretty. Congratulations! What is it?"

"Oh, just an office job. You know, taking dictation, typing, that sort of thing. But it's a permanent position. And the pay is really good."

"Such great news," Jack said, holding me by the shoulders.

"Well," my father said. "I better get going."

He left, and, while clearing the table, I told Jack how grateful I was to him for coming by, bringing my father beer and listening to his old stories. It meant so much to him. I started doing the dishes.

Jack came over, leaned against me, kissed my neck and held me.

"The beer and the lunch were for us," he whispered into my ear. "I thought your father would be gone, and I didn't know you were out."

"You're sweet." I turned around, my hands still in the sink, kissed him briefly and went back to the dishes.

"I think I may have good news of my own, actually. The *Eagle* and the *Herald Tribune*. Great interest in the articles I showed them. Too soon to tell. But still .... Very promising."

I faced him, wiping my hands.

"And you're telling me only now? The *Eagle* and the *Herald*? Jack! That's wonderful! I told you things would work out in the end. Which articles did you send them?"

"Easy, easy. Like I said: too soon to tell. But, you know, fingers crossed. Looks really good."

I started drying the dishes. Again, Jack held me from behind.

"So much to celebrate," he murmured.

"So much to celebrate, yes. But look, I have to read this book for my new boss today. Maybe I can take you out to dinner when I get my first payment? Someplace fancy. We've always wanted to go to Monte's."

He stepped away from me, and I turned around in time to catch his lips contorted, briefly, in annoyance before they flattened into a neutral expression.

"Actually, I should get going." He looked at his watch. "I need to follow up with this editor at the *Mirror*. No stone left unturned!"

"I'm so proud."

"Not yet. But soon."

He kissed me and left.

IO

At first *Bonds* was not just literature; it was evidence. And I was not just a reader; I was a detective.

There had to be clues in there. However superficially, Harold Vanner had met the Bevels—and people in his circle surely knew them as well. Some of the elements in the novel must have been based on reality. Of course there was no way for me to tell fact from fiction back then (and even after all my subsequent meetings with Bevel this distinction would still remain unclear), but I suspected that buried in the text there was a kernel of truth. What did Vanner really know about Andrew and Mildred Bevel? Why would someone as powerful and busy as Bevel go through the trouble of challenging a piece of literature? There had to be something specific in the novel Bevel needed to suppress and refute. Was it in plain sight? Had Vanner hit on something by sheer coincidence, or was he sending Bevel some sort of message coded in his book? There was some vital fact that the novel had exposed, intentionally or not, about the people on whom it was based. Perhaps the truth was in all those distortions and inaccuracies that bothered Bevel so much.

As I read on, however, the prose itself rather than the content became the center of my attention. It was unlike the books they had made me read at school and had nothing to do with the mysteries I used to check out of the library. Later, when I finally went to college, I would be able to trace Vanner's literary influences and consider his novel from a formal point of view (even if he was never assigned reading for any of the courses I took, since his work was out of print and already quite unavailable). Yet back then I had never experienced anything like that language. And it spoke to me. It was my first time reading something that existed in a vague space between the intellectual and the emotional. Since that moment I have identified that ambiguous territory as the exclusive domain of literature. I also understood at some point that this ambiguity could only work in conjunction with extreme discipline—the calm precision of Vanner's sentences, his unfussy vocabulary, his reluctance to deploy the rhetorical devices we identify with "artistic prose" while still retaining a distinctive style. Lucidity, he seems to suggest, is the best hiding place for deeper meaning—much like a transparent thing stacked in between others. My literary taste has changed since then, and *Bonds* has been displaced by other books. But Vanner gave me my first glimpse of that elusive region between reason and feeling and made me want to chart it in my own writing.

Later I would read some of the reviews that came out when the book was published. Even though most of them were more or less laudatory (*The Nation* included it among its "Notable Books of the Year," and it made the "Christmas Book-List for *Harper* Readers"), the reactions were not as unanimously positive as Bevel had claimed. *The Atlantic* ran one of the few entirely enthusiastic reviews. Part of it read:

> Our canon is saturated with stories concerned with class and conspicuous consumption, with the corseted manners or the unbridled eccentricities that come with affluence. But few novels, like *Bonds*, dwell on the actual process of the accumulation of capital. And even those narratives that attempt a critique of affluence and inequality almost always end up dazzled by the ostentatious greed they set out to demystify—a pitfall Mr. Vanner deftly avoids.

But there were also ruthless takes. Some critics dismissed the book as entirely derivative ("epigonic," *The New Republic* deemed it) and pointed out the undeniable influence of Henry James, Constance Fenimore Woolson, Amanda Gibbons and Edith Wharton. *The New Yorker* called the novel a mere *succès de scandale* that had gained notoriety only for being an obvious *roman à clef* (both French expressions are in the review) based on a prominent yet secretive couple about whom everyone wanted a story—true or false.

As soon as I finished reading *Bonds*, I started it again. From my brief meeting with Bevel I could already tell there were differences between him and Rask, an intuition I would be able to confirm over our many conversations in the following weeks. The real man was more outspoken, less elusive and reserved than his fictional incarnation. They did feel, however, like two distant relatives.

The passages describing Rask's financial transactions required a bit more effort, but even if at the time I was not familiar with many of the terms in Vanner's novel, the overall account of the operations was clear enough. Although Rask's actions defied my moral imagination, I had no doubt they were modeled on real maneuvers. And during our sessions Bevel himself would confirm this. Several times, with a sportsman's pride, he told me how he was able to think ahead of his competitors and turn them into his prey, and how later, in 1929, he had outwitted the entire market, played it against itself and made a fortune out of it. While working with Bevel, I would go through newspapers and books from that period, and they would all confirm and describe, in great detail, most of the financial operations found both in the novel (with some inaccuracies and licenses) and in his firsthand accounts to me (with some whitewashing and self-aggrandizing touch-ups). Not only that: I discovered that both Vanner and Bevel closely paraphrased some of those publications in their narratives.

Helen, Benjamin Rask's wife, was the absolute center of the book to me. I was quick to identify with her. We both had a penchant for loneliness. We both were for the most part friendless. We both had overbearing and dysfunctional fathers, consumed by half-baked dogmas. We both were young women trying to grow in narrow crevices, hoping to break and expand them in the process. And I felt that Vanner, always keeping a respectful distance, understood her—and through her, me. Perhaps because the story had such a personal resonance, I found the last portion of the novel increasingly infuriating with every reading. Why did he have to destroy Helen? Why abuse her body with such violence in the final moments of her life? And, above all, why make her mad? He had obviously taken all sorts of liberties with Mildred Bevel's story and could have given her any kind of fate. Why, then, this? Why break her mind?

Looking back after all these years, I still remember the main effect of that first encounter with the novel. After reading it, I felt prepared for my first interview with Andrew Bevel. Even more: although it was a work of fiction, the book had convinced me that I was in possession of some essential truth about his life. I was still unable to see just what this truth might be, but this did not prevent me from believing I had, somehow, the upper hand.

II

A ticket booth under the plaster medallions and garlands. By the fireplace, banners advertising different exhibitions. "Gold, Silver, Bronze: American Decorative Arts at the Turn of the Century." "Down the Rabbit Hole: Illustrations from Victorian Children's Books." Floral air freshener. Beyond the vestibule, the hall—now a gift shop. An incongruously patterned runner slinking up the staircase. The same fire-gilt sconces. The same marble-topped console. The same straight-backed chairs but with red rope tied across the armrests.

I am surprised at how territorial and indignant I feel. The architects who renovated the house and turned it into a museum made the predictable decision to disrupt the original beaux arts atmosphere with unabashedly contemporary glass cubes and tame the convoluted excess of the original design with disciplined straight lines. All the signage is in a sans-serif font, surely meant to be irreverent in its anachronistic austerity.

My irritation and possessiveness puzzle me because when I first came here, I thought the place obscene. I should be glad to see it desecrated. And yet this incarnation of Bevel's house only adds a new layer to my exasperation with it.

The gift shop I find particularly offensive. Irrationally, I am even bothered by the young man behind the counter. I peer in, wanting, for unknown reasons, to fan my outrage. Some ridiculous Prohibition-era tune is playing softly in the background. There is a profusion of pens, mugs and postcards adorned with reproductions of objects from the collection and the museum's logo. A sidewall is dedicated to Roaring Twenties tchotchkes—boater hats, feather boas, hip flasks, satin gloves, cigarette holders, flapper costumes. Next to this section stands a gondola devoted to Francis Scott Fitzgerald. Copies of all his books. Biographies and critical studies. The Great Gatsby *in different languages.*

Of course not a single copy of Harold Vanner's Bonds.

It was through Vanner that I originally saw this house. I read his book a few days before setting foot here for the first time. Although his description is quite brief, my initial perception of this place was strongly conditioned by his words. Toward the end of the second part of his novel the fictional versions of Mr. and Mrs. Bevel finally meet. Vanner offers quick, not entirely accurate glimpses into the mansion and records Helen Rask's reactions to it.

"She failed to be raptured," Vanner writes of Mildred's avatar. "Nothing, as she first arrived at Mr. Rask's fastuous home, made her tingle with desire or even feel the momentary and vicarious thrill of a life unfettered from every material constraint."

And this is exactly how I intended to react when I first came here in my youth. I was determined to be indifferent and disdainful. I failed. The house was then in its prime and did to me everything it was designed to do. It made me feel unworthy of it. Awkward and unclean. Like a beggar, even if

I was not asking for anything. I was overwhelmed, yes. But being my fa-
ther's daughter, I was also disgusted and enraged—both by the house and by
my obedient reaction to it. A far cry from Helen's apathy.

Now, as I amble about before walking up the stairs toward the library,
my experience of the house is even more contradictory. My unaccountable
possessiveness and indignation ("I know what this place really used to be
like") mixes with the indifference I failed to feel in my youth (the loveless
accumulation of Holbeins, Veroneses and Turners does not amount to a gal-
lery but to a mere trophy room) and with a sharp sense of longing (returning
to a meaningful place after several decades reveals how alien one can be to
oneself).

I walk up the stairwell, looking around, trying to compare past and pres-
ent impressions. Should I provide an inventory of the paintings, sculptures,
statuettes, porcelains, vases, clocks and chandeliers? Should I describe the
sumptuous rooms? Should I name their function and at what time of the
day each of them was supposed to be used? Should I try to convey their di-
mensions? Should I linger on the rich fabrics, rare stones and unique types
of wood used throughout the house? Should I classify the different kinds of
furniture? Should I mention the makes of the cars that used to be lined up in
the driveway? Should I say how many servants were employed here back
in the thirties? Should I list their different duties?

The Great Gatsby *merchandise for sale at the gift shop downstairs comes*
to mind. I feel no desire to indulge in the description of unattainable luxu-
ries. Just like Vanner, I am disinclined to dwell on the opulence of the place.
I am here for the documents. Nothing else.

At the top of the stairs I turn left and walk down the long hallway. A few
doors are open, revealing rooms with paintings and decorative objects on
display behind velvet ropes. I remember exactly which door led to Mildred's
room. Now, as then, it is closed. Down at the end of the corridor, the library.

They have moved things around. There are fewer books here now (most of them are probably in stacks out of sight), and I welcome the rows of utilitarian desks with functional lamps and serviceable chairs, designed for real work. A few patrons leaf through large art books and take notes. The chief librarian comes out to meet me, and we walk back to his station, where he introduces me to his two colleagues. I hand him my letter requesting access to the restricted materials, and he accepts it, apologizing for this necessary formality.

I ask him what kind of documents and books are most usually requested. He tells me most of their visitors are academics or students who research the extensive art collection. Appraisers from auction houses come almost every day.

"In fact," he says, "as a writer, you are the outlier here."

We talk about the materials I am looking for. When I request Mildred Bevel's papers, the three librarians look at one another and chuckle.

"Oh, I wish you all the best," the chief says, as the other two librarians nod along emphatically. "Mrs. Bevel had terrible handwriting."

"We call them the Voynich manuscripts," says the youngest of the three with a mischievous giggle.

Librarian jokes. The Voynich manuscript is a fifteenth-century volume on parchment kept at the Beinecke Rare Book and Manuscript Library, at Yale University. Little is known about what seems to be, from the illustrations, a treatise on unidentified plant species and cosmology. The manuscript could be from anywhere in Central Europe, and it is written in a made-up alphabet that has baffled generations of scholars. Despite considerable investments of time and resources, linguists, cryptographers and even government agencies all over the world have, as yet, failed to decipher it.

The chief librarian giggles along but is quick to resume a professional tone.

"There's so much in Mrs. Bevel's files that we haven't been able to figure out. And this has affected the way in which her documents are cataloged.

We've been forced to group things based merely on format and size, rather than on subject. So we apologize in advance if you find that the content of the boxes is somewhat heterogeneous."

I sit at one of the desks, take out my notebook and a pencil (no ink allowed here) and wait for my boxes to arrive.

2

I was told to use the service entrance, which led to a small reception area for the staff, where I was shown to a chair. I was glad to be in this intermediate space before going into the living quarters. One of the maids introduced me to Miss Clifford, the housekeeper, a grandmotherly yet somehow youthful woman who offered me a cup of tea I was too nervous to accept. She gave it to me anyway, calling me "love."

A butler who seemed to be impersonating a butler in a film came in and, addressing the room rather than me, said my name, turned around and left. Miss Clifford took my cup and encouraged me to follow him. The butler led me through a passageway, up some stairs and then down a narrow corridor. It was like the backstage of a theater. He never looked back to make sure I was following him. At last, we went through a baize door that led to the actual house. I felt like a trespasser as soon as I set foot on the carpet. We crossed an eternal parlor. The butler knocked on a door, and I was shown into Bevel's study.

Within his confined expressive boundaries, he gave me a warm welcome. We exchanged a few pleasantries, and he asked me to take a seat at the desk, behind the typewriter.

"Before we begin," he said, getting some papers from a side table, "there's an important legal obligation we need to fulfill. You are to sign these papers. They state, in essence, that under no circumstances may you discuss, share or comment on any of the things that will be mentioned here. I wanted to give you this document in person to impress on you how seriously I take this issue. If you abide by these rules, there won't be a thing for you to worry about. This document will have no effect whatsoever on your life. But I fear we'll be unable to start if you don't sign it."

I signed without reading the papers. I had no choice—and, at the time, no intention of divulging any of his secrets.

It is not unlikely that I am still bound to confidentiality by that agreement. This particular document has not come up in my archival research into Bevel's papers so far. The estate's counsel has told me that the law firm held on retainer back then no longer exists. And this is as far as I intend to take the matter.

"You've read that book by now. No need to discuss it. I know you have come to understand, simply by having visited my workplace, that I'm a serious businessman. We'll talk about that at length, of course. But I'm sure you see now how justified my anger is and how quickly we must work. Questions."

"None." I knew it was unwise to ask any of the endless questions I had about Vanner's novel in connection with Bevel's real life.

"Good. This is how we shall proceed. I will simply tell you my story as it comes out. You will take it down and, when necessary, rework the sentences to ensure the whole thing makes sense. Eliminate redundancies and contradictions. Get the order of events straight (you know how one tends to jump back and forth in conversation). Make sure nothing sounds too jarring or obscure to the average reader. Perhaps add the occasional embellishment. You know, all those little changes. Just so it reads well. I'll provide the story, naturally, but will leave all the small details and the tidying up to you."

"Of course."

Correcting his style and, in fact, *writing* his book were aspects of the job I had not anticipated. Things would become clearer along the way, I decided.

"I also trust you to provide a . . . feminine touch in the passages concerning Mrs. Bevel."

I nodded, while still trying to find my bearings.

"And since I've mentioned my wife, there's an all-important matter regarding that novel you've read. Something you should never forget. As I've said before, my wife never suffered from mental ailments of any kind. Mildred was a clear-sighted, serene woman. How could someone as good and frail as her be defamed in such a way? It's like mocking a child." He paused and looked first at the angle where the wall met the ceiling and then at his hands. "And how could anyone imply that I was in any degree responsible for her death? How could that hack writer ever conceive, let alone print, that I would subject her to some deranged medical experiment? You must realize how I cannot let this narrative stand." His eyes turned to me as if to make sure these words had been properly pinned to my mind. "It's true that she died in a Swiss sanatorium. But I lost her to cancer."

"I am so sorry."

He stopped me with a raised palm.

"No need. To work."

"Sir, if it's all the same to you, I would rather sit over there, on that sofa. I won't need the typewriter. I'll take shorthand and transcribe everything later."

He was taken aback.

"I think the conversation, as you called it, will flow better in a less office-like setting," I said.

A thoughtful pause.

"Very well. If it makes you more comfortable." He gestured to the sofa and sat in an armchair across from me. "Let's begin."

3

As I was leaving Bevel's house, the butler handed me an envelope and said it contained my first weekly salary, paid in advance, together with money for initial expenses. Perhaps I needed a new typewriter and office supplies. Or perhaps I could use some new clothes? I remember how he relished his tactless display of tact when he made this last suggestion.

I crossed Fifth Avenue and found a quiet bench in the park where I could inspect the contents of the envelope.

Because of my upbringing, I had come to consider money as something filthy. The physical dirt on the greasy, wrinkled singles and fives I was accustomed to handling was also moral since the bills were quite literally "stained with the sweat of the exploited masses." Over the years, as I shed my father's dogmas, my ethical repulsion mellowed into indifference. I no longer have thoughts in favor of or against money in its physical manifestation—I view it merely as the tangible vehicle through which we conduct commercial transactions.

Yet that day in Central Park that envelope seemed to contain more than just money. I had never held so much cash in my life. Ten twenty-dollar bills. (Our rent, at the time, was about twenty-five dollars a month.) They were unused and clung to one another. Wondering what the actual smell of money—rather than that of the multitude of hands that had touched it over the years—could be, I stuck my nose into the envelope. It smelled just like my father. But beneath the ink there was also a forest-like scent. An undertone of damp soil and unknown weeds. As if the bills were the product of nature. Flipping through them inside the envelope, I noticed they had consecutive serial numbers, which was something I had never seen before. This made me think, with a bodily sort of vividness, of the millions of twenty-dollar bills printed before and after mine and the endless possibilities they represented. The things they could buy, the problems they could solve. My father was right: money was a divine essence that could embody itself in any concrete manifestation.

That same day I went around Brooklyn running errands. As much as I disliked that butler, he was not wrong: I needed new clothes. Moreover, I considered that perhaps it had been Bevel himself who had instructed him to tell me to get a new outfit. I decided to do this immediately, since I knew my father would be out that afternoon and I did not want him to see me with shopping bags.

It took some effort to convince the saleswoman at Martin's, on Hoyt Street, that although I wanted to look sharp, I had no desire to draw attention to my clothes. She kept asking about my boss and what the office environment was like. I gave evasive answers and, invariably, picked the outfits she had discarded for being too frumpish.

"Someone as attractive as you . . . You shouldn't be hiding behind these mousy clothes," she said before capitulating to my dun, dull wishes.

My next stop was our landlady. The only reason we had not been evicted yet was that she loved my mother and therefore felt an obligation toward me. But she disliked my father and his semi-clandestine press in almost the same measure. And with each day we were late with the rent, I became more my father's daughter. It always took about an hour to pay her. She wanted the money, but she also felt uncomfortable taking it and invariably felt obliged to keep me at her door for a long time while we shared neighborhood gossip. This illusion of closeness would cool off after two weeks and utterly vanish by the end of the month.

Something similar happened at the stores where we had accounts. If I had been ashamed to add to our tab for weeks and sometimes even months, the shopkeepers were now ashamed to take the money that was rightfully theirs. Their awkwardness led to long conversations on various trivial topics, after which I was sent off with a small treat.

I had a quiet dinner with my father, who asked no questions about where all the food in the pantry had come from.

The following day I asked Jack to help me get a typewriter. I thought it would give us something to do (our time together was increasingly aimless), and perhaps he would enjoy an opportunity to show off his journalistic knowledge. He had told me he had done some work for a few small papers in Chicago, and I assumed from the description of his duties that he was well versed in typewriters and other aspects of the office world.

We met at an office supply store in downtown Brooklyn, close to the courts, that sold, rented and repaired typewriters. Jack, his hat tilted back, a cigarette dangling off his lips, asked a lot of questions and tried different machines. It was clear, however, that he knew nothing about typing. He tested several models, hammering "alalalalalalalalalalala" as fast as he could with his index fingers. While Jack talked to one of the salesmen, I quickly tried a few typewriters, hoping he would not see me. As I was settling for a secondhand Royal portable (even though the "e" was a bit over-inked, with a blacked-out eye, and the "i" often un-dotted), he came over before I realized and could stop typing. He said nothing, but I could sense his resentment. It did not help that he saw me decline the installment option and pay the $27.50 in full.

On our way back he told me about his promising leads, scoops and hunches. He was getting to know a lot of people in different news-rooms, and his hope was that soon it would all come together—he just had to find the perfect story for the perfect editor at the perfect paper. That was all he needed: to get his foot in the door. Then he would be on his way to becoming a columnist.

"It's only a matter of time," he said. "But time is getting . . ." He made an awkward pause. "Expensive."

I stopped and covered my mouth, horrified.

"I'm so sorry. I can't believe I never offered." I reached into my purse.

"Oh no! I didn't mean . . ."

"Let's not go through that whole routine." I handed him some money; he stared at the sidewalk. "Please. Take it. For me."

He pocketed the bills quickly, without ever looking up, muttering words of thanks and a promise to repay me. We walked on.

"But tell me about your new job," he said, resuming his normal tone. "Why the typewriter? Won't you be working at an office?"

"I'm not sure yet. Yesterday we worked at his house. He says he doesn't like going downtown anymore. He works from his place every afternoon. And that's why I need to type all those notes at home. Maybe later we'll meet at his office. I don't know."

"Hold on. You were at his house?"

"Yes."

"Alone?"

"Well, he has all this staff around."

"But the two of you were alone."

"Yes."

"I don't like it."

We walked along in silence. It reminded me of our quiet teenage strolls along the water, during which he would be absorbed in his calculations about when he should next kiss me.

"Who is this guy anyway?"

"A businessman."

"Does this businessman have a name?"

I stopped again.

"Look. I'm not going to ask you to trust me. I'm not going to give you names you have no use for, just to make you feel good. I'm not going to say anything to appease you."

As I started walking again, with Jack sulking a few steps behind, I realized that I had uttered those last sentences flatly, with expressionless calm. Just like Andrew Bevel.

4

evel had a severe head cold next time I saw him. Still, he kept our appointment. Since he was sick, he wouldn't feel so bad for wasting his time on "this thing" instead of doing real work, he said. It was the worst day for a cold—a hot, humid New York summer afternoon.

I handed him my typed transcript of our first session. I thought I had whittled his words down to hard, incisive sentences. The text sounded, I believed, manly. It conveyed an impatience with style, and this was intended as a tacit yet vehement denunciation of Vanner's novel. At no point had I departed from the facts he had presented in his narrative.

He read the pages right there and then. It seemed to me that he was going too fast to appreciate my subtle severity.

"Right," he said and blew his nose. He was sweating. Perhaps annoyed. "You do take faithful notes. The facts are, in essence, there. A few things ought to be emended. We'll get to that. The problem is that this doesn't reflect me."

"I can assure you that I stayed close to . . ."

"As I just said, you do take faithful notes. But if I wanted someone to merely transcribe my words, I would use a Dictaphone. Too much is lost in your transcription. This is flat. And full of doubt. Do you truly understand what my job is about?"

"No."

"Thank you for not attempting a response. My job is about being right. Always. If I'm ever wrong, I must make use of all my means and resources to bend and align reality according to my mistake so that it ceases to be a mistake."

"I should be taking this down for your book."

"I can't tell whether you're being sarcastic or naïve. Either way, don't make me regret hiring you." He blew his nose again and picked up a phone. "Tea." He hung up. "Your pages are too hesitant."

"I'll rewrite them."

"Good. I don't know for how long I'll be able to do this today, with this cold. But there's one thing about my parents. No, no need to get your notepad yet. I don't want to dignify the outrageous allegations in that novel with a response. But I do want you to know it's all false. To imagine that my father would have a double life in Cuba. He did indeed have a tobacco concern—as he had many other businesses. But to ever conceive that he would even think of setting foot south of the border." He came close to laughing at this point. "And my mother . . ."

There was a knock on the door. The unpleasant butler came in with tea for one. Gravely, soundlessly, he poured Bevel a cup and left.

"My mother," Bevel resumed after the door was closed. "A smoker? Cigars? With those . . . *friends*? For that alone Vanner deserves what he's getting." Cough. "Again, this is not something I wish to address directly. We'll find a way, though." The heat, his cough and the tea had made him break into a full sweat. "Let's go back to my charities."

I took my notepad and sat on a different sofa. Somehow, I found it important to show that my seat was my choice.

"Why don't you tell me a bit more about your parents first."

The exasperation absent from his face was all in the force with which he put the cup back on the saucer. I had made a mistake. But being decisive had served me well in the past. Perhaps I could exonerate myself by insisting on my error.

"Maybe your loss could explain how you relied on your ancestors for inspiration. And it could be a good backdrop for all your charitable work. Show what drew you to that kind of work in the first place."

"The feminine touch." Had he softened a bit? "You don't seem to have been paying attention. I want decisive pages, not mush."

He wiped his brow and suddenly looked drained and empty. He might have had a fever.

"I suppose I see your point, though. What would you like to know?"

"Why don't you tell me about some early memories. A few paragraphs with childhood scenes would be good to break the ice. Show how you became the man you are today. What do you think your first picture of your mother is?"

There was a pause. He coughed and wiped his brow. I was starting to sweat, too. The long silence was uncomfortable. But I refused to break it.

"When she died."

Another pause.

"When she died, I asked myself that. An Easter egg hunt, I think."

The silence started to rebuild itself.

"She was a very loving woman. Which made her absence difficult.

And brilliant. She was brilliant. She discovered my precocious talent for mathematics. Oftentimes she would stay for my lessons and correct the tutors. In this she resembled Mildred. Both brilliant women." He laughed, in his habitual way, through his nostrils. "Legions of tutors fired. One after the other. None of them was a match for my talents, she said. At one point she started to tell me to dismiss them. I had to inform them they were fired and explain why—what they had failed to teach me and so on. I must have been six or seven years old the first time I had to do it." He either laughed darkly or cleared his congested nose. "The confused look on that man's face."

He seemed exhausted.

"This is a pointless exercise. And I'm sick. I fear I have a temperature. Bring back those rewritten pages on Wednesday. And we'll talk about my charities."

5

We did not meet the following Wednesday. Bevel was still sick. I made use of the extra days to rewrite my initial pages, trying to follow his directions. It was true that my prose lacked the force of his presence. But this force was not solely in his speech; it was also the cumulative effect of different aspects of his personality, his surroundings and the intimidating preconceptions one had of him. Because this strength or decisiveness was not just verbal, it could not be imitated only with words and refused to come to life on the page.

All my attempts failed. The closest I could come to Bevel's voice was a caricature. An almost irrepressible desire to meet Harold Vanner took hold of me. He must have some of the answers I was looking for, from the larger facts down to the smaller details. Perhaps he might even help me with my writing. He could not be that hard to find. But what would I tell him? That I had been hired to help write a book whose main aim was to debunk and destroy his novel? And even if for some miraculous reason Vanner were to help me, Bevel would no doubt find out that I had seen him, and that would be the end of my employment, if not worse—there was that document he had asked me to sign.

My trash can was full. I could smell my own panic.

Out of that mounting despair came my first breakthrough. I would no longer try to capture Bevel's voice. Instead I would create the voice he wished he had—the voice he wanted to hear.

After filling another trash can with worthless drafts, I realized how presumptuous my new plan was. How could I, on my own, ever come up with a tone grandiose enough to captivate Bevel to the point that he would think that he could hear himself in it? I needed help.

I went to the main branch of the New York Public Library, at Bryant Park, and spent the entire day going through their catalog and looking at autobiographies written by "Great American Men." Benjamin Franklin, Ulysses S. Grant, Andrew Carnegie, Theodore Roosevelt, Calvin Coolidge and Henry Ford are some of the names I remember coming up with, riffling through the cards. If Bevel's own voice, transcribed without any embellishment or modification, was not enough, I would make a new one for him out of all those other voices. And they would all be stitched together with my father's bluster and pride. Like Victor Frankenstein's creature, my Bevel would be made up of limbs from all these different men.

I was able to check some of those books out of the Brooklyn Public Library, and during the following week I went through them in a chaotic, haphazard fashion, skipping from one to the other without much method, taking random notes without attribution. I had no training in archival research or how to properly manage a bibliography. And that turned out to be a good thing. Because thanks to my wild and uncompromisingly disorganized approach, the books started to merge into one another. What was individual about each man—Carnegie's self-serving sanctimoniousness, Grant's essential decency, Ford's matter-of-fact pragmatism, Coolidge's rhetorical thrift and so on—yielded to what I thought, at the time, they all had in common: they all believed, without any sort of doubt, that they *deserved* to be heard, that their words *ought* to be heard, that the narratives of their faultless lives *must* be heard. They all had the same unwavering certainty my father had. And I understood that this was the certainty that Bevel wanted on the page.

I was absorbed in work and barely left my room. The timing could not have been better. During this week my father and I had fallen into a hostile silence. He was angry because of my Wall Street job, and that was the way things would remain until I took the first step toward reconciliation, which meant telling him, in some way, that he was right and I was wrong. Something similar was happening with Jack. He had not come by to see me since our squabble after buying the typewriter. It was not unlikely that they both thought I had sequestered myself in my room because I was hurt. Rather than working, they must have pictured me moping, wallowing in my unjustified resentment against them.

My father exerted an emotional monopoly. His happiness tolerated no dissent. When he was in a good mood, everyone was supposed to be delighted to hear his long stories, laugh at his jokes and cheerfully partake in whatever project he had in mind—calamitous home renovations, around-the-clock printing jobs, excursions to the Bronx in search of an Italian butcher someone had mentioned. But whenever he was low or had been wronged, he made everyone pay for it. I have yet to see a face as determined as his was in anger. It was, sadly, a determination that was fixed only on itself—determined to be determined. Once he got into that state, I think he viewed any kind of compromise as self-betrayal, as if his whole being could be eroded and wiped away by the admission of a fault. I lived with my father for over twenty years, and we stayed close after I moved out. Not once, in all those decades, did he apologize to me for anything.

A few days before my next meeting with Bevel I finished writing the preface to his autobiography. If my text did not sound exactly like him, it captured how I thought he *should* sound. It is not impossible that some of the overconfidence I had given my fictional Bevel had rubbed off on me, but I was certain I had found his voice—and that it would work.

As I walked out of my room, elated, there was my father, at his press, upholding his principled anger as an example for exactly no one. I gave him a hug and a kiss.

"Come on. Don't be angry."

"Angry? I'm not angry. You're the one who's been locked up in your room for days."

"I was working. You know I was working."

No answer. He put in a slug of type.

"And I understand you don't like the job I got."

"I never said that. Those are your words."

"I'm not crazy about some things about it either. But it's the job I happened to get."

"Don't put words in my mouth."

"Would you say that a worker at Ford's assembly line is a capitalist? Would you say that a man operating a forge at U.S. Steel is an imperialist? Aren't those the very people you are fighting for? What's the difference between those men and me?"

He put down his tools. In my enthusiasm I had forgotten that if we were to patch things up, he was supposed to be right and I had to be wrong. Now he would walk away and sulk for another week. But instead the impossible happened.

"You're right," he said, and he even repeated it. "You're right. Come on, make me some coffee and tell me about this job of yours."

6

G ood. I'll make some adjustments later. Let's move forward."
This was all Andrew Bevel said after reading my new version of his text. And it was all I needed.

We spent the first half of that session mapping out the whole book, chapter by chapter. It had become clear by then that he would not tell me the story of his life in chronological order or exhaust each topic before moving on to the next. Yet, having the organized and methodical mind of an accountant, Bevel needed to know where each event would go. We therefore designed a general scaffolding, not unlike the bare structure of his new skyscraper. It was my job, as I typed out my notes at the end of each meeting, to sort the events I had recorded, decide in which chapter they belonged and weave them into a coherent narrative.

After a short preface the book would begin with a chapter on his ancestors, followed by others about his education, his business and so on. Often, when Bevel got carried away, he would skip back and forth between chapters, asking me to take down some isolated sentences, key words or just a name, which he would expand on later. The core of the book was made up of the sections vindicating his wife and those insisting on his extraordinary talent as a businessman.

It was also of great importance to him to show the many ways in which his investments had always accompanied and indeed promoted the country's growth—even in the midst of the 1929 crash. He went to great lengths to explain how his ancestors, all the way up to his great-grandfather during the Jefferson presidency, had married personal gain with the good of the country. This, Bevel insisted, was at the center of his business practice. "A selfish hand has a short reach," he would often say. Or, "Profit and common good are but two sides of the same coin." Or, "Our prosperity is proof of our virtue." Wealth had, for him, an almost transcendental dimension. Nowhere was this clearer than in his legendary string of triumphs of 1926, he often repeated. While geared toward profit, his actions had invariably had the nation's best interest at heart. Business was a form of patriotism. As a consequence, his private life had become, increasingly, one with the life of the nation. This, he said, was not always easy for Mildred.

"She was very reserved. Here's a confession for you: I was surprised when she agreed to marry me. Never did I imagine that she would consider getting involved in all . . . this." He looked around as if trying to figure out what "this" truly meant. "I can't . . . Honestly, I don't know what I would have done without Mildred. Where I would be." There was an unusual depth to these rather banal words. "She . . . I mean to say . . ."

I found Bevel's speechlessness to be his greatest show of eloquence up to that point. The man whose job it was to always be right, the man who never indulged in the luxury of doubt, was at a loss for words.

"Would you like to stop for a few moments?"

The cushioned silence deepened.

"She saved me. No other way to put it. Saved me with her humanity and warmth. Saved me by making a home for me. You probably can't see it now, but this place," he rolled his hands in gentle waves around him, "felt like a home once. Now, with each passing day, it becomes more and more like a museum. Hard. But this was a soft place not too long ago. She . . . Mildred had . . . There was always music. She was . . . We should talk about that. There was always music." Again, he was at a loss for words. "Beauty. Yes. She was a lover of beauty. And kindness. Beauty and kindness. That's what she loved. And . . . It's what she brought to the world. She would always . . ."

He stared into the past, and I did not dare bring him back from his reverie. I was coming to understand why Vanner's depiction of his wife in the novel had moved him to write his autobiography in response.

There was a gentle knock on the door. The butler came in with tea, but Bevel stopped him before he could put down the tray.

"There's two of us."

"Very good, sir."

He turned around and left.

"I wish I could have met her," I said, fearing to spoil what had seemed like a true moment of candor and, to some extent, intimacy.

"She would have liked you. Sycophants bored her."

In plain contradiction with the spirit of Bevel's last sentence, I felt immensely proud and flattered by it.

"Mildred was blessed with an exceptional clarity of vision. To her, nothing was ever too complex or mysterious. Her approach to the world was elementary and, without fail, right. She could see through false complications and into the simple truths of life. Just as you're finding a way to distill the essence of these long conversations of ours onto the page, I believe that, with my guidance, you shall succeed in capturing Mildred's spirit as well."

"Thank you. I'll do my best."

"I think I just said there was something childlike about her enthusiasm. This is true. But it's just as true that a wisdom of sorts came with her frailty. Perhaps part of her knew that her time with us would be short. Her health was always delicate, you know. This is why we were never blessed with children."

"How did you two meet?"

"The usual way. Not a riveting story, really. Mildred had just arrived from Europe with her mother, Mrs. Howland. After so many years abroad (almost Mildred's entire life) they had no friends here. At the time of their return I was finalizing some business with a certain person (names are irrelevant), and he asked me, as a favor, to attend a dinner he was hosting for Mrs. Howland and her daughter. I'm famously averse to social functions of any kind. But this was work. I was seated next to Mildred."

"Do you remember what you talked about?"

He made a long pause and stared at the space above my head.

"We . . . She talked about music."

"What kind of music did she like?" I was thinking of Helen Rask's sophisticated musical taste in Vanner's novel. "Who was her favorite composer?"

"Oh, she liked all the great ones, you know. Beethoven . . . Mozart . . ."

It seemed as if he was going to elaborate, but he did not.

"To be perfectly frank, I don't know the first thing about music. Some of the recitals we attended together, I rather enjoyed, although

I'd be unable to tell you about them. Other performances barely sounded like music at all. I always thought most people in the audience only pretended to like them. But from the way Mildred talked about those pieces afterward, it was clear that she understood what they were all about. No need to get lost in irrelevant details, though. Here's what you need to understand about Mildred," he said in the end. "Music aside, she was a simple creature. And sensitive. But somehow from that simplicity came her great depth. Simple and deep, you know."

I nodded without really understanding what he meant.

"This is what I'm trying to convey. The simple depth of those who are close to the edges of existence. Her childhood and her fatal disease. Make sure to use that: 'edges of existence.'"

I made a suitable pause.

"Did you host concerts here, at the house? Like those in . . ."

I remembered the interdiction of referencing Vanner's book, but it was too late. Bevel looked at me long enough to convey his annoyance without resorting to any gestures.

"At first not more often than anyone else. Although as Mildred got weaker and became unable to go out, she started bringing the music home. Small functions in the second-floor music room. I supported these concerts, naturally, and helped secure the best performers. But for the most part I stayed out of it. Most of the music sounded just like that moment before the performance, when the musicians tune their instruments. Still, even if I disliked most of that stuff, I admired Mildred's boldness and assurance."

"Would she, by any chance, have kept a journal?" I asked, recalling the diary in several thick volumes that the character based on Mildred kept in the novel.

"Nothing beyond a few calendars where she noted her engagements with acquaintances—and her concerts, of course."

"Do you think I could talk to some of her friends or a few of those musicians? It would help me get a fuller picture."

"Miss Partenza, I am writing this book to stop the proliferation of versions of my life, not to multiply them. I most emphatically do not want more perspectives, more opinions. This is to be *my* story."

"I understand."

"Besides, Mildred was extremely reserved. And with her delicate health she barely had a social life at all. She led a very private life, devoted to our home and the arts. That's, in part, why we got along so well—we both enjoyed our privacy. Of course she met with representatives from the institutions involved with her charities. But I don't think we should disturb museum directors and university presidents with this. After all, her dealings with those men were strictly about practicalities. I very much doubt they could throw any light on Mildred's character. For that you have me."

"Understood. Thank you."

"You just need to know about her kindness and her love for the arts. That's what needs to come to life on the page."

Again, a knock on the door, and the butler let himself in with the tea.

"Look at the time," Bevel said. "I have a call to make. Excuse me. Please call my office to arrange our next meeting. Good work, Miss Partenza."

And with that he left.

The butler looked at me.

"So. Still want your tea?" He grinned. "Madam?"

7

Jack arrived with a beautifully rustic bouquet of roses. He had never brought me flowers before. Jokingly he hid his face behind the red buds, making sad eyes. My father, who was sitting with me in the kitchen, laughed and started mocking him.

"Ah, she's got you now . . . Flowers, eh? Roses, too. They mean passion. Oh, this is getting serious! But wait. Let me count. Six? No, no, no, no. Never give roses in even numbers." He took one out of the bunch. "There. Even roses are for funerals. Uneven roses are for love."

Jack mouthed an apology as I took the flowers. He had also brought a bottle of astonishingly sour wine some friends of his made out on Long Island.

The conversation quickly turned to politics. Perhaps encouraged by the wine, my father was particularly fiery that afternoon.

"The time has come for action. Mussolini crushing Italy under his boot, Franco massacring Spain, Stalin murdering his own with his purges, Hitler getting ready to devour Europe. Yes, the time has come for action." He looked out the window. "How did we get here? How? All we have left to choose is different forms of terror. Terror and imperialism. That's all. Fascist imperialism. Soviet imperialism. Capitalist imperialism. Those are our only choices now, it seems. The time has come for radical action."

I still have no idea what "action" meant. How real that word was. How seriously it had to be taken. Most likely, not as seriously as my father would have liked. Although the vague accounts of his past contained some references to violence, I never fully believed he had been engaged in any of the acts he so dimly described. There is nothing imprecise and nebulous about violence, and I found it suspicious that his narratives were so hazy. Still, he and his comrades would often fall quiet as if by common accord whenever the conversation took certain turns (especially when reminiscing about their Italian days). This made me think they did share facts terrible or compromising enough to call for immediate and unanimous silence. Then again, the recurrent flirtations with "insurrectionary violence," the insistence on "the propaganda of the deed," the flippant reference to capsules of fulminate of mercury, the grotesquely indiscreet winks to Luigi Galleani and the Wall Street bombing of 1920 and the overall giddiness around the possibility of bloodshed made me believe it was all bluster. Who would be involved in such things and then talk about them in such a way?

Whatever my father's prevailing version might have been at any given time, the directive always remained the same for me. I was not to repeat anything I heard or mention to anyone, ever, his political beliefs. Growing up, I found this to be a source of both anxiety and excitement. Sometimes, however, the burden got too heavy. After all, my father talked almost exclusively about politics, which made it hard for me to respond to even the most trivial questions about him—it seemed anything I said could betray his confidence. But it is also true that being entrusted with this big secret often gave me a thrill.

What all tendencies, branches and splinters of anarchism—and there are quite a few—have in common is their opposition to every form of hierarchy and inequality. It should not be surprising, then, that there are no extensive records of the movement, since the institutional order required to keep such records was in obvious contradiction with the movement's tenets. This is why my attempts at determining my father's role, in both Italy and America, have led only to dead ends. But the lack of evidence is not only a result of the movement's characteristics. Anarchists were systematically persecuted in the United States, where they served as scapegoats for political and, in the case of Italians, even racial anxieties. During my research into my father's past I found that between 1870 and 1940 about five hundred anarchist periodicals were published in the United States. That virtually no trace remains of that vast number of publications and the even vaster number of people behind them shows how utterly anarchists have been erased from American history.

For all these reasons it is nearly impossible for me to know what my father meant by "radical action." But I do remember Jack seemed touched by his speech.

"I've been thinking," Jack said after a brooding pause. "Perhaps my place is in Europe. Report from there. From the front line. Like Hemingway. Maybe even *join* the front line. The International Brigades. You know? *Do* something. This idleness is killing me."

I looked at both of them, staring somberly into their glasses, and shivered with embarrassment. Their bombast. Their boyish earnestness. If they only knew how decisions really were made, if they could only hear how subdued the true voice of authority was, if they could only see how impossibly removed the two of them were from any sort of actual power.

And then I shivered with embarrassment again. This time for me. Because I realized I had just measured my father and Jack against Andrew Bevel. I had allowed him to convince me of his superiority.

My father gulped down the last of his wine, announced he had some leaflets to deliver, gave a clownish salute and left.

Jack took my hand, waited until my father had gone down the stairs and closed the front door, and then led me to my room. The floor was carpeted in stenographic notes; the bed was covered with typed pages. He picked one up before I could stop him.

"Please give me that," I said as I rushed to make a pile with the typed pages. (I was not concerned about the shorthand, which he would be unable to make out.)

He started reading.

"'A Destiny Realized' . . . Is this some kind of novel or something?"

I snatched the paper out of his hand.

"Jesus!"

"Sorry."

"I guess I can't do anything right. I express my concern about your safety with your boss, and you bark at me. I bring you flowers and try to apologize (even though I shouldn't), and that's no good. I show interest in your work, and you get all hysterical."

"Sorry. It's just that I'm not allowed to show any of this to anyone."

"I care about you. That's all."

"Sorry."

I looked down at my shoes, thinking of the embarrassed applicant in the brown suit and her eternally downcast eyes.

"Come here," he said and hugged me. "Want to cuddle a little?"

I did not. My lack of response and slight stiffness were enough to make that clear.

He let go with a grunt and left.

I rolled up the typed pages and shoved them inside the sleeve of a raincoat, deep in my closet.

8

Walking around Wall Street during the weekend, one gets the impression that the world's affairs have been settled once and for all, that the age of work is finally over and that humanity has moved on to its next stage.

Bevel disliked the excitement of downtown Manhattan on workdays. Because he avoided his office during the week, he often had his closest people come in on Saturday morning so he could catch up with paperwork undisturbed. He had asked to see me after one of those quiet work sessions at his office. There was something buoyant about him.

I handed him my latest pages, all about Mildred—her life at home, the first pronounced symptoms of her illness and how her health compelled her to host concerts at home. I dwelled at length on her sophisticated, uncompromising taste that favored radically modern artists.

"Yes. Good. The domestic passages really do capture Mrs. Bevel. A few remarks, though. These paragraphs about Mildred's experimental, untraditional ideas about music need to go." He crossed out half a page. "We wouldn't want anyone to believe she was arrogant or affected. Keep it simple. Make her love of the arts approachable for the common reader."

I would receive similar directives over the course of the following weeks. With each crossed-out paragraph or toned-down sentence my sense of betrayal deepened.

"We ought to convey Mildred's lovely softness with a bit more emphasis. I do realize that 'softness' and 'emphasis' may seem like contradictory terms. But truly, that's where the focus ought to be. Her delicate nature. Her frailty. Her kindness."

"Of course. Perhaps you have a few stories about her that illustrate this."

"Oh, I think you'd do a much better job."

I did not repress a perplexed look.

"Why, with that delicate touch of yours I'm sure you'll strike the right tone."

"Thank you. But if you could provide me with a few examples showing Mrs. Bevel's warmth and kindness. Small everyday stories, as usually the most . . ."

"Exactly right: some small everyday stories. You should impress on the reader her exquisite sensibility and how her artistic inclinations suffused every aspect of our domestic life. Regrettably, I've never had much time for books and recitals myself, so I'm unable to provide extensive details. But, again, this is for the best: we wouldn't want our readers to think she was pretentious or, heaven forbid, a snob. Which, of course, she wasn't. And we most certainly don't want any artistic eccentricities that could be taken for some sort of . . . mania." He paused to make sure the implications and importance of this registered with me. "Make it homey. As a woman, you'll do a far better job painting that picture. I'll review the pages once you're done, naturally."

This time I did my best to conceal my absolute confusion.

"Before we begin I must share a piece of excellent news." He re-arranged himself in his seat. "After long negotiations I've finally taken Mr. Vanner's slanderous book out of circulation. Because it's a novel, my case for libel and defamation was dismissed. I attempted a friendly approach first, but neither Mr. Vanner nor his publisher would accept my generous offer for his contract. Yesterday, however, after protracted discussions whose details you'd only find tedious, I managed to ac-quire a controlling stake in his publishing house. Mr. Vanner's book shall remain in print forever, which means his contract with my newly acquired publishing house will never lapse."

"I'm not sure I understand."

"As long as the book sells, Mr. Vanner will be bound to his current contract. And sell it shall. Because I will buy every single copy of every print run. And pulp them all."

There did not seem to be a correct reaction or response to this.

"What if he writes another book or exposes this?"

"He may write as many books or articles as he wishes. But I can assure you that no publisher or editor in this town (or in London, New Delhi or Sydney, for that matter) will ever touch his work. That is, if he ever finds the time to write. At the moment he must be overwhelmed with the many lawsuits my attorneys have been piling on him. We don't care to win any of them, of course. But it will be up to him and his lawyers, if he can afford them, to prove that he isn't a plagiarist and a fraudster."

"Isn't taking the book out of circulation enough?"

His eyes thinned. He let my question linger for a while.

"Could you be implying that my actions are gratuitous?"

I had finally managed to anger him.

"Are you saying, perhaps, that I am moved by spite, revenge or, even worse, that I am seeking some sort of perverse thrill in cruelty? It seems to me that you don't understand what our work here is about. It seems to me that you don't understand what any of this is all about."

"I do."

"Is that so?"

"Bending and aligning reality."

At the time, I was not entirely sure if the phrase applied to this situation. But I did know that most men enjoy hearing themselves quoted.

"Exactly. And reality needs to be consistent. How incongruous would it be to find traces of Vanner in a world where Vanner never existed?"

For the first time since meeting Andrew Bevel, it occurred to me that I should be afraid.

9

The subversive almanac was a calendar of anarchist holidays where all the religious and patriotic commemorations had been replaced with dates relevant to the cause—Bakunin's birthday, the execution of Giordano Bruno, the fall of the Bastille, different strikes and uprisings around the world and so on. My father was one of the main providers of the *almanacco sovversivo* in New York. He even printed a limited "deluxe" edition, a contradiction I never dared mention to him.

After May Day the most important holiday in this calendar was August 23, the day Nicola Sacco and Bartolomeo Vanzetti were lynched by the state. (This date also had a private meaning for my father, since 23 was his lucky number and he endowed it with powerful and mystical qualities.) We were now in July, which was a period of feverish activity—in addition to all his usual work my father had to finish many commemorative prints to be sent out in time for this anniversary. I always gave him a hand during these frantic weeks, but that year I was sequestered in my room, trying to turn Mildred Bevel's tenuous ghost into a tangible human being.

We saw each other for quick meals in the kitchen, eating open-faced sandwiches and fruit, standing at the counter, never using plates and sharing our single rusty "good knife"—it was still "the good knife" even if the blade rattled loose in the handle and the tip, broken after being used for every imaginable purpose, was square. At first he had refused to discuss my work for "the speculative machine." Although his cold silence was usually hurtful, for once I welcomed it, knowing how seriously Andrew Bevel took confidentiality and how he dealt with those who betrayed his trust. But after our last conversation about my job my father had softened a bit. And as time went by and he saw how hard I applied myself to it, his respect for me grew. "Work" was the standard by which he measured a person's worth, and I think he finally had come to see me as a "worker," the highest honor he could bestow on anyone—all the people he admired, dead or living, were "true workers."

With his respect came a newfound curiosity. Our quick lunches got longer as his questions multiplied. At first they all had to do with the technical side of my job. Was it not remarkable, he wondered, that we both had ended up working with type? A typesetter and a typist, working side by side. During these talks we discovered many shared qualities in our trades, and we discussed how they shaped our perception of the world. I told him, for instance, how I had come to experience time differently. The word I was typing was always in the past while the word I was thinking of was always in the future, which left the present oddly uninhabited. He could relate to this: as he fed one piece of type into the composing stick, he was spotting the nick and face of the next one. "Now" did not seem to exist. He also told me the biggest influence of his work in his life had been that it had taught him to see the world backward. This was the main thing typesetters and revolutionaries had in common: they knew the matrix of the world was reversed, and even if reality was inverted, they could make sense of it at first glance.

Soon these rather abstract or general conversations became more specific. My father wanted to know more about the particulars of my job. Since I did not want to lie, I tried to avoid direct answers and filled my vague accounts with irrelevant details to make them seem more substantial than they actually were. Yet he insisted and demanded more clarity—not out of some sort of inquisitorial impulse, but because he was genuinely interested. There was a sincere intensity to his curiosity he had never shown before. And it pained me to be unable to have a true conversation with him. As my father realized I was hiding something, the warmth and camaraderie began to wane. He started to barricade himself behind his hostile silence again.

One evening I made us a proper dinner and, for once, set the table. Although he was pleasantly surprised and grateful, he made sure to express, in his stony way, that this would not be enough to win him over. Halfway into our quiet meal I put my cutlery down, took a deep breath and apologized. I had not been forthcoming with him. Part of me was scared of how he would react to the truth, I said. And that was not all. They had made me sign papers that swore me to secrecy. But how could I not trust my own father? Then I proceeded to tell an elaborate lie, involving my top-secret transcripts of board meetings where complex business maneuvers and conspiratorial takeovers with Washington's complicity were discussed. I used many financial terms

I had just learned from Bevel, unsure of their meaning but certain my father would be even more unfamiliar with those words.

He was riveted.

Even if I told myself that I was protecting us both with these stories, I felt like a traitor. Instead of being loyal to my father, I had sided with one of his sworn enemies.

III

The chief librarian brings me three gray archival boxes containing file folders that, in turn, contain papers, documents and, in some cases, little parcels wrapped in brown paper tied with twine that contain fragile notepads and notebooks that sometimes contain loose sheets and even slim journals or calendars wedged between their pages.

It becomes clear, going through these materials, that no one has read them since they were stored away. When I untie the parcels, the string leaves a pale cross on the wrapping. Moving a newspaper clipping slipped inside a notebook reveals a decades-long discoloration underneath it. A ribbon marker, untouched for years, has made a slight depression on the paper. Some pages stick to each other. Some spines crack. Some brittle edges and corners crumble onto the desk.

I am the first to touch many of these documents since Mildred Bevel *handled them. This makes me experience a closeness with her that the in-surmountable distance between us paradoxically accentuates.*

Her earliest files are dated 1920, the year of Mildred and Andrew's wedding. Nothing from her previous life. Perhaps she and her mother were unable to bring more than their indispensable belongings from Europe; perhaps she wanted to start on a clean slate.

I take out the first engagement book with burgundy covers and marbled edges. "Pusey & Company, 123 West 42nd Street, Printers & Stationers. Fourteen Cylinder & Job Presses Always Busy." My father hated cylinder presses.

Over the course of this first year it seems that Mildred is trying to fill the pages in her book, even if she has few activities and barely goes out. The pages are gridded: a line for each day and a row for morning, lunch, after-noon and evening. She writes "at home" repeatedly. I can sense her boredom. Sometimes she has " fittings," but they, too, become " fittings at home."

As the librarians said, her handwriting is almost impenetrable. It helps to have only a few words repeated several times in this engagement book to teach myself how to read her script. Her "s" is just a diagonal line, barely distinguishable from her " f," her "l" and her "t," which are identical to one another. Her "n" is an inverted "v." I take note of this, knowing that longer texts will be harder to decipher. There is something runic about her hand.

In Bonds, *I suddenly remember, Vanner describes the journals Helen Rask kept day and night during her breakdown, wondering if her future self would recognize her own writing.*

Even though I hope to find the real version of those diaries in one of these boxes, most of the early documents are unremarkable. During the first months Mildred seems to make a few attempts at socializing. Some after-noons with a Mrs. Cutting, others with Mrs. Bartram, Mrs. Kimball or Mrs. Twichell—some of these names are just guesses and approximations. A few times she meets with small groups made up of these and other women.

Several "luncheons," some dentist appointments. But her efforts become more and more sporadic, and in the end Mildred seems to have simply given up on both visiting and receiving her new acquaintances. Barren calendars. Anemic address books. Still, because the latter are alphabetized, I find them helpful to learn Mildred's peculiar handwriting. I start keeping track of the variations of each letter. It is true that her writing is difficult to read. It is also true that after spending enough time with these words and looking at them in context, some can be deciphered. But no one seems to have spent any time at all with these documents. No one ever bothered.

Having known Andrew, I think how lonely and suffocated with boredom Mildred must have felt. At the same time I admire her resolute defiance. Surely all doors in New York were open to her. She could have seen anybody, gone anywhere. Artists, politicians, all the big names of the day. Parties, galas, dinners. I find something both heroic and intriguing in her refusal to yield to any of these obvious temptations. Somehow, her rejection does not feel disdainful. It does not seem to be the result of shyness or fear either.

Of course I am the one assigning Mildred these attributes. All I have is mostly empty notebooks, Bevel's account from fifty years ago and Vanner's novel.

A radical change takes place in early 1921, however. She starts attending concerts. Or at least she starts recording these outings. It is not always clear what the musical pieces are—sometimes she names both the composer and the performer; sometimes she simply writes "concert." Over the following months and the next year I notice a shift away from "opera" toward "recital." There is an "87" next to some of these recitals, which must indicate that those events are hosted here, in her home.

The formerly empty rows and columns in her engagement books become peppered (never saturated) with names. Although many weeks remain blank, she now seems to have something of a social life. But her acquain-

tances are not, for the most part, New York society ladies. She receives several men (sometimes only men), many of whom are among the most prominent musicians of the day. I am merely an enthusiast with no formal musical education, but even I recognize a few names mentioned over the years. The conductor Bruno Walter comes by with some frequency. So do violinists Fritz Kreisler and Jascha Heifetz. Pianists Artur Schnabel and Moriz Rosenthal. Composers Ernest Bloch, Igor Stravinsky, Amy Beach, Mary Howe, Raimund Mandl, Ottorino Respighi and Ruth Crawford are among the names I can make out. Possibly even Charles Ives. Later, in a 1928 engagement calendar, if I am not misreading, I spot Maurice Ravel.

If all these names are striking, there is something even more remarkable here. In the fall of 1923 I find, in unambiguous and enthusiastic block letters, "LEAGUE OF COMPOSERS—FOUNDED—$10,000." This is the first time a sum of money appears attached to a cultural institution in Mildred's papers.

I get up, walk over to the cabinet by the librarians' desk and go through the cards. The library holds a twenty-eight-page-long pamphlet titled The League of Composers: A Record of Performances and a Survey of General Activities from 1923 to 1935. *I request this document, which arrives a few minutes later.*

Reading the introduction to the slim report, I learn that this is the first organization in the United States dedicated exclusively to contemporary music. In 1935, twelve years after its foundation, the board is saturated with such luminaries as Aaron Copland, Sergei Prokofiev, Marion Bauer, Béla Bartók, Martha Graham, Leopold Stokowski and Arthur Honegger, among many others. Out of the twenty-seven members of the Auxiliary Board twenty are women. In Mildred's lifetime—and presumably with her financial support—the League commissioned, sponsored and premiered pieces by Schönberg, Stravinsky, Webern, Ravel, Krenek, Berg, Shostakovich and Bartók, to name just a few. Still, despite the profusion of European com-

posers, the League regarded "as especially important its work in introducing fresh American talent, chiefly by means of less formal recitals." Mildred's home must have been the venue for many of these concerts, which were probably not unlike those described by Vanner in his novel. These had to be the "untraditional" performances that "barely sounded like music" that Andrew Bevel asked me to edit out of his memoirs.

In Bevel's autobiography sweet, sickly, sensitive Mildred just loved pretty melodies. Like a child with a music box. From his descriptions one could almost see her nodding along with a half smile and closed eyes, keeping time, slightly offbeat, with her hands on her blanketed lap. In her husband's condescending characterization Mildred was an endearing dilettante who enjoyed music as other women enjoy crocheting or collecting brooches. I feel renewed shame for having helped him create this image of her.

Nothing like that innocent, childlike and patronizingly "feminine" picture emerges from these engagement books and calendars. According to these documents, a year after her wedding Mildred comes out of her isolation to start spending time with some of the foremost composers, performers and conductors of the twentieth century. Even if Andrew cared nothing for music, even if he actively disliked it, would this not be worthy of mention? Who would omit the fact that his wife was in the habit of hosting musicians ranging from Pau Casals to Edgard Varèse? Why present her as a dabbling little girl?

Mildred seems to have been eager to keep herself out of the press. I find only a few clippings where she is mentioned, in passing, as a benefactor or an attendee at some function, her name among others. Her passion and her contributions were private matters. I suppose people in her circle—society people—must have known about her cultural life, and I can't help but think this is one of the reasons Bevel chose me, a Brooklyn girl, for the job.

By 1925 Mildred's handwriting has deteriorated further. Her traces often can resemble a series of scratches. Some pages are too daunting to even try. It *is frustrating that her words should become more and more impenetrable just as she starts showing signs of interest in politics and current affairs.*

I open an undated scrapbook with newspaper clippings. Dense annotations and marginalia surround many of the excerpts.

"To Test Radioscope Across Atlantic: Germans Will Try Sending Script and Photographs by Air Instantaneously"; "Bond Issue Called Unsound: Smith's $100,000,000 Plan a 'Pork Barrel' to Be Spent All Over the State, He Says"; "$2,000,000 in Gold Here From Japan: Shipment Makes $9,000,000 Exported Since September to Protect Exchange"; "New Low in Coarse Grains: Corn and Oats Are Selling Below 1924–25 Figures"; "New Electric Bulb Cuts Lamp Costs: Manufacturers Agree on Standard Which Will Reduce the 45 Designs to 5."

I spend a good while going through these pages. Just like Mildred's musical activities these clippings do not fit Andrew's homey, childlike description of his wife. That incarnation of Mrs. Bevel is incompatible with someone who engages in political commentary (even if in private) or has an interest, however fleeting, in current events. And this scrapbook also feels out of place in Vanner's version of Mildred. Helen Rask, the quiet aesthete, would never dissect and gloss the news. And precisely because the image of her that comes forward in this scrapbook differs so drastically from the portrait offered by those two men, I feel this is my first glimpse of the real Mildred Bevel.

Once done with the first box, I decide to take a break from Mildred's runes and request the last of Andrew Bevel's files from the year 1938.

There is not much to see, probably because his office secretaries kept most of his records. After all, this is a collection of personal papers, and Andrew Bevel barely had a personal life. Calendars, address books, lists of gifts— items include candlesticks, billiard tables (for three different people), cuff links (for two) and a fishing rod.

The fourth file folder I take out makes the room recede.

Here is my Royal portable's distinctive "e," with its over-inked, blacked-out eye.

Here is my often undotted "i."

Here are my discreet dogears.

Here is the system of editing symbols I devised back then and still use.

Here are my tidy notes, more school-like than professional.

Here, more vivid than in any picture, at twenty-three years old, I am.

One by one I go through the pages. They are drafts of Bevel's autobiography, and there are several of his notes to my text. His comments are mostly wordless: he strikes through this line, crosses out that paragraph, moves a circled passage to the top or the bottom of the page with an abrupt arrow. Scattered all over the pages are several asterisks indicating sections to be discussed in person so that he could point out inaccuracies, correct the tone or address other issues that were too long for him to put in writing.

I pause on a passage that describes how his great-grandfather started his business:

> *William acquired a sizable loan against his father's property and then borrowed more upon that sum. He went deep into debt with the intention of buying from those who, like his parents, were unable to sell their goods. But rather than tobacco, which he would have been unable to store properly, he purchased non-perishable goods, especially cotton from farther south and sugar from the newly acquired Louisiana.*

I think of my father. He would always say that every dollar bill had been printed on paper ripped off a slave's bill of sale. I can still hear him today. "Where does all this wealth here come from? Primitive accumulation. The original theft of land, means of production and human lives. All throughout history, the origin of capital has been slavery. Look at this country and the modern world. Without slaves, no cotton; without cotton, no industry; without industry, no finance capital. The original, unnamable sin." I keep reading through the draft. Of course, not a single mention of slavery.

Yes, at the time my father and I needed the money; yes, Bevel was imposing and I was young. But none of this gives me any comfort.

I reach the section on Mildred. After having gone through her papers and getting a sense of who she truly might have been, I cringe at the trivial scenes I made up for her. I am shocked to see the extent to which Andrew pushed his wife out of his autobiography—and ashamed of my complicity. There are several segments, perfectly harmless to my mind, that he has briskly edited out. From what I have learned going through her papers today, these passages presented an extremely watered-down version of Mildred. And yet, after her death, her husband thought her presence should be reduced even more. Bevel's decision to write an autobiography was moved, to a large extent, by his desire to clear his wife's name and show that she was not the mentally ill recluse in Vanner's novel. But reading these pages, it seems that more than vindicating Mildred he wanted to turn her into a completely unremarkable, safe character—just like the wives in the autobiographies of the Great Men I read during that time to come up with Bevel's voice. Put her in her place.

Perhaps this is what Harold Vanner tried to do in his way as well. Why present that broken image of Mildred in his novel? This is a question I have asked myself again and again since first reading Bonds. *Why make her mad when she was obviously so lucid? Over the years I considered different answers—jealousy, vengeance, sheer malice—but in the absence of details about Vanner's life I always came back to the same conclusion: he broke her mind and her body simply because it made for a better story (a story he could not resist telling, even if it debased her and, in the end, destroyed him). He forced her into the stereotype of fated heroines throughout history, made to offer the spectacle of their own ruin. Put her in her place.*

The next box they bring me contains financial records of Mildred's char-

ities. *Just as the passion for music that is so palpable in her engagement books contradicts the amateurish and decidedly middlebrow picture Andrew painted of her, so these papers challenge the notion of Mildred as a passive or reckless philanthropist. Here is someone who not only knows exactly to whom the gifts are allocated but also uses her contributions to shape the institutions she supports. All her endowments seem to be tightly restricted, and Mildred specifies in each case how the dividends from the principal she donated should be expended.*

It is all written in purple ink. She uses an accounting system I am not fully able to figure out, partially because her handwriting is so hard to read (and my knowledge of bookkeeping is limited to what I taught myself fifty years ago) but mostly because Mildred's methods are highly idiosyncratic. These are not regular balance sheets. Her approach reminds me of my editing symbols, which no one understands except for me. Both of us, it seems, had to create our tools and systems to tackle jobs for which we received no formal education.

In addition to Mildred's donations that Bevel told me about (predictably, to the opera and some other high-profile orchestras and cultural institutions) she sponsors scholarships for students in the arts and sciences, expands a library or creates a series of grants. As time goes by, she becomes emboldened and has more funds at her command. She no longer supports libraries but builds them. From the dates on her sheets and some letters it seems clear that the birth of the Albany Symphony Orchestra must have been the direct result of her gifts.

By 1926 most contributions seem to be funneled through the Mildred Bevel Charitable Fund. This may explain why her personal financial records wane around this time. I remember Andrew telling me he had created the Fund for her. He made it sound like a gift. In his narrative its purpose was to provide Mildred's impulsive and chaotic donations with a method. He claimed to have endowed and managed the Fund and used it to rein in his wife's charitable splurges. These documents reveal the exact opposite—Mildred comes off as a thoughtful, disciplined philanthropist.

When I get to the correspondence, I realize that it makes up the bulk of Mildred's archive: sixteen binders containing letters addressed to Mrs. Bevel. Not a single one penned by her. I open envelopes more or less at random and inspect the contents. They are, for the most part, thank-you letters. Musicians from all over the country thanking her for pianos, violoncellos and violins; conductors from small towns thanking her for the instruments and funding for their orchestras; mayors and congressmen thanking her for a library branch; a letter from Governor Al Smith thanking her for the wing for the humanities at the State University of New York at Troy.

There is a shift in content in some letters after the 1929 crash. In addition to all her cultural patronage it is clear that she has been involved in helping those who lost everything during the crisis. Her emphasis is now on housing and on loans to businesses. The owners of factories, stores and farms write to let her know how much the aid received has done for them and their communities. But these letters are outnumbered by a renewed outpour of gratitude from the same kind of beneficiaries she favored in the past—libraries, musical institutions, universities.

There are only a few boxes left. My hope to find anything resembling the diaries Vanner mentions in his novel wanes. Bevel claimed they never existed, and if they ever did, they must have been destroyed or purged from this collection. But it could simply be true that Mildred never kept a journal—that this habit was just part of her fictional incarnation.

Several pages have been torn out of many calendars and notebooks. Concerts (fewer). Short, indecipherable formulas or computations. Small dinner parties at home. I am quite sure I spot Harold Vanner's name in three of these guest lists.

2

I da."

A young man in a pinstripe suit but, oddly, wearing neither tie nor hat was waiting for me outside my apartment.

"Who are you?"

"Let's talk inside."

"Who are you?"

"Open the door, and let's talk in the hall. You don't want Bevel's men to see you with me."

I looked around. Only a few familiar faces down the block. I refused to open the door, but we spoke hidden in the small niche of the recessed entrance to my building. I held the key sticking out between my knuckles like a dagger.

"My father and my boyfriend are upstairs. If you get any closer, I'll scream."

"So dramatic." He leaned against the wall and put his hands in his pockets to show he had no intention of touching me. "I'll keep it short. Here's what I know. I know you're Andrew Bevel's secretary. I know you go to his house several times a week, always in the afternoon, and stay well into the evening. Sometimes late. I know you're alone with him in his office. I know he tells you about his life. I know you take notes." He paused to see how his words had affected me; I gave him a blank stare. "That's what I know. And here's what I want. I want a copy of everything you write. The real thing. As you see, we have plenty of information about you. And we'll know if you're bluffing."

"Get lost."

"In a second. Here's the deal: you give me what I want, and I won't tell the FBI about your father's communist press, his political agitation and his anti-American activities. Hell, for all I know you could be spying on Bevel for him. It'd be a shame to see him deported."

"Who are you?"

"There's a soda fountain on Metropolitan and Union. If you're not there Wednesday at 1:30 with my pages, I'll talk to my buddy at the FBI. *Capisce*, Miss Partenza?"

He left.

My knees were quaking. A suffocating void in my lungs. I stared at the key sticking out of my fist. Underneath the fear, bottomless exhaustion. I collected myself and went up to my father.

3

S trike that. Tell Bevel the truth. That was the best option. An unknown man wanted information about him. I had been intimidated. Threatened. But what if Bevel thought, not unreasonably, that I had already given something away? How could I prove to him that I had not betrayed his confidence? Come to think of it, I did not really know any sensitive secrets about him. Come to think of it, our conversations had been rather banal—we had only discussed his life in broad strokes, talked vaguely about some of his business transactions, and he had shared, even more vaguely, some superficial stories about his wife. That was all. But that was hardly the point. I had signed those papers Bevel had given me. I knew what he did to those who invaded his privacy. My father and I would be crushed and erased.

"Am I boring you?"

"I'm so sorry, sir. Could you please repeat the last sentence?"

"No."

"I'm so sorry."

Strike that. I was so tired of saying I was sorry.

"Because we are meeting here, at my house, at this hour, and we are having tea, you may be under the impression that this is my leisure time. I have no leisure time."

I looked down at the carpet, retracing the maze-like pattern on it with my eyes.

"It won't happen again."

"My role needs to be made clear to the average reader. There probably wouldn't even have been a Coolidge Market without me. The president himself said so. Strike that. I plugged holes, propped things up and protected the investing public from gamblers for as long as I possibly could. The result was the most phenomenal bull market in history. The greatest boost to American industry and American business ever. Anyone looking at the economy with attention after the 1920 recession and up to 1927 can see my hand there. How I made some key stocks rise in order to make the whole market ascend in sympathy. Take the case of U.S. Steel, Baldwin, Fisher and Studebaker in 1922. That was the beginning of the prosperity market. Right there. And it was me. Me. Of course even *that* was perceived as a conspiracy. Alexander Dana Noyes or one of his minions at the *Times* called it a 'mystery move' instead of simply crediting me with it. Strike that."

Andrew Bevel would not hesitate. My father and I would be crushed and erased. He might even think that the whole blackmail scheme had all been my idea—that I had made up the story about this tieless man in the formal pinstripe suit in order to extort him, Bevel, for my benefit. Yes, that was most likely what he would think. That it was all me.

"As I've said, that was the beginning. But what we really ought to look at is 1926. When, in the history of world finance, has there ever been a success like mine in 1926? When? Unsurprisingly, there were accusations of fraud, which is the only way simpleminded journalists could account for my accomplishments, the only way those would-be novelists could explain away my unprecedented achievements. That's good, but strike it. Need I say my operations that year involved market-wide transactions? How could any swindle encompass such a vast array of securities? The sole idea that anyone could sway or penetrate every company trading on the New York Stock Exchange is laughable. I lifted the whole nation with me. And instead of thanking me, the press vilified me. I encouraged and very much drove the prosperity of those years. So I don't want to hear any birdbrained ideas about a conspiratorial consortium of bears. As if I had the time and the desire to confer with others. Strike that."

But it could also be a test. Maybe it was Bevel who had sent the tieless man to see how easily I would break. A test. To see how I would handle things. To see how loyal and self-sufficient I was. If this was the case, what was the right response? Perhaps the best would be not reporting anything at all. Perhaps he wanted me to fend for myself. Solve this on my own. Strike that. The tieless man could be more powerful than I first thought. Perhaps he represented a rival financier. Perhaps he was with the government. Perhaps he had mentioned a fictitious friend with connections as a decoy to hide the fact that he himself was the one with the FBI.

"People blame me for having cleared my decks before October 1929. Is it my fault if I saw the writing on the wall? Look, I predicted that deflation had hit bottom in 1921 and that we could expect a rebound in prices. And I was right. Nobody seemed to have detected any conspiracy there. Why? Simply because they liked my prediction. Then I anticipated the prosperity panic two years later and was right again. But in '29 I was a bogeyman, the very instigator of the events predicted. Why? Simply because they didn't like what they heard. So they decide I headed some sort of unscrupulous bear pool. Strike that."

What did I have to give? Bevel's bluster. Transactions covered by the press years ago. His hazy, incoherent stories about a wife he did not seem to know at all. And this would become public soon enough anyway. It would all be in Bevel's book. So much of it a fiction. Bevel had asked me to make up a voice for him. He had asked me to fill in several blanks about his wife with stories of my own invention. Why then not feed the tieless man another fiction, just as I had done when my father had pushed me for details about my job? Yes, that was the solution. I had created a fictional Bevel for the real Bevel; I had created a fictional Bevel for my father; I could easily create yet another fictional Bevel for my extortionist.

"My actions allowed a multitude of American businesses, manufacturers and corporations to increase their stock issues and capitalize themselves. Take United States Steel. They exchanged bonds for common stocks, thus completely doing away with their indebtedness. That was a direct effect of my actions. This is my record. This is what I've done. This is the background against which we need to look at the 1929 debacle. If I was forced to take a short position in the market, it was not only to preserve myself but also to preserve our nation's financial health, under attack from both speculating mobs and government regulators. But we'll leave that for next time. I expect to find you in better form then."

"I'm so sorry."

4

Transcribe and rework Bevel's words. Make up a life for Mildred. Compose a fiction for the tieless man. I told myself it was work that kept me sequestered at home for the next few days. But it was fear. I moved the desk away from the window and into a corner, and there, huddled over my typewriter, I labored over these stories.

Toward the end of that secluded week I realized that writing a completely made-up tale for the extortionist served as a major inspiration for the other story I was developing for Bevel. These narratives informed and fed one another. What was a dead end here proved to be an open avenue there. Having to fully make up the events in the report for the tieless man, I was able to borrow from those pages to fill in certain gaps that had been major obstacles in Bevel's autobiography or Mildred's portrait. Likewise, what proved unviable in the memoir went into the pages for the blackmailer. Passages I had written and liked but whose style did not fit in with the rest; long-winded technical expositions that Bevel had cut out; small side-scenes I had composed and he had disliked—all these paragraphs and pages were distorted and made harmless and, I hoped, untraceable before being woven into the narrative for the extortionist.

Writing all these texts at once required more research. I could tell already that my strokes were too broad and that the stories lacked those little details (a mundane object, a specific place) and verbal trinkets (a brand name, a mannerism) often used to bribe readers into believing that what they are reading is true. Reluctantly I faced the fact that I would have to leave my apartment and return to the New York Public Library's main branch. With my underused makeup kit I drew in heavy eyebrows, ruddied my cheeks and tried to add a little age to my face. I also covered my head with a scarf tied under my chin and put on my father's baggy raincoat, which helped make me look older and smaller. None of this made the subway ride into Manhattan less excruciating. From all my mystery novels I knew that the worst thing to do when one suspects one is being followed is to turn around. Even without the scarf and the trench coat I would still have been soaked in sweat.

Once again, my complete lack of method served me well. I drew from Woodrow Wilson's speeches, Roger Babson's bizarre treatise on prosperity, William Zachary Irving's *Autobiography*, Herbert Hoover's *American Individualism*, Henry Adams's *Education* (perhaps the only of the books by Great Men I enjoyed) and a number of volumes on the history of finance. Of these, the most influential was *Mystery Men of Wall Street* by Earl Sparling. Having grown up on detective fiction, I found the title immediately appealing. It was a collection of portraits of financiers, written in 1929. Jesse Livermore, William Durant, the

310

Fisher brothers, Arthur Cutten, Andrew Bevel . . . They were all in there. I found answers to many questions in those pages and drew freely from them whenever I had to describe some murky financial operation. I also looked up how Bevel and his transactions had been covered in *The Wall Street Journal*, *The New York Times*, *Barron's*, *Nation's Business* and other publications.

For the details to flesh out the personal side of Bevel's story for the blackmailer, it seemed to make sense to rely on fiction. Again, I wrote down a number of titles, which I later would check out from the Brooklyn Public Library. I tried to read Theodore Dreiser's *Trilogy of Desire* but only made it through *The Financier* and half of *The Titan*. Nathan Morrow's ill-fated bankers and brokers and his descriptions of the spending orgies of the twenties found their way into my pages. From Upton Sinclair's *The Moneychangers* I learned to draw Bevel in stark villainous lines, and I also found inspiration for the luxuries that I sprinkled all over the pages for my extortionist—yachts, palatial offices, mansions.

Because these novels were slightly outdated, I turned to the press. Most issues of *Fortune*, *Forbes* and other similar magazines held at the New York Public Library featured lengthy profiles of financiers, industrialists and patrician families. In these articles on Morris Ledyard, the Goulds, Albert H. Wiggin, the Rockefellers, Solomon R. Guggenheim, the Rothschilds and James Speyer I found details of business transactions, descriptions of residencies, travel itineraries, reports on lavish parties and a wide array of habits, idiosyncrasies and pastimes that I gave the Bevels. I also quoted from the advertisements that made up the bulk of this and other similar magazines promoting luxury goods I had never heard of. Bevel was driven around town in a Maybach-Zeppelin with a twelve-cylinder aircraft-type engine, but he sped around at 110 miles per hour in a Super Sports Delage when he went to Glen Cove, where his three-hundred-foot transatlantic diesel yacht, recently brought in from the dry docks in Bath, was anchored. Sometimes he commuted on his Fokker airplane, fitted with a sitting room and a bar, while sipping on grand cru Bordeaux wines.

It was much harder to find books that could help with Mildred's story. After reading the review of Vanner's *Bonds* mentioning Edith Wharton, Amanda Gibbons and Constance Fenimore Woolson, I had immediately looked up their work. Still, because they preexisted Mildred by a generation or two, their New York sets or their cliques of American expats in Europe felt outdated. After consulting with librarians, I read, in a haphazard way, everything I thought could be inspiring, from Emily Post's *Etiquette* to Viña Delmar's *Bad Girl*. But my focus, if one could call my slapdash approach that, was on more or less contemporary American authors whose work might, perhaps, be pertinent. Among them I remember immensely disparate writers such as Dawn Powell, Ursula Parrott, Anita Loos, Elizabeth Harland, Dorothy Parker and Nancy Hale. Only a few of them turned out to be germane to my work—and none captured the atmosphere of subdued wealth I wanted for Mildred. Still, even if I can't say I liked them all, some of the authors discovered during this intense exploration became the foundation for my personal canon, as I have written in *Before Words*—although I never revealed in my book how I first came to know them.

Writing about Mildred (in any of these versions) was, by far, the most challenging aspect of my work. There was nothing I could rely on. If none of the books I read was of help, Bevel's ambiguous and intentionally vague depiction only deepened the void at the center of her portrait. It seemed certain that Mildred's role in the musical scene in New York had been more important than Bevel was willing to admit.

But nothing suggested she suffered from the severe mental issues that destroyed her alter ego, Helen Rask, in Vanner's novel.

There were two things I had to suppress from every sentence I wrote about her. First, the undeniable complexity of her character, which came through Bevel's obfuscations and his attempts at making her image more "accessible." Second, my conviction that I understood her plight—at least to some extent. Living with Bevel. The suffocation. The loneliness. Calculating every action and repressing every impulse.

Facing this dead end, I thought of Harold Vanner. I had loved so much about his rendition of Helen Rask, and perhaps I would be able to find inspiration in some of his other female characters.

If the fear I had felt when I left Brooklyn had dissipated after hours among books and magazines, it returned in a massive wave of terror when I went through the library cards in the cabinet looking for Vanner's work. I flipped back and forth the VAM-VAR drawer, always pausing in the same place and feeling my heart leap each time I confirmed the void:

Vann, William Harvey. *Notes on the Writings of James Howell.* 1924.
Vannereau, Maurice. *L'Ornière, pièce sociale en 1 acte.* 1926.

It was inconceivable that the New York Public Library would hold an obscure essay by an unknown critic and, also, an unheard-of short play by a thoroughly unnoted French writer but not one book by the author who should have fallen between these two names. No Vanner. Nothing. Not a single title. I asked a librarian. She told me everything they had was on those cards. But I knew it was simply impossible that one of the largest, most comprehensive collections in the world would not hold any of Harold Vanner's books. His early work had been some-what successful, and *Bonds* had been widely reviewed. There was only one explanation. Bevel, one of the Library's main donors, had bent and aligned reality.

Chaos is a vortex that spins faster with each thing it swallows. Work-ing ceaselessly for days, I had no time left to take care of the house. Dishes in the sink and towels on the floor, open tins and moldy back issues of *Cronaca Sovversiva*, crusts of bread and rotten apple cores, flies and centipedes, ink-stained rags and a clogged bathtub. None of this bothered my father in the least. He would clear the area he needed, wipe some utensils on his shirt, make a sandwich or work on some components of a page and move on, leaving everything behind. Those were blissful days for him. He was happy we were spending time together, working. His joy is the only good memory I have of that period.

Jack showed up one afternoon with apologies, explanations and de-mands. I let him speak and nodded along. Once he was done, I asked him to look around the apartment and, fighting back a surge of rage that would, I knew, lead to tears, asked him if he thought I had time for his needs. He truly did look around the apartment. And when I thought he was about to leave, he took off his shirt, put it in his satchel and started to clean up the kitchen in his undershirt. It was the last gift I expected from him, and I was touched. I told him he did not have to do anything, that it was fine—all those things one is expected to say.

"No, no. Come on, now," he said with sweet sternness. "You have work to do. Go. I'll take care of this."

I kissed him, barely recognizing this new version of Jack but over-whelmed with gratitude for it, and went back to my room through my father's workshop. He was wrestling with his press, trying to adjust some inaccessible piece. I told him Jack had just arrived, but he ignored me and cursed at the machine as he kept reaching for whatever part was giving him trouble.

A couple of hours later I had almost finished the fake pages. They sounded believable. I had included all the jargon that Bevel generally edited out of his autobiography (he always said he wanted to reach a wide audience, "the common man" or "the average reader") and distorted it into a convoluted yet plausible drivel that could in no way be traced back to any real financial operations. I thought my blackmailer would appreciate something he could not quite understand. All these technical disquisitions were woven into a more sweeping narrative of Bevel's life. This version complied with every expectation I thought most people, educated by films and novels, would have about a tycoon like Bevel. There were lush, detailed descriptions of his home and his possessions; there were foreign dignitaries and limousines; there were impromptu trips to Europe and Palm Beach; there were actresses and champagne, senators and caviar. For good measure I put in some of Gatsby's Marie Antoinette music rooms, Restoration salons, and sunken baths. And there was, of course, the right dose of ennui and moral discomfort about it all.

It was almost dinnertime, and I had barely had breakfast. It would be nice to get something special for sweet Jack and my father. A roasted chicken. Maybe even some wine. After rolling up my finished pages and stuffing them into my raincoat sleeve, I got ready to leave. My father was still at his press. On my way out, I paused in the kitchen. Jack had done a beautiful job and moved on to the bathroom, where he was kneeling on the tiled floor, struggling to unclog the bathtub. I kissed him on the head and told him I was getting dinner.

"I know this isn't the right time," he said, looking up timidly. "You being so busy and all. But . . . I was wondering if you could type out this article for me. I'm showing it to someone at *The Sun*. It would look so much better. No rush. I have the pages here, but if you can't . . ."

It was the first time Jack overtly asked me for help or acknowledged my abilities.

"Of course! Anything you need. It shouldn't take too long."

"Thank you. It'll look so much better," he said again. "I'll leave the pages on your desk."

I went from store to store, reviewing the false autobiography in my head. Some details might be compromising and had to be deleted; a few of my mannerisms were recognizable and needed to be changed; a discarded passage was, on second thought, effective and should probably be restored. I hurried back home before I forgot my edits.

Jack was still working on the tub; my father was still muttering curses at his press. I left the shopping bags on the counter and went to my room to write down my notes. An envelope with Jack's article sat on my desk. I left it unopened and went back to the version for the extortionist. I corrected a few sentences and crossed out a paragraph or two. The discarded passage I wanted to bring back should have been in one of the balls of crumpled paper closest to the surface in my trash can. I took one ball and straightened it out. Blank. Another. Blank. Another. Blank. Most of my discarded pages were gone, replaced with blank paper.

Terrified and heartbroken, I pretended to enjoy dinner. It took everything I had to keep my eyes from constantly drifting toward Jack's satchel.

5

My only comfort after discovering the theft of the discarded papers was that they were all part of the fiction I was composing for my blackmailer. Nothing in those pages could compromise Andrew Bevel or lead back to me. The relief brought by this realization outweighed the anger and sadness I felt thinking of Jack. Again I was disheartened to discover that I cared more about Bevel—his rules, his standards, his threats—than my friends and family. The pain of having been betrayed by someone so close to me seemed irrelevant compared with the consequences of a breach of confidentiality. And what made it all doubly dispiriting is that it was true: suffering the loss of a friend was nothing next to facing Bevel's wrath. Such was the extent of his power. His fortune bent reality around it. This reality included people—and their perception of the world, like mine, was also caught in the gravitational pull of Bevel's wealth and warped by it.

Since my first meeting with him I had sensed that I had to push against this force. This was not out of rebelliousness. Rather, I intuited and soon confirmed that his esteem for me depended to a large degree on how effectively I managed to resist his enormous influence. We both seemed to enjoy (although this word is, no doubt, excessive) our meetings the most when I was able to overcome my fears, show some nerve and even stand up to him regarding some trivial matter. Pluck was as important as elegance, of course. He would not suffer rudeness, but acts of mild, ambiguous insolence amused him or, at least, awakened his curiosity. It was, paradoxically, on these occasions that his stiff demeanor, which I came to see as proof of a deep-seated fear of ridicule, seemed to thaw ever so slightly. And it was in these moments that I managed to steer our sessions into a more productive course.

I was determined to regain the respect lost during our last encounter. With my discovery of Jack's betrayal and my upcoming meeting with the tieless man, it was crucial to have Andrew Bevel on my side and to know how he would react to the potential publication of the stolen papers.

"I must say I'm quite pleased with your depiction of Mrs. Bevel," he said after looking at my new pages. "Quite pleased indeed." He went back to the beginning and skimmed them again. "You'll receive my notes, as usual." He paused. "Come to think of it, perhaps we should expand on some sort of pastime that would have been suitable for Mildred." He put his index finger to his lips and looked around the room until he saw a floral arrangement on a side table by a window. "Flowers. Her love of flowers. How she would match them up, make displays and so forth. A nice little scene. Speak with Miss Clifford, the housekeeper, before you leave. She'll let you know what kind of bouquets you should describe. Maybe show you the greenhouse."

I never looked up from my notepad, pretending to be absorbed in my notetaking. This was not the time to show my bewilderment.

"You have, through the power of your imagination and . . . feminine sympathy, managed to capture much of Mildred's private life. And Mildred being a private person, that means *most* of her life."

"Thank you. Precisely to make the details of Mrs. Bevel's private life richer, I was thinking that perhaps today you and I could walk around the house as we talk. I barely know it, and a tour with you as a guide would be priceless. We could include the occasional description of a room or a painting . . . A more vivid backdrop for your personal life. And Mrs. Bevel's. The average reader loves to peek into these grand houses, you know?"

I had managed to make him slightly uncomfortable—my suggestion was plainly a good one, but it also went against Bevel's fixation with privacy. And uncomfortable was exactly what I had hoped for.

"Why, yes. By all means." He tried to conceal his hesitation underneath his manners. That he thought he had to be polite to me was a great, unexpected triumph.

"Please remember I don't want an ostentatious description of the place," he said before we set out. "It's in bad taste."

He led us back down to the marble-floored foyer so that I could experience "the progression of the house." We passed a few staff members. Some were cleaning; others whisked by in three-piece suits. Regardless of their rank, they all looked away from us. It seemed as if they had been instructed to simply go about their business and ignore Bevel.

First he showed me his paintings. He paused briefly in front of each one of them, pointed at the plaque on the gilded frame, stated the artist's name and moved on: Corot, Turner, Ingres, Holbein, Bellini,

Fragonard, Veronese, Boucher, van Dyck, Gainsborough, Rembrandt. I took notes.

We reached a windowed corridor looking out onto a greenhouse.

"I'll leave this to Miss Clifford, when you see her about the flowers. I don't know the first thing about plants," he said as we walked alongside the greenhouse. "Here, in the back, is where I spend every afternoon."

He opened a door to reveal a large office with a few smaller workspaces adjacent to it. The walls in all the rooms were covered with blackboards saturated with stock quotes and mathematical formulas, and at the desks about a dozen men behind counting machines waded through binders, books, documents and reams of paper. There was a quieter mood here than at the downtown headquarters of Bevel Investments. It almost felt like a library.

"After the market closes, work starts here. In fact I like to think this is the real work. The conclusions reached here inform my trading, daily operations and long-term plans. The rest, what happens on the floor, is the mere execution of decisions made in this room. All these men you see are statisticians and mathematicians. Recruited from universities from all over the country. A veritable brain pool. They study stock records and industrial records, predict future trends from past tendencies, detect patterns in mob psychology, design models to operate more systematically. Reports, statements and prospects from every corporation or concern that is or could come under my purview are evaluated here."

He looked into my eyes until I had to turn away. I still remember his blue stare. He was either trying to extract something through my pupils or trying to place something inside me through them.

"You see, intuition has served me well throughout my career, and I owe a great part of my reputation to it. Adding science and the objective interpretation of great volumes of data to my intuition is the source of my edge. This unique combination is what has always allowed me to stay ahead of the ticker." He paused, surveyed his men and looked at his watch. "We usually go until nine o'clock."

"Did these men work here when Mrs. Bevel . . . ?" I was unable to finish my tactless question.

"Of course not."

We left the offices, and Bevel guided me through the uninhabited ground floor. He made a ceremonious pause in a parlor with mounted heads of elk and bison, a stuffed bear, the hide of a mountain lion, roaring head and all, and other hunting trophies. Presiding over these prizes were two oil portraits of a brawny, rugged man who somehow seemed to be making a great effort to hide that he was happy. The painting on the left showed him in full hunting garb, holding a rifle and a bunch of limp pheasants. In the picture on the right he was in business attire, pen in hand, looking up from a document.

"As you know, I'm very pleased with the passages about my ancestors," Bevel said before leaving the room. "Now you can probably describe Father's face. Not a bad idea this stroll around the house, after all. Come to think of it, to really understand the family history you must visit La Fiesolana. That's where our spirit resides. I'll make the arrangements."

"Thank you. That would be immensely helpful."

He never made the arrangements.

Galleries, a morning room, halls, a small library, studies, dining rooms, a den. He was unusually quiet, and his brisk step suggested he wanted to be done with the tour.

"Many of our paintings are on loan at different museums at the moment," he said, nodding toward a bare wall. "It was Mrs. Bevel's wish that they be enjoyed by the public."

"Have you made other changes to the house recently?"

"Aside from the downstairs offices and the art on loan, naturally, everything remains untouched. In Mildred's memory."

We walked up to the second floor. Ballroom, more galleries, bedrooms. There was a music room, but it was simply a large parlor with a piano and a harp—nothing like the private concert hall in Vanner's novel. The library, with its sumptuous volumes shelved at inaccessible heights, was made for someone who did not care for books. And I was still unable to detect Mrs. Bevel's homey touch. Perhaps Andrew Bevel mistook the docility he attributed to her for warmth.

Bevel paused in front of a door on the park side of a corridor.

"These were Mildred's rooms," he said solemnly.

We stared at the threshold as if we were standing at her grave. After a suitable pause it seemed the right time to be bold and carefully impertinent again.

"It would be of great help to see how she lived. I would find so much inspiration among her things. Pick up little details, small everyday things that would make the story livelier. More believable."

"You may look at the entire house, but this one door shall remain closed."

"I'm so sorry. I just . . ."

"No need to apologize. I understand how you would be curious. But there are things I would like to keep to myself."

Bevel led me on through the house in silence.

"During one of our first meetings you shared some early memories of your mother," I said at last. "You mentioned that what she and Mildred had in common, in addition to their loving nature, was their intelligence. They were both very bright women, you said."

He stopped and looked at me. His eyes stirred with what I thought was irritation. But I did not feel his vexation was directed at me this time. He walked on; I caught up.

"How would you say Mildred's intelligence manifested itself?"

"Oh, you know. In a myriad of little details. It's not easy to run a house like this, with all this staff and such. And her taste in music, of course. But we've discussed that already and covered everything that could be of use for the book. Also, to be honest, it takes someone quite gifted to keep up with me." He laughed through his nostrils. "Not easy. Not easy at all to keep up with me. Perhaps include this in the book? In a moderately humorous fashion. And by the way, you're not doing so poorly yourself, you know."

I felt my cheeks redden as my need to prod and corner Bevel vanished.

We reached the third and last story. The entire backside was the servants' quarters; the front, facing the park, was for guests.

"A number of people, many of them of great renown, have stayed up here over the years. Perhaps we should list a few names in the book. I expect readers like to hear of such things. Still, truth be told, neither Mildred nor I enjoyed having guests over for a long time. The more people partake in your everyday life, the more entitled they feel to spread stories about you. I've always found this baffling. You'd think closeness would engender trust."

"Are you saying even your friends spread rumors about you and your wife?"

"*Mainly* my friends. That's what they think friendship means: the freedom to turn you into a topic of conversation."

This was my chance to find out how he would react if the stolen papers with the fictional account of his life ever were published.

"Do you treat all this gossip and hearsay with the same force with which you're handling Vanner and his novel?"

"Dear, no. I wouldn't be able to tend to my business if I had to respond to every idiocy published in every afternoon rag. It takes too much time to keep track of all the rumors and deny them. But Vanner is different. What he wrote about my wife and me is different. And his reach is different. But I would be grateful if you avoided uttering his name from this time forth."

The tour was over. Bevel went back to his downstairs offices, and I was escorted out. Nothing about the stolen papers worried me anymore. After all, I could keep up with Bevel.

6

I arrived at the soda fountain early so I could pick a safe spot, something in plain sight and close to the door. As soon as I walked in,
however, I saw the tieless man in the same pinstripe suit. He was
sitting at the most secluded table in the place, having a sundae. The
room was mostly empty, but I was encouraged by the sight of some
children drinking milkshakes at the counter. Nothing too bad could
happen around children drinking milkshakes. I made it over to the
tieless man and sat across the table from him.

"My pages better be in there," he said, pointing at my purse with his
long-handled spoon.

"How do I know this will be it? How do I know you'll leave me
alone after this?"

"Well, sweetheart." His diction was muddled by a spoonful of ice
cream he rolled around his tongue. "You'll just have to trust me."

Suddenly, looking at him enjoying his sundae at a soda fountain, it dawned on me. Now that I saw him in his natural element, I realized this was not a conspirator working for an unscrupulous newspaper, the government or any other higher power. This was just a Brooklyn kid. Having ice cream in his only good suit.

"Tell you what." I reached into my purse. "Here's ten bucks."

He stopped eating and froze at the sight of the money.

"I know who sent you here," I said. "Say his name, and the ten dollars are yours. Otherwise, I'll just walk. And there's nothing you can do about it."

"Listen, Miss Partenza, we know about your commie father. If you don't . . ."

I got up and took a few steps.

"Jack," he said.

I stopped. What I experienced at that moment remains, to this day, the standard by which I measure hatred. I went back and stood by the table, looking down at him.

"How did he find out about Bevel?"

"What about those ten bucks?"

I gave him the money.

"He followed you. Didn't like the idea of you alone with some guy at his house, so he tailed you. Just to see who it was. It wasn't too hard to figure out who owns that mansion. Then, at your place, he happened to read a bit of the thing you were typing for Bevel. Looked like he was writing the story of his life. Jack figured he'd sell it to a paper. Highest bidder. Get a big job with that big scoop." He pointed at his ice cream and laughed like an idiot.

"Tell Jack that Bevel is on to him. He just sent me here to confirm it. Tell Jack he better forget about publishing the pages he stole from me. Tell him Bevel knows everything and he's coming after him. He'll destroy him. I've seen him do it to others. Tell him he should leave town. Right now."

7

F
ollowing the instructions Bevel had given me during our last meeting, I had made an appointment with Miss Clifford so she could show me the flowers in the greenhouse.

When I met her in the staff's reception area, she offered me a cup of tea, which I declined and was given anyway, just like my first day there. After a bit of small talk I asked her about her job, unsure of what a housekeeper's duties in a house like that might be. She explained that most of the staff was under her supervision and that her main responsibility was to ensure that everything in the house happened "naturally." I asked if she also oversaw the butler. No. She gave me a look implying we had the same opinion of the man but that she would not discuss it. Elegantly she changed the subject and asked me about my work. She was impressed that I spent so many hours in conversation with Mr. Bevel.

Encouraged by her friendliness, I decided to put into practice a plan I had devised, vaguely, over the past few days.

"We should probably visit Mrs. Bevel's room first, don't you think?"

"Mrs. Bevel's room? I thought I was to show you the flowers."

"Yes, and her room. Mr. Bevel is finishing a chapter on Mrs. Bevel, and he asked me to describe her surroundings. So I think we better start with her room. That would set the mood for the rest, don't you think?"

She hesitated for a moment.

"I suppose that makes sense." She leaned over to pick up my cup, but I took it first and placed it in the sink. "Why, thank you, love. Very sweet of you. Shall we?"

Our steps echoed concisely in the marbled spaciousness of the hall.

"Mr. Bevel would like me to provide a feminine touch to the pages on Mrs. Bevel. It would help to learn a bit more about her routine. Perhaps you have some anecdotes to share? Small stories about her daily life?"

"I'm so sorry. I wish I'd had the pleasure of meeting Mrs. Bevel, but I was hired after she passed."

She seemed a bit out of breath going up the stairs.

"I see. Maybe you could introduce me to the people working here who knew her. It would be a quick chat, I promise."

We walked down a long corridor. Thick carpets and curtains reduced our voices to a prudish hush.

"Well, you see, we were *all* hired after Mrs. Bevel's passing. Shortly after the memorial service, Mr. Bevel decided to sell this house. Too many memories. I believe he moved to a hotel for a while. Dismissed the entire staff and shut down the house. For months, maybe even a year. He rejected bid after bid. And in the end, when a suitable offer was made, well . . . Too many memories."

We paused halfway down the corridor. Miss Clifford caught her breath.

"They were going to tear the house down and build some ghastly apartment building. Mr. Bevel couldn't do it. Couldn't see the home he had made with Mrs. Bevel go. He moved back in and hired new staff." She lowered her voice. "But you know Mr. Bevel. He wouldn't want me to be standing here jabbering about his business."

She gently squeezed my shoulder and led me on.

"Anyway," she said in her normal tone. "Here we are." Miss Clifford pointed to Mildred's door. "I understand it's all quite as Mrs. Bevel left it."

She opened the door, and we walked in.

I had never seen anything like that space. The bedroom, between a parlor and a dressing room, was an angular cloud—all light-blue and gray and sunshine and somehow ozone-smelling. A bed that was a rectangle. A nightstand that was a cube. A coffee table that was a circle. In a corner, a few clean curves resolved themselves into an arm-chair. All these pieces of furniture were so elemental they appear color-less in my memory. Mere abstract lines.

The sitting room was just as serene and uncluttered. The desk and the chair had been realized with the absolute minimum of elements re-quired for a desk to be a desk and a chair to be a chair. Empty shelves, except for a few small sculptures—each of them, congealed pure form. A modest bookcase ran along the shortest wall.

There was a gentle knock on the open door. A maid needed Miss Clifford's help.

"I'll just be a minute, love," she told me as she left with the maid. "Look around, and then I'll take you to the greenhouse."

I went back and forth between the rooms. These were not the "soft," "warm" spaces of someone who had "made a home" for her husband. These were not the quarters of a sickly child-bride. In contrast with the rest of the house there was a monastic sort of calm here—what, in retrospect, I recognize as a modern, austerely avant-garde atmosphere.

The few pieces of furniture derived their elegance from their quiet functionality. And the intensity of the place came from the impression that every object (and its placement) was logically necessary.

I walked around, trying to feel like Mildred but having no idea what that meant. No trace of the journals that, according to Vanner's novel, she had kept all her life. There were few hiding spots in those ascetic rooms with their mostly empty shelves and tabletops. Foolishly, I even looked in the closets, where her clothes were wrapped up in their hangers, feeling the sleeves and pockets of some of her coats, as if she (like me) would have hidden her writings within them.

The bookcase might hold some clues, even though I was sure the books would be unread, perhaps with their pages uncut. I was wrong. They were all heavily underlined in pencil, dogeared, spotted with tea or coffee. Some of them were in French, others in German and even Italian, which made me feel unreasonably close to Mildred. Many were inscribed by their authors—whose names at the time I did not know and therefore did not retain. Harold Vanner was not among them. I leafed through volume after volume, pausing on underscored passages here and there, hoping they would tell me something about the reader.

I went over to the desk, sat down and looked at the portion of the park that Mildred must have seen every day. There was the bench under the tree where I had sat after my first session with Bevel and counted my pay. The desk drawers were unlocked. Stationery, blotting paper, pencils. The blotting paper caught my attention. It was covered in a multitude of words, numbers and symbols traced and retraced chaotically on top of one another in purple ink. Everything was backward, of course. I thought of my father and his inverted truth.

I put the blotting paper in my pocket right before Miss Clifford returned to take me to see the flowers.

8

The hand-delivered letter was typed and curt. But everything that was meant to make it impersonal had the paradoxical effect of bringing its author to the fore. Only Andrew Bevel would have someone type a dinner invitation and phrase it in such a way. No time to meet. Work over supper. Don't dress.

The same driver who had dropped off the envelope that morning picked me up in the evening and took me to East 87th Street. I felt the stares behind the dark windows as I got into the back of the limousine and could almost hear the whispers that would snake through the neighborhood the following day.

Once, when I was working at the bakery, I overheard a humorously resigned conversation between two customers. "There is a better world," a man said. "But it's more expensive." The quip stayed with me not only because it was a drastically different take on my father's utopian visions but also because it pointed to the otherworldly nature of wealth, which I confirmed during my time with Bevel. I had never coveted any of his luxuries. They had intimidated and angered me, yes, but above all they had always made me feel unwelcome and alien. As if I were a displaced earthling, alone in a different world—a more expensive one that also thought itself better.

That evening, however, in Bevel's car I experienced, for the first time, the cool rush of luxury. I did not just witness it; I felt it. And loved it.

I had never been in a car by myself, at night. New York flowed and ebbed in perfect silence outside the thick windows. If I leaned back, the city disappeared behind the tasseled velvet curtains. Pedestrians, curious about the limousine's passenger, peered in at every traffic light. This accentuated the oddity of the situation. I was out in the street while being, at the same time, in a secluded space. More than the mahogany panels, the cut-glass decanters, the embroidered upholstery and the capped, white-gloved driver on the other side of the partition, it was this strange paradox of being in private in public that felt so opulent—a feeling that was one with the illusion of suddenly having become untouchable and invulnerable, with the fantasy of being in total control of myself, of others and of the city as a whole.

When we arrived, the driver handed me over to the unpleasant butler, who escorted me to a small dining room I had not seen during my tour of the house. The table was set for two. Bevel had pushed aside his plate to work on some documents, which he turned over as he got up to welcome me.

"Kind of you to come so late. May I offer you something to drink? Champagne?"

I repressed my hesitation. There was something cowardly about declining and something awkward in accepting. And I had never had champagne before.

"That would be lovely, thank you."

"Well done. Nothing more exhausting than a timid guest."

Bevel gestured to the butler with his chin, and the servant left, closing the door behind him. We sat at the table, and I took out pen and pad.

"Do you know how far away the moon is?"

He did not want an answer.

"Roughly 238,000 miles," he said. "Do you know what the loss in security values was in the crash? Roughly fifty billion dollars."

He rearranged his plate and silverware on the table and looked at me. My features somehow managed to twist themselves into the baffled yet engrossed expression I thought he expected from me.

"If you lined up fifty billion dollar bills end to end, you could make ten trips to the moon. And back. Ten round trips to the moon. And you would still have quite a bit of change to spare."

Now I looked at him with genuine disbelief.

"Striking, isn't it?" he asked, nodding. "I made the calculations."

But my perplexity was not over this absurd computation. It was over Bevel. He had never said anything this inane before. And I had never felt embarrassed for him.

"Fifty billion dollar bills could go around the Earth's circumference almost 195 times." He spun his index finger. "Almost 195 times around the Earth. That's how much money was swept away in stock values in October 1929."

The butler returned carrying a salver with one glass of champagne on it. Bevel was not drinking, and now I would be stuck with that stupid prop.

"Such was the magnitude of the crash. And this was somehow *my* fault? Cataclysms like this have never been and can never be the result of one single person's actions."

Two maids came in with bowls of soup, placed them at the exact same time before us and left.

"A nation's prosperity is based on nothing but a multitude of egoisms aligning until they resemble what is known as the common good. Get enough selfish individuals to converge and act in the same direction, and the result looks very much like a collective will or a common cause. But once this illusory public interest is at work, people forget an all-important distinction: that my needs, desires and cravings may mirror yours does not mean we have a *shared* goal. It merely means we have the *same* goal. This is a crucial difference. I will only cooperate with you as long as it serves me. Beyond that, there can only be rivalry or indifference."

He took two or three shallow spoonfuls. Having soup made him look old and weak.

"There's nothing heroic about defending other people's interests just because they happen to coincide with yours. Cooperation, when its objective is personal gain, should never be confused with solidarity. Don't you agree?"

He seldom wanted my opinion.

"I think I do." And I think I thought I did.

"True idealists, in contrast, care about the welfare of others above and especially *against* their own interests. If you enjoy your work or profit from it, how can you be sure you're truly doing it for others and not yourself? Abnegation is the only road that leads to the greater good. But you don't need me to tell you this. It's something you must have learned from your father's doctrines and his example."

I stopped writing. Bevel had never made a reference to my father's political activities. It could not have been Jack who sold us out—not after the threats I had made through his accomplice. Bevel must have been spying on us all the time, ever since my first interview with him. Had he known all along? To give my body something to do, I reached for the glass. Up close, the strings of effervescent pearls coiling up to the surface became audible.

"Oh, you are mistaken," I said. "His cause is his one luxury. And from his self-denial comes his self-importance."

I took a sip and put the glass down with a worldly casualness I did not have, knowing at once that I had disgraced myself by describing my father in those terms. While having champagne. Days later I would find myself mumbling in public, responding to my words. Moaning. Screwing my brow. Physically cringing. Even now, recalling and transcribing my pathetic aphorisms, I feel ashamed.

Bevel noticed and enjoyed the agitation behind my stiff nonchalance, I could tell.

"Have your chowder."

I had my chowder.

"Surely, you see where I'm going with all this. Those who today complain most loudly about the depression are the same who caused it in the first place. All those egotistical individuals now crying out foul play in the press . . . All those petty speculators playing roulette on margin suddenly turned into champions of justice and fairness . . . None of the people attacking me over my actions in 1929 is close to your father. He, a committed revolutionary without sin, is one of the few who could cast the first stone."

The maids came in again. Subdued rustle of fabric on fabric; muted chimes of silver and china. They took away the bowls and put down plates with boiled chicken, asparagus and peas, over which they poured a white sauce.

"I should imagine someone as uncompromising as your father would object to your working for someone like me."

The maidservants left.

"He believes in the dignity of work," I said with what I judged to be the right amount of defiance.

Bevel nodded gravely as he troweled, with the delicate touch of an artist, some gravy onto a piece of chicken.

"Anyway. I should let you know that we can't continue to work in this fashion."

I tried to swallow the food in my mouth. It was impossible.

"I'm far too busy to take off valuable time in the afternoons. You saw for yourself how much there is to do in my downstairs office."

"Sir, if I may. Perhaps you could record yourself with a Dictaphone whenever you find it convenient, and then I could transcribe and edit the . . ."

"Please." He rearranged some of the items on the table by moving them a fraction of an inch in this direction and that. "I've rented a furnished apartment for you. Walking distance from here." He looked at me and then away. "This will allow us to work before the opening bell or late nights, like this evening. We're moving much too slowly, and the book is behind schedule. Having you close ought to help."

I failed to find a response.

"You're expected at the apartment before the end of the week. Call the office if you need help with your things. Now, back to 1929 and the ensuing depression. People want a culprit and a villain. And there is, in fact, a culprit and a villain: the Federal Reserve Board." He gestured toward my pen and pad. "You'll want to take this down."

9

My father opened the door as he heard me walk up the steps. He was visibly distressed. I was convinced he had seen me getting out of the limousine. Instead, he told me Jack had come by the apartment to pick up some papers he had left in my room. He was in a hurry, my father told me, since he had just received a job offer from a newspaper in Chicago. But they wanted him to start at once, so he was heading back there immediately. Did I know anything about this? Yes, I lied. It had all been so sudden, but I was very happy for him.

Except for the envelope with Jack's article nothing seemed to be missing from my room. I was not only relieved to know him gone; it also made my new circumstances simpler. Had Jack been around, moving to Bevel's apartment would have led to fits of jealousy, fights and ultimately a melodramatic breakup.

I remember feeling excited—almost aroused—by the possibility of independence, an idea I seldom dared to entertain. But other physical sensations disrupted this thrill. Anger, like a wound in my throat. Outrage, like a bruise on my chest. Bevel had never proposed this new arrangement to me. He had never asked me to consider his suggestion. He had simply rented the place and told me to move in at once. And even if I liked the thought of living on my own, it was insulting to be taken for granted and to be ordered around. Still, rejecting such an opportunity because of the objectionable way in which it had been presented seemed both vain and unwise.

Knowing how dependent my father was on me, I had never allowed myself to fantasize at length about moving out. He was increasingly unable to support himself. If I ever left, I would have to keep paying his rent in addition to mine. But it was not just about money. My father had never been capable of coping with basic daily responsibilities—cleaning up, feeding himself and so forth. On his own, chaos would engulf and drown him.

Now, even though I could hardly believe it, money was no longer an issue. Bevel would pay for the new place, and my salary was more than enough for the Brooklyn apartment. This allowed me to convince myself that I could take care of my father and manage his many needs—needs he himself was unaware of having. I would visit him a few times a week to make sure things did not get too out of hand. Perhaps give our landlady some money (behind his back) to drop by and discreetly do some chores. A chance like this would not come twice. I had to swallow my pride, forget the demeaning terms in which Bevel had presented his plan and accept his "offer."

My interests aside, there was a crucial consideration impossible to ignore. Bevel had asked me to move out after bringing up, for the first time, my father's political activities. This could not be a coincidence. Perhaps Bevel thought he could control any potential threat by having me away from my house; perhaps he merely wanted to make me choose between my father and him. (I now understand he could never have cared enough about me to engage in this kind of reasoning.) And although we, of course, needed the money, once again I found myself siding with Bevel over my father. It did not make it any better to tell myself that I was, in fact, shielding my father by pleasing Bevel and submitting to his demands.

I was deserting my father for the enemy. The charges would be unequivocal, and there would be no appeal after the verdict. I could already hear him. Wall Street had gone to my head. That boss of mine had brainwashed me. Next I would become interested in clothes and hairdos, go on vacations, pick up hobbies. I would be on my way to becoming a bourgeoise *lady*. Or perhaps something even worse. Because my father was sure to bring up the fact that no old man would rent an apartment for a young woman just so that she could take dictation for him. A fight would ensue, after which I would be summarily sentenced to years of tight-lipped rage.

Others in my place might have been concerned about Bevel's intentions. Looking back, perhaps I should have been as well. But I remember considering and immediately dismissing the notion of Bevel wanting to take me as his mistress. His body seemed to be an infelicitous but tolerable accident to him. I could not imagine him wanting anyone to touch it.

Fears, desires, suspicions, affronts. None of it mattered. Bevel's plan was nonnegotiable. If I wanted to keep my job, I would have to move uptown. It was a relief to realize I had no choice.

There was no point in delaying the confrontation with my father. After a mostly sleepless night I told him everything over breakfast (except for Bevel's name and the true nature of my work). He listened in silence, with downcast eyes. I finished speaking. We stared into our coffees. Just when I thought a natural pause was hardening into one of his fits of icy wrath, he reached across the table and took my hand.

As a child, I found his callused fingers and palms, hardened by years of feeding type and handling abrasive chemicals, fascinating. How they were part of his body but also things. I used to pinch and poke his rubbery skin and ask him if he felt anything. Invariably he would pretend to be unfazed and tell me he had not even noticed I had touched him. This was my cue to pinch him harder, as hard as I could, until my fingers trembled and whitened with the effort. He would just yawn or make some remark about the weather, as if nothing were happening.

"This is not what I imagined," he said at length. "I'm not sure what I imagined, but it wasn't this."

I held his hand tighter.

"But it's time. You are wise, and I trust your judgment. Even if I disagree with you." He looked up and into my eyes. "It's time. It's past time. You should go."

With these last words he, too, held me tighter and gently pulled me toward him. Without letting go of his hand, I got up, walked around the table and hugged him.

"You know you can always come back to this mess," he said.

We spent the day together in an atmosphere of warm melancholy. Although my love for my father had surged after our brief conversation, it is also true that there was something unpleasantly incorporeal about my presence in the apartment, as if now that my departure was imminent I had become two-dimensional. There was also the pressure to comply with Bevel's request as soon as possible—and perhaps above everything else I was curious about my new place and eager to move in.

I started packing the following morning, while my father was out delivering some cards. He had offered to help, but I explained the apartment was furnished and I needed to bring only a few things. Since I would be going back and forth for a while, it would be best to move out in stages, I said. The truth was that I wanted to pack and leave while he was away, to spare him the heartache of seeing me go.

There was not much to do after I had folded my work clothes and picked some books, toiletries and random objects to take on my first trip. Was I forgetting something obvious? Perhaps I should take one of my father's posters. No matter what the new apartment looked like, one of the silly, loving posters he printed for me during my childhood would make me feel right at home and in his company. I went to his room and looked through the drawers of his flat file cabinets. There were signs commemorating the Haymarket massacre, placards announcing meetings at L'Aquila Social Club, old copies of *Il Martello* and *L'Adunata dei Refrattari*, flyers in Italian demanding bread and freedom, broadsides addressed to strikers at different factories, back issues of some of his anarchist newspapers. And interspersed with these political advertisements, bulletins, pamphlets and documents, in no particular order, I found some of the beautiful posters my father had made to cheer me up or celebrate the accomplishments of my childhood. "Ida Partenza! Ten Wild Lions! One Performance Only! This Thursday! Carroll Park!" "EXTRA! Miss Partenza Emerges Victorious from Third Grade!" I remembered with almost tactile vividness each one of these occasions. Misty eyed, I kept going through these disorganized prints, among which, toward the end of a bottom drawer, I saw the papers.

Letter size.

Uncrumpled.

Typed.

The "e" was a bit over-inked, with a blacked-out eye.

The "i" often undotted.

I O

A tautly upholstered sofa in an ocher living room in an odorless building on an unknown street in a foreign neighborhood on a different island.

When I was not working with Bevel or transcribing my notes from our sessions, all I did was sit on that hard sofa, drawing concentric circles in my mind that went out from my new apartment to the whole city. Voids encircling voids. And just beyond the outer edge of the largest vacuum containing all others stood my father. Remote, small and shipwrecked.

Why he had stolen my discarded drafts and what he had done or planned to do with them did not concern me—they were fake anyway and could not hurt me or upset Bevel, even if he had taken them with the intention to show off this "piece of intelligence" to his comrades or print the contents in one of his leaflets. All I knew, all I felt, all I cared about was that he did not hold me anymore. Messy, dictatorial, irresponsible and whimsical as he was, he had always held me. He had, perhaps against his doctrines and even his own will, encompassed my entire world and endowed it with meaning and something resembling lawfulness, however precarious this last term might have been when applied to him. His was such a confident chaos. Over time and through a mysterious transmutation I had derived a sense of safety from all that was erratic and unstable in our life together.

Despite everything, I had consistently chosen to respect and look up to him. Only now did I realize how active and conscious that choice had been. Sometimes he made it easy for me, and it was a joy. More often it fell entirely on me to make a father of him. Year after year I had made up for his shortcomings. Helped him be my parent. And I had loved our hard, complicated life. And I had loved him for his dim yet unbending principles and passions and for his wild notions of freedom and independence. But now I had to find a way to love a new, still shapeless idea of him.

A few days after leaving, I sent my father a short letter. There was more work than anticipated, and I was needed at all times, even during the weekend. I would come over to Brooklyn in a week or two, as soon as things calmed down at the office. "I miss you," I wrote at the end. He would never know how deeply I meant those words.

I did not miss Jack, though. Learning that he had not stolen my papers did not change that. I was not proud of myself for having forced him out of town, but still, given that he had followed me and sent someone to extort and terrorize me, I was relieved to know he was gone.

My notes from those days are not clear about how many times Bevel and I saw each other after I moved into my new apartment. Six? Nine? We never met in the morning, as he had intended. Only for supper.

Without fail (and without being asked) I was given a glass of champagne with our bland meals. He joined me two or three times, creating an illusion of moderate closeness—an illusion that, I knew, he did not share.

Perhaps because he was tired and therefore slightly unguarded, our evening sessions were much more productive than our daytime meetings. He also seemed more receptive to my work and skimmed the pages I handed him before our first course with brief nods of approval, giving occasional minor notes. For the most part he corrected inaccuracies regarding his business transactions and kept editing the passages concerning Mildred. His main concern was to make both his financial operations and the portrait of his wife as accessible to the "common reader" as possible. He also told me we should focus on his gift for mathematics, which had been crucial in his career. The wonders and difficulties of being a "child prodigy," his years under Professor Keene at Yale, the development of his financial models—this should all be laid out in great detail, while making it plain enough for a wide audience.

Meeting over dinner might have predisposed him more favorably, but it is also true that I had finally managed to inhabit the voice I had created for him and was able to write fluently in a Bevelian tone without having to think about it. My work on the apocryphal version had freed my writing and expanded the latitude for invention I allowed myself. As a result, my style and the memoir as a whole became more self-assured, which was what Bevel had always demanded. At our new pace we might have been able to finish the book by the end-of-the-year deadline Bevel had given himself.

Our last dinner did not have the gravity of endings because neither of us knew we would never see each other again. I found him, as always, working at the table, and, as always, he turned the pages over when I walked in.

"I believe I'll join Miss Partenza tonight," he told the butler as he was leaving to get my customary glass of champagne.

"I must say I'm pleased with the shape the book is taking. It's rewarding to see one's achievements laid out in clear succession." As was his custom, he rearranged some of the objects on the table with millimetric fingers. "I am confident that my memoirs will help the general public understand my accomplishments and their place within our nation's recent history. Vilified as I was after 1929, they won't fail to see that through my actions I upheld the very order they are now crediting others with saving."

"Others?"

"Needless to say, the president should never be named. Feuds are beneath me, but the implication ought to be abundantly clear in the book." He swept the table with the back of his hand. "What I'm driving at is this: the resilience of the individual. Fortitude. What should come through is this one main fact: what I've made, I've made on my own. Alone. Completely by myself. And that, in part, is what I proved to everyone during the crash. Regardless of the circumstances there is always room for individual action."

"Well . . . You weren't completely by yourself. Your ancestors . . . And your wife was at your side. You did say that Mrs. Bevel saved you."

At once he lost the impetus his brief speech had given him.

"That I did." He made the salt shaker rotate between his fingers. "And how true it is. Nothing gives me more satisfaction than restoring her image. Thank you, again, for that lovely paragraph with the bouquets in Gainsborough and Boucher."

The butler came in with our drinks and left.

"To your health," Bevel said, barely raising his glass in my direction, and drank. "Why don't I allow myself this more often?" He seemed to be speaking to the wine.

"How about your wife? Did she enjoy champagne?"

He laughed through his nostrils.

"Hot cocoa. That was her one indulgence. Regardless of the season." He folded his lips inward in a repressed smile. "Her simple pleasures." He nodded. "And her enthusiasm. She always retained that unabashed sense of excitement we are taught to tame in our first childhood."

I put pen to pad, hungry for even the smallest morsel concerning Mildred's life and character.

"You know I don't much care for books, but what a delight it was to hear her retell one of the novels she had just read and enjoyed." He went back to his salt shaker. "Murder mysteries. A mere pastime, of course. But she was always trying to outsmart the detectives. She'd remember every detail, every piece of information and narrate the whole plot back to me. A book could take up a whole dinner. And I'll confess to it: through her I came to enjoy those silly little mysteries as well. Such was her passion. She'd light up telling those stories. Sometimes I'd be so delighted looking at her that the food on my plate would grow cold. How we'd laugh when we noticed . . ."

I knew I was not drunk. But that was the first explanation that came to my mind. I put my pen down and looked at Bevel, who was still twirling the salt shaker. That was *my* story. The retelling of detective novels over dinner. Bevel had read it in my pages. It was one of the scenes I had made up for Mildred, following his request to create homey episodes using my "feminine touch." I had based it on my dinners with my father, who listened, riveted, to my recounting of the latest Dorothy Sayers or Margery Allingham book I had borrowed from the Brooklyn

Public Library branch on Clinton Street. And here was Bevel, telling me my story to my face.

Later, over the years, both at work and in my personal life, I have had countless men repeat my ideas back to me as if they were theirs—as if I would not remember having come up with those thoughts in the first place. (It is possible that in some cases their vanity had eclipsed their memory so that, thanks to this selective amnesia, they could lay claim to their epiphany with a clean conscience.) And even back then, in my youth, I was acquainted with this parasitic form of gaslighting. But someone presenting one of my family stories as theirs?

"Most of the time I'd solve the crime with the clues she had given me, but I was careful to never let her know it." Bevel picked up his glass, seemed to smile to himself once again and took a deeper drink. "I'd always blame some secretary or the butler and pretend to be shocked when Mildred revealed who the murderer in fact was."

Now, this was something I had not written into Bevel's memoir. Pretending not to know who the culprit was and pointing a condescending finger at the obviously wrong suspect was not something I had included in my narrative about Mildred and him. And yet this is exactly what my father would do each time I retold him one of the novels I had just finished reading. The killer, he invariably said after dutifully following my red herrings, had to be the spoiled stepson or the slighted heiress apparent. It was embarrassing to realize only now that he had merely been humoring me all along. And it was doubly depressing to see that Bevel's mind worked just like my father's: in the fictional world I had created for him, Bevel had added a scene of his making where he reacted to his wife exactly like my father had to me in real life.

We had our meal and, for the first and last time, a second glass of champagne. He denounced, as he often did, those who claimed his best days were behind him and his approach to business had become obsolete, despite all his recent triumphs. Then he revisited several moments of his life that we had already covered, always emphasizing how his personal interests converged with the nation's well-being. This recapitulation revolved around his extraordinary success starting in 1922 and his almost superhuman prescience dating back to 1926, leading, of course, to the events of 1929. It was a "perverse paradox" that his greatest stroke of genius (what had made him one of the richest men in the world while correcting the unhealthy tendencies of the market) had also caused so much damage to his public perception. This was, he supposed, his cross to bear, and he would do so with dignity until history realized that he had been unjustly burdened with it.

At the time, this all felt redundant, and I left the house thinking it had been our most unproductive session yet. The only thing that stood out was his fake story about Mildred's detective novels. There was a bizarre sort of violence in having my memories plagiarized.

Soon, however, even the most trivial and repetitious aspects of this dinner would become saturated with meaning. That second glass of champagne would be remembered as a farewell toast. The somewhat tedious reexamination of events Bevel had discussed several times would resound like a coda—the main motifs of his memoir woven into one final phrase.

I spent the following days typing down and editing my notes, as always. Roughly two weeks had gone by since I had moved, and I was still a visitor in my own apartment. Waking up in the middle of the night not knowing which way I was facing. Being somewhat intimidated by doormen and neighbors. Trying to keep everything unused and tidy because nothing was mine. In an attempt at reconciling myself with my father, I put up one of his posters. "Ida Partenza! Ten Wild Lions!"

I I

It must have been about five days after our last dinner (Bevel had sent word canceling our usual mid-week meeting) that I found myself leaving a shop on Third Avenue where I had bought a pocket-knife for my father. I had seen it in the window many times and had always, for mysterious reasons, felt drawn to it. With its straight blade and horn handle it was deceitfully rustic—the simple design concealed a great elegance. I knew my father would love it, and that morning I had finally gone into the store. We had never been apart for so long, and I thought it would make things easier to have this object to talk about when we met. Perhaps seeing his enthusiasm over the knife would make me forget how angry and hurt I was.

The owner of the shop (which sold kitchen supplies, hardware, stationery and knickknacks) was Italian, and I was happy to learn from him that the pocketknife was, in fact, a stiletto from Calabria. He insisted this was no coincidence: part of me knew. The knife had called out to me, and my Italian instinct had responded.

Summer's last gasps were mixed in with the first breaths of autumn. Instead of getting on the subway right away, it would be nice to walk down along the park and take the train to Brooklyn at 59th Street. I crossed Lexington and glanced at the newsstand on the corner.

"ANDREW BEVEL, NEW YORK FINANCIER, DEAD OF HEART ATTACK"

It was only after taking three or four steps that I understood the words. I walked back to the newsstand. It was on the cover of *The New York Times*. It was on the cover of every paper.

The Sun: "DEATH TAKES ANDREW BEVEL"

The American: "ANDREW BEVEL, GREATEST FINANCIER, DEAD AT 62"

The Post: "ANDREW BEVEL, RULER OF TREMENDOUS BANKING EMPIRE, DIES"

Il Progresso: "ANDREW BEVEL È MORTO"

The Wall Street Journal: "ANDREW BEVEL, 62, DIES"

The Herald: "BEVEL DEAD"

Without deciding it, I started making my way at great speed toward Bevel's house. I remember thinking, absurdly, that I would confirm the news of his death at the next newsstand. My fast walk would turn into a trot once or twice every block. It was not grief that I felt but an unexplainable sense of urgency.

As soon as I turned on East 87th Street, it became evident that something was off. There were slightly more people than usual moving slightly faster than usual. After crossing Park and reaching Madison, I realized it would be impossible to complete my urgent and unclear mission. Jogging reporters, curious passersby and police officers were making their way toward Fifth Avenue and congregated in a disorderly throng at the end of the street, right in front of the entrance to Bevel's house, from which, I knew, I would be turned away.

A silent confusion disfigured the next few days. I kept working on Bevel's memoir, shifting different sections around, correcting random passages and creating and discarding new scenes, imagining what his edits might have been. I had Mildred's blotting paper propped up against the wall behind my typewriter. The backward writing in purple still refused to yield any answers.

Meanwhile, although the story of Bevel's death stayed in the press, the reports became shorter and were buried deeper in the papers. If no one disputed the cause of death (sudden cardiac arrest; found in his room three to four hours after the event; could probably have been saved if someone had been around him when he collapsed), there were already disagreements about his estate. Having no immediate family, he had bequeathed most of his assets to charity. I knew, from our conversations, that this was of the utmost importance to him—the seal that would, once and for all, make people remember him as a great philanthropist and benefactor. His will was the cornerstone of what he called his "legacy," which was also the title of the last chapter of his memoir. But as I had learned during my sessions with Bevel and later confirmed reading about the disputes over his money, a fortune seldom has one single owner. Many interests and parties are tied to it. Rather than a block of granite, wealth resembles a river basin with multiple tributaries and branches. Mounting claims and lawsuits from associates, creditors and investors resulted in a freeze of Bevel's estate. A great part of it remained in this legal limbo for decades, until the late 1970s, which is when the renovations that finally turned Bevel's house into a museum began.

Every day I expected a call from the office asking me to surrender all my notes and documents and vacate the apartment at once. This never happened. Bevel's death was so sudden he must have failed to make any provisions in this regard. I did, however, get a call from Mr. Shakespear, the man who had interviewed me before I met Bevel. We briefly expressed our shock and sadness through a few commonplaces. There was a pause, after which I was certain he would bring up the apartment. Instead, he talked about our interview. He remembered my qualifications and my eloquence and wanted to hire me at once. I asked about his secretary, the one who worked there when I met him. He told me I should not concern myself with that. My new position, he said, would not disappoint me. He would be delighted if I accepted. After an adequate period of mourning, of course. Suddenly I detected a touch of deference in his tone. It was not about my qualifications or my eloquence. He just wanted Bevel's private secretary.

I took the job, mainly because moving back in with my father was a complete impossibility.

Visiting my father could no longer be postponed. Walking down Lexington with the knife I had bought for him felt like a shallow re-enactment of the events of the previous week; the subway ride was fraught with anxiety. My highest hope was that my father would bring up Bevel's death. Because under normal circumstances he would never have mentioned such an event, any reference to it would be a tacit admission of guilt—an acknowledgment that, through the papers he had taken from me, he knew of my association with Andrew Bevel. That would have been a lot for a man who never apologized.

He received me with humorous pomp.

"The return of the prodigal daughter! Ah, I thought you had forgotten all about your old father! Had almost given up all hope!"

Big hugs, prickly kisses. He pushed some tools and garbage off a chair and offered it to me.

"Not as good as your uptown apartment, I'm sure. I would have tidied up, if you'd told me you were coming."

The place looked frightening. Dangerously and irreversibly filthy. It smelled of madness. But all this only deepened the love I felt for him right then. A love so tightly intermingled with pity that from that day on I was unable to tell one apart from the other.

I gave him his present and he unwrapped it.

"Ah! No, no, no, no!" He dropped the box over a pile of cheese rinds, nails and wilted leaves as he recoiled. "You don't know this? You should know this. Very bad luck. The worst."

"Bad luck?" I feared I would be unable to repress my irritation and masked it behind a little laugh. "Really? Bad luck? What kind of anarchist are you?"

It was such a relief to finally say this. The satisfaction of popping his thin dogmatic bubbles. I knew, even then, it was a petty (and insufficient) form of revenge for his theft of the papers, but it was still gratifying. It was also a dare: would he, despite what he had done to me, play the wounded party, shut down and sulk?

"No, no, no, no." Surprisingly, there was no anger or resentment in his voice; only grave concern. "When you give someone a knife you cut the ties with him."

"What?"

"Yes. If I take this knife, it will be bad luck. We will fight. It will cut the ties between us."

I had always believed his mild superstitions were mere relics from his hometown, like the legends, anecdotes and recipes he had brought from there. But he seemed oddly serious about this. I shrugged and motioned to pick up the box.

"Wait," he said. "There is a solution. Money."

I looked at him.

"Money," he repeated. "I buy the knife from you. That's how it's solved. Then it's not a gift." He rummaged through his pockets and proffered me a penny. "Here. Will you sell me that beautiful knife for a penny?"

I took the coin; he picked up the box.

"Ah, look at this!" Beaming, he inspected the blade with his thumb. "We used to have one like this, remember? You whittled arrows with it. Ages ago. But this is so much better. A work of art. It must have cost a fortune. Thank you so much, my dear."

We used the knife to cut some salami and cheese, which we ate standing at the counter as we chatted like in the old days—I had been away for just a couple of weeks, but my time with my father had already become the old days. Bevel was not mentioned once. Not that day. Not ever.

I still have the penny that saved us.

IV

The reading room has darkened and emptied. There are only a few islets of light here and there. I notice all the remaining patrons are women. They are studying art books. From the loose, wide movements of her hand, one of them seems to be copying a picture from the volume on her desk. I am, by far, the oldest person here.

This makes me think of the remaining years of my youth, following Bevel's death. My brief period working for Mr. Shakespear while saving up for school. My time at City College. My cheap, lovely apartment on Thompson Street. My first job as a writer (advertisement copy for Bonwit Teller). My first published fiction, a forgettable social realist story in The Parallel Review. My first piece of reporting, for Today, on four girls from different backgrounds orphaned by the war. Harold Vanner's death, which went almost completely unnoticed. My job at Mademoiselle. My first book.

Through these initial steps of my writing life I stayed close to my father. He *died some twelve years after Bevel. Toward the end he was fully dependent on me. Now, after all these hours reviewing Mildred's life, he reminds me, once again, of Mr. Brevoort, the troubled father of Helen Rask, the fictional incarnation of Mildred Bevel in Vanner's novel. And although I realize we can't be related to each other by a literary character, this connection brings me closer to Mildred.*

The question about who she might have been never stopped plaguing me. She could not have been the haunted woman in Vanner's last chapters. And I always knew she was not the insubstantial shadow in Bevel's unfinished memoir. But after looking at her papers and learning how profoundly different she was from the "accessible" character her husband asked me to create, I find it hard to forgive myself for having helped him perpetrate that fiction, even if it remained unfinished and unpublished.

I skim the documents in the last box. More letters addressed to Mrs. Bevel. More bookkeeping. I am distracted. Tired. I open a ledger book. Its few entries seem related to the Charitable Fund. I have no strength to decipher the handwriting or the patience to figure out the arcane accounting system. All I can do is flip through it. Until I find a slim notebook wedged into the middle section of the ledger. A dim rectangle remains on the ruled surface when I remove it. On the cover, in Mildred's hand, is the word "Futures." The first few sheets have been ripped out. The remaining pages contain short paragraphs and isolated lines in purple ink. There is a pressed leaf halfway into the notebook. The ghost of a leaf, rather—translucent veins in a pale red frame.

Different times of the day followed by text. Without reading it, I can tell it is a journal. The writing is much smaller, more cramped and even more illegible than in the other documents. It will take days, possibly even weeks to decrypt the diary—if I can ever make out the contents at all.

I am shocked at myself as I hide the journal among my papers and pack it into my bag. The only other theft in my life I can think of is when I took

Mildred's blotting paper from her room. That makes this my second time stealing Mildred's writing, almost half a century later. I wonder, vaguely, if the blotting paper will match some page in the journal.

But this is not theft, I tell myself. This is a conversation starting after a decades-long delay. A message finally arriving at its destination. These pages have been waiting a lifetime to be read. If they can be read.

Still, I am bothered by my arrogance—the feeling that the words in there are addressed to me. I am bothered by how easy it is to convince myself that I have a right to this notebook. (Who knows Mildred better than I? Didn't I even forge her a past out of my own? Are we not then, in some oblique way, connected?) I am bothered by my certainty that Mildred would have liked me to have these papers. And yet I get up, thank the librarians and walk out of the building and into the cold with Mildred Bevel's diary in my bag, thinking how lovely it would be to finally hear her voice.

Futures

———◆◆———

MILDRED BEVEL

AM

Nurse's thick accent somehow makes me feel my English is improper. "Can I touch you?" Once she does, she's assertive. Her hands have the authority her voice lacks. How can someone so meek be so strong? Facing down, forehead on forearms, I wonder if Nurse undergoes a transformation when I don't see her. At least, her face must look different from the exertion. Once done, she covers me with a sheet that first balloons with a breeze of camphor and then settles with a waft of, I suppose, Alpine herbs. Gooseflesh. "So," she always whispers before rustling out, leaving me on the table, where I try, and sometimes succeed, to become a thing.

PM

They warm up my clothes before I get dressed. If only I'd learned about this luxury before.

AM

The modest yet relentless torment of a crumb-filled bed.

Headachy.

AM

Good to resume journal after such long time. Miss my thick Tisseur notebooks, tho.

Box of books from London. Short-lived excitement: unable to read. As if the words had to jettison their meaning to make the trip from the page up to my eyes.

PM

Church bells. D F♯ E A. Followed by retrograde response: A E F♯ D. The most conventional chime. (Same as Big Ben?) Archaic in its pentatonic simplicity, it condenses most of our musical past: tonal hierarchies, symmetry, tension, release. But here the E bell is louder + more sustained than the others. And a tad flat, in the most exquisite way. If the call/response motif contains our history, that strange lingering 9th is the sound of our musical future. Grazing against the D, it makes the air oscillate. I feel it with the hairs on my forearms.

Never seen the church.

AM

Andrew called from Zürich, hiding his business qs. under a great display of concern for my health. I know he's genuinely worried about me, so I don't mind his little ruse.

Less than an hour later, he called again. Attempt at fatherly instructions + caring, stern commands supposed to carry me through his absence.

Already tired of milk + meat diet.

AM

New, dispassionately determined pain. My insides are trying to get out, fleeing from it.

Won't tell Nurse. Don't want morph.

EVE

Now able to read. Went through box of new books.

Started "Voyage in the Dark." Welsh (?) author seems to have grown up in the West Indies. Reads like a memoire of sorts.

"A plant made of rubber with shiny, bright red leaves, five-pointed. I couldn't take my eyes off it. It looked proud of itself, as if it knew that it was going on for ever and ever."

"The orchestra played Puccini and the sort of music that you always know what's going to come next, that you can listen to ahead, as it were."

So nicely put. This defines the classical form. Music that one almost doesn't need to listen to, because its development is all implied by the form. Just as Rhys says in her passage, "you always know what's going to come next." This music creates an unavoidable future for itself. It has no free will. There's only fulfilment. It's fatal music. Just like the chime I hear every day. D F♯ E A plants + grows the seed of A E F♯ D in the mind before the ear can hear it.

AM
Morph.

EVE
Re. morph. Narcosis may be pleasant (I enjoy the sedation, tho I emerge from it melancholy + irritable) but surely makes for dull narratives. Never cared to read about any sort of paradis artificiel + certainly don't care to write about my own stupor.

PM
A back from Z this AM, looking tired. Organized a surprise picnic for me. Set up a tent by the forest. Even tho picnic was overstaffed + overfurnished, he was uncomfortable. Kept looking at the sun filtering through the twiggery as if affronted by it. Smacking non-existent bugs on his face. But kindly looked after me. Even attempted humour. After reviewing the minutiae of my treatment and the diplomatic intrigues of the nurses' station, he tiptoed around his concerns about Zürich deals. He has a way of presenting his questions as categorical statements. I made him see it was unwise to hold K, G, T positions. He then came to the conclusion he should telephone in the AM and change course.

He fell asleep in the tent after lunch. I slipped away for a short stroll. Seldom alone these days.

The sight of rock against sky creates the illusion that the entire orb is in the orb of the eye.

The squirrel's dexterous fingers, the petals' scented colours, the stone beak encrusted in the bird's face and the lovely implausibility of its flight. All of life's peculiarities result from a long series of mutations. I wonder what the cells mutating within my body would turn me into, if they didn't kill me first.

EVE
"From a long way off I watched the pen writing."

AM
Sickish

PM
Out. All the way to the edge of the woods.
Nature is always less gaudy than I remember it. It has much better taste than I.

AM
Barely slept.

A off to Z again. Part of it is business; part of it is that he finds my illness unbearable. He's often angry at it (and it, of course, is in me). I realise now how poorly I've managed this whole thing. Should've done as so many times before: nudge him gently enough in the right direction so he could believe he was in command. Once I learned about the tumour, I should've told him I was unwell, let his doctors "discover" the illness + allow him to be in charge (nothing to be done anyway). It was a mistake to present him with the hopeless truth, supported by tests + examinations conducted behind his back. More than sad, he looked disoriented. And then I told him we were coming to this place. He followed, dutifully. I never let him be of help.

Unreasonable menu:
Beef tea thickened with tapioca
Meat jelly
Milk

PM
I speak imperfect German with Nurse. She sticks with her imperfect English. We both pretend this is all perfectly natural.

AM
To the baths and back. Twice a day, in every weather, with bloated retinue.

Just learned that Paracelsus was this spa's 1st physician in 1535 + wrote a treatise on the healing properties of the waters. Don't know anything about Paracelsus but remember Father bringing up the name in connection with his Hermetics, Rosicrucians + such.

Wonder if I learned about Paracelsus' link to this sanatorium through him during our years in Switz. and then repressed it. Was this the unconscious reason that made me pick this place over the others? Or just a coincidence? No way to know. But how fitting that Nature's Final Mystery will be revealed to me here!

Massage. "So."

Andrew called from Zürich. Wondering about best approach to Kolbe. Told him we could only get him through Lenbach. I could hear the whole thing coming together in his head as I explained it.

Now that we're truly alone here, I see how lonely he + I have been.
It's not that I'm tired of him. I'm tired of the person I become around him.

Hemicrania

EVE
AM
Nuit sans fin

AM
A called from Z. More questions about K + L. Asked him to get me a copy of "Zauberberg." Would be amusing to finally read it here. One would expect to find a copy in the nightstand drawer of every reputable spa room in Switz.
Bathed at length.

PM

Nothing more private than pain. It can only involve one.

But who?

Who is "I" in "I hurt"? The one who inflicts the pain or the one who suffers it?

And does "hurt" refer to the inflicting or the suffering?

AM

Morph.

EVE

Did something cruel. Would like to blame morph. + its sour sequels. A, back from Z, came for tea. Struggled to find conv. He ended up talking about La Fiesolana. Said he wished we'd spent more time together there. So much of the place he would've liked to show me. Family hist., etc. If only we'd gone up more often, he said.

Kitsch. Can't think of Engl. trans. for this word. A copy that's so proud of how close it comes to the original that it believes there's more worth in this closeness than in originality itself. "It looks just like . . . !" Imposture of feeling over actual emotion; sentimentality over sentiment. Kitsch can also be in the eye: "The sunset looks like a painting!" Because artifice is now the ultimate standard, the original (sunset) has to be turned into a fake (painting), so that the latter may provide the measure of the former's beauty. Kitsch is always a form of inverted Platonism, prizing imitation over archetype. And in every case, it's related to an inflation of aesthetic value, as seen in the worst kind of kitsch: "classy" kitsch. Solemn, ornamental, grand. Ostentatiously, arrogantly announcing its divorce from authenticity.

This, I told A, is why I went to La Fiesolana only a handful of times. That "Tuscan" incongruity is a cathedral to kitsch.

I'm ashamed of the rush of vitality that coursed through me as I spoke.

After writing the above, I went over to A's rooms to apologize. He said he didn't know what I was talking about + was very gentle. We sat in silence for a while. After gathering some courage, he asked if I'd mind it if he gave me a bracelet. Given what had happened a moment ago, it seemed insensitive to make my usual stand on the matter of jewellery. I smiled. He brightened up + produced a box from his pocket. "Good! Because I already got it!" It's a slender band of white gold. It'll be rather lovely once it fades.

PM
A off to Z.

It's only through a great effort that I can convince myself that I'm here today.

Body was massaged, bathed, fed, laid.

AM
Head. Belly.
  Massage.

PM

Mail. Thrilled to find unexpected word from friends. All tactful + apologetic for writing, since I never told them where I'd be. (For once, I'm glad I failed to keep one of my secrets safe.) Bundle forwarded from home. Some good news about Charitable Fund. Several business letters, destroyed after reading. Two long ones from HV, who wrote with delightful NY gossip + tableaux. (Should tell him about crackpots here!) Blissful to find letter from TW and then saddened by its content. Tells me Berg is in a tight spot, forced to sell score of Wozz. (3 vols., £250) + Lyr. Suite (£125). Heartrending + infuriating that he should find himself in this position. Instructed TW to buy scores straightaway at 4x the price + donate to Lib. of Cong. He signs off "your old and loyal bore," which at least made me smile. Mother. Responding to her show of concern will consume a whole PM. Should prob. write her after robust dose of morph.

AM

Back from taking waters. Something disgusting about bath at body temp. Feels like getting into someone else's tub. I try to picture millenary streams cutting through strata of glittering rock, chipping away healing minerals that then filter through my pores, but fail. May just stop coming.

Fruit juice. Berries + rhubarb.

PM

Mandatory 90 min. rest, wrapped up on chaise longue under warmish sun, is loveliest time of day.

Air like French horns.

AM

The loneliness of animals.
I aspire to.

PM

Seized with toothache. Loose molar.

Overheard: "The most charming garbage."

EVE

Tried to have supper at restaurant for 1st time. Of course, stares + murmurs as I walk in. How much those stares feel like tongues. Always. Sit down with Cocteau. Feel better a few pages in. But when consommé arrives, a French woman, about my age, gets up and recites a cloying poem on friendship ("amitié" is made to rhyme with "chocolatier"). Immediately after, another patient, accompanying himself at the piano, proceeds to descale, gut and behead Schubert's trout. I'm amused. A little girl (patient? visitor?) starts singing a cappella in Russian. All of a sudden, I'm blinded by exasperation. Enraged at how charmed everyone is. Enraged to a shocking, disproportionate extent. The girl's followed by someone playing a tremulous mandolin of sorts. My fury keeps mounting. Diners either transported by this "artistic moment" or delighted by the drollness of it all. Anger + angst in my sternum. Impossible to make an exit unnoticed. I sweat, am short of breath, feel faint. Get up as discreetly as possible and leave. The tongues.

Even in the midst of my frenzy I understood, with absolute clarity, what was happening to me. It was a distorted version of a recurring childhood scene. Being here, in Switz., with my parents. Dinners with travellers + émigrés from all over. And the performances afterwards. Sometimes a middling artist; more often, painfully fervent dilettantes. One after the other, leading up to the main attraction.

Mother would dim the lights + ask guests to read a few sentences from different books. Then I'd repeat them in different order. Sometimes she'd bring a deck of cards so I could perform other feats of memory. Maths was always the main act. Mother asked guests to come up with qs. + problems for me. People have no imagination for maths, so the calcs. were usually dull + falsely convoluted. Over the course of the interrogation, a change always took place in the audience. From entertained to murderous. For some reason, they felt they had to destroy me. Their faces disfigured as they squinted + grinned with the impossible effort of thinking up problems larger than their minds. They kept going until I was defeated by their absurdities. Once it was all over, they pinched my cheeks + patted my head, congratulating me for my efforts, like gracious victors.

I was 11. This went on for about a year. Ended because I no longer looked like a child.

Never told this to anyone in its entirety. Especially after marrying A.

AM

Rereading the above "confession" made me think about diaries. Some journals are kept with the unspoken hope that they will be discovered long after the diarist's death, the fossil of an extinct species of one. Others thrive on the belief that the only time each evanescent word will be read is as it's being written. And others yet address the writer's future self: one's testament to be opened at one's resurrection. They declare, respectively, "I was," "I am," "I'll be."

Over the years, my diary has drifted from one of these categories to the next and then back. It still does, even if my future is shallow.

Massage

PM

Nurse puts my hands and feet in scalding water while sponging my head. She also soaks a flannel in boiling water, wrings it with sticks and applies it on my neck. Once it cools down, she replaces it with a mustard leaf. Primitive as this all is, it brings some relief from headache. For a while.

EVE

Listless
Fitful
Listless

AM

Little sleep.

Denied fruit juice for inscrutable dietary reasons.

PM

Andrew back. Happy with outcome in Z, which he now (as usual) describes as the result of his "intuition." I had to be careful not to snap at him. Coming out of morph. Prickly.

AM

White night.

A had fruit interdiction lifted. Glorious juice with oranges, chinotti + peaches he brought from Z.

Writing letters. Distracted by unseen birds unable to break their bondage to their 2 or 4 notes. Wish I had some knowledge of ornith.

PM

Sent out batch of letters. Mother. PL, Fran, HV, G. Smuggled out responses to business letters in envelope to D.

As I gave Nurse the bundle, I thought of myself dying as all my letters were en route. Each sheet a ghost.

AM

I know my days are numbered, but not every day is a real number.

Among my new books, "Le chant du monde." Gave up after 2 ch. Something simplistic about Giono's simplicity. Something dishonest about his nostalgia for nature + primitive state. Almost as if he were glad that nature is lost to us, because this allows him to show how deeply he mourns the loss. Reminds me, in a diagonal way, of Stifter's "Bunte Steine." Would like to like.

So many things I'd like to like. Scriabin, oysters, NY . . .

PM
Dullish

Massage

EVE
A just did a lovely thing. Hired a string quartet from a Z hotel and put together a little recital in the library. Also brought hotel waiters, refreshments + juices, just like home. Invited director, drs. + other people I didn't know. Short, predictable program. Reductions of Vivaldi's "Spring," followed by "Kleine Nachtmusik," J. Strauss + other viennoiseries. Still, very touched by A's gest.

Despite the trite selection, it was plain the musicians were 1st rate. They somehow managed to "find" something even in that overtrodden répert. After perf., I approached them for a chat. Violist studied under Hindemith. Cellist played at Verein. 2nd violin collaborates regularly with Barcz. They all met in Berlin, but left after Hitler became chancellor. How lovely to talk to true artists! Told them they could come to me for whatever they needed. Cellist suggested, with shy humour, one-way tickets to America + visas for all. I said they could consider it done.

A looked at me from the back of the room as I talked to the musicians. Stoically sulky. Just like back home.

AM
A in Z.

Belly

Walked with Nurse to the edge of the forest. Some trees creaked with age. Delicious greenness. Pressed my hand into a mound of warm moss. Watched it spring back slowly, erasing my impression.

Seized with pain. Had to lie down under a tree. Can't remember when I last lay on grass, leaves, lichen. Rested my head on Nurse's lap. She stroked my hair. Sweet, damp sounds + smells from the ground. Clusters of clouds against the unwrinkled sky. She must have thought my tears were of pain.

EVE
Head

Massage becoming hard to take. The touch. Don't want to offend Nurse by refusing.

AM

Music started out from noise. After a long journey, it's going back home.

PM

Lost offending molar. Don't think there'll be time for the hole to close.

EVE

Reading Arduini's latest. A lovely little poem about Thales of Miletus:

Il

greco che

fece entrare tutta

Cheope nella propria ombra

AM

Juice. Rhubarb, berries, mint.

Overheard: "Everyone knows I'm here incognito."

Lassitude

PM

A just called from Z (again), asking for advice. Kolbe, Lenbach, London, NY, etc., etc., etc., etc. As always, he mistakes doubt with depth, hesitation with analysis.

I drifted away.

"Are you there?"

He thought we'd been disconnected during my long silence after his long q.

"No," I said.

I can't explain the relief that word gave me. Not all the opium in the world.

"Hello?"

True. I was not there.

"I'm such a brute," he said. "You should rest."

"I've been doing this for too long. Done."

Silence between 2 is always shared. But 1 of the 2 owns it and shares it with the other.

"But you live for this," he said at last. "You . . ."

He regretted his words.

"Exactly. And now it's over."

I hung up, gently, before we got trapped in another silence, which would say nothing except that there was nothing else to say.

EVE

Sleepless after conv. with A. Rereading the above. Too long. Started in 1922, when he 1st saw that the small sum he'd given me for the Phil. had done better than his funds. He looked at my books. Had me explain them. Weeks later, said he'd tried my approach with disappointing results. Showed me his work. He'd merely replicated what I'd done but at a much larger scale. He'd accounted for market impact, yes, but it had all been done with a lifeless, artificial sense of symmetry. The right notes without any sense of rhythm. Like a player-piano. I made him a new sketch for his volume. And it worked.

We'd been married for about 2 years before this. An amicable, respectful, exhausting period. Few effortless moments. We cared for each other, but care's demanding. Did our best to fulfil what we imagined the other's expectations were, repressed our frustration when we failed, and never allowed ourselves to be pleased when we were the recipients of those same efforts. It's unsurprising that we should soon slip into politeness. No graceful way out of manners.

Keeping busy with music + charity helped. Board meetings + donations. Recitals at home. New friends. All this drew me away from A, but he encouraged it, understanding that our time apart improved our time together.

It was a good life, once this balance was found. We could prob. have gone on in such a way forever.

But after he saw my books, we started a collaboration of sorts. He taught me the rules of investment. I showed him how to think beyond their boundaries. I found great pleasure in the work.

For 1st time, we were true companions. And, I should say, happy.

With full access to funds, results were almost instantaneous.

Numbers so large there were few things outside the realm of nature they could've been applied to.

People started speaking of Andrew + "his touch" with awe.

We complemented each other. He understood he'd never be able to uphold the myth forming around him without my help. I understood I'd never be allowed to operate at such heights if it wasn't through him. For a while, we both enjoyed this alliance.

Soon, tho, an imbalance became obvious: what he could teach me (nature of instruments, procedures, balance sheet analysis, etc.) was finite, while my domain was inexhaustible. Rules + defs. are fixed; conditions + our reactions to them change hourly. True, he'd provided capital. But after a year or so, I'd more than repaid + could've, in theory, broken away on my own.

We fell into our rôles. Where there's a ventriloquist, there's a dummy. The latter word only sounds worse than the former. He disliked being told what to do. I disliked being pushed further into the shadows + speaking only through him.

It all came tumbling down in 1926. Back then, I believed it was the end of our marriage. In time, I understood that was when it really started. For I've come to think one is truly married only when one is more committed to one's vows than the person they refer to.

As so many times before, I've underestimated the salutary effects of confession! I may just be able to sleep after this.

PM

A by my side, asleep on sofa, still in his travel clothes. I must've been sleeping since yesterday AM, when I woke up in awesome pain and was given morph.

When I saw him, my 1st thought was this notebook. Seemed untouched, in the exact position I'd left it in drawer, with pen on it at the same angle. Now hidden inside charity ledger. He's never been able to read my hand anyway.

Sun stain on blanket on my feet. Pleasant then clammy.

I smell.

EVE

Beef-tea. Bicarb.

Massage too much. Asked Nurse to suspend. No. Says muscles need it.

AM

A delighted to see me wearing the gold band. No mention of Z etc.

I look down at him from my wheelchair. Such an odd sentence.

He seems content, spread out on his chaise next to me, leafing through "The Times."

I didn't want the wheelchair. Nurse insisted. She was right.

The lovely, shapeless rustle of the newspaper.

Jutting crags mantled with eternal snow, bare blue ridges, sawtooth edges + horn-shaped peaks enclose the valley on every side. No roads in sight. Seems hard to believe there's a way in/out. Should I ask A to bury me here? Perhaps in the bell churchyard?

PM

Overheard: "The game is not worth the candle."

EVE

Is the strawberry in my mouth alive?
Or is its flesh, speckled with the unborn, already dead?

AM

After sleepless night, looking at the latest Colette. Admirable, as always, but don't have the strength to read about marriage. Picked up new Woolf. Biography of Elizabeth Barrett Browning's cocker spaniel!

EVE

A brought phonograph. I pretended to be delighted. Nothing sounds the way it should.

AM
EVE
Droll!

I'm Adam, Eve. Mad, am I?
D F♯ E A / A E F♯ D

PM

Reading "Flush." Superb, even if dog's perspective is inconsistent, which I find distracting. The dog's loving submission to its bedridden mistress is wonderfully suffocating.

EVE

Woolf quotes Barrett letter to Browning: "You are Paracelsus, and I am a recluse, with nerves that have been broken on the rack, and now hang loosely, quivering at a step and breath." Why all this Paracelsus suddenly?

"The Waves," "Flush" . . . Curious about what VW's next title will be. Put together, her 3 latest books could form a sentence!

AM

Ailing. Compassionate weather, tho.

Massage replaced by a passive sort of callisthenics. Nurse moves my limbs for me.

This made me realise how little I know about "my will." I want to move a leg. Then I'm aware of its moving. But what moved it? At what point does the sum of anonymous electric impulses + twitching muscles become me? Can I rightly call that force "I"? What's the difference, regarding my participation, between the nurse's moving my leg and the leg's moving "on its own"?

Hemicrania. Hot water, sponge, poultices.

PM

A back from Z. Doing his best to become someone else for me. His efforts only underscore how little time I've left.

Something endearing about his stiff softness. But I've the feeling he's (unknowingly) trying to create a bank of future memories for himself. These are the scenes he'll go back to when I'm gone. He'll see his own hand arranging my pillow and stroking my cheek.

EVE

Sleepless. My above thoughts on A say more about me than him.

Perhaps finishing with confession started a few days ago will absolve us both.

Or at least let me sleep tonight.

Between 1922 and '26 I spun the cobweb. Thanks to discovery of "stickiness" in maths, the web's nodes + entanglements spread out in every direction. Results were repeatable. It was an applicable model that drew everything toward it. Even became 3-dimensional.

A followed my instructions.

Our profits during those years dwarfed original Bevel fortune.

I discussed stickiness principle + cobweb architecture with A countless times. He either pretended to follow my explanations or lost patience. My fault. Never been good at explaining maths. But this added to resentment.

The more we prospered, the more estranged + embittered we became.

He felt unmanned, he once said.

I found his vanity repulsive.

Still, our queer collaboration continued. I was obsessed with the process; he was addicted to the results. But it'd be dishonest to claim it was only an intellectual exercise for me. I discovered a deep well of ambition within. From it I extracted a dark fuel.

Toward the end of this period (early '26?) I turned my attention to an increasing flaw in the Exchange, a flaw that became more pronounced as our transactions + profits grew: traffic.

During rallies + plunges, the ticker always fell far behind. There could be a gap of up to 10 points between selling price on the floor and ticker quotation.

I decided to make these delays mine.

By trading in outsized amounts + inciting bursts of general frenzy,

I started creating the lags. The ticker fell behind me, and for a few minutes I owned the future.

Andrew became a legend. Everyone thought he was a clairvoyant, a mystic.

Truth is all this was made possible by obsolete + overwhelmed machinery:

brokers couldn't cope with the flood of orders;

then clerks fell behind phoning in the brokers' backed-up orders to the floor;

then each order had to wait for its turn to be executed;

then the updated quotations went to the ticker keyboard operators, also backed up;

then more time went by between the release of the already obsolete quote and a new order based on that quote;

then the circle of delays started all over again, increased.

This deficient mechanism created arbitrage opps.

Bizarre that nobody had thought of profiting from these lags before.

I made the most of them.

In passing, I once told A that our whole financial system relied on 4 people: the keyboard operators in charge of feeding all the quotes into the New York Stock Exchange ticker. It would take 1 of them to bring the whole market to its knees.

Imagine, I said, if 1 of the 4 keyboard operators could be bribed to provide all the quotes before punching them into the machine. The delays would make it possible to act on this information unnoticed.

Some weeks later, Andrew did just that.

It was obvious, looking at the tape.

The scheme lasted only for a few months. But he made an incalculable fortune. And the myth of Bevel grew till he became a god.

I called him a criminal. He said I couldn't suffer his success.
We barely spoke to each other for about 2 years.

AM
A off to Z.

Inert callisthenics.

PM
Pain outside me, like the surrounding mountains, swelling in wild-crested waves, petrified right before breaking.

AM
Waking up from morph.

This place seems full of simulacra.

PM
A back from Z. Tells me someone's taking care of visas for quartet musicians.

EVE
Sleepless. Never fail to find an exasperating sound, an awkward memory, a sore spot, a grievance.

AM

Overheard: "Un visage comme une brioche."

PM

Some bells in music:

Zauberf. (tho the celesta in the pit never felt like bells to me)

Parsifal?

Tosca (matins)

Symph. Fant.

Mahler in almost every symph.? Sleigh bells in 4th so lovely.

The leap from percussion to melody took music out of prehistory into its history.

Bone bells.

A femur must sound lower than a tibia.

EVE

The Doppler effect of memory. The pitch of past events shifting as they rush away from us.

AM

Restful night without morph. Odd sense of pride in owning my sleep.

Writing letters.

A bit better. But this only makes me realize I've forgotten what it feels like to be completely well.

PM

I've never heard the Stock Exchange bell.

AM

Language annoying today.

PM

A diarist is a monster: the writing hand and the reading eye are sourced from different bodies.

EVE

Overheard: "He just pretends to pretend."

Looking through these pages one would think I've a passion for bells. Never gave them a thought before coming here. Not sure I even care now. They just keep ringing.

Mostly fruit

Hemicrania

Unable to do much

PM

Quasimodo, deafened by bells, loves ringing them.

AM

Ill

Confined to bed

PM

A back from Z with giftlets. Hadn't realised he was gone.

A few berries.

EVE

No pleasure in juice

AM

Ill

Head

AM

Ill

AM

Ill

AM

Better. Went out. Valley encased by stone under shell of nacre sky. Inside a mollusc.

Found tattered copy of Heine.

Overheard: "She forgot to swim."

PM

Nurse never feigns gaiety. Never makes shows of sympathy. Never pretends to know what I feel. Calling her a friend would be an insult to the dignity of her impersonal care. And yet.

EVE

Read Heine aloud in my room, hearing Schumann in each syllable.

AM

Ill
Befogged

PM

Can barely stand the violence of eating.

AM

Asked Nurse to cut my hair, because constantly wet from sponge, hot flannels, plasters. She declined. Started doing it myself with little scissors in letter opener set. I'd never seen Nurse frightened before, so I stopped. Not sure what she found in my eyes while we looked at each other, but she told me to wait and left. Returned with proper scissors. She didn't ask for directions or try to appease me with a little trim. I could feel the blades snipping close to my skull.

PM

Just read Harland's latest. Perfect morph. novel. Enjoyed not being able to fully follow it.

Something miraculous + sad about the glass on the table. Water disciplined into a vertical cylinder. The depressing spectacle of our triumph over the elements.

EVE

La campanella.

A good thing about my situation: there is no risk of being subjected to Paganini, Hummel, Berlioz, Paderewski, Quilter, Saint-Saëns, Tosti, Franck, Lindner, Offenbach, Elgar, Dubochet, Rachmaninoff ever again.

AM

Overheard: "No, no: Odessa, Texas."

PM

A back from Z. Shocked by haircut. He tried to be angry. Looked at me with awe.

EVE

A took coffee with me. He's off to Z tomorrow. Showed commendable restraint and never asked a single business q. I was touched + grateful. Asked him to lie by my side. We held hands, looked at the ceiling in placid solitude à deux.

I distrust the surge of well-being within me when I make him feel good.

PM

Managed to read Clouvel's latest. Short. Perhaps perfect.

In books, music, art I've always looked for emotion + elegance.

AM

New nib. A left for Z, flaunting self-sufficiency with the restrained agitation of a very busy man.

Reminded me of his behaviour during our long estrangement after ticker argument. Then, like now, I stepped away from business. Then, like now, he hid behind a show of earnest industriousness. We never crossed paths in the house. Only spoke to each other in public. He spent most of his time at office + Fiesolana.

Poured myself into music + philanthropy. At first, out of curiosity,

I followed his work. Safe, reasonable, unremarkable. Soon, I lost interest. My only connection with business was managing Charitable Fund.

Looking back, I saw that we'd never truly spent time together except during our business collaboration. Knew very little, almost nothing, about each other.

In many ways, we seemed to have returned to the first years of our marriage, before our collaboration, when we learned to be together from afar. But the gap between us had widened, which was not bad. Things found their place again. This courteous estrangement would, from now on, be our life, I thought.

But then a blanket of exhaustion descended on me. The oddest thing: it smothered me under its weight while also providing me with a bizarre sense of comfort.

Couldn't get up. Felt I'd break whenever upright. Constant fear of fracture. Of cracking.

Yielding to the heavy fatigue was the only relief.

Eventually, A learned I was bedridden. During his first short visits, he was dismissive + irritable. Kept asking about my "nerves." More than caring, his questions seemed to dare me to tell him I was unwell.

It took pain to make him pay attention. And only when he could see how much weight I'd lost did he truly worry.

First dr. found nothing. Also said neurasthenia. Sedatives I didn't take.

My weakness allowed A to show, after such a long time, the feelings that bitterness + jealousy had been unable to extinguish. And it allowed me to see that the forgiveness I'd withheld from him had crystalized, in my clenched fist, into spiteful pride.

This may've been our best time together.

In early 1929, 2 conflating events upset this precarious harmony.

Not events, really, since they both lay in the future. I should say 2 predictions.

1st, my realization that the market would crash before the end of the year.

2nd, my cancer diagnosis, according to which I'd be dead not too long after that.

PM
Priest came with soggy offerings of comfort.
God is the most uninteresting answer to the most interesting questions.

Bells, bells, bells. The Jingle Man.

Sun stain on blanket. Each particle of light has travelled from the sun to my feet. How can something so small have made it so far? Up close, the stream of photons would look like a meteor shower. My feet play with it. The vertigo of scale (the space between a photon and me and a star) is a foretaste of death.

Without revealing my condition, I gradually started giving Andrew financial advice again. Because I was effective, he welcomed me back. But with a tinge of caution. I sometimes had to find new ways for him to adopt my ideas. They had to become his thoughts first. Call and response: I gave him D F♯ E A so he could think he'd come up with A E F♯ D on his own.

Despite impending débâcle, he was sceptical about my plan and kept saying mkt. was shock-proof. But I knew it was just a matter of time. I started creating short positions.

In early Sept., after almost a month of advances, I liquidated, creating a sharp break.

To preserve value, investors started selling holdings during decline, with the obvious consequences, leading up to the final week of Oct. 1929.

No need to expand. Most accounts of the crash are, in general, correct, except for the omission of my name. For this single error I am thankful.

Peal of bells from the unseen church.

My 1929 plan was much like the bell motif.

Short selling is folding back time. The past making itself present in the future.

Like a retrograde or a palindrome.

D F♯ E A / A E F♯ D.

A song played in reverse.

But going against the mkt., everything is turned on its head: the more a stock is depreciated, the larger the profit, and vice versa.

Every loss becomes a gain, every increase a drop.

All intervals in the song are flipped, turned upside down.

A major third up (D F♯) becomes a major third down (D B♭), a step down (F♯ E) a step up (B♭ C), a fall of a fifth (E A) a proportional upward jump (C G).

D F♯ E A becomes D B♭ C G.

But backwards.

The inversion of the retrograde.

A song played in reverse and on its head.

Call and response.

"The orchestra played the kind of music where you know what's coming next, where you can listen ahead."

In 1929, everyone heard D F♯ E A and, listening ahead, thought A E F♯ D.

But when I heard D F♯ E A, the response ringing in my mind was G C B♭ D.

In '29 no bells were knelling in my mind.

But looking back, this seems like an accurate allegory of what I perceived + thought.

My wager against the mkt. was a fugue that would read backwards and upside down.

Where every voice would result from vertical + horizontal mirroring of orig. motif.

A radical version of Musik. Opfer.

Or, perhaps better, Schön.'s Suite for Piano.

I don't believe in magic, but the viciousness of cancer after the crash didn't feel like a coincidence.

Finally had to tell Andrew about illness.

He seemed more concerned about his solitude than my absence. Still, he was a good companion.

After '29 devastation, I tried to organize a recovery plan. Give most of money away. But was too sick. Dimming. Consumed by failed treatment after failed treatment. Andrew made a number of contributions: a sprinkle of libraries, hospital wings + univ. halls. Mortified to learn he'd given away these crumbs in my name, I asked him never to use it again.

A asleep in chair next to me. Old.

Feel I've been here for decades. Has time slowed down or sped up?

Every object is an activity.

All of this bowl's strength is consumed in showing itself.

Have read little since finishing Clouvel. Can barely manage Sutherland's little diptychs.

"Imagine the relief of finding out
that one is not the one one thought one was"

Juice sweeter than usual.
People look at me differently now. As if I weren't one of them.

Impossible to hear my voice as a child. I remember entire conversations but can't remember what I sounded like.

Ill

getting untidy behind my eyes

ill
till
still

Something teething within

Woke up to find left ankle in a cast.
Broken while moving me under morph.
No recollection or pain.
Nurse was dismissed.
I demanded they bring her back.
She's here now.

My good foot sometimes touches the plaster. The encased foot doesn't know.

When I say I think of all the things I haven't done,
what is the content of those thoughts, really?

No more baths. Nurse rubs eau de cologne between my toes + inside joints. A cool burn.

A's impatience.

So lovely to be outside again
Cradled by the world

But each time I blink, the mountains are gone

Ferns within ferns within ferns within ferns

Bird-crowded trees

Some leaves reddening at the edges
La fauve agonie des feuilles
Keeping one here, suspended in its agony

A bell in a bell jar won't ring

The terrifying freedom of knowing that nothing, from now on, will
become a memory

It took me a while to realize the hum was only inside my head
Is a waveless noise still a sound?

Nurse just filed my nails, blowing away the dust as she went

Words peeling off from things

In and out of sleep. Like a needle coming out from under a black cloth
and then vanishing again. Unthreaded.

ACKNOWLEDGMENTS

I am forever grateful to the New York Public Library's Cullman Center for Scholars and Writers, the Whiting Foundation, MacDowell, Yaddo, and Artist Relief for their invaluable support.

All my thanks to the incomparable Sarah McGrath and everyone at Riverhead, particularly Jynne Dilling Martin, Geoff Kloske, and May-Zhee Lim. And my endless gratitude to Bill Clegg, Marion Duvert, David Kambhu, Lilly Sandberg, and Simon Toop.

For their generosity and support at different stages of this project I must thank Ron Briggs, Heather Cleary, Cecily Dyer, Anthony Madrid, Graciela Montaldo, Eunice Rodríguez Ferguson, and Homa Zarghamee.

A few friends in particular have made this a better book. I am indebted beyond measure to Pablo Bernengo, Brendan Eccles, Lauren Groff, Gabe Habash, Alison Maclean, and James Murphy.

For too many years, Jason Fulford and Paul Stasi have been my long-suffering interlocutors and the stoic readers of premature drafts. I owe them more than I can express here.

Anne, Elsa . . . Properly thanking you would take a whole other book.